Another Man's Child

D1344063

JUNE FRANCIS

Another Man's Child

CANELO

First published in the United Kingdom in 1999 by Judy Piatkus

This edition published in the United Kingdom in 2019 by

Canelo Digital Publishing Limited
Third Floor, 20 Mortimer Street
London W1T 3JW
United Kingdom

Copyright © June Francis, 1999

The moral right of June Francis to be identified as the author of this work has been asserted in accordance with the Copyright, Designs and Patents Act, 1988.

All rights reserved. No part of this publication may be reproduced or transmitted in any form or by any means, electronic or mechanical, including photocopy, recording, or any information storage and retrieval system, without permission in writing from the publisher.

A CIP catalogue record for this book is available from the British Library.

Print ISBN 978 1 78863 582 0
Ebook ISBN 978 1 78863 516 5

This book is a work of fiction. Names, characters, businesses, organizations, places and events are either the product of the author's imagination or are used fictitiously. Any resemblance to actual persons, living or dead, events or locales is entirely coincidental.

Look for more great books at www.canelo.co

Printed and bound in Great Britain by Clays Ltd, Elcograf S.p.A.

Chapter One

'Yer'll give up that room and come and live here!' A moment ago the voice had sounded thin and drained of life but now it had gained new strength.

From eyes swollen with weeping Molly May stared at her mother-in-law, the bane of her youthful life since marriage. She drew the black shawl more securely about her slender shoulders and trembled inwardly. She had never had to fend for herself in her whole life but she couldn't let the woman who so patently disapproved of her take her over now. 'No,' she said shakily.

Ma Payne's salt and pepper eyebrows twitched together, hooding her protuberant eyes as she folded skinny arms across her non-existent bosom, scaring the life out of Molly May. 'I didn't hear that,' she said tersely. 'Our Cath'll go with yer. Help carry what yer've got for the baby.'

Molly May swallowed nervously, one hand straying to her swollen belly. She couldn't. She just *couldn't* let this overbearing, self-opinionated woman get her claws into Frank's child. 'No,' she repeated, voice barely above a whisper.

'Don't be so bleeding stupid, girl!' the woman said wrathfully. 'How are yer going to manage on yer own with no husband and nowt coming in? Yer too near yer time to find yerself some work.'

Molly May lowered her head and swallowed, her brown eyes fringed by reddish-gold lashes full of trepidation. 'I'll manage.' How she wished her mother was still alive. Mabel wouldn't have allowed Ma Payne to boss her like this. Nor would Nanna. She drew on all her resources of courage and stammered, 'You might rule the whole bl-bl-bloody street but you–you're not going to rule *me and mine*. With Fr-Frank gone there's no reason for m-m-me to be as nice as pie to you and yours anymore. I'm-I'm off!'

There was a concerted gasp from Ma Payne and her two daughters. 'The cheek of her, Ma!' said Josie, the eldest, who was tuppence short of a shilling. 'She needs a clout round the earhole for swearing at yer like that. Her and her stupid accent.'

'You–You just try it,' said Molly May, wishing the ground would open and swallow her up. I'll-I'll knock the spots off you.'

'Yous? Yous couldn't punch a hole in a paper bag!' crowed Josie. 'Yerra heretic and yer'll go to Hell! Our Frank should never have married yer! Yer not one of us. You tell her, Ma.'

'Shut up!' Ma Payne turned on her daughter. 'How could I stop my boy? He was well past twenty-one. We've just got to make the best of a bad job, that's all.'

Molly May's heart sank. That was how Ma had viewed her from the start – as a bad job. It was so very different from how Nanna had seen her. 'I don't want you making the best of me,' she said, clearing her throat nervously. 'I know you–you never thought me good enough for F-Frank.'

Her mother-in-law fixed her with a baleful glare. 'Too right but you were his choice and I had to go along with it. Now I want that baby so I'm prepared to put up with you and yer slapdash ways. Spoilt, that's what you've been, girl! But I'll soon knock yer into shape once yer living here.'

Molly May didn't want to be knocked into shape. Nanna and Frank had thought her perfect as she was, so why should she change for this woman? She decided to make a move and tilted her head defiantly. 'I'm going. Maybe I'll see you again one day, and maybe I won't.'

She headed for the door but was brought to an abrupt halt by a tug on her hair. Molly May clutched her hat as it slid sideways and turned carefully to face Josie, who stood grinning at her like a Cheshire Cat.

'I got her, Ma,' she crowed.

Molly May's heart plummeted even further as she took a grip on the hair which hung down her back almost to her waist and tugged to free it. But her sister-in-law, who sometimes scared her out of her wits with her wild laughter, hung on like grim death to the handful of curls she had seized. 'Let g-g-go!' insisted Molly May though her teeth chattered with fright.

'Not so fast,' said Ma Payne, long black skirts brushing the floor as she marched across the room. She thrust her face close to her daughter-in-law's. Determined eyes as dark and evil-looking as brackish pools in a marsh gazed into Molly May's and the girl's knees shook with terror as she sent up a quick prayer for deliverance. 'Yer haven't any understanding of a mother's luv, have yer, girl?' said the older woman, shaking her head. 'That babby is my boy's and it belongs to us as much as you do. So yer staying here!'

'No! You-you can't m-make me,' she said, struggling to keep her voice steady, trying to be neither browbeaten nor scared. Her mother had often said in the exasperated tone of voice she'd frequently adopted with Molly that it gave your opponent an advantage if you showed weakness. Tears threatened as the girl remembered her mother who had died only eighteen months ago in childbirth. They had moved to Bootle three years after the old queen died in 1904, the widowed Mabel May having met her second husband on a trip to Southport. Until then mother and daughter lived with Nanna in Burscough, an agricultural village in Lancashire which had gained some importance when the huge mere at Martin had been drained and the new Leeds–Liverpool canal was built.

'Can't I?' Ma Payne's voice was silky and heavy with threat. 'Cath, help Josie get her upstairs. She can go in the front attic now it's empty. The door has a lock on it.'

Josie's expression was jubilant as she seized Molly May's arm. 'Haven't got much to say for yerself now, have yer? If yer cheek me again, I'll give yer a swipe!'

3

Oh, God! How Molly wished she dared tell her to take her filthy paws off and then give her that look Mabel May had used to demolish her enemies, but she just didn't have the guts.

'Maybe I'll hit yer anyhow,' said Josie, eyes glistening, and her hand came up.

Ma Payne seized hold of it. 'Control yerself! We've got to look after her. Don't want her going into early labour and losing me boy's babby.'

'That's right,' said Molly May, relieved. 'You've got to take care of me.'

'I am a caring woman,' said Ma Payne solemnly, adjusting a strap beneath her frock. 'But many a mother dies in childbirth... so think on that.'

'I do,' said the girl honestly, forcing down the fear which drenched her in perspiration every time she imagined going into labour.

'Good,' said Ma Payne, sounding pleased. 'It's a fact of life, girl, as yer know. Now, if yer had any sense you'd throw in yer lot with me and mine. After all, we share a common grief since the sea claimed my boy.'

Her boy! There had been times when Molly May had felt like exploding on hearing those words. It was that possessiveness in Ma that filled her with dismay. She thought of all the times this woman had interfered, not only in her and Frank's lives but in so many others, with her rigid morality and fixed ideas on what was best for them all. Due to her one of the girls in the street was ostracised for falling for a baby while she was unmarried. Her own parents had cast her out and the poor girl later drowned herself in the canal.

'Well, are we moving?' said Cath impatiently. She was twenty and the brains of the family, with dark red hair and a creamy skin. 'Is Moll being locked up or not? I think you're daft meself. She's going to be nothing but trouble.'

'I wanna do it,' said Josie, almost jumping up and down with impatience. She brought her face close to Molly May's so the girl could smell onion on her breath. 'You'd better start being nice to me,' she said in a sing-song voice.

Molly May shuddered, scarcely able to believe this was happening. It was like something out of a penny dreadful. Oh, how she wished Nanna or Frank were here! She fought every step of the way but when Josie lost her footing on the stairs, almost dragging her down with her, realised there was a real danger of falling and losing the baby, maybe even her life, so stopped struggling.

She walked into the front attic without being forced, her heart banging away beneath her ribs as she heard the key turn in the lock. She wanted to burst into tears as she stood in the middle of the room, gazing at the whitewashed walls. On one there were hooks for hanging clothes and beneath the window a single bed. A chest of drawers and a washstand stood opposite. It was a terrible room and had been the lodger's until he'd left a week ago. Before that it was Frank's.

Oh, Frank, Frank, why did you have to die? Tears trickled down Molly May's cheeks and she wiped them away with her hand. How many times had her mother told her crying would not solve a thing when she came home from work to find Nanna pandering to Molly May's every little problem with soft words, a large embroidered handkerchief ready to mop her tears, and the delicious buttery homemade scones and jam sponge permanently on offer? 'You spoil her,' Mabel May would say. 'Poor little mite,' Nanna would reply. 'She's got no father to look out for her and thee's never here.'

'I've got to do something to keep us,' Mabel May would reply irritably. 'You can't do it with your game leg.'

She'd always been irritable with Nanna and herself as long as Molly May could remember. Nanna said it was ever since Molly's father had been killed in that terrible accident. Still she was dead now and the girl would have had her back in an instant for all she'd been forever finding fault. Mother had looked after her in her own way, even marrying again to provide Molly

May with a better standard of life or so she'd said. Though how rooms over a pub in Bootle could be better than Nanna's cottage with its roses round the door, a roaring fire in the grate and delicious smells coming from the oven, was something the girl had found hard to understand. It was true she had seen a lot more of life there, even though the fights that broke out most Saturday nights had soon sent her diving for cover under a table in the farthest corner of the saloon bar.

She sniffed back tears, thinking it didn't do to remember the past. She had wept enough when the agent from the White Star line had called to tell her that Frank's ship had gone missing during a hurricane off the coast of Maryland. She and Frank had only been married nine months: Since June 10th, 1908. He had been twenty-six to her eighteen years.

She sighed shakily, remembering him coming into the pub on Stanley Road where her stepfather was the licensee. Her mother had been dead only a short time and he and Molly May were finding life hard and frustrating. She considered it her duty to stay and try to look after him but he expected too much of her in her opinion. It seemed almost as if he wanted her to take her mother's place: cleaning, working behind the bar, cooking, shopping.

It was not what Molly wanted from life and she just could not live up to his expectations. She was seriously thinking of going back to live with Nanna when Frank had appeared on the scene. Dark-haired, brown-eyed, broad-shouldered, and with a voice that could charm the sparrows from under the eaves, he made her laugh with his impersonation of Vesta Tilly (of all people!) singing 'Daddy Wouldn't Buy Me a Bow Wow'. He soon had the whole pub looking on. She was collecting glasses and stopped to watch him. Their eyes met and that was that. Here was a man she felt certain would look after her, a seaman like so many of the men who came into the pub, bringing with him the flavour and freshness of the wide oceans he sailed. He opened her eyes to a whole different world: exciting and romantic. He was strong and caring but not always there to criticise her slapdash housework. And if her cooking failed there was always the shop round the corner which specialised in roasted hearts, pig's trotters and steaming hot spare ribs. But now Frank was gone and she did not know how she would survive without him.

She took a deep quivering breath and moved slowly over to the window to kneel on the bed. She pulled aside one of the curtains, staring at the rivulets of rain making their way down the window pane. It was difficult to see out so she unfastened the sash lock, forcing up the lower window to gaze out on the glistening pavements below.

The lamplighter was doing his rounds and she heard him greet one of the neighbours. Her ears caught the faint plop as the gas mantle ignited and a pool of warm yellow light was reflected in the water rushing along the gutters. A couple of boys were splashing about. Racing sticks, she thought, listening to their voices above the noise of the rain. She lifted her eyes to see the huge drumlike containers of Linacre gasworks looming behind the shining roofs of the houses. She took several deep breaths of the smoky, damp air before withdrawing her head and closing the window.

The sight of so much water and the sound of it rushing along the gutters reminded her of the canal with its locks. Her father Joseph, of whom she had no memory at all, had been crushed against a lock wall after falling into the Leeds–Liverpool canal. The childless Nanna Fletcher was Mabel May's foster mother and had taken them in without hesitation. It was she who'd looked after Molly May when Mabel found work in Ainscough's flour mill repairing grain sacks. She was just a plain seamstress but Molly May had been taught fine embroidery by the vicar's daughter at St John's National School. Not that it had proved of much use since moving to Bootle.

She frowned as she gazed at the floor, absently noting the cracks in the brown linoleum. She must get away from here and

Nanna Fletcher's house was the very place to go. It was three months or more since Molly May had paid the old woman a visit although she wrote to her regularly, knowing Nanna would get someone to read the letters to her. A bargee's daughter herself, Nanna had attended school only infrequently. Any news from her was passed to Molly May via Jack Fletcher, a distant relative, who worked for Williams coal and timber merchants, Liverpool. He plied the canal daily, using a steam-driven tug which pulled four to six barges laden with coal from Wigan. Some of his load he would drop off at Linacre and Athol Street gasworks before going on to Williams's depot in the city of Liverpool. Then he would do the return trip loaded up with timber for Tyrer's boat-building yard at Burscough.

Molly May lifted her head, hope stirring faintly inside her. If she could somehow get to the coal depot at Linacre then Jack Fletcher would certainly take her as far as Burscough Bridge.

The baby moved inside her and she placed one hand protectively over her belly. Her and Frank's baby. The muscles in her throat constricted and she had consciously to relax them to force down a lump that felt like an egg in her throat. She had not thought of a baby when she had married Frank but did not want to wish it away now, however difficult it would make her life. Nanna would help her cope… if she could just escape this house.

Feeling weary to the bone she decided there was nothing she could do tonight. With difficulty she bent and unfastened the buttons on the boots which were the last present her mother had given her. She wriggled her squashed toes, cold and damp because one of the soles had a hole in it and let in the rain despite the cut-out cardboard she had placed there, and undressed down to her camisole before gingerly pulling back the blankets. She was aware of the smell of damp and bug powder and shuddered, remembering Nanna's lavender-scented sheets. Still, no use dwelling on them right now. She must not allow this or anything else to prevent her from resting. She needed to conserve her strength. She must think of a plan to get out of the house. But within moments, with the abandonment of an exhausted child, she fell asleep.

Molly May woke from a dream in which she was clasping her baby to her breast. But hands, two hands, were clutching at it, determined to take it from her. It was still dark and a figure was bending over her, covering her mouth. 'Don't make a sound if you know what's good for you!' hissed Cath's voice in her ear.

Molly May's blood, already chilled by the dream, froze. The whole family were at it! Mad! Nervously, she tried to bite her lower lip but instead bit the hand covering her mouth. Cath caught her a stinging blow across the cheek with the tips of her fingers. 'Stop that!' She sounded exasperated. 'I've come to help you. You want to get out of here, don't you?'

Molly May let out an exclamation, scarcely able to believe that help could come from such an unexpected quarter. 'Of course I do. But why are *you* helping me?'

'I want you out of here and best now before you really begin to get on Josie's and Ma's nerves and I suffer for it,' Cath hissed. 'So are you going to shift your carcase or do I do it for you?'

'No need for that,' said Molly May, rejoicing, swinging her legs nimbly over the side of the bed. 'What time is it?'

'Just gone six. Here, get your boots on.' Cath nudged them with her foot in her sister-in-law's direction. 'Now if Ma wakes and catches us, we say you're going to the lav. Hurry, though, because I'd rather we didn't bump into her.'

'Me neither,' said Molly May, quaking at the thought of bumping into Ma Payne.

Heart hammering, she crept down the top flight of stairs. She felt like a heroine from a Victorian melodrama as they paused on the landing, listening intently, before creeping down the next flight of stairs. She forced down a nervous giggle. 'I never thought you'd do me a favour,' she said when they reached the kitchen.

Cath did not answer but led the way into the scullery and out into the yard. She opened the back gate and would have pushed

Molly May through it unceremoniously if she hadn't resisted. 'I *do* need the lavatory,' she said in as dignified a manner as she could. 'So if you don't mind…?'

Cath shrugged. 'I'll leave you to it then. But don't look back and keep on going. I wouldn't even go back to your rooms if I were you. That's the first place Ma'll look.'

'Why are you doing this really?' she said, puzzled. 'You're able to stick up for yourself. I can't see why my being here would make that much difference to you.'

Cath flashed her a smile. 'I never could stand the way Ma treated our Frank, as if he was a little prince. The last thing I want is his brat lording it over us like he did. Tarrah!' And with that she went back up the yard.

Molly May was surprised to hear Cath had felt like that about her own brother but did not linger to discuss it. Instead she hurried to her lodgings near the Diamond Match Works opposite the Methodist Mission, where she speedily packed her few worldly goods. The furniture had come with the room so it was no hardship to leave that behind. Soon she was walking in the direction of Litherland Road and the Leeds–Liverpool canal. With any luck Jack Fletcher would be at the Linacre depot already. He would need to go into Liverpool to unload the rest of his cargo but she did not mind that. Once aboard she would feel safe from Ma Payne.

'Thee all right, Molly May?' Jack Fletcher sounded concerned for her.

A happy smile warmed her elfin features as she gazed down at him from her perch on the cabin roof. 'Better than I was.'

She thought how nice it was to have a man caring for her again, even if this one wasn't Frank and old enough to be her father. Jack wore the heavy dark blue seaman's gansy and khaki corduroys of the canal boatman. His big feet were shod in thick woolly socks and brass-buckled clogs, and on his greying hair was a cap which served to protect him from rain and sleet or to keep the sun out of his eyes. Nanna said he had once been in love with Molly May's mother and would still have had her after she was widowed if he hadn't already married another bargee's daughter who'd inherited her father's boat.

Molly watched him carefully steer his way past a muck barge carrying night dirt and horse manure from Liverpool to sell to Lancashire farmers, her small tip-tilted nose wrinkled in distaste. It was pulled by a horse, as was the Bradford flyer with its load of cotton they had passed earlier.

'Soon be there,' said Jack.

The words were sweet in her ears. Relief swamped her anxiety and grief like a flood. She glanced up at the sky. The rain had cleared and ribbons of silver-grey cloud hung as if suspended by invisible wires against a pale blue sky. To either side of the canal there were green fields and every now and again birds flew across with bits of twig or moss in their beaks. Hard to believe Frank really was dead. That the bottom had dropped out of her world on such a beautiful day. She longed for Nanna, to be held close to her soft bosom and comforted with kind words and buttered scones.

'Are thee coming down?' Jack said to her as one of his sons emerged from the cabin.

'Aye,' she said, accepting Rob's hand as he helped her from her perch on the roof.

'I hope thee finds the old woman fit,' said Jack. 'I haven't seen her awhile. I'll drop thee off at the Packet House. Thee won't have far to walk then.'

She thanked him and her soft lips brushed his weatherbeaten cheek.

'I don't know what I'd have done without you, Uncle Jack,' she said warmly.

'It was nowt, lass.' His face had turned brick red. 'Thee look after theeself now.'

Molly May waved to father and son as she paused on the bank a moment, then made her way up to the red brick Packet House Inn. A brisk wind had risen, fluttering her skirts and teasing the fringes of her shawl. She settled the latter more securely about her shoulders and walked on in the direction of Orrell Lane. According to Nanna it had once been called Gobbins Lane and as a child Molly May had imagined goblins living there. Every All Hallows Eve she'd pictured them coming back to haunt the place and had thrilled deliciously to her own imaginings.

Children were playing out with hoops and skipping ropes. One or two cast a glance in her direction and she found herself imagining her own child skipping to school. The heaviness at her heart lightened a little. She passed the grocery store, hoping Nanna had plenty of food in.

At last she came to the house and to her surprise found the blinds drawn. Her heart began to beat unevenly as she pushed open the gate, hesitating a moment before sounding the black-painted wrought-iron knocker.

Almost immediately a neighbouring door opened and a plump, middle-aged woman looked out at her. 'Thee's not going to get an answer there, lass. Hasn't thee heard?'

Molly May stared at her, wide-eyed. 'Heard what?'

The woman hesitated only briefly. 'There's no easy way of saying this – Mrs Fletcher's dead.'

Molly May's heart felt as if it had slipped its moorings to settle like a lump of lead in the pit of her stomach. 'Dead!' She could not believe it and had to put one hand on the wall to steady herself.

The woman's eyes were sympathetic. 'Aye. She's still up there on her bed. We're not sure when the funeral's to be. The vicar was going to get in touch with you.'

'Well, he didn't,' said Molly May indignantly, feeling a sudden need to sit down. What a shock! She inserted one hand through the letter box, found the string and pulled the key out to open the door. Oh, Lord! What am I going to do now? she thought.

'Do you want me to come in with you?'

She nodded, thinking: Of course I do. 'It's Mrs Smith, isn't it?'

'Aye.' The neighbour smiled. 'Fancy you remembering. I never thought you took much notice of me. You'll be able to stay here a few days for the funeral and that, if you want? I know the rent's paid 'til the end of the week.'

'I'd planned on staying longer than that,' said Molly May, voice shaking. 'Poor Nanna. Do you know if there's any food in the house?'

'Not much, lass. You fancying? I've just done a baking so I could let you have a loaf.'

'That's kind of you.' She smiled gratefully and went through to the kitchen. Immediately her eyes sought out the rocking chair with its knitted cushion set to one side of the black-leaded grate and her eyes filled with tears, remembering the times Nanna had sat there making some garment or other for her while she herself embroidered cushion covers, chairback covers, or did some fine smocking for the ladies round about.

'Must have gone in her sleep.' Mrs Smith was busying herself with the makings of the fire. 'Seeth thee down, lass,' she said, lapsing into Lancashire dialect. 'How long before thy baby's due?'

Molly did not answer but lowered herself carefully on to the rocking chair. She felt dizzy all of a sudden. 'Jack Fletcher... He doesn't know about Nanna. We'll have to get in touch but it'll need to wait until tomorrow now. He'll have left the Bridge.'

'Don't you be worrying. If it's too much for you, the Reverend Russell will arrange things.'

'You think?' The girl's eyes closed and she slumped back in the chair, feet neatly together on the rag rug. Then she sat upright. 'Nanna... she... she was in the burial club?'

'Aye. That's one thing you don't have to worry about, lass.'

'Marvellous!' Molly May's laugh was hollow and tears filled her eyes. She searched for the scrap of embroidered linen up her sleeve, scrubbing her face with it before blowing her nose.

'I'm sorry,' she said in a muffled voice. 'Only I've just lost my husband at sea and what with this on top and worrying about the baby, I don't know what I'm going to do.'

'You poor thing!' Mrs Smith's wrinkled face was full of sympathy. 'You don't look much more than a child yourself.' She struck a match and a tongue of flame ran along the edge of the newspaper, weaving in and out of the kindling and sending narrow twists of smoke up the chimney.

Molly May watched, mesmerised, waiting for the whole lot to burst into glorious flame. She began to undo her boots, kicking them off and stretching out her toes to the warmth. 'That's lovely. Thanks.'

'Don't mention it.' The woman got to her feet, rubbing her knees. 'I'll go and get that loaf.'

'Thanks again.' Molly May continued to gaze at the fire, reluctant to move. Although she knew she must go upstairs and view the body. She was feeling nervous, worrying about breaking down. She was apprehensive about lots of things: arranging the funeral, the birth of her baby. She wondered what would happen to it should she die? Lord, she couldn't bear thinking about it! She stifled the thought quickly, telling herself it was not going to happen.

–

'You're looking a bit pale round the gills.' Molly May's Good Samaritan gazed at her in concern as she placed a tray of jam butties and a steaming cup of tea on a stool next to her. 'Have you been up yet?'

The girl shook her head and sipped the tea, the colour slowly seeping back into her face. 'I'm Molly Payne really. Mam and my stepfather used to give me my full title because I was a May and not a Shaw like them. It's a bit childish. Perhaps I should drop it now I'm a widow?'

The neighbour smiled and said teasingly, 'Right you are, Mrs Payne.' Then her smile faded. 'Sad about your man and the old woman. No wonder you're upset.'

Molly agreed, before taking a large bite of bread and jam. Not as good as one of Nanna's scones but delicious all the same. 'I was planning on living with Nanna,' she said sadly. 'I feel guilty about not being here when she died, but what with getting married and setting up home, I just didn't have time. Now it's too late. Too late,' she repeated. 'Aren't they the saddest words in the English language?'

Mrs Smith sat opposite her, clasping her hands in the lap of her pinafore. 'If you have enough to pay the rent for a few weeks, you could stay on here. You never know, something might turn up.'

Molly sighed. 'I've only a few bob. Nanna and Mother always saw to the housekeeping so I've never been very good with money. I've hardly anything for the baby either.'

'If I were you I'd look in that big chest of drawers in Mrs Fletcher's room,' said Mrs Smith, nodding sagely. 'She was always knitting.'

Molly's expression brightened. 'It would be just like her to have made a whole layette.'

'There you are then! Go up and have a peek. Perhaps you'd like me to come up with you?'

'Yes. It would be best for me to get it over with.' Molly swallowed the last of her bread and jam and stood up.

As they climbed the linoleum-covered stairs her heart was pounding. It made her feel even more peculiar than she already felt. There was a peculiar kind of stretching pain beneath her bump and an aching sensation in her lower back as if she was about to start her monthlies. Surely, surely, it couldn't be the baby? No! Not now! It was much too early.

They entered the front bedroom where a large iron bedstead stood against one wall. On top of the knitted multicoloured bedspread lay a still figure dressed in a red flannelette night-gown. 'Right stuck on red she was,' said Mrs Smith, going over to the bed to gaze down at the corpse. 'I looked for white but she didn't have any.'

'She believed red was warmer.' But it wasn't going to keep her warm in the grave, thought Molly, mouth quivering as she gazed down at the well-loved face.

'She had a good innings.' Mrs Smith smoothed a strand of hair on the corpse's head. 'Will you be all right here on your own? Only I've a hotpot on and I want to see it's all right.'

'Of course,' Molly said brightly, asking herself what there was to be scared of. Nanna had loved her in life so it was hardly likely she would hurt her in death, even if she could have got off that bed and haunted her like one of Dickens's ghosts. Gingerly, she sat on the wooden chair by the bedside, remembering the many things she had shared with the old woman.

It was Nanna who'd dressed her in her Sunday best for St John's Walking Day. A brass band had played and Molly had felt fit to burst with pride, walking along with the other girls. Then there were trips to the Thursday market at Ormskirk during the school holidays, and once they'd travelled with lots of other people to Preston during Guild Week. She recalled picnics on the canal bank, trips on barges and walks to Burscough Priory ruins. She thanked God for Nanna's generosity of spirit and, no longer fearful of the dead, pressed her lips lightly against the wrinkled cheek before going over to the chest of drawers in the corner and pulling out one drawer after another.

It was as Mrs Smith said. In the bottom one there was a small pile of matinee coats, bootees and bonnets, as well as a cobweb shawl of the purest, softest three-ply wool. She held the latter against her cheek, her eyes damp. She should have come before. Forcing down the grief which threatened to engulf her, she placed the tiny garments back in the drawer. Then she looked down at Nanna again before leaving the room.

The bedroom which had once been Molly's was not very big and she needed to squeeze past the foot of the bed to reach the window. A shaft of sunlight fell on the Wellington lockstitch sewing machine, made in Oldham. Her mother had sewed curtains and covers and clothes on this, never allowing Molly near it for fear she might break it. Pity, thought the girl. It could have been useful now, knowing how to sew.

She left the room to go downstairs and finish her bread and jam, conscious of that ache in the small of her back once more. She told herself not to worry. It was probably the bending down or that lousy bed in Ma Payne's. Just thinking of it made her itch and she scratched her arm, then her neck, hoping she hadn't caught a flea. At least she had escaped Ma's clutches, she thought, biting into the bread and jam again. Then despair took hold of her as she thought of Frank and the forthcoming birth.

She forced the scary thoughts away, and placing her hands on the wooden arms of the rocking chair, pushed herself up to kneel on the rag rug and place more coal on the fire. She felt another twinge of pain and her teeth caught on her lower lip. The pain ebbed. She must move more carefully. She probably just needed rest after rushing from one place to another. She levered herself up using the chair and went upstairs, hesitating outside Nanna's room before going into her own.

Molly removed the woollen skirt and the well-worn braided velour jacket Frank had brought her home from his last trip. In the high-necked blouse she had embroidered with flowers and her tie-waist drawers, she eased her bulk beneath the blankets. The pillow was of feathers and so was the mattress which enveloped her. She wriggled around, imagining how warm and safe a cygnet must feel beneath its mother's wings. Comfortable now she closed her eyes. A stillness settled over the room but she could not ignore the ache in her heart nor the one in her belly. It seemed to ebb and flow as she drifted on the borders of sleep, wondering how she was going to cope. She had to find someone to help her.

It was a long drawn out pain which brought Molly back into a shocked awareness of her surroundings. For a moment she could not think where she was. The room was dark and she felt frightened. Instinctively both her hands cradled her belly. Oh, God, that hurt! She sat bolt upright, stiff with fear.

The pain eased and her head flopped back against the pillow. She lay for a few minutes recovering, hoping it was a false alarm. Then it returned, slamming into her with the force of a sledgehammer. She gasped and sat up again, clutching the wooden post of the bedhead, breathing hurriedly. Then the contraction passed and she sank back against the pillow, sweating and trembling. 'This isn't nice. If I didn't know better I might believe Ma Payne had put a curse on me,' she said aloud, trying to make light of the situation.

She forced herself up and rolled off the bed, feeling a trickle of moisture down her leg. She tensed, trying to hold the water in, but it was no use. When the pain returned with what felt like double the force, she screamed, gripping the foot of the bed. Why did Nanna have to die? She should have been here to help. Now Molly was going to have to help herself.

The pain subsided slowly and for a few moments she was able to breathe deeply – in, out, in, out – trying to get as much air into her lungs as she could. But she ended up feeling dizzy.

'Oh, Lord, help me,' she whispered, wanting to believe it was possible that an angel would appear and magically help her to have a painless birth. Of course it didn't happen and she'd only managed to reach the door when she felt another contraction. She clung to the door jamb and screamed and screamed.

There was a thudding of feet on the stairs and Mrs Smith appeared on the landing with another woman. 'Oh, dear. Oh, dear,' muttered Molly's neighbour. 'I thought you were closer than you said. It's a good job you've a healthy pair of lungs.'

Molly said in a faint voice, 'I need a midwife.'

'You're in luck, lass. This is my sister-in-law and she's had eight of her own. She knows what to do. Isn't that right, Em?' Mrs Smith turned to the woman next to her.

'Thee knows it is.' Em's eyes were scanning the room behind Molly. She had a rawboned look about her and the girl noticed her large hands. 'Have to get the lass out of there. Too small. What about the front room?'

'Have you forgotten?' whispered Mrs Smith, nudging her. 'The old lady's laid out there.'

'The other one?'

'Full of junk. No bed.'

'Then there's nothing furrit,' said Em cheerfully. 'We'll have to move the old woman out. She won't mind.'

Mrs Smith looked uneasy but her sister-in-law seized hold of her arm and the next moment they'd vanished into the front room.

Molly couldn't believe it. Moving Nanna off her bed with no coffin to go into didn't seem right, but she doubted Em would take any notice of her objections. Anyway when the pain came again she would not have cared if they'd laid Nanna outside alongside her and she'd given birth in the lane with the whole neighbourhood watching. Just so long as she could get it over with. The two women came out of the front room carrying Nanna's body in the multicoloured bedspread. 'Where are you putting her?' gasped Molly.

'Nothing for it, lass. Got no choice but to put her on your bed,' said Em cheerfully. 'Now shift your carcase. Oops! Didn't mean to joke.'

Molly moved out of the way, considering Em far too cheerful in the circumstances. No doubt she would sing as Molly screamed in childbirth, too, considering her pain nothing to get upset about. She went into the front bedroom and gazed down at the spot where Nanna had rested. Mrs Smith entered the room, looking hot and flustered. 'I've got to walk thee, lass. Em's gone to get her bag of tricks.'

'I can walk on my own,' said Molly, shivering slightly. She didn't like the sound of that bag of tricks. 'I wouldn't mind a cup of tea, though.'

'I'll see to it. You just think about this baby.'

'I can hardly think of anything else,' she said crossly. A groan escaped her then, and she wished she could go to sleep and that when she woke the baby would be there. Still she walked up and down, up and down, knowing now why Nanna had never told her having a baby would be like this. Fairies and gooseberry bushes were all that had figured when Molly asked about such things. She paused as a pain gripped her again.

A smiling Em reappeared, wearing a spotless white pinny. 'Bad are they, dear?'

'That's a bloody daft question,' muttered Molly through gritted teeth, shocking herself by her own turn of phrase.

Em tutted. 'Wash thy mouth out with soap! Things always get worse before they get better.'

'Sorry,' said Molly meekly.

'It's OK, dear.' She rubbed her hands. 'Get on the bed and let's be seeing how far on you are.'

Reluctantly Molly climbed on to the double bed. 'You'd better have washed your hands,' she said. 'I've heard about women like you going from the dead to the living and mothers dying. It happened to my mam. Septicaemia.'

'Little knowall, aren't you?' said Em, rolling up her sleeves.

'Let me see your hands close up? Let me smell the soap,' said Molly bravely, still suspicious despite the spotless apron.

'You're a right doubting little madam,' said Em sniffily, holding out her hands.

Molly inspected them, her small nose almost resting on the woman's fingers. 'OK,' she said, submitting herself to her inspection.

Em surfaced with a pleased expression on her gaunt face 'Won't be long now, dear.'

Molly smiled with relief but the next contraction soon wiped the smile from her face. There was something different about this one and she told Em so.

'That's what I like to hear,' said the midwife briskly. 'Now pushhh! Pushhh! Stop – take a breath. Pant!'

Molly did as she was told, pushing, panting, gasping, resting, and pushing again until with a supreme effort her baby was finally delivered.

'She's perfect,' said Em, face flushed and eyes shining.

'She?' asked Molly doubtfully, lifting her head. 'Frank wanted a boy.'

'Well, she's a beautifully formed girl. Straight limbs. Lovely head. Here, have a hold of her. Then cups of tea all round, I think, don't you, Ada?'

'I'm on my way,' said Molly's neighbour happily.

Molly felt really proud of herself. She had achieved something that nobody else could have done for her. She began to weep from joy, sadness and relief all mixed up, not minding at all that she had a daughter. They had both survived, thank the Lord! But how she was going to keep them both was a different matter altogether.

Chapter Two

Molly rested against the pillow, nursing her baby and sipping tea. A frown furrowed her brow as she nervously listened to the noises and murmuring voices below. Oh, Lord, what was she going to do? It was two days since the birth and today was Nanna's funeral. Yesterday the undertaker had arrived with a coffin and until this morning the old woman had lain in state in the front parlour. Jack Fletcher had popped in to pay his respects but Em had not allowed him to visit Molly, saying she needed to rest. The girl would have liked to have seen him, certain he would have found some way to help her in the difficult position she was now in. She had also wanted to get up for the funeral but Em said certainly not. The weather had turned bitterly cold and what if she caught pneumonia? What would happen to her baby then? She mustn't be thinking of herself all the time, there was the little one to consider now. Then Em went off to attend another confinement.

Was she selfish? thought Molly, gazing at her suckling daughter, feeling sympathy for the woman whoever she was, having to go through what Molly had just suffered. Her heart swelled with love and a smile softened her face. Her milk had come in with a rush yesterday and very uncomfortable it was, too. Her breasts felt like water-filled balloons. But at least she possessed the means to prevent her child from going hungry so she was doing something right. That was as long as she could keep it up. Em had said she must eat properly to keep good milk coming but where Molly was to find the money to buy food she had not said. Perhaps she and Mrs Smith thought there would be a nice lump sum left over after paying out for the funeral but there would be barely enough to cover the costs and Nanna's savings had dwindled to virtually nothing in the last year. She had managed before, only with help from Molly's mother.

Molly eased her daughter from her left breast and placed her over her shoulder, patting the tiny back to bring up any wind as Em had shown her. She gnawed on her lower lip, wondering if she could eke out a living by taking in washing and ironing, not that she was very skilled at those things. Perhaps she could grow her own vegetables, as well as helping in the fields at harvest?

Her mother had told her of women who did such things when they'd lived here. They'd all feared the workhouse just as Mabel May had done. Where were they now? thought Molly. Where were their daughters and sons whom she had passed on her way to school with Nanna? She had never played out much with them. Nanna had always been nervous of her catching some infectious disease. Molly had made few friends so there was no one from her schooldays to whom she could turn. Reluctantly she accepted that Ma Payne had spoken the truth when she'd said Molly had not given enough thought to how she would manage. Without husband, family or friends her situation was desperate.

She set her baby to the other breast, resting her pointed chin on its downy head and wishing her mother was still alive, knowing she would have thought of some way out of this predicament.

Ten minutes had passed when Molly's thoughts were disturbed by footsteps and voices below. Surely the funeral was not over already? She recognised Em's surprisingly high-pitched tones but the other voice was deep. A man's? Uncle Jack?

There were footsteps on the stairs and, despite her daughter's mew of protest, Molly hastily made herself decent, buttoning up the flannelette nightgown and placing the baby in the top drawer of the chest which had been moved next to the bed. She reached for her shawl and pulled it about her shoulders.

It was not Jack Fletcher. The man who entered the room with the midwife looked to be in his early-twenties, of medium height, his face pale and drawn with high cheekbones that seemed to be threatening to break through the skin. He wore a green jumper and creased dark brown corduroy trousers. A dusting of what looked like sawdust clung to his hair and the wool of his jumper.

'Molly, this is Mr Nathan Collins,' said Em, coming to, stand next to her.

The name seemed vaguely familiar but she could not place it. 'Hello.' A hesitant smile hovered on her lips as she held out her hand.

His eyes were bleak but he gazed at her intently as he clasped her hand firmly. 'Mrs Payne.'

'How do you do?'

His grey eyes shifted to the drawer which contained her baby and he took a deep breath which shuddered through his wiry frame. 'I can pay you five shillings a week. Is that acceptable to you?'

'What?' Molly's tone was incredulous. She darted a look at Em but found no help there.

'Midwife seems to think you'll do it. I hope you'll find it in your heart to agree.'

'Pardon?'

'She was right when she said you're small. The strong part I'm not so sure about... but I'll see you get plenty of milk and good food down you. It's up to you then. Don't let me down.' His eyes met hers briefly and she felt as if he'd looked at her in such a way once before but could not think where. Then he turned and walked out of the room, clogs noisy on the wooden floor.

'What was all that about?' whispered Molly, looking at Em, scarcely able to believe her fortunes had changed so swiftly.

She smoothed the coverlet. 'A job only you can do but he insisted on having a look at you first. His wife died in the night after giving birth. Their first child, a girl, and she's struggling to live.' There was sadness in her eyes. 'I told him the little I know about your situation and suggested you might be willing to act as wet nurse to his child. You will, won't you? You'd be a fool not to.'

Help a tiny baby to live and do herself some good at the same time! Molly could not believe it. She had pints of milk. It oozed from her nipples even when she wasn't feeding, seeping through her camisole and the bodice of her nightgown. She could have fed half a dozen babies with it. The mouth that was a little too wide for her narrow face broke into a delighted grin. 'Of course I will. Praise the Lord! Tell him: Hurry, hurry!' She waved her hand frantically towards the door.

'Wise lass.' Em hurried out of the room.

Molly hunched her legs and wrapped her arms round them. 'What a Friend We Have in Jesus' she hummed to herself, thinking five shillings wouldn't pay the rent but it would certainly help. And food! He was going to provide her with nourishing grub. She felt like getting up out of bed and dancing round the room but Em would have her life. Who was he? She wished she could put a name to his face. A couple of years older than her at St John's? The name Nathan was from the Old Testament. Hadn't he been some kind of prophet to King David? The King who'd sent Bathsheba's husband to the front line after seeing her bathing on the roof of her house one evening.

The baby wailed and Molly reached for her. She lay back against the pillows and closed her eyes. Suddenly Frank was in her thoughts and tears rolled down her cheeks. 'What would he have made of it? Me feeding another man's child,' she murmured. 'I don't think he'd have liked it. But what else can I do? We've got to live, haven't we, baby sweetheart? And I have to help Mr Collins. Me and him, like, we're almost in the same boat.'

She fell silent, feeling rather foolish. It was the first sign of madness, talking to oneself. She opened her eyes and looked out of the window. The sky was a uniform grey but even so she wanted to be out there in the fresh air. She was fed up of being bedridden, using the po, feeling strangely haunted sometimes by Nanna for sleeping in her bed.

Don't think of her being buried in the churchyard! Don't even think of death! Frank filled her thoughts again but she shut him out quickly. Think of that other baby. What would she be like? Fair? Dark? Nathan Collins's hair was that pale brown shade that might turn golden in the sun. She looked down at her daughter, noticing she had no eyelashes worth speaking of. After a few minutes Molly removed her from the breast and put her back in the drawer, then she slid out of bed.

Her gait was unsteady as she made her way over to the window. She unlocked it and pushed up the lower sash so she could lean out and take deep breaths of air tinged with smoke from the chimneys. As she rested her elbows on the windowsill, her eyes searched the street. She spotted a dog snuffling in the gutter on the other side of the lane where the houses backed on to another street beyond which was the canal. She thought of Ma Payne and would dearly have loved to see her mother-in-law's face when she found Molly missing. What tale had Cath made up to explain her absence? Molly put her tongue in her cheek and her eyes gleamed. How she wished she could have been an invisible spectator at that scene. Was it possible she and Cath could have become friends in time? It would be lovely to have a real friend.

'Molly, what are you doing at that window?' It was Em, standing in the street below bearing a muffled shape in her arms, rawboned face upturned to hers.

'I was getting some fresh air. Is that the baby?'

'Aye, poor mite. Now, shoo! I'll expect you in bed by the time I get up there.'

Molly did as she was instructed because if the truth be told she was feeling a little shaky on her pins.

Em entered the room. 'Here she is. Do your best. She's already been christened just in case. Jessica Esther.' The baby was placed in Molly's outstretched arms. 'Her paternal grandmother'll be coming to see her. She keeps house for her half-brother, Mr Barnes. You probably don't remember him but he helped set up that candlemaking factory the other side of town. Apparently he wanted Mr Collins working for him but the lad wasn't having any, so Mr Barnes went back to Liverpool where he has his main candlemaking business and put someone else in charge. Last I heard he was trying to persuade the lad to move to Liverpool.'

'So Mr Collins isn't poor?' said Molly, easing back a fold of shawl and gazing on the shuttered, crumpled face of the baby.

'She's worn out. Put her to the breast right away. I'll look in on you both later. I'm fair whacked.' Em squeezed her shoulder gently and was about to leave when Molly repeated her question concerning Nathan Collins.

Em rubbed her nose absently. 'He's got a trade. Joiner or cabinetmaker, one or t'other. He married a lass from Newburgh way. Now she's dead, perhaps he'll go to Liverpool.'

'He told you all this?'

'Eee, lass, not all.' Em smiled. 'Next-door neighbour who's known the family for years told me. I'll leave you in peace now.'

For a few moments after she went Molly sat staring into space, trying to remember what she knew about Nathan Collins, but the memory proved elusive. Shaking back her hair, which was in two plaits for convenience's sake, she began to undo her buttons. She rolled the baby's name round her tongue. 'Jessica Esther. Posh name for a little scrap like you,' she said, stroking the corner of the tiny rosebud mouth. She had been taught by Em how to encourage a baby to root for the breast. Her daughter had caught on right away but this one was not overly interested. Molly persisted, squeezing droplets of milk from her nipple so they fell on the baby's lips. The tip of her tongue caught a drop. Immediately Molly eased a nipple into the tiny mouth. Feebly the baby suckled, stopping after a few moments as if it was all too much effort. 'Come on, Jessica! I'm not having this,' Molly chided. 'You're going to keep us out the workhouse, my girl.' She stroked the smooth cheek again and the tiny mouth worked.

The next two hours were frustrating and tiring for Molly. Her mind wandered, pondering what Em told her about Nathan Collins and his uncle. What were the odds he would leave Burscough now his wife was dead and take his child with him? Would he take her as well? Molly's heart sank and she felt scared all over again. Dear Lord, she hoped so much he would want her and her baby! She gazed down at Jessica, no longer suckling, and lightly pinched her in an effort to get her to fight and feed. It was only her daughter's crying that caused her to give up.

She placed Jessica at the other end of the large drawer, hoping Mr Collins would bring spare clothing and nappies next time he called. She was going to be stuck if he didn't. She lifted her daughter, yawned and stretched out on the bed to start the feeding process all over again.

Nathan Collins turned up early the following morning. Fortunately Molly was awake, dressed and having a cup of tea. If anything he looked worse than he had the day before. The rings beneath his eyes were so deep they looked like bruises. He was carrying a wooden cradle and without speaking placed it just inside the lobby. She noted that it contained blankets and clothing for the baby.

'Ta. I was wondering about those,' said Molly, making an effort to sound cheerful and friendly.

His only response was to take hold of her right hand and press two half crowns into it. 'There's your money. I'll see you again next week. And I've told the grocer up the road to deliver some provisions to you. Good morning.'

'Hang on!' called Molly as he turned away, taking her courage in both hands. 'Don't you want to see your daughter?'

'What?' He stumbled on the step and appeared to lose his balance.

'Steady. You don't want to break a leg,' she said, taking his arm. His head turned and there was an expression in his eyes that sent a quiver right through her. If looks could kill, she thought. 'I'm sorry, I just thought it would help you to see her,' she stammered.

'I'm not paying you to think!' He sounded quite savage and suddenly Molly remembered who he was and was half scared, half annoyed. Fancy it being him! Did he remember her? Oh, Lord! She couldn't resist opening her mouth and repeating just what she had said then. 'Yes, Nathan Collins. Three bags full, Nathan Collins!' She tugged an imaginary forelock.

'Don't you be giving me any cheek,' he said wrathfully, his face colouring. 'I'm paying your wages and don't you forget it! My mother'll be round some time today to see the baby. Now I've things to do. A funeral to arrange.'

'Yes, Mr Collins. I'm sorry, sir,' she said meekly, lifting the cradle with both hands. She turned her back on him and kicked the door with her heel. It was not her intention it should close with a slam but it did and she wondered what he'd made of that.

Grimacing, she walked through into the kitchen. It was not until she'd placed the cradle on the stone floor that she felt ashamed for reacting to his rudeness in the way she had, but it was odd he had not asked to see his child. Speaking of whom… Molly hurried upstairs to feed the babies, wondering when Mrs Collins would arrive. Not that her vague memories of the woman made her keen to see her.

By dinner time there was still no sign of Mrs Collins but the delivery boy arrived with the provisions. Lots of lovely bacon and eggs, butter, cheese, potatoes, carrots, cabbage, onions and potatoes, as well as milk. Molly emptied the milk in the boy's jug into another and returned his to him. As she put the groceries away she realised how weary she was but there was still washing to do.

She had brought rags with her to bind herself and a day's supply was all that was left. Em had given her three tiny night-dresses, brushing aside her offers of payment, two of which were

29

also in soak. Molly was finding that babies were messy and time-consuming and hoped she could cope. For the first time in her life there was nobody to correct any mistakes she might make and that was scary, as well as a challenge.

She lit a fire under the copper in the outhouse, which wasn't easy because the wind blew beneath the door and kept shifting her waxed taper. In the end she managed it but her fingers were sooty. She put everything in to boil together.

Hunger gnawed at her insides as she fried bacon, onion, sliced potato and cabbage in the blackened frying pan. It was her most substantial meal in days and tasted heavenly when washed down with two cups of sweet, milky tea. She felt almost a new woman and her worry about being pert to Nathan Collins eased. Even so she must be nice to him. It was obvious the poor bloke was feeling pretty dreadful about losing his wife. She knew what that was like so should have been more under-standing. A yawn escaped her and within minutes Molly was asleep.

She woke to hear a baby's screams. Feeling stiff, she hurried upstairs. It was chilly in the bedroom so she carried both babies downstairs. Placing Jessica in the cradle she saw to her daughter's needs first, knowing she would have to give more time to Nathan's child. 'I should give you a name,' she said, cuddling her daughter. 'Perhaps I should name you after your gran.' She kissed the fluffy, soft-as-silk hair, placing her at the opposite end of the cradle to Jessica and lifting her out. Molly kissed her, too, thinking: Poor little mite, having no mam.

The child was lethargic and took hardly any milk. Molly was worried and hoped Em would call as promised. She hung the washing on the line, dismayed to find that the whites were no longer white but streaked pink and red. Stupid! Why hadn't she thought of washing Nanna's red flannelette nightie separately? Still, no use worrying now.

She made another attempt at feeding Jessica but could not wake the child so sat in the rocking chair, nursing her. Molly dozed off. When she woke the fire was almost out, a baby was crying and there was someone knocking at the door.

'Wait! Please wait!' she called, placing Jessica on the chair.

It was not Em as she'd hoped but a woman she realised must be Mrs Collins.

Her gaze swept over the bedraggled Molly, who involuntarily glanced down at herself and saw that her skirt was soiled. 'You are Mrs Payne?' The older woman's tone was chilly.

'That's right.' She made an attempt to appear in control of the situation. 'P-Please, come in. I'm-I'm afraid you've caught me offguard. I-I fell asleep.'

Mrs Collins stepped over the threshold. She was of medium height with a well-corseted figure, dressed neatly in a black jacket and a long black serge skirt. Her grey hair was almost concealed by a black bonnet. 'You're very young but I appreciate what you're doing,' she said stiffly.

'I'm grateful for the job,' said Molly, leading the way in, certain the other woman had not recognised her. She went to the rocking chair and picked up Jessica. She was about to say, 'Here's your grand-daughter,' when she saw something in the baby's face that turned her own heart to stone. Molly pressed her cheek to the child's. It was cold and she could feel no breath in her.

At the same time Mrs Collins spotted the cradle and hurried forward, bending over the crying baby. 'Shouldn't you feed my grand-daughter first?' she said impatiently, reaching in and lifting up Molly's daughter.

The words 'That's not Jessica' died on Molly's lips and her mouth went dry. In a voice she barely recognised as her own, she said, 'If you'll just give me a minute, I-I must change my skirt.'

She hurried out of the room, up the stairs and into the front bedroom with Jessica clutched to her bosom. She felt sick, really sick. Trembling, she sat on the bed, staring down at the dead child in her arms. She could hear her own baby screaming downstairs. What was she to do? Oh, Lord, what do I do? she thought frantically. Mrs Collins called upstairs, demanding that she hurry.

Swiftly Molly placed the dead child in the drawer and covered her up. Then she glanced down at her own soiled skirt and revulsion struck her. Shaking she went over to the alcove in the corner of the room and pulled back the curtain. Behind it hung several skirts and a coat that had been Nanna's. She took out a skirt and found a clean rag in a drawer. With trembling fingers she undressed, taking out a clean blouse to replace the one that was damp with milk.

Feeling faint, she leaned heavily on the bedpost, trying to slow her rapidly beating heart. After a few moments she felt a little better but could not bear to look in the direction of the drawer where she had placed the dead baby. Trying to blank out all thoughts of Jessica, she went downstairs to find Mrs Collins standing by the fire, fingers in her ears.

'There you are! And about time, too,' she said crossly, lowering her arms. 'I can't stand hearing a baby cry. Feed my granddaughter immediately. She'll give Nathan something to live for once he's done with mourning that woman.'

Molly dredged deep inside her for the right way to say that this baby was *her* daughter. That if Nathan Collins's future depended on his child's being alive then he didn't have one. But a thought struck her, as painful as a blow from a dagger. What if they blame me for the baby's death? I might end up in prison! And what will happen to my baby then? Oh, Lord!

She sat down and with trembling fingers unfastened her blouse. As her child began to suckle Molly's mind worked over-time. What were the odds against Nathan Collins recognising his own child? He had scarcely given either baby a glance, for all his mother seemed to believe his child would be his saving grace.

Molly looked at Mrs Collins and saw the woman frowning as she watched her. She forced a smile, wondering what was going on in the visitor's head. She couldn't possibly have any suspicion that the baby Molly was feeding was not her granddaughter. After all, she had laid claim to her herself. Nevertheless Molly felt guilty and closed her eyes, wanting to shut out the older woman's face. Suddenly she thought of Em and Mrs Smith and felt chilled to the marrow. Would they be able to distinguish which baby was which?

'You shivered,' said Mrs Collins abruptly. 'I hope you're not coming down with something.'

'No, I'm fine. Just tired,' murmured Molly, willing herself to keep her nerve.

'I think I knew your mother,' said the elder woman, eyes narrowing. 'Wasn't she Mabel May?'

'Yes.'

'I thought so. She was one for the lads. People used to say how attractive she was.' There was a peculiar note in her voice. 'You're not like her, though. You're no beauty.'

That's a bit of an insult, thought Molly indignantly. Who was this woman to say such things about her and her mother? 'No better than she should be,' she remembered Nanna saying about Dorothy Collins once. As for her son... Molly remembered once coming across him with his bum hanging out of his pants when he'd been scrumping plums. The owner had suddenly come out of her house and Molly had called to Nathan, telling him to hurry but to be careful and not break a leg. He'd come down that tree too fast and torn his pants and she had laughed and laughed, partly from nerves, thinking he might get shot and she'd be implicated as well, and partly because his expression was so comical. He'd been furious and boxed her ears and told her not to tell anyone, that he was depending on her to keep it quiet. In those days he and his mother had been as poor as she and hers, his farm hand father having been kicked in the head by a cow and killed.

There was the sound of someone at the door and Mrs Collins went to open it. Em entered the room and Molly's heart began to pound. The moment of truth. She took a deep breath. 'My little one hasn't been too good today. I wonder if you could take a look at her, Em? She's upstairs sleeping.'

'Course I will,' said the midwife, stopping in the middle of the room and running a hand over the cradle. 'This is a lovely piece of craftsmanship. Your son's got a real talent, Mrs Collins.'

'It's not what I wanted for him,' she said stiffly. 'But he's always been stubborn, like his father before him. I believe I've you to thank for saving my grand-daughter.'

Em sighed. 'I was only sorry I couldn't save the mother. Sad it was.'

'Aye. But he married against my wishes, you know. Still he's only young and can marry again and have a son the next time.'

'Well, that's up to the good Lord,' said Em shortly. 'I'll go upstairs, Molly, and take a peek at your little lass.'

'She seems to be having trouble breathing.' That was true all right, poor little mite. 'I've wrapped her up well and put her to sleep in the drawer.' She lifted her head, knowing there was no need to pretend to look worried because she was scared out of her wits.

Em's expression softened. 'Don't thee be fretting, lass. I'll see to her.'

As the midwife left the room Molly's back ached with tension and her ears strained to catch every sound overhead. When Em's footsteps stopped Molly fixed her eyes on her sleeping daughter. She must start thinking of her as Jessica. She rocked her gently as Em's footsteps came hurrying downstairs. She held the dead baby in her arms and anyone looking at her would have known instantly that something was terribly wrong.

'What is it?' said Molly, voice trembling.

Em's eyes fixed on her face and the girl had to force herself to hold that stare. Did Em suspect? Surely she delivered so many babies she couldn't possibly remember what each individual looked like? Em sighed and said gently, 'I don't understand it. Molly, I'm sorry but your baby's dead.'

'No!' she screamed, rising in the chair and thrusting her own child at Mrs Collins. The woman caught it to her hastily as Molly held out her arms for the dead baby. Em hesitated only a second before handing her over. The tears the girl shed were real as she went through the motions of verifying Em's statement. She only had to dwell on Frank's death or Nanna's to be filled with sorrow.

Mrs Collins appeared embarrassed and although she expressed sympathy, kept her distance. Then she said unexpectedly, 'I don't know if I should let you take care of my grandchild any longer. I mean — to allow your own child to die says something, doesn't it?'

Molly was dumbstruck but Em turned on the woman. 'Molly hardly allowed it! There but for the grace of God goes your son's daughter, Mrs Collins. It is the Lord who decides who to take and who to leave. If it weren't for Molly you wouldn't be holding a live baby in your arms right now.'

'You've got a nerve, speaking to me like that,' said the older woman, turning scarlet. 'This is my grand-daughter, and I'll say what's right for her.'

Terrified she was going to be parted from her baby, Molly found her voice. 'She's not your child, though, is she, Mrs Collins? Your son hired me to look after her. I think he should have the final say as to whether I'm fit or not to look after her.'

'I agree,' said Em, folding her arms across her chest. 'And I'm willing to go and see Mr Collins right now in his workshop and tell him what's happened here.'

Mrs Collins looked affronted and her eyes flashed. 'You do that! And tell him to come right away.'

Em hurried out.

Molly and Mrs Collins stared at one another resentfully. She hates me, thought Molly, wondering why. Am I mad to put myself in a position where this woman has a say in my daughter's future? Might as well have stayed with Ma Payne. Might as well tell the truth. Yet where would that lead?

They'd want to know why I pretended it was my child who was dead. They might think I deliberately killed Jessica. She glanced down at the dead baby in her arms and realised just how thick her eyelashes were. Had Em noticed? Had Nathan Collins? Terror gripped her as she imagined the hangman's noose.

Without a word to Mrs Collins she left the room and went upstairs. Once more she placed the dead baby in the drawer and covered her with a blanket. She thought of Nathan Collins and his attitude to the child; of Mrs Collins and the way she spoke of her son being stubborn. Molly considered how Mrs Collins had called her daughter-in-law 'that woman' and so obviously been against the marriage. Could it be that there was little love lost between mother and son? Molly smiled tight-lipped, convinced it was so, and thought, surely he wouldn't have noticed such a thing as the length of his daughter's eyelashes? When he arrives I'll put on the act of my life, playing the role of grieving mother with such conviction there won't be any doubt in his mind that the dead baby is mine. I also have to convince him that the surviving child cannot possibly survive without me.

—

Nathan leaned against the dresser, arms folded, staring at Molly. The tears were still damp on her cheeks. They were alone except for the baby sleeping in the cradle. He had told his mother to get out. She had refused at first but when he had shown signs of evicting her forcibly had left, protesting volubly.

Suddenly he spoke and although Molly had been waiting for him to do so, she jumped. 'Sorry!' She cleared her throat and although she'd heard what he said, asked him to repeat it.

'I said, won't you find it upsetting, Mrs Payne, feeding my child when your own is dead? Taking care of her as if she was your own?'

'I think that goes without saying, Mr Collins.' Molly's voice was low but distinct and she resisted the urge to pleat the skirt of her apron between her nervous fingers. She wished she could read his thoughts. He knew who she was all right. Probably had done immediately Em had mentioned Nanna's death and gave him this address.

'I don't want you breaking down...'

'I won't,' she said earnestly. 'I care about Jessica's well-being.'

He raised his thick dark eyebrows. 'Maybe.'

Molly took a deep breath. 'What are your choices if you sack me? Will your mother feed her with cow's milk from a bottle? Em says that can upset a baby's stomach. Or will you search for another woman who's just given birth? The trouble with that is, her husband might not like the idea of her feeding another man's child.'

His expression froze. 'Is that how your husband would have felt? You're a very young widow, Mrs Payne. Did you really have one?'

Her cheeks flamed. 'That's an insult! If my mother were here to hear you say such a thing, she'd swipe you one! You're not a very old widower, Mr Collins. What kind of girl do you think I am?'

'I wouldn't know. I don't know you very well.'

'You do know me, though?' she challenged.

'Aye, I remember you,' he said softly. 'You told the whole school about me falling out of that tree and tearing my pants so my arse stuck out. You told them I was a scaredy cat.'

'I said nothing of the sort!' she said indignantly. 'That must have been Anna Hepple-white. I happened to meet her going home after it happened. I was crying because you really hurt my ear when you boxed it and she wanted to know what was wrong. Bum... that's what I said to her. And "the whole school's" an exaggeration. And weren't you scared? Old Mrs Howarth had a shotgun.' She folded her arms. 'Anyway what's that got to do with here and now? It's no good reason for implying I lack morals.'

'I think it's everything to do with it! You lack respect for me.' His eyes did not leave her face.

'I do have respect for you,' muttered Molly. 'Although Nanna always said respect must be earned.'

'What!' He glared at her and took a step forward. 'Are you saying I have to earn your respect?'

'No!' she squeaked, stepping back a pace. 'I'm sure you're very respectable now. And so am I. I only said what I did because I was hurt. Of course I had a husband. I must have done if I'm a widow, mustn't I? You didn't doubt it before the baby died. Or did you? Perhaps you didn't but do now because you think I killed her?' Molly said boldly.

He looked astonished. 'Have you gone off your head?'

'Of course not!' Her dire situation struck her afresh. 'I've just had one shock on top of another. It's not surprising I'm in a bit of a state. Aren't you feeling terrible with your wife dying?'

He said nothing but his lips tightened as he went over to the cradle and looked down at the sleeping child lying snugly wrapped in a shawl so that only the top of her head showed. He put out one hand. 'Don't disturb her!' Molly's heart danced a crazy, terrified he might suddenly remember what his baby had looked like. She hurried over to him. 'Look at her, so peaceful.' Her voice was soft and loving. 'Let her sleep. Why don't you come and see her tomorrow when she's awake?' It was a daft thing to say because how was he to know when the baby would be awake?

'The funeral's tomorrow.' The pain in his eyes reminded her of a dog her stepfather had once kicked. The poor creature hadn't understood why it was booted out of the pub just for cocking its leg.

Nathan moved away from the cradle and slumped into a chair. He dropped his head into his hands. 'You didn't know my wife.' His voice was muffled. 'She wasn't from the village but Newburgh. Near enough so she could visit her family when she wanted.'

Her family! Molly's heart performed that crazy rhythm again and she felt dizzy, reaching out to clutch the cradle. She hadn't thought of his wife having sisters or a mother. Perhaps she should take her daughter and run?

'Are you all right?' His words seemed to be coming from a long way off. Molly made no answer, fumbling with the blanket instead. He sprang to his feet and took her arm. She struggled but he forced her across the room and down into the rocking chair, gazing down at her remorsefully. 'I'm a selfish sod, I haven't even said I'm sorry about your baby.'

'Your wife's family?' she said faintly. 'Will they want to take her?'

'Hell, no! Her brothers have families of their own. Jess was like a mother to them for years after her own ma died.'

Molly felt giddy with relief. She watched him sit down opposite her in a wheel-backed chair, elbows on his knees. 'She was a few years older than me but there was a goodness and understanding in Jess that drew me to her. She let me talk and would really listen, She encouraged me to stick to my guns and do what I wanted when Ma was at me all the time to drop my apprenticeship and go into my uncle's factory. She hit the roof but I married Jess anyhow.' He stared at her. 'So who was he, this husband of yours?'

She told him how she'd met Frank and about his being lost at sea. 'If it hadn't been for the baby, I might have given up.' Molly's voice cracked and tears stung her eyelids.

'Don't be upsetting yourself,' said Nathan roughly, clasping his hands tight between his knees. 'I was wrong, I shouldn't have said what I did. It's lousy to lose your baby as well as your husband.'

'Terrible,' she managed in a choking voice, feeling guilt-ridden, hardly daring to look at him. 'If it wasn't for you and Jessica, I'd throw myself in the canal.'

'You mustn't do that!' he exclaimed. 'You can stay on here, looking after little Jess. I'll see if I can find you extra money.'

That was good news. Surprising, though. She rubbed her face with the back of her hand, relieved. 'How?'

He was silent for so long she thought he'd gone into a trance like she did sometimes when unable to think straight.

'I'll ask my uncle for it.'

'The one with the factory?'

He nodded. 'He turned Papist but he's strong family feelings for all that.'

She looked at him and said dubiously. 'Will he give you money if you aren't going to work for him?'

'That's the big question. He wants me to be an ecclesiastic candlemaker.' Nathan sounded disgusted at the prospect and held out his hands, staring down at them. Molly stared at them, too. His fingers were long and straight, skin roughened in places, fingernails short. 'I've got a trade in these. I love working with wood.' His voice held a fierce pride.

'You're his nephew. Are you sure he actually wants you making the candles?'

'If I'm not making them, he'll have me in an office. I'd have to give up all I've worked for.'

'What is it you've got exactly?' she said real interest.

'Don't you start!' He rubbed one hand over his stubbly chin, frowning. 'It takes time to build up a business.' Molly said nothing, staring at him, thinking she wished she had a rich uncle who wanted her for his heir. 'You're thinking I'm stupid, aren't you?' growled Nathan. 'But candles are a thing of the past.'

'I was reading about a church in Liverpool being wired for electricity.'

'Exactly!' He got to his feet. 'I must tell my uncle that. I bet everybody'll be using electricity one day.'

'Maybe. They said gas was dangerous but lots of people have it now. St John's is lit by gas.'

'I'm not interested in gas,' said Nathan, pacing the floor. 'Wood, Molly, that's what I enjoy working with.'

'Nice. I'm good at embroidery.' She looked at him but could tell he wasn't listening. She sighed and got back to the subject in hand, the one that really interested her: his paying her more wages. 'But if you don't go and work for him, how are you going to get more money to pay me?'

He didn't answer but sat down again, elbows resting on his thighs. 'I don't know. People might talk, but you could always come and live with me?' he suggested tentatively.

She was astounded. 'What d'you mean — might? I'm not having my reputation torn to shreds.'

'You'd be perfectly safe.' He scowled at her. 'I've just lost my wife. I'm not about to start fancying you. Anyway, let's give it a week then see what happens. In the meantime...' He hesitated.

'In the meantime, what?' Molly's eyes alive with interest.

'Your baby.' His expression was sober. 'It'll have to be buried, won't it? And that'll cost money.'

The brightness in her face faded. Another thing she hadn't thought about. She felt sick.

'I know it must upset you but you have to think about it. You can't leave her up there.' He jerked his head ceilingwards.

Molly almost choked on her guilt and her eyes filled with tears.

'Don't cry!' He hesitated before taking one of her hands in his and squeezing it.

'That hurts,' she mumbled.

He dropped it. 'I've an idea. I've got a nice piece of oak in my workroom. If I go home now I can knock something up to place her in. It won't be a proper posh coffin but you can wrap the baby up snug and she'll be OK in it. She can be laid to rest with Jess. That would save you money.'

Looking into his embarrassed face, Molly was almost too moved to speak. A tear escaped and rolled down her cheek.

'Don't! Don't cry, I keep telling you!' he shouted. 'It makes...' His voice broke. Getting to his feet, he strode out of the room, hands in pockets, head bent.

Molly was so astonished by his behaviour she scrambled to her feet and rushed after him. But he was already out of the house and halfway down the street by the time she reached the front door.

Nathan was as good as his word, arriving late the following morning with a plain oak box, sandpapered smooth as silk and so newly varnished the surface was still tacky. He looks dreadful, thought Molly. 'You must have been up all night,' she said, guilt-ridden again, taking the tiny coffin from him.

'It had to be done,' he muttered, fumbling in his pocket and bringing out some large nails. 'You'll have to nail the lid down.'

At this blood seemed to drain from her face, leaving her dizzy and shaking to think of shutting a tiny baby away in a box. Still she managed to thank him, eyes avoiding his, fixing instead on his neck where the starched white collar had caused a red weal on his skin. He was dressed in a black suit, which made his skin look even paler. She cleared her throat, feeling she needed to say more. 'I appreciate what you've done. I'm grateful, too, that you told the vicar about the baby.'

'He came to see you?'

Molly nodded. 'He was kind. Mabel May he christened her.' She cleared her throat again, hoping that God didn't mind the dead baby's being christened twice while her own child wasn't baptised at all.

Nathan made no comment, swaying with weariness. He placed a hand on the door jamb to keep himself upright. She felt concerned for him. 'D'you want to come in? See Jessica? Have something to eat?'

'No food.' He followed her indoors.

The baby lay in the cradle, eyes wide open, waving her tiny fists in the air. He stared down at her and Molly's heart began to beat in a crazy manner but Nathan did not comment or touch the child and after a moment said he would have to go.

After seeing him out, she hurried indoors and picked up her daughter. Molly cuddled her, rubbing her cheek against the petal soft face and covering it in kisses before placing her in the cradle. Then, with a deep sigh, she bent and picked up the tiny coffin. Bowed down with sadness, she went into the parlour. She had refused Em's offer to lay out the baby, fearful that even at that late hour she might suddenly recognise Nathan's daughter.

Earlier Molly had dressed her in one of the nightgowns Em had brought, fastened a bonnet Nanna had knitted on her tiny head and wrapped her in a blanket. Now she lined the coffin with red flannel cut from one of Nanna's nightgowns. Red for warmth, she thought, wanting to believe it would do just that for Jessica Esther in the grave.

Mrs Smith had volunteered to look after the baby while Em accompanied Molly to the church at Burscough Bridge. She remembered Nanna telling her that St John's was a Waterloo church, built as were many others in the 1820s and 30s with money put aside for memorials to that momentous battle. It was built of stone, some of it carried by barge from Parbold quarry not far away. Molly had been christened in that church and remembered singing there lustily in later years alongside her mother and Nanna.

The service was as she'd expected a sad and sombre occasion. After a swift glance at Nathan and his mother, Molly kept her gaze averted. The sight of him caused her more guilt and anguish and she was glad that the old-fashioned hat with veiling which she'd found on top of a cupboard concealed her face.

It was not until they were standing in the churchyard at the grave, the tiny coffin already in the ground alongside the larger one, that Mrs Collins approached Molly. 'I'm not pleased with you,' she said, looking down her nose at the girl. 'What right have you to bury your child here at my son's expense?'

Molly felt like saying, 'You choose your moments, don't you?' but instead gazed down at her boots, the heels of which had sunk into the grass. She closed her eyes and prayed, tears oozing from beneath her lids. She thought of Frank, wondering what he would have made of her burying another man's child as theirs.

'Tsk! You're as bad as your mother. She could turn on the waterworks at the drop of a hat,' sneered Mrs Collins.

'What! Not my mother,' said Molly in surprise. 'She was strong.'

'Humph! Not at your age, she wasn't. She knew exactly how to softsoap the men.'

'Leave her alone, Mother. Where's your heart?' snapped Nathan.

Mrs Collins sniffed and walked away. Molly's eyes met his briefly before he turned and left the graveside.

Em touched Molly's arm. 'Time to be going, I think,' she said gently. 'You don't want to linger. Best say your goodbyes and go.'

Molly nodded, her heart a little lighter because of the midwife's words. She must have convinced her the baby in the grave was her own. But now she had to look to the future. 'Can you point out Mr Collins's uncle to me?'

'He's not here, lass. Had an accident.'

Molly was put out. She wanted to see the kind of man Mr Barnes was for herself. What did he feel about his nephew having a daughter?

'Pity you didn't think of placing the little one to sleep with Mrs Fletcher,' said Em.

Molly realised her mistake and her heart sank. 'I haven't been thinking straight. I'll visit her grave now.'

'Natural in the circumstances.' Em took her arm and they walked between gravestones until they reached a freshly heaped mound of earth. There she left Molly alone with her grief.

It was here Jack Fletcher found her. 'You've heard?' she said when he spoke her name, and looked up at him with limpid eyes.

'About thy baby? Aye, lass. And I'm more sorry than I can say.' He took one of her hands between his two large ones and held it there. 'I've come to see if there's owt I can do for thee? If thee wants to go back to Bootle, I can take thee.'

'Thanks, Uncle Jack,' she said warmly. 'But I've been hired to look after Mr Collins's baby. You probably heard his wife died?'

'Aye. But I'm not sure thee's doing the right thing there, lass. His mother's a poisonous woman. She hated your mam. Thee's best not having anything to do with that family.'

Molly could see his point but she had made her decision and she was not going back on it. 'The baby needs me – and it helps knowing I can do some good.'

He frowned and shifted his stance. 'If that's what you want, but keep your distance, lass.'

What did he mean by that? thought Molly. Distance from whom? Mrs Collins? She cleared her throat. 'Mrs Collins wants her son to work for his uncle. Do you remember him?'

'He could do worse,' he said grudgingly. 'Barnes is a good man. Does thou know where his factory is, lass?'

'Liverpool.'

'Aye, not far from Athol Street gasworks.'

'Not the most salubrious of districts,' said Molly wryly. Athol Street was a long thoroughfare starting at the junction between Stanley Road and Scotland Road and ending in Great Howard Street where the North Docks Good Station was situated. The Leeds-Liverpool canal cut through it.

'His uncle's a warm man. Got no kiddies of his own. The lad'll come into it all if he uses his head and accepts the offer.'

If, thought Molly, thinking there was little hope of her persuading Nathan to see the sense in what Uncle Jack was saying. He would have to reach his own decision. Then what a future there could be for her daughter! Molly's heart lifted. She pictured her little love as the darling of both uncle and nephew. Plenty of food, pretty dresses, and handsome, rich beaux one day.

'Are you listening to me, Molly May?'

'What?' She fixed him with a vacant stare.

'It doesn't matter, lass.' Jack patted her shoulder. 'Thee just remember, if thee needs any help...'

She nodded and thanked him as they left the churchyard together. They parted at the bridge. The days ahead were not going to be easy, she thought. Playing the role of grieving mother and widow should not be difficult but hiding her love for her baby would be. No one must guess the truth if her daughter was to have that rosy future. And if she herself was caught out in such a deception? Molly shivered. It was just as easy for her to imagine climbing the steps to the gallows while her poor daughter was taken from her to some dreadful orphanage as it was to imagine her child the daughter of a rich man.

Chapter Three

New book reveals secrets of the Feminine figure. 100,000 free copies of The Royal Blue Book of 1909 Styles to give away. The world's highest salaried corset designer on How to Put on a Corset...

Molly crumpled the sheet of newspaper into a ball, placing it in the grate. She couldn't understand anyone wanting to wear such instruments of torture but she'd enjoyed reading the article and dreaming of her daughter one day being rich enough to wear splendid gowns to go with the corsets.

The herring Molly had eaten for supper last night had come wrapped in a double sheet of the Liverpool *Echo*, providing her with enough reading material to while away the hour after she gave Jessica her last feed of the evening before going up to bed herself. She read every bit of the newsprint, including all the advertisements. *Zam Buk heals limb that doctor said should be amputated! Pink Pills for pale people are unique for they supply that new pure blood, 2s 9d per box. Private Detective Agency: Charles Williams & Son, Dale St. Enquiries of all kinds accepted.* Molly had never imagined there being a detective agency in Liverpool. What kind of investigating did they do?

She sat back on her heels, smiling at her baby lying on a blanket on the rag rug, kicking her feet in the air. Em had told Molly off for not wrapping Jessica up tightly so her limbs would grow straight, and sadly the two women had fallen out over this. Molly too much enjoyed seeing these signs of development in her child to do as she was told, saying swaddling was old-fashioned and that she had read somewhere that muscles not regularly used wasted away. She'd tried to explain this to Em but the older woman had said if it was good enough for the baby Jesus, then it was good enough for her.

Easter had been and gone and financially Molly was no better off because Nathan's uncle had refused to give him money with no strings attached. Disappointed, and seeing her dreams for her daughter's future fading away, Molly had almost told him he was a fool. When Nathan had suggested once more that she go and live in his house, she'd refused. He had shrugged his powerful shoulders and not seemed at all put out by her refusal. But at least when the sole came off her boot and he noticed her walking oddly he'd made her a pair of wooden and leather clogs.

Molly had resorted to pawning things to pay the rent and so far had rid herself of the single bed, a chest of drawers and all the junk in the spare bedroom. But still it wasn't enough and now she was considering climbing into the attic and seeing what paraphernalia there was up there.

She was not completely without resources, though. On Easter Monday Nathan's brothers-in-law had dropped by en masse to see the baby. The eldest, Johnny, had placed a shiny gold sovereign in the baby's hand, tears in his eyes. His brothers did likewise before they all shuffled out of the cottage without a word. That was the last Molly had seen of them. She supposed if she was really desperate she could go to them and ask for help but felt it would be a bit cheeky, particularly since she was deceiving them all. Besides, she did not see Nathan liking that one little bit. Which was why she had not told him of their visit. She considered the gold coins ill-gotten gains and had hidden them in a pot beneath the floorboards. Things would have to be really desperate before she would touch them.

Now Molly sighed, knowing she couldn't go on the way she was. There was talk of a shortage of wheat, which meant the price of bread would rise. She contemplated pawning her wedding ring but was reluctant to do so. Besides it would only temporarily solve her money troubles and it was obvious she could not rely on Nathan to do any more for her. She must use the gift that God had given her.

Upstairs was the sewing machine and a box containing reels of cotton in every colour of the rainbow. Having got herself into a proper mess working out how to oil the machine, she sat in front of it, searching her memory, trying to remember exactly how her mother had set things in motion and what she had said about lockstitch machines.

Dead handy, that's what she'd said. Molly smiled. They used two threads. The thread from the needle above picking up another thread from a shuttle beneath the plate, so locking the stitch and enabling a continuous thread to be used. It had revolutionised the sewing machine industry, which had first sought to imitate hand-sewing by trying to get a needle right through the cloth. But that could only work with short lengths of thread. The first successful sewing machine was a chain-stitch machine, patented by a French tailor and used for making army uniforms in the 1830s.

Well, Molly didn't need to work on anything as tough as khaki serge. She just wanted a few larger baby nightgowns. After several attempts, pricked fingers, useless turning of the balance wheel, and a whole lot of muttering under her breath of swear words picked up in her stepfather's pub, she gave up and stood, easing her back and looking out of the window. It was then she saw the booklet on the windowsill half hidden by the curtain. She picked it up and whooped with delight. It was the instructions which must have come with the machine, yellowing and dog-eared but still legible.

Immediately she set about reading and soon was practising stitching on a piece of another of Nanna's red flannel night-gowns. Within the day she had made her daughter the nightgowns of which she was sorely in need. Delighted with her own achievement, Molly decided to drum up some business.

Wrapping the baby in a blanket, she bound her to her with her black shawl, knotting the ends where she could reach them

49

easily. Then with a wicker basket on her arm, she set out for School Lane. The first few doors she knocked on proved a waste of effort. Two were opened by maids who said their mistresses already had a woman to do their sewing. At the third house the owner appeared to believe Molly a gypsy and set a yapping Dachshund on her, which made her nervous and inclined to give up, which irritated her no end.

It was not until she'd reached the safety of the other side of the gate that she plucked up the courage to shout, 'My dog could make mincemeat of yours!' despite having no dog.

The thought made her smile. Three more doors and if she continued to get negative replies she would try another road, she decided. Bracing her shoulders, she banged the knocker of the next house. No answer.

Three doors further down, still having had no luck, Molly decided to try one more house. The sky was rapidly clouding over and she was fed up, her confidence in her ability to make money draining from her. She marched up the next path, which was flanked by overgrown laurels and rhododendrons, and wielded the knocker several times before hearing footsteps in the hall. 'Hold your bloody horses!' shouted a male voice she recognised. She groaned, unable to believe her luck.

The door was flung open by the overall-clad figure of Nathan Collins. His hair was coated in sawdust. 'What are you doing here?' he demanded, frowning. 'Is something wrong with the baby?'

'No! And how would I know you were here if there was?' Molly said in what she considered a reasonable tone. 'I'm trying to drum up work and not having much blinking luck.'

'You trying to make me feel guilty? Think I'm a skinflint?'

'Of course not! I'm sure you're being as generous as you can be.'

He rested one shoulder against the door jamb and folded his arms, eyeing her up and down. 'You look like a gypsy. What kind of work? This place is empty right now. I'm fitting extra cupboards for the new owner.' Molly saw her opportunity and jumped in. 'Perhaps you could mention me to the lady of the house? I've a machine for seams and I can do fine embroidery by hand as well as smocking.'

'Can you now?' he drawled. 'I must give you my shirts. I've buttons missing on a couple of them and a rip under the arm of another. Now you'd best get home before the rain comes and you're drenched.'

'I expect payment if I do sewing for you.'

He raised one eyebrow. 'Did I say I wouldn't pay you for the extra work?'

'No, but you do cry poverty a bit.' She peered into the lobby, wishing he would ask her in. She would have enjoyed looking over such a house.

'We're no different then, are we?' he said sharply. 'Now I've work to do to pay your wages.' He slammed the door in her face.

As the first drops of rain fell on Molly she scowled, thinking he could have given them shelter from the rain. Placing one arm protectively over the baby's head, she hurried down the path. When she arrived home it was to find a stranger sheltering under a large black umbrella on her doorstep.

'Mrs Payne?' said the man.

'That's right.' She eyed him curiously as he doffed the umbrella as though it were a hat. He was middle-aged and balding, his face round with fine purplish blood vessels criss-crossing his cheeks and rather squashy nose. He wore a brown suit and highly polished shoes splattered with rain. 'Just the young woman I want to see.' He smiled. 'I take it this is little Jessica?'

She nodded, continuing to stare at him as she reached inside the letter box for the key on the string.

'May I come in?' He folded the umbrella.

'I don't know about that. You might look like an elderly cherub but that doesn't mean to say you're an angel. How do I know I can trust you?' Molly said suspiciously.

He threw back his head and roared with laughter. There was something very infectious about that sound and she smiled too. 'It's true!' she said. 'But I suppose I can take a chance on you.'

'Thank you, my dear,' he spluttered. 'If I tell you I'm this child's Great-uncle William, Mr Barnes, will that ease your fears?'

The man with the brass. Hope tingled in her veins. 'You don't look a bit like I expected.'

'Ah! What has the lad been saying about me?'

'Not much.' She presumed by the lad he meant Nathan. 'Only that you want to turn him into a candlestick maker.'

'I want to make him my heir,' he said, wheezing slightly as he followed her indoors. 'But I will not hand everything I have to him on a plate. He has to work for it – do something for me in return. Wouldn't you say that's fair, Mrs Payne?'

'I would. You don't get naught for nothing in this world.' Molly was starting to realise that in a way she had never done before. There had to be give as well as take. She entered the kitchen which was dark due to the miserable weather outside and waved him to a chair, thinking she would have to light the fire to make the place appear a bit more cheerful now she had such an important guest.

He sat down heavily, leaning on the handle of his umbrella. 'He's a young, hotheaded fool and will end up with nowt if he's not careful. As for you, my dear, you're just like your mother.'

'You knew her?' said Molly, although perhaps it shouldn't have come as a surprise. 'Your sister says I don't have her good looks.'

He clicked his tongue against his teeth, gazing down at the baby where Molly had placed her on the rug. 'My sister's a sight too keen to say what she thinks. Is the child all right on the floor? Can I not…?' There was a wistful note in his voice.

'Of course you can hold her. That's if you want a wet and smelly knee you can.' Molly put a match to the fire, thinking how easy he was to talk to. 'She needs changing and so do I,' she added ruefully, gazing down at her skirt.

'Are there not such things as rubber pants, my dear?' he said gently. 'I have looked into the items a baby needs since my great-niece's birth.'

His great-niece! Oh, Lord! Another person she was deceiving. It hadn't seemed so bad when she hadn't met him. Still, too late to go back now. Molly cleared her throat. 'If there are, I can't afford them. And neither can Mr Collins.' She sat back on her heels, picking up her baby, feeling a sudden need to stake a claim to her. 'So what can I do for you?'

'I came to see the child and suggest you and she come and live in my house.'

Molly almost dropped Jessica. It was the last thing she'd expected him to say. Her spirits rose instantly, imagining herself in a big house, bigger than the ones she had visited this morning, with enough food in her stomach and fuel in the winter and nice clothes for Jessica and no worries about where the rent was coming from. Then the vision faded. 'Have you asked Mr Collins?'

'No.' He sighed. 'But he might come round to my way of thinking if I had you and little Jessica living with me. A bird in the hand, my dear, is worth two in the bush. I could threaten that I'd change my will and leave little Jessica all my property. So what do you think about coming with me now and I'll have a note popped through his door saying where you've gone?'

Molly's jaw dropped. She was tempted to do as he said. She really was! It was a short cut to her dream coming true. Her daughter, heiress to all this man possessed! Then as if someone had stamped the image on her brain she pictured Nathan as she'd first seen him and the corners of her mouth turned down. Molly shook her head. 'That wouldn't be very loyal of me, Mr Barnes, would it?' she said gently. 'Nathan's my employer and has only just lost his wife. For me to do the dirty on him wouldn't be right. Jessica's all he's got.'

'You wouldn't be doing the dirty as you put it. You'd be doing him a favour.' Mr Barnes settled himself more comfortably in the rocking chair, placing the tips of his fingers together under his treble chins. 'My sister seems to believe this lovely little baby upsets him. Reminds him too much of his wife's death.'

'That may be true sometimes but he'll change,' Molly said confidently.

'He's stubborn.'

'He loves her, I know he does!' Molly argued fiercely, wanting to believe it. 'He's just frightened of letting himself feel too much at the moment. After you've lost someone you love, you're frightened it's going to happen again.'

'That may be so, my dear, but I don't want to wait until he comes round to seeing things my way or yours. I'm not getting any younger.'

Molly wrinkled her nose, seeing his point. 'Why can't you find him a job in his own line? He's a craftsman.'

'We make candles, incense burners and sanctuary light holders, my dear, not furniture.' Mr Barnes rubbed his chin against the tips of his fingers. 'He has accused me of being a moneygrabbing shyster, lacking an eye for beauty and without a soul. What d'you think of that, hey?'

'Not very wise of him,' she said, not surprised. 'You'd think he'd know which side his bread was buttered on, wouldn't you?'

'You would indeed. But there it is, my dear, you see what I'm up against.' Mr Barnes spread both his hands in a gesture of helplessness.

She knew all right and her spirits sank as she saw the promise of the good life fading into the distance. There was silence except for the crackling of the fire as she tried to think of some way of convincing Nathan to take up his uncle's offer. 'Isn't there *any thing* he could do with wood in your factory?'

'We're thinking of going into the vestments and church hangings business next, so I'm afraid not.' From a pocket he took a packet of cheroots and with exquisite civility asked if she minded his smoking. She nodded her agreement graciously, considering him a real gent. Not snooty at all but well-mannered and considerate of even the likes of her. He lit the cheroot and drew on it. 'There is also my partner, Mr Braith-waite, who is in charge of the Leeds factory. I have to think what he might say.'

'I see.' Molly chewed her lip, wondering if Mr Braithwaite had an heir. The baby in her arms woke suddenly and began to root against her breast. She sighed. 'Nathan made Jessica a beautiful cradle. It's a pity you've never thought of making church furniture. Pews, pulpits, screens, lecterns... couldn't you do them instead of vestments?'

'We've already bought the sewing machines, my dear.'

Molly sighed. It was a shame. She could not think of anything else to say so sat watching him smoke, wishing she didn't have a conscience and could do what he suggested and go off with him right now.

Finally Mr Barnes threw the butt on the fire and stood up. 'Your advice has not been wasted on me,' he astonished her by saying, 'I have a room standing empty at the moment. If my nephew can raise half the money then maybe I could find the rest from my private income. He would have to drum up business himself, visit churches and see what comes of it. You must put it to him, though, seeing as you appear to have his and Jessica's best interests at heart.'

'I'm sure it would be better coming from you,' Molly said hastily. 'I know nothing about business, sir.'

'But you can sketch in an outline of your idea. If he's got an ounce of Lancashire nous, then he'll be hotfooting it to my door.' Mr Barnes smiled, fumbling in an inside pocket and pulling out a Morocco leather notecase. From it he extracted a five-pound note and handed it to her. 'I think you'll be able to buy some rubber pants with that and maybe a pretty white lace-trimmed frock for when you bring my great-niece to visit me?' Molly could not disguise her joy at such largesse. 'I'll do that as soon as I can, sir. Thank you very much.'

'And here's my card if you need to get in touch with me. I've enjoyed our conversation, Mrs Payne.'

She managed to get to her feet, still clutching the baby. 'I'm sorry I couldn't offer you a cup of tea but I'm going to have to feed Jessica now.'

'Of course. She's looking very well. No, no.' He held up a hand as she made to follow him out. 'I'll find my own way. You see to the child.' And on those words he limped out of the room.

Molly glanced down at his card. There were two addresses on it, a business one in Liverpool and his home address in Blundellsands. She placed it under the clock on the mantelshelf, and as she fed her baby, pondered on the best way to approach Nathan with her idea.

—

As soon as Molly set eyes on Nathan she could tell he was in a bad mood. His brow was furrowed like a newly ploughed field. He flung three shirts and a pair of trousers on the dresser and sat down in front of the fire. 'D'you know, the owner of that house had the nerve to complain about my work?' he muttered, a brooding expression on his face.

She did not know what to say so picked up one of the shirts and inspected it.

'I don't know how I stopped myself from hitting him. He wanted a cheap job and I told him good workmanship doesn't come cheap.'

Molly saw an opening. 'You're a craftsman. Cupboards are beneath you, really.' Her tone was casual. 'When you think of the workmanship in old churches… it's wonderful, isn't it.'

'Old churches! What are you going on about?' He knuckled his eyes and yawned. 'He thought I was green behind the ears. Too young, not enough experience.'

'I hadn't thought of pews and pulpits and things until today,' said Molly, sticking to her side of the conversation. 'But your uncle called and he made me think about the craftsmanship involved in such things.'

'My uncle?' Nathan blinked and stared at her. 'What the hell did he want?'

'To see Jessica, of course.' Molly began to root through her sewing box. 'He wanted us both to go and live with him.'

'Bloody cheek!' Nathan's scowl deepened. 'Big house, rubber pants, lacy frocks, no bugs, and enough coal and food to make anyone happy,' murmured Molly, picking out a reel of pale blue cotton and biting off a length.

'Rubber pants?' His expression was puzzled.

'You wouldn't have a wet knee then if Jessica sat on it.'

'I didn't know you could get such things.' Nathan paused. 'I suppose he went on about me working for him?'

'He thinks you should go into business for yourself making church furniture. He's got an empty workroom you could have and he must know lots of churches.'

'Maybe,' said Nathan, getting up.

'You could give it a try.'

'Shut up, Moll.'

She began to set neat stitches, glancing up at him out of the corner of her eye. He was clasping the brown teapot in both hands. 'Where d'you keep the tea?'

'In the caddy on the mantelshelf. There's not much. Are you going up to see Jessica?'

'Maybe.'

She felt impatient with him, wanting her daughter to have a proper father who cared about her. Molly had missed out on that herself and knew it was important. But how could he be a proper father if he blew hot and cold towards the baby? Sometimes he wanted to nurse her, sometimes he didn't.

'What's this?' said Nathan.

'What's what?' She did not lift her head.

'My uncle's card. Why's he given you this?' She jumped to her feet, dropping his shirt on the floor and snatching the card from him. She had a sudden inspiration. 'It's for me if I need to get in touch with him. He's opening a sewing room. I thought there might be a chance of a job in it.'

'You'd leave Jessica?' He looked dumbfounded. 'I thought I could depend on you. I'd have to find someone else to look after her then and I've got used to you, Moll.'

She was touched, thinking she had got used to having him to talk to as well. There really wasn't anyone else in her life except Mrs Smith and the delivery boy. She'd wanted to speak to the other mothers round about but was too shy. Still she kept silent, thinking if he wanted her round that much he might change his mind about a few things.

He turned his back on her, fingers gripping the mantelshelf so the knuckles shone through the taut skin. Molly took the teapot from near his hand and made tea, covering the pot with a teacosy. Then she went upstairs and brought Jessica down. 'Your wife gave her life for this child. Was her sacrifice for nothing?' she said quietly.

He whirled round and his eyes were shiny with unshed tears. Molly felt guilty then. 'Bitch!' he said passionately before reaching out and putting his arms around her. He almost squeezed the life out of her and the baby. Then he began to cry with great sobs that wracked his body, shocking her to the roots of her being. He upset her so much that she began to weep as well.

–

Molly watched Nathan eat the last of the bacon, sliced fried potatoes and two eggs, and some of her guilt evaporated. It had been terrible watching him go to pieces but he'd soon pulled himself together. To get them both past that moment of weakness she had handed him the baby and poured two cups of tea, asking when he had last eaten. 'A round of bread at breakfast,' was his answer.

Now he wiped the plate clean with a chunk of bread, ramming it into his mouth and chewing. After swallowing that last morsel, he said gruffly, 'I promised Jess I wouldn't go back on what we'd decided about building up my own business and staying on in Burscough. She wanted our child brought up round here, near her family.'

'I suppose that's understandable, but if it's not what's best for Jessica then maybe you have to think again. She's your responsibility now,' said Molly earnestly.

Nathan nodded. 'I'll get in touch with my uncle.' He was careful not to look at her as she fed the baby.

She suddenly remembered something she had forgotten to say and her heart sank. 'He mentioned you'd need to raise half the money.'

'What! You didn't say that before.' He groaned and snatched at his hair, tugging on it. 'Where am I going to find that sort of money?'

'If you go and live with him, you'll sell up here. There'll be some money then.'

'My few sticks aren't going to raise much.' He lifted his head, glancing at her before quickly looking down at his plate.

She remembered the gold sovereigns and thought it was not going to be easy trying to explain why she hadn't mentioned them before. Even so she had to do it, but before she could speak Nathan spoke again.

'I'll have to work for him for a while. Do what he wants,' he said heavily. 'I'll save. Then when I've enough money and have looked into things myself, I'll have a go.'

She felt a rush of relief. 'Right, Mr Candle and Church Furniture maker. Do I get packing Jessica's things right now?' Molly wanted to dance with delight.

A smile tugged at the corners of his mouth. 'Hang on, lass. Not yet. Let me see my uncle first. I'll take the train to Liverpool tomorrow. Might as well have a look over this factory.'

'Can't we come?'

He glanced at her and the baby and the breath seemed to shudder right through him. 'No. You'll be in the way,' he said gruffly, pushing back his chair and getting to his feet. 'I'd appreciate it, though, if you could sew the buttons on one of those white shirts this evening? I'm going for a walk. Need some fresh air. Be back soon.' He was out the house before she could speak.

Chapter Four

Molly sat back on her heels at the bottom of the front step, eyes screwed up as she gazed up the lane, scrubbing brush dripping water down her arm. Was that Nathan? It was two days since she had last seen him. She dropped the scrubbing brush in the galvanised bucket and shaded her eyes with her hand. Yes, it was him! She scrambled to her feet, wiping her hands on her apron, aware that the curtains in the house across the road twitched and several of the neighbours stopped gossiping and were watching her every move.

'Mrs Payne.' Nathan inclined his head, doffing his straw boater. 'Everything all right with you?'

'Fine. Just awaiting your orders.' Her eyes were bright with expectation as she took in his smart appearance.

He twirled the hat between his hands and grinned. 'Get packing.'

She thought he wasn't bad-looking when he remembered to smile, and returned it. 'I want to take my mother's sewing machine. It'll come in handy. Nanna's furniture I'll need to get rid of.'

'I'll see to all that. You leave today and I'll follow on in a few days. I'll square everything with your landlord.'

'Do I go straight to Mr Barnes's house?'

'That's what he wants.' Nathan's expression clouded and his eyes were thoughtful. 'You're going to have to cope with my mother too. I hope you won't find yourself regretting this move, as I might?'

Molly groaned inwardly. She had forgotten about his mother. A picture of Ma Payne popped into her head and she wondered if she had exchanged the frying pan for the fire. 'Is it a very big house?' she stammered.

'Big enough.'

'Then I suppose there's room for all of us.'

'That's my girl,' he said, ramming his hat on the back of his head. He reached into a pocket, drew out some change and gave it to her. 'Take the train from the Bridge to Southport and change there to the Liverpool line. Get off at Blundellsands. It's only a short walk to the house. You've his address still?'

She nodded, thanking him as she placed the money in her apron pocket. Nathan strode off up the lane and she stood for a moment watching him, a delighted expression on her face. That vision of Jessica dancing in a lace frock floating before her eyes. There was no need to worry about anything. Nathan would be there, seeing his mother didn't get on her high horse where she was concerned.

–

Molly sauntered up the road which led to the sea, gazing about her with interest. She was in no hurry despite her burdens of baby and holdall. The breeze was bracing and she filled her lungs with the salty air, unaware of the glances she received from residents, servants and tradesmen going about their business.

On both sides of the road stood large houses in expansive gardens. It was here that many a businessman retreated at the end of a working day spent in the crowded, bustling, streets of Liverpool ten miles to the south along the coast. Molly passed Warren Road and was soon turning right. It was somewhere along here that Mr Barnes's house was situated. She wondered whether to march up to the front door, carrying the alleged youngest member of the family, or go round to the back entrance. There would be servants to cope with and she could not help wondering where *she* would fit into the household.

Here it was. Falconstone. And very imposing it looked, too, with stone pillars decorating the porch and a long shrub-lined driveway. Molly felt suddenly nervous, wondering how she was going to cope with Mrs Collins. One thing was for sure: Nathan's mother was not going to make her life easy.

There was a bell next to the door with a rope attached. It jangled discordantly as she tugged on the rope. No one came rushing to answer it. Perhaps there was nobody at home? Or maybe they were just round the back of the house. She pulled the rope again and listened. This time she heard footsteps and took a deep calming breath.

The door was yanked open. 'Hey, yous! What d'yer think yer doing, ringing our bell? No hawkers or gypsies. No beggars either come to that!' The voice was pure Scouse and nasal as they came.

'I'm none of them,' said Molly, relieved it wasn't Mrs Collins, thinking this slip of a girl didn't look anybody to be scared of, 'I'm Mrs Payne and this here is Miss Jessica Collins. I think you'll find we're expected.'

'You don't look old enough to be a Mrs,' scoffed the girl, her mousy hair barely contained by her white mob cap. Her head just about reached Molly's shoulder and she wore a voluminous apron over a black frock which brushed the floor. She looked to be no more than fourteen or fifteen years old.

'Well, I am,' said Molly with a toss of the head. 'I'm nineteen and a widow. So why don't you shift yourself and let me in?'

'Hummph!' said the girl, narrowing herand folding her arms across her thin bosom. 'Hoity-toity, aren't we? How do I know yerroo yer say yer are and not a thief out to pinch the family silver?'

'Do I look like a thief?' said Molly indignantly. 'You're mad!'

'Who is it, Doris?' called a male voice, echoing round the high-ceilinged hall. 'What have I told you, girl, about keeping people standing on the doorstep?'

'Mr Barnes, it's me!' said Molly, trying to get round the maidservant. 'Mr Collins sent me and Jessica on ahead.'

'Come in, lass.' There was warmth in the man's voice.

'See, he knows me!' hissed Molly to Doris. 'I'm not a thief. So get out of my way and let me through.'

'Yer could have been,' she said with a toss of the head, moving aside awkwardly.

Molly stepped into the hall and smiled at Mr Barnes, who was standing in the doorway of a room to her left, leaning on his stick. 'How are you, sir?'

Before he could answer Mrs Collins's face appeared at his shoulder like some malevolent spirit. 'Look at the cut of her! What does she think she's doing, carrying the baby tied to her like that?' Her tone was scathing. 'What'll the neighbours think?'

'Do you suppose they've nothing better to do than notice what's going on here?' He sounded exasperated as he beckoned Molly forward. 'The girl looks worn out. I say send her to the kitchen and get Cook to provide her with a posset and a nice ham sandwich. But first let me have a hold of my great-niece. Did you buy those rubber pants, my dear?'

'Yes, sir.' Molly hurried over to him, untying her shawl as she went. She eased back the bonnet so he could gaze upon Jessica's dainty features. 'See how well she looks.' His plump face creased with delight as he bent over the child. 'She's a little beauty. Reminds me of Mother, wouldn't you say?' A comment which caused Molly to marvel at the way people could deceive themselves.

'Perhaps. Although I can't see it myself,' said Mrs Collins. 'Anyway, girl, give the child to me.' She glared at Molly, holding out both arms. 'I want to see if you've been treating her properly.'

Reluctantly she handed her daughter over. 'She'll need feeding soon.'

'Look at those bonny legs,' said Mr Barnes, watching his sister inspect the baby's limbs, even going so far as to lift her lacy white frock and shift and peer at her tummy. 'Mrs Payne might be young but I think she knows what she's doing. I'm looking forward to the day when Jessica'll be dancing round this hall, cheering us all up.'

Molly thought how wonderful it was that his thoughts should run along the same lines as her own and stood smiling at him, reluctant to leave her baby in Mrs Collins's hands.

Mr Barnes glanced at Molly. 'You don't have to wait. Get yourself to the kitchen, my dear, and see Cook. Doris will show you the way. When you've had something to eat you can feed the baby. If she cries, we'll call you. Dismissed.'

Molly thanked him, bobbing the briefest curtsey, having little experience in dealing with the moneyed middle classes.

As she followed Doris, who had a most peculiar gait, through a green baize door, Molly felt an overwhelming urge to burst out laughing with relief and wonder. She could easily picture Jessica dancing round the hall in this house. It was Christmas and there was a huge tree decorated with baubles, candles, tinsel and presents. Molly hummed 'Silent Night,' and Doris gave her a look. 'Yer not sickening for somethin', are yer? Christmas is months off.'

'Sorry, I was just imagining what it might be like here then.'

'Nuthin' to write home about. Although it'll probably be different with a baby here. It's more fun at our house.'

'And where's that? I mean, I know it must be Liverpool but whereabouts?'

But Doris did not answer her because they had reached the kitchen which was warm and full of delicious smells.

Cook was even fatter than Mr Barnes but she was just as welcoming. 'You be seated, luv. We've been hearing all about your charge and it's been a real tonic listening to the master looking forward to the little one's coming. I'm sure she's not going to be the nuisance a certain person in this house would have us believe,' Cook added darkly.

Molly could guess who that might be. 'You're very kind,' she said, seating herself on a straight-backed chair with a crocheted cushion in green and blue. The coals glowed red in the huge black-leaded grate and on a gas stove a couple of pans simmered.

'I believe you're a widow and that you lost your own little one?' Tears glimmered in Cook's bright eyes which were like currants in a mound of dough.

Molly thought of Frank and the poor little mite in St John's graveyard and a tear instantly rolled down her own cheek.

'There now,' said Cook, patting her shoulder. 'I shouldn't have mentioned it. Sorry, dear.'

'Master says yer to give her a posset – his cure for all ills – and a nice ham butty,' said Doris, dipping her finger into one of the pans.

Cook slapped the back of her hand with a wooden spoon. 'You're plain daft you are! You'll scald yourself.' She removed one of the pans, replacing it with a smaller one on the gas ring. 'Now pass me that there jar of treacle and an egg.'

Doris did as she was told. Molly was content to watch. 'Where do you live, Doris?' she repeated.

'Near Athol Street. Me dad works at the master's factory.'

'By the gasworks?'

'More up Scottie Road end. Know it, do yer? Yer not from round our way.'

'I've had a scouse pie from Block's. I know a bargee who unloads at the gasworks.'

Doris stared at her. 'What's his name? Me dad goes drinking with some of the boatmen and me sister's going out with one.'

'We don't want to hear about your dad's drinking,' said Cook, busily whisking egg and treacle. 'Me and my brother signed the pledge when I was twelve. Anyway, hadn't you better be getting upstairs.'

'I've got too much to do since Ethel went,' muttered Doris, dipping her finger in the pan again.

Cook aimed a clout at her but Doris dodged the blow. 'I'll be back for yer, probably in half an hour, kid,' she said to Molly. 'They'll be wanting me to show yer where the nursery is. Yous'll be sleeping up there. Although why the master wanted a big place like this with a nursery, I'll never know. He never looks at the women although he likes kids. See yer!' Doris waved cheerily and vanished.

'You'll have to excuse her,' said Cook, beckoning Molly to the table. 'She's had a tough life. Got rickets as a child and her legs are bowed ten times worse than a jockey's. She feels it but puts on a good show.' She poured hot milk on to the eggs and treacle and grated nutmeg on its surface before placing the bowl in front of Molly. Then she took up a knife and removed a muslin cloth to reveal a juicy pink ham which she began to slice.

'She hasn't let it get her down by the sound of it,' said Molly, fearful of all the ills that could claim her child's life. She felt a fierce surge of protective love for her and wanted to leave the food on the table and run upstairs to see that she was all right, but she knew she needed to control such feelings. No one must suspect Jessica was hers.

Half an hour later Doris came into the kitchen with the baby and took Molly upstairs to a large sunlit room. There was a single bed but no cot because Nathan would be bringing the one from Burscough. Cream-painted cupboards covered one wall and there was also a tallboy. Next door was a smaller room with all the practical necessities.

Molly wandered back into the main room.

There were bars on the window which looked out over a large walled garden to the rear of the house. She gazed and gazed at the view. The sun was cutting a swathe of shimmering palest gold through the surface of the sea. It looked so calm and beautiful that it was difficult to believe in another part of the world the sea had claimed Frank's life. She spotted a dredger working to keep the channels between the sandbanks clear for shipping and a liner. Poor Frank, she thought, turning away with a sigh.

After being shown the contents of the cupboards, which contained brand new baby clothes, proper nappies and bedding,

Molly was left alone. She went over to the fireplace and sat down in a basket chair. 'We're lucky ducks,' she said to her daughter as she changed a sodden homemade nappy for a brand new one. There were enough clothes and to spare, at least until Jessica passed her first birthday. As she fed her child, Molly was counting her blessings and looking forward to exploring her new surroundings.

–

'Where are you going with the child tied to you like that?' demanded Mrs Collins, face like thunder.

Apprehension tightened Molly's throat as she paused, her hand on the front door. 'It's easier to c-carry her like this,' she stammered, annoyed with herself for doing so.

'It won't do and you should be going out the back way. The neighbours'll think the gypsies have come to town.'

'You really think so?' Molly raised her eyebrows, thinking sardonically that perhaps she should buy a pair of gold earrings with one of the sovereigns she had hidden at the back of a cupboard, as well as a red scarf to cover her hair. She was fed up of being accused of looking like a gypsy.

The older woman's eyes narrowed. 'You're right hardfaced, you are. I'd have you out of here if I had my way. Right now you're not leaving this house with that baby until you're dressed properly. I'll have a word with my brother about a uniform for you.' She hurried in the direction of the sitting room whose French windows opened on to a large garden.

'What I need is a baby carriage to wheel her out in,' called Molly. 'Perhaps you could have a word with him about that, too?'

Mrs Collins swung round to face her, resting her hand on a three-tiered whatnot. 'I don't like your tone, my girl.'

'I'm sorry.' Molly could not understand what there was about her tone to dislike. The request she had made seemed eminently reasonable to her.

'No, you're not. And call me Mrs Collins when you address me.'

'Yes, Mrs Collins,' said Molly woodenly, trying to keep all emotion from her face.

The woman's eyes narrowed. 'Don't be impudent! You don't fool me. And don't be trying to get round my brother. He's speaking to the gardener and I don't want you wasting your time sucking up to him. You can tidy the nursery.'

'I've already tidied it, Mrs Collins.' Molly seethed inside. It was a blinking lie to say she sucked up to Mr Barnes who liked to talk to her, not only about her mother but his own early working days at Lever Brothers, the soap manufacturers. And she enjoyed listening to him, and was learning a lot.

'You can help Doris clean the brasses then. Give the child to me.'

Molly felt like saying, 'I wasn't hired as a maid and I don't work for you.' She hesitated.

'What are you waiting for?' snapped Mrs Collins, shooting out her neck like a reptile. 'Hand her to me and get those brasses done.'

Reluctantly Molly relinquished her daughter and, turning on her heel, went in search of Doris who exploded when Molly found her and told her why, saying exactly what she thought of Mrs Collins.

'Don't let her get to yer. She's a jumped up madam and I don't suppose her son'll be any different.'

'Oh, he is. That's why there's no love lost between them.' Molly wrapped one of Doris's large white aprons about her waist and began polishing a brass statuette of the Greek hero Jason which usually stood in the dining room.

'Give people a bit of power and it goes to their heads,' muttered Doris darkly. 'They think they're as good as the king.'

'Well, you've heard the rumours about him,' murmured Molly.

'Eddyweddy, who are yer taking to beddy? Talk about sailors having a woman in every port,' said Doris with a giggle.

69

'My husband was a sailor.'

'Yeah, well, so are a couple of me brothers. No harm meant, Moll.'

'No harm taken,' she said, remembering that Frank had been a very physical lover. Too blinking physical sometimes. But each homecoming had been exciting. It was like being married all over again every time but he'd always brought her a present, making her feel special, and handed over her housekeeping. She felt that familiar tightness in her chest, remembering, and rubbed extra hard on the brassy curls framing Jason's handsome features, trying to picture Frank's good-looking face instead. To her dismay she couldn't conjure it up and had to force herself to think of something else.

She was polishing the front door bell when Nathan arrived. He was bareheaded and there was a smut on his cheek. His jacket was slung over one shoulder and his shirt collarless and unbuttoned at the throat. Molly was surprised by how pleased she was to see him but he looked vexed.

'What the hell d'you think you're doing?' he said, frowning.

'I'm polishing the bell.' She paused, duster in hand.

'Well, stop it. I don't pay you to do that. I pay you to look after my daughter.'

'You tell your mother that, Mr Collins,' she said promptly, dropping the duster with glee. 'She doesn't listen to me.'

'Well, she'll listen to *me*.'

Molly wiped her damp forehead with the back of a hand. 'I wanted to take the baby for a walk but she says I'm not properly dressed and I should have a uniform.'

He looked exasperated. 'What's she think I am? Made of money?' He turned to a youth standing behind him, wearing the insignia of the Yorkshire & Lancashire Railway. 'What are you gawping at, lad? Help unload that lot.' He indicated with his head the handcart piled with a cardboard suitcase, a large toolbox, several bundles, Molly's sewing machine and Jessica's cradle.

'I don't think she intends you to pay for it,' said Molly. 'I told her I needed a pram, too.'

'Well, it's going to have to wait.' He seized hold of his toolbox and heaved it off the cart. 'Give us a hand here. You grab something.'

Molly took one of the bundles. 'Your uncle would probably buy one. He's besotted with Jessica.'

Nathan turned on her, face flushed with anger. 'Don't you dare go asking him for anything for her! She's my daughter. Isn't it enough that you've got me here? I'm not going to be able to call my life my own from now on.'

'I'm sorry!' Colour flooded Molly's face but she was not going to take that lying down. 'But excuse me, Mr Collins, you're not here for me but for Jessica.'

'Don't answer me back,' he muttered. 'Just you remember, I'm your boss not them. Anything you need, you come to me.'

'That's why I'm asking you about the pram,' she said, wondering if she had made a mistake in beginning to rely on him. But before he could respond to her words another voice spoke.

'So you've arrived.' Mrs Collins hung over the banister, seeming to hover above them like a bat. 'Why aren't you wearing a collar? You look like a workman.'

'I *am* a workman, Mother.' He stared at her from beneath dark brows.

'Not any longer – and you've a smut on your face – and what's that the lad's carrying?'

'A sewing machine. I should have thought you'd have seen one of them before.'

She frowned. 'Don't speak to me like that! I'm your mother. What's it doing here? What do I need a sewing machine for?'

'It belongs to Mrs Payne.'

'Her?' The tone was scornful. 'What's *she* want with it? I wouldn't have thought she'd have the brains to know how to use it. Anyway where's she going to put it?'

Brains! thought Molly indignantly. I've got more brains in my little finger than you've got in your whole body. I'll show you, Mrs Collins!

'It can go in the nursery for now,' said Mr Barnes, coming out of his study and limping across the hall towards Nathan. 'It's good to see you here, lad.'

Molly watched the two men shake hands. 'I'll do my best to match up to your expectations of me, sir,' said Nathan stiffly.

'I'm sure you will.' The older man clapped him on the shoulder. 'But relax, lad. You're not at the factory now. This is your home. Why don't you go up and rid yourself of the dirt from the journey? I'll send Doris up to run a bath for you.'

'I'll get rid of my stuff first, if you don't mind, sir.'

'Aye. You do what you think best, lad. Just remember, anything you want you only have to ask.'

Nathan mumbled something that Molly could not catch before turning to the boy and ordering him to follow. He headed for the stairs and Molly hurried after them before Mrs Collins could do anything to prevent her.

Molly was in the nursery with the boy when Nathan came in carrying Jessica's cradle. He tipped the boy and told him to scram then glanced about him. 'The sewing machine OK on that table?'

'It's fine, Mr Collins,' she said politely.

'So what are you planning on doing with it?'

'Sewing.'

'Sewing what?' He brought his gaze back to her face. 'You do know that sarcasm is the lowest form of wit? And you haven't any big ideas still about working for my uncle in his factory, have you?'

Molly smiled. 'Not at the moment I haven't.'

'That's OK then.' He leaned against the cupboards. 'Where's my daughter?'

'Your mother took her.'

'You mustn't let her do that.'

'And how am I going to prevent her, Mr Collins? She's your mother.'

'I'll speak to her.' He straightened up. 'She didn't have Jessica with her when she came into the hall.'

'Perhaps Cook's got her.'

'Go and look. I want to see her.'

'Yes, Mr Collins.' She moved towards the door.

'Hang on. I've something for you.' He hurried past her, reappearing a few minutes later with a pair of highly polished tan boots. 'I thought you might like these. They belonged to my wife but she had hardly any wear out of them. I got rid of everything else but I thought you couldn't go on wearing clogs here and these might fit you.'

Molly took them from him, pleased that he should have thought of her, and tried the boots on there and then. They were a tiny bit too big but she only had to stuff some tissue paper or a rag in the toes and they'd be fine. 'Thanks.' She gave him a delighted smile.

'It's nothing,' he said brusquely, waving her towards the door. 'Go and find Jessica.' She hurried off in the new boots and down the backstairs. As soon as she reached the passage leading to the kitchen, she could hear her daughter screaming and hurried to her child. 'What's wrong with her?'

A scarlet-faced Cook said, 'Thank goodness! I don't know what the missus was thinking of, handing her over to me when I've dinner to prepare. But she was like this when she reached me. I haven't done anything.'

Molly took Jessica and rocked her in her arms but still she carried on crying. She checked her over and discovered one of the nappy pins had come undone and scratched her hip. 'Poor love,' she murmured, making it secure, puzzled as to how it had come undone as she was always careful with pins.

Doris entered the room with an air of suppressed excitement about her.

'Where've you been?' demanded Cook. 'I needed you.'

73

She sniffed. 'I haven't got two pairs of hands. The master told me to run a bath for young Mr Collins. I offered to scrub his back but he refused to let me.'

'You never did!' exclaimed Cook, scandalised.

Molly's lips twitched. 'She's having you on.'

The older woman tut-tutted. 'She shouldn't be saying such things. But you take it from me, that air of tragedy he has tugs at the heartstrings. You mark my words, there'll be wedding bells before we know it once word gets round he's here.'

Doris rolled her eyes, putting both hands over her heart and fluttering her fingers. Molly's smile faded. 'Why should he want to marry again when he's got all he needs here? I can carry on looking after Jessica for him.'

'Aye, well,' muttered Cook, bustling over to the table, pan in hand. 'I'll only say a young man has his needs.'

'Why don't yer call a spade a spade and say he needs his oats served up every day?' demanded Doris.

Cook's eyes bulged. 'Your mouth! You shouldn't be knowing about such things at your age!'

'I'm over twenty-one. It's better to know what the fellas are after than end up in trouble.'

'Enough said,' barked Cook, mouth working. 'Get on with peeling those tatties.'

Molly left the kitchen, feeling uneasy. What if Nathan did marry again and have more children? How would that affect Jessica's position? She hadn't done all this for Jessica to have her nose put out of joint by a second marriage. She sighed. What could she do to stop it? She braced her shoulders, remembering how he had wept for his wife, and was comforted.

Molly was just settling the baby down to sleep when Nathan entered the nursery, his hair still damp from the bath. 'Where did you find her?' Molly told him what had happened and he gazed down at the child and touched her cheek. 'She seems all right now.'

'Of course she is. But it still puzzles me, how that pin came open.'

He said nothing, stroking the baby's cheek.

'Why don't you pick her up? She needs to get to know you better.'

'I don't want to hurt her.'

Molly smiled. 'Babies are tougher than you think.' She picked up her child. 'Hold out your arms.'

He obeyed her, taking Jessica, weighing her in his arms. 'She's heavier than I thought.' He placed a finger on the baby's palm and her tiny fingers curled about it. She gurgled up at him and he smiled. 'Look at that.'

Molly was looking, thinking, This is the moment I prayed for. He's fallen in love with my daughter.

'What's going on here?' The voice was sharp and they both jumped.

A muscle tightened in Nathan's jaw as he turned and looked at Mrs Collins. 'What d'you want, Mother?'

'I heard the baby screaming. Just came to see if she was all right. Mrs Payne's only young. What does she know about children?' She darted a venomous look at Molly.

'She's doing all right so far.' Nathan lifted the baby up into the air and smiled into her face. 'You're fine, aren't you, lass?' The baby gurgled again, still clinging to his finger. 'Look at that grip.' He gave a shout of laughter.

'All babies do that,' said Mrs Collins disparagingly.

Jessica's gurgle turned to a whimper and Nathan hushed her, bringing her against him and rocking her gently.

His mother looked far from pleased. 'You'll spoil her, you know. Put her back in the cradle,' she demanded, moving towards him with a rustle of silk.

'I haven't spoilt her at all.' His voice hardened and he held her closer. 'Perhaps it's time I did.'

'Stuff and nonsense! Discipline, that's what's important. You'll rue the day you took on this girl to look after your child.' She flounced out of the nursery.

Molly felt shaken and stared at Nathan. 'You won't rue the day, will you?' she whispered. 'I only want what's best for Jessica.'

'I know you do, Moll. Take no notice of my mother. She can't help herself. She's always been a jealous woman. Why I don't know. I think it must be that she's never got over my father's death. He spoilt her rotten, so Uncle William said. He was a lot older than her. I can't say I remember much about him.' He handed the baby over to her and left the nursery.

From that day on Molly expected trouble from Mrs Collins but the next day was reasonably peaceful because the older woman went to Southport and when she returned was kept busy because a guest was expected for dinner.

When Nathan returned from his first day at the factory he came straight up to the nursery, pausing in the doorway when he saw Molly feeding the baby. 'You'll be getting your baby carriage. It's to be delivered the day after next,' he said, going over to the window and gazing out.

'Thank you.' She was delighted.

'It's for Jessica. There's no need to thank me – and you must call me Mr Collins. And another thing, you must wear a uniform.' His voice was stiff.

'Yes, all right, I agree.' She wondered what had made him change his mind.

'It's not for you to agree or disagree, Mrs Payne.'

She stared at his ramrod-straight back and felt the colour rise in her cheeks. 'Yes, sir, Mr Collins!'

'Don't make this hard for me,' he groaned, still not looking at her. 'All this kind of thing is as far from my upbringing as it is from yours. But just because we knew each other when we were young and went to the same school and I've been poor like you, we can't carry on being familiar with each other.'

'I didn't know we were familiar?'

'Don't interrupt.' He spun around, his eyes like steel. 'I've rehearsed this and you throw me off my stride when you answer me back. For God's sake, we've got to have a strictly regulated boss and employee relationship.'

Suddenly she understood. First day at the factory. His uncle had probably been talking about such things as working relationships with the staff. 'I understand, Mr Collins,' she said, knowing the best thing was to pacify him.

'I hope you do.' His gaze met hers briefly, taking in the suckling baby before looking away again. 'This uniform…'

'I could probably run one up in no time if I could get the material.'

'That's what I was thinking, knowing you have the machine. Uncle William buys cloth by the roll for his suits from his partner in Leeds. He suggests you not only utilise one of the smaller back bedrooms for your sewing but that you make use of his material. There's also a roll of cambric that would do you for waists… blouses… call them what you will. The fabric's upstairs in one of the attics. You can go and have a look. The sooner the better if you want to wheel Jessica out.'

'He's a lovely man, your uncle.' There was warmth in her voice. 'I don't know why you ever took against him.'

'He's OK,' he said, with a careless shrug of the shoulders, hands in his pockets. 'His partner's OK too. He's a widower with one daughter, Charlotte. She's involved with the suffragettes, the daft girl. Anyway, that's the Braithwaites though I doubt you'll be having much to do with them. Now I've to bath and change. There's a Colonel Walker coming for dinner.'

'He's the oil merchant Mr Barnes gets his paraffin wax from. Has he any daughters?'

Nathan looked surprised. 'How the hell would I know or care?' He went out, closing the door behind him.

Molly smiled and began to hum 'Onward Christian Soldiers' beneath her breath, thinking it was obvious he wasn't interested in acquiring another wife. She looked forward to going up to the attics and delving into the treasures there. She would start sewing within the day.

Molly fingered the fine white cotton and decided to embroider flowers on the collar and cuffs. It was her second waist and as she worked she sang softly, thinking of the trip she'd made to Madam Val Smith's, a wholesaler's in Liverpool. Artificial flowers, feathers, ribbons, veiling, straw and felt hats! What a pleasure it had been browsing there. The shop stood between Bunny's departmental store and the new Woolworth's where everything cost no more than sixpence.

The city had been full of bustle, lifting Molly's spirits. This was what she missed out at the house in Blundellsands. People, noise, and big shop windows to press her nose against while drooling over the contents: clothes and accessories, furniture and nick-nacks. She could not afford anything but enjoyed looking anyway. She had gone on to watch the Punch and Judy show on St George's Plateau, thinking she would take Jessica there when she was older. After that she'd walked to the Pier-head to stare in wonder at the Royal Liver Insurance Building, still under construction. Architecturally it was not as pleasing as that of the Customs House with its pillars and dome. Old salts sat on the steps, smoking their clay pipes and telling far-fetched tales about sea monsters and natives on tropical islands to anyone who cared to listen.

Molly had fed the seagulls with the remains of her packed lunch and bought an *Echo* for the return train journey. Then wished she hadn't because there was a report of a Liverpool liner being in collision with an iceberg. Fortunately no lives were lost and it had managed to limp into port in Newfoundland. How she wished Frank's ship had reached port! She wouldn't be worrying about being parted from her daughter then.

She was glad to arrive home, knowing Jessica was due for a feed and needing to reassure herself of the child's safety. To Molly's horror she found Mrs Collins trying to get Jessica to feed from a bottle but the child was refusing the teat and screaming. The woman slapped her right there in front of Molly who snatched her daughter away and screamed at her, saying she was cruel. Fortunately Mr Barnes arrived on the scene then or Molly did not know what might have happened. Doris was there so Molly hurried out with the baby, leaving him to deal with his sister and hoping Doris would explain. Nathan was in Leeds or Molly would have spoken to him about it. But she knew his mother would have it in for her even more now.

Yesterday evening Mrs Collins had repeatedly come into the room where Molly was sewing and stood silently at her shoulder, watching all she did. Molly told herself she must not allow herself to feel threatened and that the woman was doing it on purpose to unnerve her. It was not easy, though, ignoring that brooding presence. She just wished Nathan would come home soon.

–

Wearing her new suit and hat, Molly wheeled Jessica out in the pram the next day. She strolled along the tree-lined thoroughfare, enjoying the sunshine and feeling proud as anything, knowing she looked the part of nursery nurse. She noted the names of the houses on pillars and gates.

No plain old numbers for the well-to-do, she mused, savouring each name. The Shanty must surely belong to a retired sea captain. Cairdhu was owned by a Scot or Irishman. Newstead, Doris told her, boasted four cotton brokers and a solicitor, all in the same family, while The Dunes was situated not far from the beach. Molly vowed each day to vary her walk to take in either the shops or the seafront. It was all a far cry from her previous lives in Burscough and Bootle.

'Molly, is that really you?'

Her head turned as Nathan drew alongside her, carrying a suitcase. She was so relieved to see him she beamed up at him. 'Do I look very different, Nathan?' His name tripped off her tongue and she waited for him to scold her but he didn't.

Instead dancing eyes took her in from top to toe. 'I never would have believed such a change possible. It's frightening!'

'Frightening?' she said, taken aback.

'The uniform. I feel like saluting you.'

She laughed, not believing a word he said, knowing the snugly fitting suit did wonders for her female figure. 'I don't know why you should say that?'

'You remind me of my commanding officer.'

'Who?' She flashed him a startled glance.

'That's a joke. But I am one of Haldane's men.' There was a proud tilt to his head. 'I joined the Lancashire Fusiliers Special Reserve the other year when I was feeling a bit browned off. Jess and I had quarrelled. It was before we married.'

'I thought you were mad about each other?'

He stared down at her, a thoughtful expression in his eyes. 'We got mad at each other at times. Didn't you and your husband?'

She hesitated. 'Frank was away at sea a lot.'

'So you never had fights?'

'We had so little time together. In some ways I hardly knew him. Besides, I wouldn't have dreamed of answering him back. He was my husband and eight years older than me. Knew so much more about life, had been to so many places. The only quarrel I had with him, really, was over Ma.'

'Ma ?'

She grimaced. 'I shouldn't have mentioned her. He's dead and that part of my life's over.'

There was a silence. Then Nathan said abruptly, 'I'll be going to army camp in summer for a month. Uncle William's put out. We almost had a row about it but I was adamant about still going. I enjoy it, you see. Roughing it, cross country training and all that. It demands something of a bloke. He was astonished when I told him my instructor last year wanted me to sign up to be a regular soldier. I used to shoot pigeons so I'm a good shot. The instructor was of the opinion there was certain promotion in it for me.'

'You told Mr Barnes that?'

'Aye. And he seemed impressed, if still annoyed with me.' He smiled and changed the subject. 'You know, Moll, I still find it hard to believe you made that uniform yourself. It looks so professional. Turn round. Let me see it from all angles.'

Slightly embarrassed she did a twirl, revealing a neat pair of ankles in the buttoned tan boots.

'Very nice.' Then he changed the subject again. 'They all say time heals. D'you believe them?'

'The shock passes but it still hurts. It's just a matter of getting on with it.'

They both fell silent and he stared at the child in the pram. 'I'll pop up and see her later,' he said eventually.

Molly carried on with her walk, thinking about him being away a whole month. If only it was Mrs Collins going instead!

Later Nathan popped into the nursery as he'd said he would. Molly had finished bathing the baby who was now clad in a clean nightgown and smelling deliciously of Pear's soap. As she emptied the bath in the other room she caught the faint sound of a lullaby and smiled to herself, thinking once again that Nathan was a funny mixture. Who had taught him that? She could not imagine Mrs Collins ever singing to him.

That visit to the nursery was the forerunner of many over the following weeks. Molly was pleased by Nathan's growing fascination with her child. When he did not come she was keenly aware of her own disappointment. When he did they talked not only of the baby's welfare but of the factory and his plans, and of the changes going on in the world: of airships and votes for women, the visit of the Csar and Csarina of Russia.

Mr Barnes had given Molly leave to read whatever took her fancy from his bookshelves. He recommended *Her Benny* which was set in Liverpool during Victorian times and was about a poverty-stricken pair of orphans. The book made her cry and she told him so when he asked what she'd thought of it. Afterwards they discussed poverty and David Lloyd George's intention to improve things for the poor on top of the old age pension which he had already introduced.

Molly was well aware of Mrs Collins's disapproval of her son's daily visits to the nursery and of her brother's desire to educate her further. As Molly pushed Jessica in the pram in Alexandra Park she tried not to think about the growing physical attraction she felt towards Nathan, telling herself she couldn't possible be in love with him, but there was no doubt in her mind just how much she enjoyed the time spent in his company. She told herself she mustn't get too fond of him, that way lay heartache. Yet she could hardly ask him to stop visiting the nursery. Maybe if she absented herself during the time he was there...

But when Molly tried that ploy he was visibly annoyed. 'Where are you off to again? I need to talk to you about Jessica.' He paced the floor, hands in his pockets, eyes on her face, to catch her every expression. 'Has my mother been saying things to you? If she has, forget them. She doesn't rule me. I say stay so you stay. Understand?'

Of course she understood. But she wondered if he understood what was happening between them. Because she would have to be daft not to realise he felt something for her. She would catch him staring at her and he would look away almost immediately. Yet not soon enough to slow the racing of her heart at the expression in his eyes. Their hands would brush apparently by accident, but was it?

It was August when Nathan informed Molly he would be leaving for a training camp in Wales the next day. She was expecting the news but even so her spirits plummeted.

'Jessica's just getting to know and recognise you. Your voice, everything. She's going to miss you.' Molly could not disguise the catch in her own voice.

'Don't you think I'm going to miss her too?' Nathan pressed his cheek against the baby's as she bit on an ivory and silver rattle. 'You as well, of course,' he added softly, staring at Molly.

She lowered her eyes, finding it hard to smile. 'You'll be too busy enjoying yourself crawling through undergrowth and taking potshots at the wild life,' she murmured.

'I aim to enjoy it, but being with the lads won't be the same as being with you. That's a daft thing to say, I know, but it's true. I really am going to miss you, Molly.'

'You mustn't say anymore.' She lifted her head. 'Here, give me Jessica. I'll put her down.'

He handed the baby over, watching as she placed Jessica in the cradle. 'She's going to need something bigger soon.'

'I know.' Like she'll need weaning, thought Molly. And what about me then? Mrs Collins would say they should get a proper trained nurse. It wouldn't be the first time she'd expressed such an opinion.

Molly straightened, not realising how close he was standing. When had he moved? Her heart began to hammer as his arms went around her. She knew it was foolish not to resist but it felt so good. With a sigh she placed her head on his shoulder and put her arms round his waist. For a moment they just held each other then she looked at him and felt a rush of excitement at the expression on his face. When his mouth came down on hers it caused a tingling in her veins. Her lips yielded and they kissed, long and deep.

After a while Nathan reached behind her to unfasten the strings of her apron and pull it over her head. Then, with fingers that trembled, he began to undress her. Molly knew she should stop things there and then but didn't have the willpower. She wanted him to make love to her. His hands moved over her body and he nuzzled her neck as he carried her over to the narrow bed. She felt so alive. Like a scrunched up sheet of paper set afire, his body the taper that ignited the flame at her heart. As he cuddled, caressed and took her.

She came to herself, aware of Jessica gurgling in her cot, and was suddenly reminded of the pain of childbirth. What if she became pregnant? What had she been thinking of, giving way to her emotions?

Scared stiff now, she pushed at him and he rolled off her. She glanced at him as he lay with one hand across his eyes and murmured, 'I shouldn't have done that.'

'A bit late now, Mr Collins,' she said shakily, getting out of bed and clutching her drawers to her.

'God, it was good, though.' His voice was almost reverent.

Molly could have agreed with that but chose not to. She mustn't encourage him to think they could do it again. Suddenly she noticed the nursery door was not quite shut and hurried to close it. 'We must have been mad!' she whispered. 'You'd better get dressed and get out of here before someone comes.'

'In a minute, Moll. We have to talk.' He did not move.

She shook him. 'Mr Collins… Nathan… your mother or your uncle… anyone could come along.'

He shifted, scooping up the clothes she threw at him and staring at her with a frown. 'What's happened to us? It's only five months since Jess died.'

'I know. It's the same with Frank.' She went into the other room.

'It must be me going off to camp that caused it,' he called after her.

Molly did not argue.

When she re-entered the room, dressed, he surprised her by catching her to him. 'Twenty-eight days, Molly,' he whispered against her mouth. 'It'll pass.'

'Not thirty-one?' she said flippantly, near to tears.

'I'll be counting the days.' He kissed her lightly on the lips before releasing her and going over to the cradle. 'You'll take care of Jessica?'

'Of course! That's my job, Mr Collins.' Her whole body felt stiff with dread of what might happen once he had gone.

'Nathan,' he said softly, gazing at her. 'You can't call me Mr Collins after that.' His head indicated the bed. 'Bye, Moll. Thanks for everything.'

She almost said it had been a pleasure but restrained herself. 'Don't get in the way of any bullets.'

'I'm not stupid.' He smiled, blew her a kiss and left.

Molly went over to the cradle and lifted out her baby. Tears shone in her eyes. 'Lovely precious,' she whispered, rubbing her cheek against the light brown hair. 'He loves you. Whether he really loves me as well, we'll just have to wait and see.'

Chapter Five

'Bitch!'

'Pardon?' Startled, Molly stared at Mrs Collins. She had just felt a tooth while feeding Jessica and it had not only hurt but dismayed her. Now Nathan's mother was acting up again.

'Thee thinks I'm a fool, don't thee?'

'Why should I think that, Mrs Collins?'

'*He* thinks I'm a fool,' she snapped, folding her arms and pacing the nursery floor. 'He forced the child on me, thee knows. I wanted our cousin's.'

'What child? What cousin?' Molly felt like asking, 'And why all the thees and thous all of a sudden?'

'Him!' She jerked her head in the direction of Jessica. 'And thee knows who I'm talking about.'

'She's a girl,' said Molly.

'Took the other one from me. It had golden hair, just like his.'

Who was she going on about?

'Stop staring at me!' Mrs Collins shook her head. 'Oh, thee's useless! I thought thee at least would understand.'

'Understand what, Mrs Collins?'

'What are you calling me that for? I never wanted his name. I'm going.' She swept out of the nursery.

Molly stared after her in amazement, wondering what was wrong with her, then carried on changing her daughter's nappy.

Half an hour later Mrs Collins came up to Molly as she was buckling Jessica into her harness in the pram. 'What do you think you're doing?'

'Taking Jessica for a walk, Mrs Collins.'

'Let me look at you.' The woman inspected her appearance, stepping forward to fiddle with her collar and adjust her hat. 'Don't be dawdling. I've got work for you to do.' She prodded her in the back.

'Yes, Mrs Collins,' she said, tight-lipped. 'I'll be back within the hour.'

'You'd better be. I've got my eye on you.' Molly wheeled the pram down the drive, aware of Mrs Collins standing in the doorway watching her.

'Wait for us, Moll!'

She turned to see Doris hurrying after her. 'She's going queer, that woman,' she said in a breathless voice.

'I know. She called Jess "he" and went on about another baby.'

'What d'you think's wrong with her?'

'God only knows. I'm worried, though. I'm going to have to start weaning Jess and I'm sure she'll try and get me out before Mr Collins returns.'

'Wouldn't surprise me. But yer could do with some time away from Miss Jessica anyhow. Come to our house with us tonight. Mr Barnes said we could have time off 'cos he's going to some party with Lady Muck.'

'I'd like that,' said Molly wistfully, 'but I don't know whether Cook'll be that keen on keeping her eye on Jessica. She's teething.'

'Ask Flo, the new maid. She's from a big family. Yer too attached to Miss Jessica. Yer wanna take care. I know yer think Mr Collins'll stick by yer, but I wouldn't bank on it, Moll. He's only using yer.'

She stiffened. 'What d'you mean?'

'You and him!' Doris stopped in her tracks, biting her lip as she stared at Molly. 'I was passing the nursery the evening before he left. Yer a fool to yerself. There's a big gap between you and him.'

'That's where you're wrong.' Molly's cheeks were scarlet. 'We went to the same school.'

'That was *then*. Things have changed for him. If you were to get caught...' She nudged Molly in the side. 'Yer'd be an embarrassment. He'd be rid of yer like a shot.'

Molly's stomach seemed to fall like a stone in a well. 'You don't know him. He feels like a fish out of water here.'

Doris rolled her eyes. 'Holy Mary! He might have at first but not now.'

'OK, OK!' Molly shot out her hands as if to ward her off. 'I see what you mean. Let's change the subject. I'll come to your house if Flo agrees.'

The new maid was willing and Molly started looking forward to an evening out. She settled Jessica to sleep and was just about to leave the nursery when Mrs Collins swept in, dressed to the nines in a blue eyelet embroidered evening gown which was far too young for her. She was carrying an armful of brown velvet material. 'I want you to make curtains out of this. I saw it in the sales and thought it would be just right for the house.' She dumped it on the bed. 'You can get started right away.'

Molly couldn't believe it. 'That isn't part of my job, Mrs Collins. Your son spoke to you about this.'

The older woman's eyes flashed. 'Don't you talk to me about my son! I'll tell you what's what here and if thee doesn't like it, thee can scoot.'

Molly's heart sank and she had to dredge up the courage to reply. 'I'll speak to Mr Barnes.' Molly made to push past her but the other woman caught hold of her arm, gripping it with a strength that surprised her and bringing her mouth close to Molly's ear. 'Don't thee dare open thy mouth. Thee's said enough to him. I'll not have thee taking him away from me. Thee's a troublemaker.'

'I don't know what you're talking about.' Molly's voice shook.

'Ha! Think I believe that? Thee's good at sewing. Well, get sewing.' And Mrs Collins waltzed out of the room.

The woman was mad. She had left no measurements and which windows was she talking about?

'Are yer ready?' demanded Doris, entering the nursery.

'That woman's crazy. She's just asked me to make curtains. Wants me to start right away.'

Doris shook her head in disbelief. 'Wharra you gonna do?'

Molly hesitated, then reached for the new velour jacket she had made and buttoned it up. She placed the matching hat at a saucy angle, shoving a hatpin through the fabric to secure it. 'I'm not doing them, am I?'

'That's the spirit,' said Doris, grinning, seizing her sleeve and hurrying her out of the room. 'I'd better warn yer now, though, yer'll be expected to do a turn at our house. Yer don't mind, do yer? You can do any old thing.'

Oh, Lor'! thought Molly, despite knowing a whole repertoire of songs from her pub days, and her tummy quivered with nerves.

After the spaciousness and relative quiet of the house in Blundellsands, Doris's home in Ascot Street was not only noisy and overcrowded but the area itself much dirtier than Molly remembered, and due to the gasworks it definitely ponged a bit. At least the welcome was warm. Despite all the chairs being taken by the older generation and her having to share an orange box with Doris, while one of her brothers gave them a rendering of 'Home, Home on the Range' with comb and tissue paper, Molly began to enjoy herself.

Her heart was bumping when she was dragged up by Doris to do her turn. There was silence as she stood there, thinking and getting her nerve up. But after a shaky start she did a rather good impersonation of Nelly Powers singing 'The Boy in the Gallery', encouraging everyone to join in the chorus. When she finished they clapped and cheered and Molly found herself curtseying and blowing kisses, enjoying herself no end.

Several of the children got up and danced, to be joined by a young man who did a clog dance. To her surprise Molly recognised Rob Fletcher and as soon as he'd finished she went over to him. 'I didn't expect to see you here. How's your dad?'

'The same as always. I'm walking out with Marie, Doris's sister.' He wiped sweat from his eyes with the back of one hand. 'Some's been asking after thee, by the way.'

'Me?'

'Yeah, you!' He grinned. 'I can't tell thee who he is, though. Dad said but I've forgot.'

'Can't be important if you've forgot.' She poked him in the ribs and soon forgot about it. Until she was on her way home. Then she wondered whether the man was her stepfather. But what could he want with her?

'Moll, wake up! Lady Muck wants to see yer right away,' said Doris loudly in her ear.

Molly groaned and tried to force her eyes open. She could hear Jessica crying and managed to crawl out of bed. 'It'll be those damn' curtains, I bet. She must have crept in while I was asleep and noticed I haven't done them. Well, she'll have to wait. I need to feed Jess first.'

'Lady Muck made her a bottle and gave it to me to give to her.' Doris looked uncomfortable.

Molly did her best to conceal her apprehension. 'She won't take it. Where is the woman?'

'Sitting room. Yer'd best go. I'll see to the baby. It won't be the first bottle I've given.'

Molly hesitated, then nodded. Best get it over with. She went into the adjoining room and splashed cold water on her face.

Mrs Collins was standing by the window looking out over the garden when she entered the sitting room. 'You wanted me,' said Molly.

The older woman turned and there was a gleam of triumph in her eyes. 'A man called. I told him he shouldn't have come to the front door but he left this message for you.' She waved a cigarette packet at her.

A man? What man? thought Molly, reluctantly taking the battered packet from her and flattening it out. She read: *Dear Moll, this is going to come as a shock to you but I'm not dead.* The world seemed to tilt sideways and she felt herself in danger of falling off. She took a deep breath to steady herself and read on. *I'll wait at the gate post. Your loving husband, Frank.*

Oh, Lord, it couldn't be true!

'Well?' said Mrs Collins. 'Who is he? He's not the first boy thee's had, is he? Thee always were one for the fellas. Jack, he liked thee, but thee weren't satisfied with him… you stole our cousin?'

'What are you talking about?' cried Molly, crushing the cigarette packet between her fingers. 'You know who he is. You've read this!' She threw the packet at Mrs Collins.

'He says he's thy husband. Thee'll have to go with him.'

Molly's mouth had gone dry and she was trembling. Her mind was in turmoil and her heart beating fit to burst. 'My husband's dead! This is a trick of yours. I have the baby to see to. I have to go.'

She turned but Mrs Collins's voice stopped her in her tracks. 'I'll look after the baby. I'm good with babies, whatever they say.'

Molly looked at her and saw she was smiling. At least her mouth was smiling but her eyes appeared to be fixed on something in the distance and were unfathomable. 'No, I can't leave her,' croaked Molly. 'I can't!'

'Thee has to. Thee's another husband now. I'll manage. I told them I was good with babies.'

'She'll scream the place down,' said Molly, feeling desperate. 'I'll take her for an airing.'

'No. Thee must go and not come back, Mabel.'

Molly stared at her and suddenly understood. 'You're jealous of me because I remind you of my mother,' she gasped.

'No.' Mrs Collins shook her head. 'Thy mother's dead. Why should I be jealous of her?' She hunched her shoulders and said petulantly, 'And why should I be jealous of thee? Go! Thy husband's waiting.'

Molly hesitated, unsure whether to rush upstairs or see if Frank really was outside. She couldn't think straight. How she wished Nathan or Mr Barnes was here.

'Go on!' Mrs Collins pushed her in the direction of the door, almost sending her flying.

Molly made a decision. She had to see if Frank really was there.

She saw her husband at the same moment as he caught sight of her. It was the most peculiar feeling. He couldn't be a ghost. She thought she was going to faint. He was a stranger., yet not a stranger as he came striding towards her. 'What the hell were you playing at, Moll? You've had me bloody worried.'

'Have I? You're the one supposed to be dead.' She gazed up at him in a daze. He was just as handsome as ever, brown eyes full of life.

He seized her by the shoulders and she reached up and ran one hand over the sleeve of his coat, feeling the firm muscles beneath. 'You are real,' she whispered, and her knees buckled.

Frank's arms went round her, stopping her from falling. He laughed, teeth appearing white against his ruddy skin. 'Well, I'm not a damn' ghost, you daft girl!'

She cleared her throat and managed to find her voice. 'What happened? Where have you been all these months? I cried and cried. I thought my heart would break.'

'I'm sorry, Moll. Give us a kiss.'

She gave him a tentative peck.

'What d'you call that?' He squashed her against him and crushed her mouth with his. She was suddenly frightened, not ready for this. She cut the kiss short. 'Not here, Frank,' she whispered.

'What the hell d'you mean, not here? You're my wife. I'll kiss you where I want. It's been months. I thought you'd be glad to see me?'

'Of course I'm glad to see you! But here's not the place.'

'You would have said what the hell once and kissed me anywhere.'

'Would I?' She wasn't so sure about that. 'Anyway I don't want to give the people round here a peepshow.' She squeezed his arm. 'Let's go somewhere quieter. We need to talk.' She pulled on his arm, tugging him in the direction of the sea, frantically trying to sort out her thoughts. 'Were you the man who asked Jack Fletcher my whereabouts?'

'Not me. A private detective. I arrived home to find you missing and Ma had no idea where you were. I tell you, girl, that was one in the eye for me. What were you thinking of, going off the way you did?'

'Does it matter right now? How did he know to speak to Jack Fletcher?'

'I remembered your Nanna but couldn't remember where she lived. So I went to your stepfather, didn't I? But for the life of him he couldn't remember either. I think he's going senile. Anyhow, I'd got meself another ship. Needed to get back into the routine of things and make some money. I just happened to see this advert in the *Echo* about a detective, so I set him to find you while I was at sea.'

'I remember that advert,' she said slowly. 'How long ago was this?'

'Three weeks.'

'Only three weeks!' She couldn't believe it. 'Where have you been all this time?'

'Don't get shirty with me, Moll.' He scowled. 'You've been missing, too, remember, girl. I was dead lucky. I've always been a strong swimmer. Thrown in the canal as a nipper, had to sink or swim. Anyhow I managed to find a bit of wreckage and hang on to it. I was picked up by this father and son fishing from Ocean City in Maryland.'

They had reached the sand dunes and he dragged her up the nearest one, their feet sinking in the soft sand as they balanced on the top. 'If you were found that quickly, why didn't we hear sooner?'

He squeezed her hand. 'I was done in, wasn't I? Must have banged my head at some time. I couldn't remember things properly. When I started remembering bits of things, like the name of the ship I'd been on and where I'd come from, it was months later. When I finally got home, you'd flown the coop.'

She felt terrible, really sick, thinking of Nathan and their making love, of Jessica, and all that she had been through believing him dead. 'I wish I'd known – and I'm sorry, Frank, for not being there when you came home. But I couldn't have stood it with your mother. But you're here now. I take it Nanna's neighbour, Mrs Smith, gave the detective Jack Fletcher's name?'

'The bargee? Yeah. And he gave him this Nathan Collins's name. So here I am.' Frank smiled.

But Molly wasn't smiling. She'd committed adultery, and how was Nathan going to feel when he returned from Wales and discovered her husband was alive? Whatever there was between them it had to be over now.

'What are you thinking? What's wrong?' Frank smoothed back her hair. 'I know this must all be a shock to you.'

'I wish you could have found me earlier,' she said miserably.

'Bloody hell, girl! Don't you think I do too?' He cupped her face between his hands and kissed her several times and she responded automatically. 'You should have let Ma look after you and then you might not have lost the baby,' he said against her lips.

Darling Jessica! It was as if a dagger had been thrust into her heart. What was she going to do? How could she explain?

'It was a lousy thing to happen,' continued Frank. 'But at least we can have another now I'm back. I wanted a boy anyhow.'

She tried to speak, to say how wonderful little girls were, but couldn't get the words out.

'There now,' he said, hugging her close. 'I can see how upset you are. But you're not to worry, luv. If you'd been brought up with sisters like me, you'd want a boy, too. Girls can be a pain in the backside.' He was smiling and she could have hit him.

At last Molly found her voice. 'I can believe that of your sisters, Frank. But our little daughter, she's—'

'Dead! I know, and it's sad, Moll. I'm not blaming you,' he said impatiently. 'As I said, we can start all over again. Ma says—'

'I don't want to know what Ma says.' Molly felt a familiar resentment.

'I won't tell you then. But it surprises me that someone as nice and easygoing as you are is so stubborn when it comes to doing what Ma says. She's more experience of life. You should have listened to her and not run off like that. She only wanted to help.'

'Did she tell you she locked me in a bedroom and was planning to keep me prisoner?' said Molly, tight-lipped. 'She wanted to take possession of our baby, body and soul.'

Frank's mouth set. 'Don't be melodramatic! She shouldn't have locked you up but she was worried about you.'

'Lovely way of showing it.'

They were both silent. Molly was aware of the waves lapping against the shore and the sound of children playing. Oh, Lord, what was she going to do? How could she tell him what she had done? He'd never understand how desperate she'd felt. How, right now, she was anxious and sad, exasperated and confused.

'Anyway, there'll be other babies, Moll.' He ran one hand slowly down her body. It came to rest on her bottom.

'Don't do that!' she whispered, darting glances all around. 'What'll people think?'

His eyes hardened and he pulled her against him. 'I keep telling you – you're me wife. I don't care. I'm making the decisions, Moll. We're going to have to live with Ma for a while, whatever you say.'

That did it. Her pent-up emotions exploded. 'I can't believe you, Frank Payne! What have I just been saying? *I will not live with your mother.* We'd drive each other mad.' She wrenched herself free and began to run.

He jumped after her, quickly catching up. 'What's the matter with you?' he said, with an air of helplessness that unexpectedly tugged at her heart strings. 'I thought with me being back from the dead you'd do anything for me.'

She felt a similar helplessness. 'I'm really glad you're alive, Frank, but it's a shock. I need time to get used to it. I've built a whole new life for myself now. I've had to.' She placed one hand gingerly on his arm. 'Let's take things slowly. Not rush into anything.' His expression froze.

'And what's that supposed to mean? You can't stay here.'

'Why not?' She laughed. 'You'll be going back to sea soon. What difference does it make to you where I live while you're away?'

'I can't believe this!' He looked like thunder as he kicked up a pile of sand. 'Where am I supposed to sleep when I come home? In the nursery with you and this Mr Collins's child?' He flung the words at her. 'Get this, girl. I don't want my wife in service. I may not have much money at the moment but I'll get some.' He seized hold of her wrist. 'Come on, we're going.'

'No!'

He stared at her. 'Have you forgotten you're married to me?' His voice was heated.

'I won't live with Ma. I've got money. We can find some-where else to live while you're home.'

He took a deep breath. 'I don't want your money. For now you'll have to make do at Ma's.' He headed for the road, dragging her behind him.

'No, no, no! Frank, wait!' She tried to free her wrist but he was too strong. Molly sought another way to get round him. 'If we go and live with Ma she'll be listening for every squeak of the bed!' she rattled on, tripping over the kerb. 'I'll never be able to let myself go at your mother's. And think of living with your sisters.'

'It won't be forever.'

'Frank, sweetheart, listen to me,' she said, determined to have her way and struck by what she thought was a brilliant idea. 'If you'll take the money I've saved we can find somewhere else. Doris the maid lives by Athol Street near Scottie Road. There's a refreshment house there and I'm sure they let out furnished rooms. We could stay there.'

'Why the hell should we? And if you're talking about a seamen's lodging house, it's not a fit place for you.'

'I'm not. It's nothing fancy but I can find somewhere else once you're back at sea. This is just a temporary measure. We need to be on our own, Frank.' Her voice was gently persuasive as he stopped and looked at her. She ran one hand down his chest and brought it to rest on the top button of his trousers. 'We could go there tonight. The Rotunda Theatre's only walking distance. We could see a show, have a fish supper and then go home together. I could get the money right now. You just have to mention Jack Fletcher's name. Say you're an old friend of his and I'm sure they'll give us a room.'

'I don't know the man.'

'But he knows me.'

Frank was silent, staring at her in a way that made her feel uncomfortable. 'It was him who gave you the lift to Burscough.'

'What's wrong with that? Think of living with your sisters... we'll be better on our own.' Molly kissed him but he did not respond.

'It's all right to kiss me now, is it?' His voice was cool. 'Doesn't matter if anyone's looking now. Think you can twist me round your little finger just because you know I want you.'

'I'm not so sure about that. You stayed away so long. Do you still love me?'

'I'd be a liar if I said I didn't – and you know how I hate liars.'

'Then be patient with me, Frank. Do what I ask. Take the money I've saved and get us that room.'

He hesitated. 'I'm not happy but I see you're going to get in a state if I force you to go to Ma's. Perhaps we do need to be alone. Get the money then we'll go.'

She kissed him, this time in gratitude. His lips tasted salty and cool from the sea breeze. 'Wait here. I won't be long.'

Molly ran all the way up the drive and round to the back of the house, thinking to pick up Jessica and explain to Frank once she had her. It was quiet and there was no sign of anyone. She avoided the kitchen and sped up the backstairs to the nursery, praying Jessica would be in her cradle. She had to have her daughter. Hopefully Frank would understand. But there was no sign of the baby. Molly found her savings and her hand hovered over the cache of gold sovereigns. She took two of them but hid the rest right at the back of a drawer. Then she frantically dashed downstairs to the kitchen, hoping to find Jessica with Doris.

'Lady Muck's taken her out,' said her friend.

'Why?' Molly sank into a chair in despair.

Doris stared at her curiously. 'What's up? What did she want you for?'

'She didn't tell you?'

'You're joking! Tell the likes of me her business?'

'My husband's turned up.'

'Holy Mary!' Doris's jaw dropped and she crossed herself. 'What are yer going to do?'

'What d'you expect me to do?' Her voice trembled and she buried her head in her hands.

'Oh, yer poor thing,' said Doris, patting her back. 'But it's for the best, luv.'

'What are you saying that for, you daft girl?' said Cook, wagging a finger at her. 'I know she'll miss us all – especially Miss Jessica. But it's like a miracle, her husband coming back from the dead.'

Molly lifted her head and stared at her from wild eyes. Leave Jessica! How could she leave her sweet, precious daughter? She would go to Frank now and explain and then come back for her. She rushed out of the kitchen, trying to work out what to say to her husband. Surely he would understand?

—

'You seem to have been ages,' complained Frank. 'Where's your things?' He seized her hands. 'Did that Mr Collins want you to stay?'

'He's not here. I've got to tell you something else, Frank,' she panted. 'Something important. But first, here's the money.' At the last minute she had hidden the two gold sovereigns in a pocket of her petticoat. 'I've got to go back for my things. I've wages due and must see Mr Barnes. He's Mr Collins's uncle. I'll follow on.'

'No!' He seized her arm. 'You're coming with me now.'

'Please, Frank! I have to speak to Mr Barnes. We need that money.'

He hesitated. 'OK. But you won't be late?'

'No, I won't be late.' She wondered how late was late and wished she wasn't finding it so difficult to tell him about Jessica.

Back at the house Molly went upstairs and packed her belongings. Then she sat gazing out of the window at the gleaming expanse of the sea, thinking how different the view would be in Athol Street. Her mind roamed backwards and forwards, trying to decide what was the best thing to do for her daughter. She was still sitting there when she heard Mr Barnes come home.

Molly hurried down the main staircase, pausing when she saw him below in the hall talking to Jessica who was sitting up in her pram, gnawing a rusk. Mrs Collins was there and Molly's heart misgave her. How she longed to carry her daughter off but commonsense had asserted itself. If she tried to explain things to Mr Barnes he would be so disappointed in her and

99

she valued his opinion. He might believe one of two things about her. Either that she was a loony who couldn't accept her own daughter was dead or that she had killed his great-niece and lied to cover it up. If she tried to run off with her daughter he would call in the police, she did not doubt that. Why, oh why, had she set out on such a path? *Thou shalt not bear false witness.* She had broken one of the ten commandments and was paying for it now.

Molly cleared her throat. 'Mr Barnes?'

He looked up as she descended the stairs. Jessica, dribbling madly, waved the rusk at her, making baby noises. Molly felt as if herwas bleeding.

'I told you to go,' snapped Mrs Collins.

'Hold on there, sister,' Mr Barnes said, holding up his hand. 'Give the lass a chance to speak.'

His sister hunched her shoulders and turned her back on Molly.

'I ain going. I just wanted to thank you for all your kindness to me, sir, and to ask if you could see your way to taking me on at the factory once my husband's back at sea? We haven't any money because he was injured and lost his memory.'

Mrs Collins made to speak but Mr Barnes held up his hand again. 'Come and see me at the factory, my dear. I'll see what I can do.'

'Thank you.' She smiled gratefully. 'I'm due two weeks' wages as well, sir.'

'I'll speak to my nephew. I'm sorry you have to go, Molly. I've enjoyed our little talks. As for this young lady, she's going to miss you a lot.' He chucked Jessica under the chin.

'I'll miss her too, sir.' Molly's voice shook and her eyes were luminous with tears.

'I'll see you soon no doubt. Goodbye for now, my dear.' He lifted Jessica out of her pram and carried her into the sitting room.

Molly gazed after them, the tears trickling down her cheeks.

'You've got a nerve,' said Mrs Collins, glaring at her. 'I know what thee's up to. Thee can't let go, can thee?'

'I am letting go and you don't know how hard it is for me!' she said on a sob. 'Not that you care. You hated my mother for some unknown reason, so now you hate me too.' The older woman's face quivered. 'I didn't used to hate you. But now...' Her eyes glinted and she rushed at Molly, catching her unawares. She slapped her across the face so hard that the girl lost her balance, falling against the staircase, banging her head and sliding to the floor.

There were hurrying footsteps and Doris entered the hall. 'What's going on?'

'Get her out of here,' cried Mrs Collins, whirling her arms like a windmill in full sail. 'I can't stand the sight of her.'

Doris made to say something but was told to shut up. Hurriedly she helped Molly to her feet and hustled her out of the house. 'I think she's flipped her lid. Yer can see fingermarks right across yer mush. What's wrong with the woman? Yer don't think she's guessed, do yer?'

'Guessed what?'

'Yer don't have to pretend with me, Moll. Jessica's your kid, isn't she?' Molly did not know what to say. 'No resentment, that was yer mistake – and the way you weren't happy leaving her for a minute. Why did yer do it?'

'I thought they might arrest me for murder and I'd end up on the gallows,' she said miserably. 'Mr Collins's daughter just didn't want to live.'

'Wanted to be with her mam, I suppose. What about yer husband?'

'He wanted a boy.' Molly felt absolutely wretched, as if the heart had been torn from her.

'So yer not going to tell him?'

'No. They might still have me arrested if I told the truth now. You don't know how even the nicest people will behave if they know you've made fools of them. Anyway,' she sighed,

'I did it all for her. So she'd have a better chance of surviving. She'll get plenty of good food here and pretty dresses.'

Doris sighed. 'It's a mess. Not that yer could ever have married young Mr Collins. As I told yer, Moll, he's above yer now. Yer've got to forget him.'

'I know.' She squared her shoulders. 'But I can't forget Jessica.' Her eyes met Doris's. 'I expect you to keep me posted on how she's getting on. You'll be visiting your mam.'

'Yeah?' Doris looked puzzled.

'Well, I've asked Frank to get us lodgings at Block's. Hopefully we'll be able to get a house nearby in a few months.'

Doris wrinkled her nose. 'But why there? Can't you afford better?'

Molly took a deep breath. 'I'm hoping to get a job at the factory, in the sewing room. Mr Barnes said I could call in and see him.'

'Yer mad!' cried Doris. 'Mr Collins works at the factory, remember. Yer should be keeping your distance.'

'I'm sure once he knows my husband's back there'll be no trouble there,' said Molly, on her dignity.

'I hope you're right. Anyway I'll look after Jess for yer.'

'I'm banking on it. Just watch Mrs Collins. I don't trust that woman.' Molly touched her face gingerly, wondering about the older woman's relationship with her own mother.

Doris slipped her arm through Molly's. 'I'll walk yer to the station and yer can tell me where yer husband's been.'

They walked along the road, Molly talking easily, but her legs felt as if they were made of lead as each step took her further away from her daughter.

Chapter Six

'I wish I could afford better for you, Moll, but considering it's not far from Scottie Road it could be worse.' Frank slid both arms around her waist as she gazed about the sparsely furnished room, in the centre of which was an iron bedstead. 'Although why you want to live round here beats me.'

'The people are friendly and it's not far from town,' she murmured, not daring to mention its close proximity to Mr Barnes's factory. She thought of what Doris had said about a bit of grandeur spoiling you. It was true. But at least here she wouldn't have Mrs Collins continually looking over her shoulder. Although without Jessica she felt as if she was missing a limb.

'It's a tough neighbourhood but at least the food's good... cheap and plenty of it.' Frank nuzzled her neck and cupped her breasts in his hands. Molly turned in his arms to face him, thinking she could already be pregnant. If she was there had to be no doubt in his mind that the child belonged to him. She drew down his head and kissed him. Within minutes he had her on the bed. It felt strange being with him after so long and the palliasse, stuffed with straw that prickled, only added to her feeling of disorientation. She kept thinking his voice was all wrong, that it should be deeper, a baritone like Nathan's, not a tenor. His lovemaking did not last long and that seemed wrong too.

'It won't be over so quick next time.' Her husband lay on his side, watching her go over to the washstand. 'But I needed that. I've had to wait a long time.'

'That's OK.' She tried to concentrate on the times they had made love satisfactorily. It wouldn't have worked tonight even if he had set out to pleasure her. She was too anxious, yearning for Jessica and filled with guilt. If Frank was ever to learn she had been to bed with Nathan, God only knew what he would do to her.

As if he could partly read her mind, Frank said, 'What was he like, that bloke you worked for?'

'Just a bloke.' She felt panicky and needed to take a deep breath. Careful to keep her voice expressionless, she added, 'Heartbroken when his wife died. Didn't want to look at the baby at first. It was the midwife's idea I should act as wet nurse. Not only to help him out but me, too.' She allowed distress to seep into her voice. 'I was on my uppers, Frank! There was me believing you dead and Nanna gone and then the baby... It was terrible.'

'I can imagine. But you should never have run away. Ma would have seen you and the baby were OK.'

Molly was silent as she went back over to the bed and sat on the side of it, gazing down at him. He had beautiful eyes, the colour of dark chocolate. A much deeper shade than Molly's but the same as Jessica's. Molly considered it fortunate that Nathan's wife's eyes had been brown. Her heart. She was missing him as well as her daughter.

'You've got to start thinking of yourself as part of a family, Moll,' continued Frankie, 'We're in this world to help each other. We firemen aren't paid a fortune. What working man is? But if we support each other, then we can get somewhere.' She wondered what he was talking about. 'And that reminds me, I must give you the money that was over after paying for this room. It's ours for a month. Let's hope you can find somewhere else soon.'

'I'll try. Are we going out now?' She smiled at him, pulling down the bedclothes, telling him to get a move on, wanting to be doing not thinking.

They walked along Scotland Road, which was still alive with people despite the late hour. They gazed into brightly lit shop windows. Clarkson's the pawnbrokers was doing a roaring trade as women redeemed their husbands' Sunday suits or shirts. Come Monday they would be returned to the pawnshop. Poorly clad people lingered outside butchers' shops and carts selling fruit and vegetables, waiting for the hour when a joint or a handful of bones, veg or fruit would be sold off cheaply. There was more than one drunk reeling from pavement to gutter as the pubs began to let out just after midnight.

Molly and Frank made their way back to their lodging where he made love to her again, this time with less haste. She found the experience pleasant enough. They slept and when they woke he asked whether Mr Collins had ever made any advances towards her. The question stunned her and she sought frantically for words to allay any suspicion he might have that there could possibly have been anything untoward between them. 'He's not as handsome as you,' she managed. 'Why should you think I'd fancy him?'

'I wasn't thinking of you fancying him,' he said, curling a strand of her hair round his little finger. 'More of his taking advantage of you.'

Molly's mouth was dry but she managed a laugh. 'Why should he? I'm not exactly a raving beauty, Frank.'

'No, but you've got something.' He drew her close. 'And these rich blokes — looks have nothing to do with it, Moll. I remember reading somewhere that in the olden days the lord of the manor had his way with a man's bride before the husband got to sleep with her.'

'That's terrible!' She shook her head in disgust. 'But Mr Collins is no lord. It's his uncle who owns everything and he's a gentleman, always as nice as pie to me.'

Those words seemed to satisfy Frank but she realised she needed to be on her guard about what she said if Nathan came up in conversation again.

It being Sunday Molly went to church and gazed about her with interest, wondering if this was one of the churches Nathan might do work for. Frank had a lie-in. Then they took the ferry to New Brighton. On Monday, after a huge fry-up with four Irish eggs, Frank said he had to go down to the docks. 'Can't hang about, Moll. Funds are short.'

'So soon?' She felt put out, having thought he would stay with her for a while. The last few days had been reasonably enjoyable. Frank could be very good company.

'Sorry, luv, but you knew how it is. I'm short on funds. I'll have to go and see Ma as well. She knows I've traced you so'll be wondering what's happened to us.'

'I'd say, she knows me well enough to have guessed,' said Molly lightly.

He frowned. 'You're wrong about her, you know. Why don't you come with me?'

'I've had one mother, Frank. I don't need another.' She reached up and caressed his cheek. 'Besides, I'm sure you'll find she prefers having you all to herself.'

He did not deny it. They kissed and he went out.

Molly went upstairs to tidy their room and wash a few things. She draped drawers and stockings over the back of a chair, then took out the two sovereigns and gazed at them. Why had she taken them? For security, with Frank saying he had little money if Mr Barnes changed his mind about giving her a job? Yes, they were for if anything should go terribly wrong and she had to fend for herself. She hadn't really stolen them though she had been given them under a false premise. What about the other four left behind? She wondered. She should have taken the lot, she decided. It probably wouldn't be long before Doris discovered them. She must have a word next time she saw her. Molly returned the coins to their hiding place and went out, having decided to visit Doris's mother.

The house was only a few minutes away on the other side of the road in an area known as the race course district. Aintree

Street was straight opposite the corner where the refreshment house stood, and Ascot Street ran off it. There were signs of poverty on all sides. Some of the children playing in the streets were barefoot; those who had shoes or boots more often than not wore no socks and their footwear was well–worn and often split across the toes. Tiny tots were sometimes clad in nothing but a grubby shirt or vest. There were houses with broken windows that had never been replaced, the holes blocked up instead with cardboard or filthy rags. Yet on this sunny August morning Molly could hear the sound of laughter and children at play and her ears caught the occasional snatch of song. Women were out scrubbing their steps and gossiping.

She found Mrs McNally cleaning windows with a handful of newspaper that smelled strongly of vinegar. 'Hello, luv! What are you doing round here? There's nuthin' wrong with our Doris, is there?'

'There wasn't last time I saw her.'

'Then what can I do for yer?'

'Could you keep your eye out for a house for me?'

'Round here?'

'That's right. Me and my husband have lodgings in Athol Street.'

'Husband?' Her eyes widened. 'I thought yer were a widow?'

'Me too. But it was all a mistake.'

'Really!' Mrs McNally stepped down off the chair. 'Why don't yer come in and tell me over a cuppa?'

They went inside and Molly explained as the tea was poured.

'Well, fancy that,' said Mrs McNally, eyes as round as doorstops as the tale was told. 'But you're going to miss the family, aren't yer? And be a bit lonely once yer fella goes back to sea.'

'I'm hoping to work in Mr Barnes's factory. Frank'll be against the idea but he won't know until he comes back.' Molly bit into the Wet Nelly she'd been offered and syrup ran down her chin.

Mrs McNally shook her head in disbelief. 'You've got a nerve, girl, going against yer man. What if he finds out?'

'Then I'll do something else. Work from home. I've a sewing machine. Hopefully I can have it delivered once I've got a house.'

'Yer've got it all mapped out, haven't yer, girl? Well, I hopes it works out for yer.'

So did Molly, although she knew that the best laid plans didn't always come to fruition.

Frank arrived back an hour after her. She was surprised to see him so soon. 'I thought you'd be ages at your mother's?'

'I've got a ship and it's sailing tonight.'

'Tonight!' She could scarcely believe he would leave her this soon. 'Where's this one going?'

He hesitated and looked a bit sheepish. 'China.'

She gasped. 'But that's the other side of the world, Frank! You'll be away months.'

'I'm sorry, Moll.' He pulled her against him and rested his face against her hair. 'But you knew what it would be like when you married me. I'd rather have a shorter trip but the money's better, and besides, I've never been to China. I'll be able to bring you some real nice trinkets.'

'Trinkets?' It took her all her self-control not to shout the word. 'Why should I want trinkets, Frank?' she said as calmly as she could. 'Don't you think it would be better if you found another ship?'

'Jobs aren't that easy to come by, Moll,' he said, frowning. 'I have to take what I can get.' She saw then there was little use in trying to persuade him to change his mind. He wanted to go to China because he loved travelling. She thought of how she had left Jessica and had to quit her job, all for the sake of being with Frank for a few days. But she could not say any of that without him getting annoyed. So instead she drew away and poked him in the chest playfully. 'You save your money and maybe we'll be able to get a decent place one day, Frank Payne. I don't want to live in a hovel for the rest of my life. Now what about your advance note?'

'I had to pay that 'tec the rest of his money and give Ma a bit for my keep but I've some for you.' He pulled her back into his arms. 'I know you're upset, I can understand that, but the sea's my life, Moll,' he said earnestly. 'And don't tell me what to do with my money. I like buying you things, so shut up and let me have my way. I won't spend up.'

She was angry but put on a smile, knowing she wasn't going to change him. 'China! You'll have to watch yourself, Frank. The Tongs and all that.'

He grinned and swayed sideways with her, to and fro. 'Britannia rules the waves, Moll. There'll be British warships out there guarding our interests. Besides I can look after myself.'

'Aye, I suppose you can,' she said dryly. 'If you can survive a hurricane.'

'A guardian angel that's what I've got.' He kissed her neck. 'We sail from Birkenhead but you can see me off at the Pierhead. The sooner I go, Moll, the sooner I'll be home.'

There was no denying that, she thought. But how could he say he loved her when he was prepared to leave her so soon after not seeing her for months, as well as giving money to Ma before her?

–

The bed felt empty that night. Surprising how quickly you could get used to sleeping with somebody, thought Molly. How quickly you could get used to having them around. The next day she felt low-spirited and decided to catch a train to Blundellsands, hoping to see Jessica.

But when she called at the back door Cook told her Doris had gone out for the day with Mrs Collins and they'd taken the baby. 'They're having trouble with her but the little love's got a sunny nature as you know and'll soon settle. God bless her,' said Cook.

Feeling utterly dejected, Molly returned home.

The next day she decided she had to buck up her ideas. Putting on her Sunday best, she set off in search of the factory. She had been told it was situated off Vauxhall Road so walked down Athol Street in the direction of the docks. It was a long street and contained the local bridewell and fire station. All was hustle and bustle. It was here shipowners of the small trampers and bum-boats came to buy equipment from the marine chandlers, while ordinary seamen visited the grocers for straw to make up beds for when they were at sea. Mothers shouted at children with noses pressed against windows of sweet shops and herbalists. Yet they themselves paused to gaze at the displays in the pawnshops, which were a hotch-potch of the useful, the tawdry, and all that was most precious to those who had deposited items there.

Men, moustached or with beards covering half their chest, puffed on pipes as they gazed at the tools in one open-fronted chandlers' store with its hooks and shovels, buckets and cobblers lasts. The shop drew the eyes of small boys and Molly had a picture of her own son doing likewise one day in her mind. Could she be already pregnant? If she was, whose child was it?

She reached Vauxhall Road. Here was where the wealthiest men had their businesses. Her fascinated eyes took in the names of seed crushers and oil refiners; merchants selling tallow, paper, coal, timber and marble. Soap manufacturers rubbed shoulders with beer distillers and sugar refiners, and they in their turn gave way to the Anglo-American Oil Company.

She came to the factory, a red brick building with lots of windows. A short flight of steps led to the entrance. She took a deep breath to steady her nerves and opened the door.

'Can I help you?' said a voice.

Molly approached a hatch in the wall to her left and saw a young man leaning back in a chair, toying with an elastic band and a matchstick. 'I need to see Mr Barnes,' she said, putting on her poshest voice.

He jumped to his feet and fixed her with a stare. 'You were at the McNally s' the other week. If you're looking for a date, I don't mind taking you out. There's a good show on at the Roundy.'

Molly could not help smiling. 'I'm glad to see my efforts weren't wasted. But I've come to see the boss.'

'Oh, yeah! And why's that?'

She leaned across the counter and whispered, 'I'm a secret agent from another factory and I want to know what magic makes his candles burn longer than any others.'

He grinned. 'You're mad! Why are you really here?'

She drew herself up to her full height. 'I told you – to see Mr Barnes. He said there'd be a job for me here.'

'You're out of luck, luv. He's gone to Yorkshire.'

Molly's face fell.

The man looked sympathetic. 'What job was it?'

'In the Sewing room, I hope.'

He scratched his thatch of fair hair. 'In that case you could perhaps see Mrs Arkwright. She's from up Lancashire, with an accent you can cut with a knife. You're a woollyback, too, by the sound of it. You didn't fool me with your put on accent.'

'That's rich coming from a Liverpudlian! You lot talk through your noses. We've a county steeped in history,' she said proudly.

'We've got plenty of that here too. If you'll keep your eye on things, I'll fetch her. Although I'm not supposed to leave my post unattended.'

'Then you shouldn't be leaving it, should you, Jimmy?' said a cold voice.

Their heads swivelled.

Molly stared at Nathan, her heart performing the most peculiar somersault. He was nursing a broken arm and did not look pleased to see her one little bit. 'Mr Collins,' she stammered. 'You've hurt yourself.'

'Clever of you to spot that. You're the last person I expected to see here, Mrs Payne.' His grey eyes reminded her of shards of broken ice, chilling her to the marrow.

For a moment she was lost for words, remembering how he'd behaved when they had parted. Had he really loved her then? Or had he used her as Doris had said? Molly knew so little about men. At last she managed to find her voice. 'I came to see your uncle. He said he'd give me a job.'

'Did he now?' Nathan placed a hand on a door marked WAITING ROOM. 'You'd best come in here then. We'll discuss it.'

She hesitated only a moment before walking into the room, head bowed.

He closed the door behind them. 'You were flirting with Jimmy.' His tone was definitely unfriendly.

Her startled eyes lifted to his. 'That lad? You must be joking!'

'You were making eyes at him.' Nathan flung the words at her as he paced the floor, right arm stiff between its splints.

'I was being friendly, that's all.'

'You were distracting him from his work.'

'Well, I like that!' said Molly indignantly. 'I thought dealing with callers was his work.' She placed her hands hard down on a table in the middle of the room, never having thought they would be having such a conversation.

'To do with business, aye.' He paused on the other side of the table.

'I am here on business. I told you, your uncle promised me a job.'

His angry eyes rested on her flushed face. 'It's out of the question, your working here.'

'Why?' she said stubbornly. 'I need the money.'

'You're a married woman. Let your husband keep you. I don't want you here.' He cradled his right arm in his left, looking exhausted all of a sudden.

Her ready sympathy was roused and she moved round the table towards him. 'Does it hurt?'

'Of course it bloody hurts.' He turned his back on her. 'I think you'd best go now.'

'But I don't want to go. Let me explain about Frank…'

'I don't want to know. I just want you out of here. That's an order. And I'm the boss here.'

'Nathan, I had to go with him. He's my husband.'

She touched his shoulder and he turned, looking no friendlier than he had minutes ago. 'Funny. There was me believing you a widow when all the time you were just a runaway wife, trying to make your husband jealous.'

She was astounded. 'That's not true! I believed him dead!'

'So you say,' he sneered, lip curling. 'But what does it matter in the long run? The end's the same. You're still married. So just go, Mrs Payne. I owe you some wages. I'll see you get them.'

Molly was so hurt she lost her temper. 'You can stick your money where Paddy stuck his ninepence, Mr Collins!' she said in a quivering voice. 'I was no runaway wife and I am no liar! Good day.' She flung the door open and marched out.

'Molly, come back here!' he yelled. 'I haven't finished with you.'

'But *I've* finished with *you*! I'm not being spoken to like that.' Her heart was thudding so fast she thought it was going to burst through her skin, lift off and take her with it. Who did he bloody think he was, calling her a liar? She heard footsteps behind her and, not wanting to speak to him again, she lifted her skirts and ran.

She raced along Vauxhall Road, aware of feet thudding behind her. The interested faces of carters, labourers and dockers flashed by but Molly took no notice of them, putting on a spurt before darting down Lightbody Street by the gasworks. Her breath was burning in her throat, her face was hot and she could feel the perspiration beneath her hair and between her breasts. She stopped on the canal bridge, gasping.

When Nathan caught up with her, chest heaving, he said, 'I've a good mind to throw you in. It might cool that hot temper of yours.'

'I haven't got a hot temper.' She turned on him, eyes flashing. 'It's you with the temper. You shouldn't have chased me. People will think I'm a thief. Why did you have to follow me?'

'I would have thought that was damned obvious. We hadn't finished talking.'

'You told me you wanted me to go. Well, I did as you told me although you're no longer my boss, Mr Collins.' She turned away from him, resting her chin on her arm against the handrail of the bridge. 'I was not a runaway wife,' she said through gritted teeth.

'I know! It was just something my mother said. I was so angry about everything, I wanted to believe it so I could hate you.'

She whirled round and stared at him. 'And do you?'

He wiped his brow with a handkerchief. 'I wish I could. It would be easier. Your husband's alive and we thought he was dead.'

She nodded. 'I should never have gone to the factory. I realise now it was stupid, as you said.'

There was silence.

'Does he know you were visiting the factory?'

She hesitated. What if she told him the truth? That Frank had already gone back to sea. That he would be away for months. Months when she would be alone. He had said he did not hate her. Did that mean he loved her? Would he see her words as a sign of encouragement for them knowingly to commit adultery this time? She wasn't sure if she loved him or not. She fancied him. Wanted to kiss that mouth of his that curved so sweetly in a smile that caused her heart to flip over. To be wrapped in his arms and be possessed by him.

She struggled with her emotions, her conscience, thinking of Frank leaving her so soon to fend for herself What had he thought she was going to live on? Did he think that by leaving her again the way he had she'd be forced to go and seek help from his mother? Perhaps. Even so, was that any excuse for her to break her marriage vows? She gazed at Nathan and managed to force out the words, 'We're hard up. Of course he knows. I'll just have to find something else.'

'You surprise me. A man who can't support you. How can you love him? How can you respect him?'

'He's my husband. I have to love him.'

'Have to?' Nathan's lips twisted in a humourless smile as he took a step towards her. 'You mean, you should but you don't?' She was silent. He was only a breath away from her and her body swayed treacherously towards him. He caught her to him and whispered against her mouth, 'Did you tell him what happened between us?'

'Do you think I'm mad? He'd – oh, I don't know what he'd do. He can be unpredictable. It might sound melodramatic but you must keep away from me – for both our sakes.'

Abruptly Nathan released her, his expression fixed in stern lines. 'I'll pay you a month's wages. I'll give the money to Doris. I presume she knows where you're living?'

'Yes.' Her voice was dull. 'I need my sewing machine too. Can you see it gets to me?'

He nodded.

She managed to stumble from the bridge and on to the tow path. She began to walk alongside the canal, her emotions and head in a whirl.

'Molly May! Where are thee going, lass? Thee'll be in the water if thee's not careful.' Two strong hands took hold of her and she looked up into Jack Fletcher's face. She sagged against him. 'Oh, Uncle Jack,' she said in a shaky voice. 'Why does life have to be so darned difficult?'

'There, lass. What's wrong?' His deep voice softened. 'Is it that husband of thine?' His sympathy was too much for her. Unable to speak she nodded, throat aching with the effort of holding back her tears though several rolled down her cheeks.

He handed her a scrap of clean rag. 'Maggie Block was telling me you're lodging with her. Said your husband's gone back to sea already?'

She dabbed at her eyes, thankful he didn't appear to have seen her with Nathan. 'We need the money. He spent most of his searching for me. I have to find some work.'

'Ask Maggie Block. She lost a lass last Saturday, just upped and went.'

'I'm not a very good cook,' sniffed Molly. 'She'll soon teach thee. Just simple fare. Scouse, pig's cheek, spare ribs.' He smacked his lips and patted the dish he carried. 'Got a bowl of scouse here.'

'Right,' said Molly, pulling back her shoulders. 'I suppose it's worth a try.'

She did not waste any time in approaching Maggie who seemed perfectly willing to take her on. She would work for her food and lodgings. It was not what Molly wanted out of life but at least it was better than living with Ma Payne. As for her daughter, far better Jessica was safely out in Blundellsands being brought up as a rich man's child.

Chapter Seven

Molly pushed open the door of the grocer's which stocked straw and took a deep breath of air laden with the fragrances of faraway places: nutmeg, cinnamon, allspice. A few weeks ago the smell of paraffin in the shop had turned her stomach but she was no longer suffering from morning sickness. So far she had managed to keep her pregnancy a secret from her employers and would carry on doing so as long as she could. The work was menial but not so demanding that it exhausted her. She washed dishes, peeled vegetables, waited on tables and at the counter, and she put in extra hours to earn more money. Which was just as well because Frank was still away.

She thought of the letter postmarked Hong Kong, reassuring her of his safety. He described scenes vividly so she could almost visualise the ports he visited but the most important news was that he hoped to be home for Christmas. Molly had to find a house before then. He mentioned Ma and moving in with her if she didn't. But that could wait one more day. As soon as Molly had changed the straw in her palliasse she was going to Blundellsands to see her daughter and Doris.

Her friend was waiting at the station, wearing Molly's old uniform which swamped her body, making her look tinier than ever. 'Guess what!' Her eyes were shining.

'What?' Molly smiled at Jessica, who was sitting up in the pram, playing with a wooden-jointed duck. 'Sweetheart! Precious!' She ducked her head under the hood and kissed her daughter, who wriggled and tried to push her away. Molly was upset. 'She's forgetting who I am. Oh, Lord! I dreaded this happening.'

'Never mind that! Listen to me,' said Doris. 'This concerns you.' Molly ignored her, her attention on her daughter, holding one dimpled hand and pressing it against her own cheek.

'They want to see yer.'

'They? Who's they?' said Molly absently. 'The solicitor and Mr Collins! He asked me if I was still in touch with you and I said I'd be seeing yer today.'

Molly straightened. 'What are you talking about? Is it about my sewing machine?' Doris wrinkled her nose. 'Why should it be about yer sewing machine? Haven't yer heard? Didn't yer read it in the *Echo*?'

'I don't have time to read the papers. What's happened?'

'Mr Barnes died a week ago of an apoplexy.'

Molly stared at her stupidly. 'You're joking?'

Doris looked exasperated. 'As if I'd joke about such a thing. He was a very kind man.'

'I know he was.' Molly felt even more upset now. 'That poor man! I was very fond of him. He was good to me.'

'He must have been fond of you, too, because as I said his solicitor and Mr Collins want to see yer. It has to do with the will.'

'The will?' said Molly, still feeling stupified.

'Mr Barnes's will! Are you going daft or something? He left me twenty pounds! Wasn't he a sweetheart?'

'Yes,' said Molly, thinking she still hadn't mentioned the sovereigns to Doris. Of course, her friend might have found them and, having no idea where they'd come from, given them to Nathan.

'Wake up!' Doris nudged her arm. 'Yer eyes have gone all glazed.'

'That's because I'm in shock.' Molly seized the handle of the pram. 'Race you to the house!' She took off, the hem of her skirt swirling about her ankles.

'Yer crackers! And mean, 'cos yer know I can't keep up with yer,' shouted Doris, scuttling after her.

Molly slowed to a walk, smiling at her daughter who was chuckling as she clung to the side of the hood. They continued at a more sedate pace with Molly in sober mood, remembering her last meeting with Nathan. So much for them keeping their distance! What had he made of his uncle's remembering her in his will? That was a real turn up for the book.

'Yer'll find Mr Collins in the study most likely. At least, that's where they were when I left the house,' said Doris.

'How's he taken his uncle's death? How's his mother?'

'You'll find out yerself when yer see him. Here we are,' whispered the maid, stopping outside the study door. 'I'll see yer later.'

Molly stood a moment, smoothing her hair and straightening her felt hat with its wide brim. Her heart was beating uncontrollably fast but she hoped she presented a calm exterior. She took a deep breath before knocking on the door.

'Come in!' called Nathan.

Her heart leaped at the sound of his voice and her knees shook. Don't be stupid! she told herself. He's only a man. When you see him you might find you don't fancy him after all.

She entered the room. A man she presumed to be the solicitor was seated on a chair to one side of the desk. Nathan sat behind it. At first glance he appeared cool, calm and collected but desirable for all that. 'Please sit down, Mrs Payne.' He waved her to a chair. 'This is Mr Taylor, my uncle's solicitor.'

'Pleased to meet you, sir,' she murmured, sitting down.

'Mrs Payne, no doubt you're wondering why we've asked to see you?' said Mr Taylor gravely.

'I presume it's to do with Mr Barnes's will. I'm really sorry to hear he's dead. I had no idea until I met Doris at the station.' Her voice trembled and tears filled her eyes.

'Quite so.' He shuffled some papers on the desk. 'He has left you some shares in the company.'

'What!' Her startled eyes turned to Nathan.

'That's what Mr Taylor said,' he murmured, toying with the inkstand, avoiding meeting her gaze directly.

'But why? I can't believe it! What do I know about business?'

'He believed you to be very astute,' said Mr Taylor, smiling frostily. 'You asked him questions about the business and seemed to take in all he told you.'

Molly smiled. 'He liked to talk and I was interested. He was a good listener, too, wanting to know all about my life. He knew my mother when she was a girl. Maybe that's why he was so kind to me. He asked how I'd have coped if I hadn't got the job of looking after Jessica.'

'You told him having a regular sum of money coming in, however small, could make the different between managing and the workhouse,' said Mr Taylor.

'It's just commonsense. You only have to think of the five-shilling old age pension Lloyd George brought in for those over seventy. They shouldn't have to resort to the Poor Law. People have their pride. That five shillings really helps families with children trying to help out elderly parents as well. Although in my opinion it doesn't go far enough. Mr Barnes agreed with me. He was a philan–philanth-th–'

'Philanthropist,' supplied Nathan.

'That's the word.' Molly's eyes met his briefly and the blood tingled in her veins.

'Yes, yes,' said Mr Taylor impatiently. 'All very true but someone has to pay for those pensions, my dear Mrs Payne. And people with money are already giving to many charitable works.'

'When it takes their fancy,' said Molly promptly. 'And most make sure it doesn't hurt their own pockets. They want to try being poor. They'd soon see things differently. Young Mr Collins knows. He hasn't always had money.'

'That's enough, Molly,' said Nathan, a slight tremor in his voice. 'I'm sure we all want the law changed to help the poor.

But right now it's you and these shares we need to talk about. Of course, this will was made before your husband turned up. How do you think he'll feel about it?' He sent her an unexpectedly challenging stare.

'He'll want me to sell them,' she responded without hesitation.

'There!' Mr Taylor rested his hands on the desk. 'I *knew* your uncle was wasting his time.'

'I won't, though,' said Molly, jutting out her chin. 'I'd be going against Mr Barnes's wishes if I did that.'

There was silence.

'But what if you were desperate for money?' said Nathan.

She lowered her eyes, pretending to pick an invisible thread from her sleeve, not sure whether to say she *was* desperate. In the end she lifted her head and stared at him. 'I'm having a baby. That's quite a difficult situation to be in with your husband at sea and no money coming in till he returns. It would be nice to have a lump sum. But, as I say, I'll go along with Mr Barnes's wishes. I've a job with board and lodgings, and I don't doubt that when Frank comes home from China a small regular income for years to come will make much more sense than blowing a lump sum in one go. The baby's not due until May so I'm sure I'll manage somehow.'

There was another silence.

Molly could almost hear Nathan counting the months in his head. His eyes hadn't left her face. Mr Taylor cleared his throat and Molly gave him her attention. 'Right. I will see that you have the share certificate once everything is sorted out, Mrs Payne.'

'Send it to the factory,' said Nathan, getting to his feet. 'Mrs Payne can pick it up there. She should see over the place now she has an interest.'

'Our business is finished then,' said the solicitor, shuffling his papers together. 'At this point, Mr Collins, your uncle always brought out the Madeira. A particularly fine one, as I remember.' He rubbed his hands. 'I think a glass for young Mrs Payne wouldn't go amiss. She's had a shock.'

'A very pleasant one,' added Molly hastily, thinking she would enjoy seeing over the factory. But what was Nathan thinking of, actually suggesting it?

He pushed the bell next to the fireplace and seconds later Doris came into the room. She glanced at Molly who only stared blankly at her. Doris shrugged and addressed Nathan. 'What can I do for yer, sir?'

'A bottle of my uncle's Madeira, please, three glasses – and some of Cook's little almond biscuits.'

'Three?' Again Doris glanced at her friend and this time Molly winked.

'Three,' repeated Nathan, coming from behind the desk and approaching Molly. 'I presume you've seen Jessica, Mrs Payne?'

'Yes, Mr Collins.'

'And how do you think she's looking?'

'Very well.' Her face softened. 'I hope you're not having too much trouble with her now?' She paused, adding in a low voice. 'Your mother – how is she?'

A shadow darkened his eyes. 'Do you really want to know?'

'Of course I do.'

'She's furious about the will,' he murmured. 'Angry that my uncle left you shares and her just some *objects d'art* – and, of course, she's to live here for the rest of her life.'

'Lucky you,' said Molly, then blushed. 'I'm sorry. I shouldn't have said that.'

'No. But then she accused me of poisoning my uncle,' Nathan said, tight-lipped, 'and I didn't find that very funny.'

Molly was shocked. 'You must be worried sick about her! I take it – he did make you his heir?'

'Of course. But it's not only that, I'm afraid, Mother's now saying Jessica's your baby.'

Molly almost dropped the glass Doris handed to her. 'She must be m-mad,' she stammered, not knowing where to look.

'She's definitely getting worse. Remember you told me she thought you were your mother at times? I mentioned it to my uncle and he said they used to be friends but fell out over some cousin. He doesn't know the whole story because he was living away. I want her to see a doctor but she's refusing.'

'I see,' said Molly, relief flooding her that he hadn't taken his mother's remark to heart. Even so she felt weak and tossed the wine off in one go.

'Go easy,' said Doris disapprovingly. 'That's good stuff that is.'

'Fill Mrs Payne's glass again, Doris,' said Nathan, draining his own. 'And mine. This is a day for shocks.' He took his glass and went over to speak to Mr Taylor.

'And why's it a day for shocks?' asked Doris, taking in Molly's pale face.

'Mr Barnes has left me shares in the company,' she whispered. 'And I've just told Mr Collins I'm having a baby. He's counting the months.'

Doris's mouth fell open. 'Oh, my sainted aunt, yer don't mean it? He can't really believe... it could be your husband's!'

'Of course it could. But it could just as easily be his.' Molly was starting to feel slightly hysterical and took a grateful gulp from her refilled glass.

'Don't rush that one down, it's a waste of good Madeira,' said Doris. 'Why did yer have to go and tell him? Keep yer distance, that's what I say. Here, have a biscuit with it. You mustn't get drunk.'

Molly nibbled at the biscuit. There was a bubble of laughter inside her struggling to get out. Why she should find the whole situation funny she did not know. Perhaps she was the one going mad, not Nathan's mother? She half-listened to the men's conversation about dividends, church furniture and electrical fittings. Then, feeling even more that her life had become unreal, she slipped out of the room.

Doris was hovering in the hall and pounced on her. 'Feeling better now? At least yer've got yer colour back.'

'I've got to get out of here.' Molly seized Doris's arm. 'Where's Jessica?'

'With Flo. Well?' Doris's eyes searched her face as she pushed open the baize-covered door at the end of the passage. 'Did he say anything else to you? Will you be seeing more of him?'

'I might have to. He wants me to pick up my share certificate at the factory.'

'Convenient,' said Doris, giving her a knowing look.

'It doesn't mean a thing. Nathan's got a lot on his plate now with having to run the factory – as well as having a dotty mother. He's not going to have time for me.'

'If you say so. But I don't believe a word of it.'

Neither did Molly but she pretended not to hear the remark, saying she was going to see Jessica, and headed for the kitchen.

–

In the days that followed not an hour passed when Molly was not thinking of Nathan's getting in touch with her. But it was to be three weeks before she received a letter from Mr Taylor informing her that her share certificate was ready to be collected, and adding: *Mr Collins assures me that any time this week will be convenient for you to pick it up from the factory.*

Molly decided to go on her next day off. She dressed in her Sunday best and with what felt like a score of butterflies in her stomach, made her way to the factory. 'Good morning, Jimmy!' She popped her head through the hatch, enjoying watching him scramble to his feet, dropping his newspaper and cigarette in his haste. 'Is Mr Collins in?'

'Oh, it's you.' He picked up the smouldering butt and blew the end into glowing life. 'I thought it was someone important.'

'I *am* important. I'm a shareholder in this company.' Molly discovered she enjoyed the sound of the words rolling off her tongue. 'A shareholder,' she repeated.

He grinned. 'Fancy your chances now, do yer? You must have been closer to the old man than I thought. All we got out of it was a morning off for the funeral and a half crown in our wages last week. Not that I'm complaining. Most bosses wouldn't remember their staff. He was a real gent was old Mr Barnes.'

'And the new boss?'

Jimmy glanced over his shoulder. 'Not as confident as he seems, if you ask me. Lets fly when things go wrong. You made your quarrel up?'

Molly fought against a rising tide of colour. 'None of your business,' she said, tilting her chin. 'Perhaps you can let him know I'm here?'

'I could.' He drew on his cigarette. 'But you know I'm not supposed to leave my post. I'll give you directions.'

Molly felt like swiping him one for making her feel small. 'Thanks,' she said, tight-lipped. 'But get a move on. In a way I'm one of your bosses now.'

He had the grace to look discomfited and hurriedly told her where Nathan's office was.

Molly hurried along a corridor and up a flight of stairs, glancing at doors as she went, aware of the sound of machinery. EMBROIDERY AND GARMENT ROOM, she noted, and felt a thrill of excitement, determined to see what lay on the other side of that door later. She came to the office but there was no sign of Nathan.

A woman was working at a typewriter. 'Can I help you?' she said.

Molly felt that hot tide of colour envelop her again. How she wished she could control it. 'I'm Mrs Payne.' Her voice sounded husky and she cleared her throat. 'Mr Collins asked me to call. I'm one of the shareholders,' she said loudly.

'Oh, yes.' The woman's haughty expression thawed. 'He's been expecting you, Mrs Payne. He's in the furniture workshop. I'll take you there.'

Furniture workshop! He hasn't wasted any time. Molly felt that thrill of excitement again.

The workshop was downstairs towards the rear of the building. As the secretary opened the door Molly caught sight of Nathan, sandpaper in hand, with another man turning a length of wood on a lathe watched by a youth. For a moment she was lost for words then the secretary spoke and Nathan turned and saw Molly. He smiled. 'I wondered when you'd turn up. What d'you think?'

She said the first thing that came into her head. 'It smells gorgeous.' She glanced round at shelves containing a range of chisels and planes, mallets and saws. There were tins of nails of all sizes and shapes.

Against a far wall planks of wood were piled while the floor was littered with woodshavings and sawdust.

He laughed. 'Better than a bottle of scent! Come over here and I'll show you what I'm doing.' He nodded dismissively to his secretary and she closed the door behind her.

Molly walked slowly towards him.

'Feel this wood,' he ordered.

She dropped her bag on a bench and he seized her hand, placing it on a chair he was working on, moving her fingers along its length. There was a sensual feel about the act and Molly's heart beat a little faster. 'It's like touching satin,' she murmured.

'Walnut.'

She glanced into his face, suddenly realising it was only inches away from hers. His hand stopped moving as their eyes met and held. There was no need for words. Molly felt heat engulf her. She removed her hand quickly, aware of the man and the boy only yards away. 'What other woods do you use?' Her voice sounded louder than she'd intended and she blushed again. I have to stop this, she thought, vexed with herself. I am a shareholder in a company. I could be somebody one day.

'Pine – that comes from Canada. Oak, from Wales, elm – mahogany occasionally,' said Nathan.

'Can I see over the rest of the factory?'

'Of course. That's why you're here.' He removed his khaki apron, dropping it on a bench and reaching for the jacket that hung on a hook.

He ushered her through the door. 'How many shares do I have?' Molly felt as if she was walking on a tightrope. One step in the wrong direction and she would fall off. They had to keep their relationship on a businesslike footing and it wasn't going to be easy. Perhaps she should sell the shares? she thought miserably, guessing what Frank could make of all this.

'Five. Mr Braithwaite has thirty, his daughter twenty. I have thirty, Jessica fifteen. Of course, until Jessica is twenty-one I control her vote. We have as many votes as shares when it comes to making decisions. Mr Taylor explained it to me. Not that I couldn't have worked it out for myself, I'm not an idiot. But you know what lawyers are.'

'No, I don't,' said Molly, thrilled to bits that her daughter should have fifteen shares. 'But my arithmetic's good enough for me to work out that my five are important. Mr Braithwaite and his daughter can't outvote you so long as I vote on your side.'

'Which I hope you always will, Molly?'

'I can't see myself doing otherwise at the moment. Why? Do you think he'll vote against you? How does he feel about yourworkshop?'

'I put the money my uncle left me into it so there was no argument.'

'What about electrical fittings?'

'They're for the future. We haven't the money to invest at the moment. But we should live long enough to see the fruits of our new ventures. We're young enough.'

She liked the way he used the word 'we' despite her being such a small shareholder and having a husband in the background whose presence Nathan must resent if he still wanted her. I shouldn't be thinking of him wanting me, she thought. Oh, Frank, why do you have to be away so long? I could cope with my feelings for him better if you were around and I wasn't so lonely.

Nathan stopped in front of a door which had CANDLE ROOM emblazoned on it and opened it. 'Candles are made two ways,' he said, leading her over to where several men stood dripping wax from a height on to lengths of wick. She did not interrupt as he went on explaining, although his uncle had previously described to her the different processes. Cheaper candles were made in moulds; the more expensive by the method of wax being built up in layers on dangling wicks, each layer being allowed to harden before the next was applied.

The Wickroom and the Finishing and Packing room followed on. He left the Embroidery and Garment room to the last.

They entered to the clatter of machinery, foot treadle Singers and flashes of colour. Molly had seen similar machines in a shop in the city centre. There were four of them here and all were in use. But there were also women measuring or cutting out from rolls of blue and cream cloth. A dumpy elderly woman was putting the finishing touches to a Celtic cross on a purple chasuble with exquisite tiny stitches, while a girl sewed a golden fringe onto a green figured satin stole. Lastly Molly noticed a young girl folding a flame red altar frontal in tissue paper and placing it in a cardboard box.

'I could be happy here,' she murmured.

Nathan nodded. 'You feel about fabrics the way I feel about wood.'

'It's the differences in texture and colour and what you can make of them.' Something far more than warmth gleamed in Nathan's eyes as he took her elbow and she trembled inwardly. It really was madness their being together. 'Come and meet Mrs Arkwright. She's been watching us for the last few minutes. She knew some cousins of my uncle and mother in the old days. One of them died of stomach trouble. He worked in a weaving shed in Colne with her.

'Colne. That's near Pendle, isn't it?' said Molly as she took Mrs Arkwright's hand.

She was a woman of medium height with greying hair caught up in a twist on the top of her head.

'Aye, missus, but the witches are long dead. Poor misguided women. You're a Lancashire lass, too, I believe?'

Molly smiled, thinking her accent wasn't as bad as Jimmy made out. 'That's right. Your women are turning out some lovely work.'

'Aye, there's some churchmen who are right peacocks. Mr Collins tells me you can embroider and use a machine?'

'Yes. And that reminds me.' Molly turned to him. 'My machine?'

He said ruefully, 'You don't have to tell me. I forgot. What's your address?'

She hesitated before telling him and he frowned. 'It must be hard work cooking and waiting on tables. You must take care of yourself.'

'I'm fine,' Molly insisted.

He surprised her by saying, 'If you're wanting to do sewing work from home instead of what you're doing now, I'm sure Mrs Arkwright could find you something.' He turned to the woman. 'My uncle would have recommended Molly. Her embroidery really is exquisite.'

'I'll see what I can do, Mr Collins.'

They left the room and walked towards his office. Suddenly she wanted to be away, apprehensive of what he might say when they were alone. 'This baby,' he began.

'I know what you're going to say,' she said swiftly. 'And, yes, it could be. But how am I to know? In the meantime there's Frank, and as I told you before, if he ever suspected there had been anything between us, there'd be real trouble.'

'I don't want to cause you trouble.'

'Then best forget this baby could be yours.' She fiddled with her handbag. 'I should never have told you. I don't know why I did.'

'Well, you did and I can't forget it. If it's a boy—'

'Don't you start,' said Molly, exasperated all of a sudden. 'Frank's bad enough, going on about a son. I should never have come here.'

'But you did.' Nathan seized her hand and raised it to his lips. He gazed into her eyes. 'I want you, Moll, but I won't pester you. I don't want you getting hurt. Don't cut me out of your thoughts. I think we belong together and one day—'

The door to his office opened and his secretary stood there. 'I thought I heard your voice, sir. There's a letter here I need your help with.'

'One minute.' His tone was abrupt.

'I'll go,' said Molly, dragging her hand from his. 'It's been really interesting, Mr Collins. Goodbye.'

'I'll see you get that certificate,' he called after her.

She raised a hand in acknowledgement but did not look back.

Chapter Eight

'Belong together… one day be together,' muttered Molly under her breath, entering the refreshment house in a rush, having walked round town to rid herself of some of the tension inside her. Now she was hoping to reach her room without having to talk to anyone. *The only way for Nathan and me to be together is for Frank to be dead again,* she thought, and she couldn't wish him dead. *It'd be wrong. Besides she still felt something for him.*

'Molly!'

She glanced about her and was more than surprised to spot Frank's sister Cath sitting at one of the tables. She waved Molly over.

'What are you doing here?' she said warily.

Cath flicked back her dark red hair and gazed at her from amused green eyes. 'We had a letter from our Frank and Ma thought it was time one of us popped round to check up on you.'

'Why? What does she think I'm up to?' said Molly, annoyed.

'Don't ask me. I just do as I'm told,' said Cath, leaning on her elbow, chin in her hand. 'I'm fed up of it actually. So how's tricks?'

'OK. I'm sure Frank's told your ma everything I'm up to, so if you don't mind I've got things to do. Tarrah!'

'Hang on!' Cath sprang to her feet. 'I made the effort to come here. The least you can do is talk to me.'

Molly eyed her up and down. 'What do you want me to say?'

'You could ask why I'm fed up.'

'Who's fed up?' said a male voice.

Both of them spun round. Jimmy closed the door. He held a brown envelope in his hand.

'None of your business,' said Molly. 'What do you want?'

'Who's this?' said Cath, smiling. 'Introduce us, Moll.'

The last thing she wanted was any of Frank's family knowing her business. 'Why can't you take a great big hint and go, Cath?'

'This place is open to the public, isn't it?' said Jimmy, returning Cath's smile. 'We don't really need someone introducing us. How about a cup of tea, luv?'

'Got one. But I don't mind your joining us at our table.' She held out her hand. 'I'm Cath Payne, Moll's sister-in-law. Not that she wants to let on we're related.'

'Why are you here, Jimmy?' said Molly, getting in between them.

'Boss sent me with this for you.' He held out the large brown envelope.

'Thanks. You can go now.'

'I'm in no hurry.' He stepped round her to shake Cath's hand.

Molly hesitated, trying to think of something cutting, and Maggie Block called her over. By the time she returned Jimmy and Cath had disappeared. Damn and blast! she thought, wanting to smash something. She could only hope Jimmy would keep his mouth shut about Nathan and her connection with the factory.

–

Molly kicked off her boots and wriggled out of her apron and frock before crawling beneath the bedcovers. How she wished she had Nathan to cuddle up to! But that was like wishing for the moon. The weather was freezing and so many people were seeking shelter in the steamy warmth of the refreshment house that she was rushed off her feet. She would be glad to give the job up, had in fact given in her notice. Fortune had smiled on her in the last week in the form of a dividend payment. She had not expected to benefit so soon from her role of shareholder and was delighted.

Tomorrow she planned on visiting Mrs McNally's landlord. A house had come empty in Ascot Street, the previous tenants having done a moonlight flit. Molly was impatient to get the key and see over the house. She needed to move in and get settled and to plan her confinement. She felt a quickening and placed her hand over her belly. She was strangely convinced she was carrying a boy this time. But the only positive thing she felt about his parentage was that she was the mother and the last thing she needed was Nathan putting in a claim for this child when he already had her daughter.

The following morning she walked down Ascot Street with the key to the house in her pocket. It came as something of a surprise to find Doris scrubbing her mother's front step. 'What on earth are you doing here at this time of day? I'm supposed to be visiting you and Jessica later, remember?'

'Well, yer won't be visiting me at Blundellsands no more.' There was a smouldering expression on Doris's face and she folded her arms across her chest. 'I quit.'

'Quit? But you can't quit!' Molly was dumbfounded. 'What about Jessica?'

She sniffed. 'That's your problem, Moll. I've stood enough from that woman.'

'But how am I going to get to see her?'

'Don't ask me. I don't know why yer can't just let her go. Yer having another baby. Put all yer luv into this one.'

Molly closed her eyes tightly and counted to ten before opening them again and glaring at Doris. 'You don't under-stand! You never will unless you have a child of your own. You don't know how it hurts, not having her with me.' The words caught in her throat.

Doris was unperturbed. 'I understand yer only thinking of yerself. Yer'd be best putting her out of yer mind altogether and accepting you caused this to happen. Now yer've given Mr

Collins somebody to love, yer've got to let her belong to him properly.'

'I've done that! But—'

'Yer haven't. Or there'd be no buts.'

'Well, there are,' said Molly irritably. 'What was Nathan thinking of, letting you go?'

'In Leeds on business, isn't he? Lady Muck's in charge.'

'Oh, Lord, I've got to do something. The woman's mad!' She clenched her fists, the door key to her new home digging into her palm.

'Don't be daft! She's just a bad-tempered, jealous old cow.' Doris got to her feet. 'Anyway, he'll be back today. He'll sort things out.'

'Perhaps I should go there?' Molly gnawed on her lower lip.

'Oh, no, yer shouldn't. What if your husband…?' Doris paused abruptly before adding, 'And speaking of husbands, there's a bloke just turned the corner who looks just like that photograph you showed me of your Frank.'

Molly whirled round. It *was* Frank. She realised there was no chance now of her going to Blundellsands.

He came running, lifting her off her feet and swinging her round and round before kissing her. When he set her down on the pavement Molly's head was spinning. She clung to the front of his navy blue reefer coat until the world steadied. His eyes searched her face as he smoothed back loose tendrils of her hair. 'Maggie Block told me about the house. She didn't say you looked peaky, though, and that you'd lost weight.'

'I haven't lost weight,' said Molly, collecting her wits and forcing a smile.

'He's not a bad looker,' said Doris, gazing at the pair of them. 'Introduce us, Moll.'

She did so.

'Nice to meet you.' Frank gave Doris a brief nod as he took Molly's hand. 'Let's be going, luv. We've a lot to discuss.'

'You couldn't have chosen a better time to come home,' she said, as he drew her away from Doris. 'I've got the key and I'm just on my way to see a house.'

'That's good. So how have you been?'

'Fine,' she said brightly, in a dreamlike state. 'I can scarcely believe you're home at last. Sure you're not a ghost?' She felt all the way down his arm.

He grinned. 'You're crazy! I know it's been a long trip but it's really me, alive and well, and I can't wait to get you alone.' Immediately she felt on edge, yet it was no more than she'd expected of him. 'Well, we'll be able to be alone, won't we?' she said, switching on a smile. 'Our own little house, Frank. A parlour house. We're lucky to get it.'

'I'll decide that once we're inside.'

She said no more but waited until she'd put the key in the door and stepped over the threshold.

'Needs some work on it,' said Frank, standing in the middle of the kitchen with his arm round her waist.

Molly gazed at the grubby walls and filthy black grate and her heart misgave her. 'There's nothing wrong that a good scrub and a coat of paint won't cure,' she said firmly. 'At least we've our own lavatory and running water. There's courts not ten minutes from here with only two lavs and a stand pipe between the lot of them.'

His brow creased. 'That's the trouble. What are we doing living round here, Moll? I'm sure we can get better.'

'We will one day,' she said swiftly. 'But this'll do us for now. I've got to know people and there's lots going on – and we're not far from town.'

He didn't look convinced. 'What's the rent?'

She had paid a month's rent in advance and it had taken all her dividend money. 'Nothing for you to worry about. It's paid,' she said lightly, reluctant to tell him about being a shareholder.

'How? You haven't been near Ma to borrow money from her and you've shamed me by working at Block's for your keep.'

'Shamed?' cried Molly, and would have said more but the expression on his face silenced her.

'I thought you'd have come to your senses and gone to Ma – but not you.'

'No, not me,' said Molly, trying to smile and keep things light. She knew he barely had his anger under control by the nervous tic that beat at the corner of his left eye.

'If you've got yourself into debt with some moneylender then tell me now,' he said, tight-lipped.

'I haven't.' Molly paused and with reluctance said, 'To tell you the truth, I was left money by Mr Barnes in his will.'

He stared at her and said incredulously, 'You mean – the man who owned that house where you were a nursemaid?'

'Yes. He died a short while back. He used to like to talk to me. Knew my mother when he was young.'

'Why didn't you mention it in your letters?'

'It wasn't that long ago.'

He was silent for what felt a long time. She held her breath until eventually he said, 'Did that Doris get money as well?'

'Yes.'

'OK, I believe you. Have you any of it left?'

She breathed the easier. 'I paid a whole month's rent and it took all of it. But now we've got this house we're going to need furniture.'

'I take it you haven't any other money tucked away?'

Molly thought of the sovereigns. 'No.' She linked her arm through his, relieved he hadn't blown his top. 'I'm hoping you've got some, though.'

He smiled. 'I'm quids in at the moment. We'll have a night out on the town tonight. A show and a nice little supper some-where, just the two of us.'

She decided that now was the time to tell him about the baby. 'Three of us, Frank.'

'Three?' He frowned.

'I'm having a baby.'

His expression immediately changed and he pulled her into his arms. 'Why didn't you tell me straight away, luv?' His eyes shone.

She laughed. 'You didn't give me a chance! Too busy telling me off.'

'Well, now I know, I won't have you slaving away and losing this baby.'

'I've already given in my notice.'

'*Now* you're showing sense.' He kissed her. 'You've no objection, I hope, to my telling Ma?'

'I'd rather you didn't right away,' she said easily. 'She'll only start fussing me and that'll drive me mad.'

'But she'll be over the moon.'

Molly managed to resist saying, *Going there on her broomstick, is she?* 'I'm not saying not to tell her. Just let it be our little secret a bit longer,' she said persuasively. 'Until after Christmas. Let's get this place sorted out first. It isn't fit for anyone to call until I've brushed and scrubbed, and blackleaded the grate with Zebo. We'll need to order coal, too – and get a decent bed. Then we'll be snug as two bugs in a rug.'

'So we're just having a bed, are we?' he teased, putting his arm round her waist. 'I'm glad you've your priorities right, Moll.' She flushed. 'You know what I mean.'

'Yeah, I know what you mean. Let's find some better lodgings while we sort this place out. You deserve a treat.'

And so I do, she thought. But if you knew everything I'd been up to while you were away, you wouldn't think so.

Much to Molly's amazement they went to the Compton Hotel opposite St Peter's in Church Street. 'I thought your pay was lousy,' she whispered, sitting on the double bed which felt as if it was packed with feathers, watching Frank unpack his things.

'It is. But with its being a long trip I managed to make extra money cutting the crew's hair and shaving those who didn't want to grow beards. It mounts up. I bought you this.' He dragged a tissue-wrapped parcel from his canvas bag.

She unwrapped it slowly to reveal a jade green dress. She stood up to hold it against herself. It had a mandarin collar and there were slits up both side of the straight skirt. On the bodice was embroidered a long dragon.

'It's silk,' he said with a pleased smile, watching her.

'It's so soft.' Molly held it against her cheek, revelling in the feel of the material. 'I must try it on.'

'You're not very big.' He frowned.

Her stomach turned over with sudden fear. 'I've been working hard, Frank. It's due in May.'

'Right. You must feed yourself proper.'

'I will now you've got money to give me while you're at sea. I had to work, Frank – I couldn't be beholden to your ma.'

'OK, OK, let's forget that now.' He helped her with the buttons on her blouse and no sooner was she undressed than he had her on the bed. She thought of Nathan while he had his way, although she knew she shouldn't. What did the Bible say? It was sinful even to look at someone with lust in your eyes.

Afterwards she put on the dress and gazed at her reflection in the wardrobe mirror. 'I like myself in this,' she said, lifting her hair and twisting it into a knot on top of her head.

'I wish you'd leave your hair down. It's pretty.'

She dropped her arms and the red–gold tresses rippled down her back. She had to keep him happy and free from suspicion. 'If that's what you want.'

He came up behind her, wrapping his arms round her. 'We'll go to the Empire and after the show have supper in Connelly's Oyster Bar. You'll wear the dress.'

'Of course. Although, it's very daring, Frank, with these slits up the side.' She was four and half months pregnant but hardly showing.

'You wouldn't be able to walk in it without the slits. You'll start a new fashion.'

Maybe. Who knows? she thought, imagining designing her own clothes.

'I bought you something else, too.' He lifted his canvas bag on to his knee and delved into its depths. 'Two things actually.' He flourished a fan, holding it up to his face and fluttering his eyelashes at her over the top. She could not help smiling, he looked so funny. She took it from him, batting her eyelids at him and practising closing and opening it.

'It's only made of paper and black lacquered wood,' he said. 'Didn't cost much.'

'I like it,' she said, fanning herself 'What's my other present?'

'It's for the house.' He drew out another tissue-wrapped parcel. She unwrapped it to reveal a china vase with a bearded man in long robes painted on it.

Molly inspected him carefully. 'I like it. He looks friendly and wise.'

Frank took the vase from her and placed it on the dressing table. 'And there's one more thing I've got you.'

She shook her head at him, feeling terribly guilty. 'You shouldn't spoil me. I'm not worth it,' she said seriously.

'Of course you're not but you're the only wife I've got.' He sounded cheerful about that and she felt even worse. From the very bottom of the bag he drew out a pair of embroidered slippers. 'They bind women's feet in China, you know. They shuffle along as if they're crippled. It makes me sick thinking about it but these should fit you.'

They did. And of course went perfectly with the dress.

It was an enjoyable evening and as Molly lay listening to Frank's steady breathing later in bed, she thought that if he stayed at home she would have to put Nathan out of her mind. She had made vows. She had to be faithful to her husband. Perhaps thinking positively about him being the father of her child would help.

She asked him about giving up the sea as they were unloading the secondhand furniture they had bought. 'You're not serious, Moll?' Frank paused in the middle of the pavement, letting down his end of a sofa. 'What would I do? I won't be a docker. You have to be in with the right ones or there's no chance of making a living. You're treated like cattle, having to go in them pens, waiting to be picked out like you were prime beef.'

'I wasn't thinking of the docks,' she said easily. 'You stoke boilers at sea for a living, don't you? What's wrong with a wash house or a public baths? There's a couple not far from here.'

He screwed up his face. 'Women coming and going? They're gossip shops. You don't know what you're talking about. I'll stick with the sea, thanks very much. Conditions might be lousy and the pay could be better, and you know I hate leaving you, but the sea's in my blood. I'll tell you what, though,' he said, once they had the sofa inside, 'I'll try and get on the Atlantic run. We'll see more of each other then. Would you be happier with that?'

What could she say but yes?

With Christmas only a few days away, Molly was determined it was going to be a happy time for her and Frank. It would be the first one they had spent together. She had no intention of being persuaded to go to his mother's. 'I want to spend it here, just the two of us,' she said in wheedling tones. 'You were at sea last year, remember.'

'I was hoping we'd go to Ma's.'

She gave him a look and after a few minutes he said, 'OK. I'll give into you for this year because of the baby. I'll just nip up there meself later in the day.'

Pleased to have got her way, she hugged him.

Late on Christmas Eve they went to St John's Market, hoping to get some bargains. Molly bought a pair of rabbits for half a crown and potatoes at elevenpence a peck. Frank purchased two bottles of port for three shillings. 'I'll take one to Ma and you can have the other with a drop of lemonade. I'll get a couple of bottles of beer from the pub for meself.'

Christmas Day passed peacefully and on Boxing Day Frank went to play football with some old mates. She was pleased to have the house to herself for a few hours. There was a Charles Dickens book she had borrowed from the Free Lending library to finish and rabbit pie to make for their dinner.

It was as she was rolling out pastry that Doris popped in. 'Just come to say Ma's invited you and Frank to our New Year's Eve party. It'll be fun. The whole family'll be there.'

'I'll tell him. He's not planning on going back to sea until New Year.'

But Frank was far from pleased when she mentioned the invitation. 'We're not going,' he said firmly. 'Ma wants me to first foot for her. Besides we're invited to another party and I've accepted for both of us. It's at Bernadette McGuire's mother's house. You remember Bernie? She came to our wedding.' He placed his arms round Molly as she stood at the sink, peeling potatoes. 'She's just been widowed, poor kid. Husband died from galloping consumption so she's moved back home. Brother's home from India, too, invalided out of the army.'

Molly remembered Bernie all right. She was the one Ma'd had in mind to marry Frank. That was another thing the old woman had against her. She didn't want to see Ma, certain it would lead to trouble, but realised she had no choice.

'So he got you to come?' There was a triumphant gleam in Ma's mud-coloured eyes. 'What did I say to yer, Sadie?' She turned to her neighbour who was sitting next to her in the overcrowded kitchen.

'That he shouldn't be letting her wear the trousers,' said Mrs McGuire, hitching her enormous bosom higher as she fumbled with a strap. 'But I'm not surprised she's ashamed to show her face, losing the baby the way she did. If she'd listened to you yer'd be a grandma now.'

Molly had expected Frank to be at her side when facing his mother but they'd no sooner entered the house than he was seized upon by Mrs McGuire's whey-faced daughter in her widow's weeds. Now Molly felt vulnerable but steeled herself to say, 'I don't think that's any of your business, Mrs McGuire. So why don't you just leave me alone?'

'That's a lovely way to speak to yer elders!' said the woman, sounding scandalised. 'Yer want to get your Frank to give her a good clout round the earhole, Joan.'

'Our Frank would do no such a thing. He's not a violent man,' said Ma, placing her glass of Guinness on top of the piano. 'Tell me now, where's the baby buried, Moll? I'd like to visit her little grave sometime.'

'Why?' she blurted out, flabbergasted.

'She's flesh of my flesh, isn't she? I hope yer had her baptised before she went?'

'Of course,' said Molly, moistening her lips. 'Mabel May.'

'No saint's name?' Ma sighed gustily. 'Baptised one of your lot then?'

Molly's knees began to shake. She wasn't in the mood for this. 'Why not?' she said defiantly. 'We're Christians too, you know.'

'So yer say. But you don't have the Pope. So where is she?'

Molly felt trapped. She did not want her mother-in-law poking her nose round Burscough Bridge.

'Well?' demanded Ma Payne when she didn't answer.

'St John's,' said Molly reluctantly. 'There's no gravestone or anything – and it's a long way for you to go. You'd be wasting your time. You wouldn't be able to find it.'

'If I want to waste me time, I'll waste it, girl.' Ma jutted out her chin. 'I'm sure the minister will help me.'

Molly did not know what else to say and knew she had to get away. Suddenly she saw Cath and Jimmy and made them her excuse. 'You'll have to forgive me. I want a word with your Cath.' She turned, pushing her way between people, but would have avoided the couple if Cath had not seized her arm.

'You've disappointed me, Moll,' she said, shaking her head.

'I bet Jimmy you wouldn't show up here and you've let me down.'

'You shouldn't bet,' she said. 'Your ma's got too much influence still over Frank.'

'You don't have to tell me that,' drawled Cath, her arm linked through Jimmy's. 'Too much influence over everybody. That's why I want out. She's always telling me what I should and shouldn't do. I was wondering if you could help me?'

'Me?' said Molly, startled. 'In what way?'

'By letting me have one of your spare rooms. I've been hearing all about the new house.'

'But you don't like your Frank.'

'I don't have to like him. He'll be at sea most of the time. I want to be near Jimmy and I can give you something for my keep. That'll be a help with you having a baby.'

'Who told you?' Molly glanced about, hoping nobody had heard. Frank would have a fit if somebody else went and told Ma.

'Doris's mother told Jimmy's. They both think it's lovely, with you having lost the last one.'

Molly sighed. 'Talk about the blinking grapevine!'

'So what about it? Can I come and live with you? I'd be company while Frank's away. And I'll be around to help when youthe baby.'

'What do you know about babies?'

Cath smiled. 'Nothing, but I've a good pair of legs to run for the midwife and I can boil kettles. Besides if you say no I'll tell our Frank you've shares in Mr Collins's company and how you quarrelled and he ran after you. You can't have told him about it because then he'd have told Ma and I'd have heard.'

Molly darted Jimmy an angry look. 'I thought it was only women who gossiped? That's my private business, you know. I hope you haven't told anyone else?'

He smiled. 'No. And I'll carry on not telling if you let Cath lodge with you. We can see more of each other then.'

'This is blackmail,' said Molly through gritted teeth. 'But drop in tomorrow after you finish work, Cath, and we can talk about it.'

'Thanks. We're going off to the McNallys' party now. It'll be much more fun there.' Cath winked and they left.

Frank materialised at Molly's side, swaying slightly. 'What were you and our Cath yacking about?'

Molly pinned on a smile, linking her arm through his. 'Never mind her. What about Bernie monopolising you? I feel real jealous.'

'No need, luv. It's her brother, Charlie. He's lost a hand, apparently, and is feeling a bit low so I've invited him and Bernie round to ours tomorrow.'

Molly could have screamed. She only hoped they wouldn't turn up when Cath visited.

The next morning Frank and Molly had a lie-in. She was wakened by a rat-a-tat-tat on the front door. She forced her eyelids open and glanced at Frank who was not moving. She swung her legs over the side of the bed, shivering as her feet touched the cold linoleum, and hurried downstairs.

Molly flung open the door and her heart turned over. Nathan stood on her front step with Jessica in his arms. For a moment she just stared, thinking, I know I'm not dreaming but what's he doing here?

'Did I get you up, Moll?' His grey eyes were dark with worry. 'I wouldn't have disturbed you only I couldn't get an answer at Doris's mother's and Jimmy had told me you'd moved here.'

'It doesn't matter.' Molly gazed hungrily at her daughter and held out her arms.

'It's my mother.' Nathan prised Jessica's fingers from his hair, wincing as he did so, and handed her over to Molly.

'What about her?' The child whimpered. Molly hushed her, pressing her to her bosom, staring at him.

'She's gone crazy. Could you look after Jessica until I get back?'

Her daughter forced her head up, staring at Molly with a mixture of curiosity and bewilderment. She looked down at her and noticed two bloodied scratches on the girl's cheek. 'How did she hurt herself? What happened?'

He clenched his fist against the door jamb and his eyes were angry. 'Since Doris left we haven't been able to keep a girl. Flo quit yesterday – and Cook. Mother's really off her head.'

'You mean, she did this?' Molly touched her daughter's cheek in horror. 'How could she? Jessica's still only a baby!'

'She went on and on about us getting rid of Jess, saying she didn't belong to us. Talked about that cousin and Mabel and two babies. I wish I could get to the bottom of that. It's wicked, isn't it?'

'Mabel was my mother's name!'

'There you are then! She's still harping back to the old days when she knew your mother. It's as if she's living it again.'

'So what are you going to do?'

'The doctor's coming when he's finished his surgery. I've locked her in her room for now. That's why I'm in a rush. I've got to look in at the factory and be back within two hours. Will Jess be all right with you 'til later?'

'Of course! You go.' She touched his shoulder and for a second he covered her hand with his before leaving them.

Jessica wailed, wriggling strenuously in Molly's hold and crying, 'Dadda, Dadda!'

Molly shushed her as she carried her indoors, wondering what to say to Frank. Jessica continued to bellow until she caught sight of the cat. Then the girl held out her hand, making a 'pusss-sss' sound.

Molly put her down. For a moment Jessica stood there, swaying, clinging to Molly's skirts. Then suddenly she let go and toddled unsteadily over to the cat. Her legs buckled and she sank on to her bottom, seizing a handful of fur. The cat spat at her and feigned a blow with a front paw. The child blew a raspberry in its face. Molly chuckled, feeling intense joy. Jessica looked up at her, eyes gleaming. She hit the cat's head with her fist and the cat hissed and aimed another blow.

'She'll scratch you,' warned Molly, scooping up her daughter who screamed, hitting out at her. Molly caught her hand. 'No!

Naughty to smack.' She kissed the scratch on her daughter's face. 'Kiss it better.' Jessica touched the spot and held her cheek out to Molly, who kissed the scratch again. Then she carried her upstairs, slightly nervous, wondering what Frank would say, but prepared to lie through her eye teeth if necessary.

Bleary eyed, he stared at them both from an unshaven face framed by the bedcovers. 'Is it *that* that's making all the racket?' Jessica pointed a finger at him. 'Man.'

'Yes, funny man. Grouchy man. This is Jessica.' Molly smiled at her husband, feeling extremely uncomfortable, but proud of her daughter for being able to talk and walk at such an early age. 'Remember the little girl I used to take care of? Her grandmother's been taken ill and Mr Collins has asked me to look after her. You don't mind, do you? It's only for a few hours.'

His dark brows puckered. 'What happened to the nursemaid who took over from you?'

'That was Doris. Now all the other servants have quit, too. His mother's gone peculiar.' She placed her daughter on the bed and Jessica and Frank stared at each other. 'Doesn't it hurt you, Moll?' he said. 'What?'

'That she's here and our daughter's dead.'

'Of course!' She looked away. 'But having another baby makes it much easier.' Her eyes were on Jessica crawling up the bed towards Frank. She pressed a hand against his nose. 'Beep,' she said.

'Beep,' he repeated.

She did it again. 'Beep, beep,' said Frank.

Molly's eyes filled with tears. Jessica giggled and she would have repeated the action but Frank stopped her and told Molly to get her off the bed. 'I've just remembered, I was going down the docks. I've to get a ship. Money's running low.'

'We've visitors coming too, don't forget.'

He groaned, scrubbing his unshaven chin with his hand. 'I must have been drunk. I could be gone tomorrow. You'd best get Doris to look after the kid. You're going to have enough on your plate.'

'Doris is out. But I'll try and catch her later.' The last thing Molly wanted was to get rid of her daughter. Somehow she would manage. Although she did not kid herself it was going to be easy, having a toddler playing around her feet.

Molly was on edge as she made preparations for her guests, imagining what would happen if Nathan and Frank were to arrive back together. What would they say to each other? What would they make of each other? The two men in line to be her son's father. The knocker went and she rushed to open the door, praying it would be Nathan.

'You are expecting us?' said Charlie anxiously. He had receding hair, was stocky but strongly built, and dressed in a reasonably decent overcoat.

'Of course. Come in.' She managed a smile. 'Frank's not back yet but he shouldn't be long.'

'You mean he's not here?' said Bernie, with obvious disappointment.

Molly explained and was about to close the door when it was pushed from the other side. 'It's me,' said Doris. 'Mrs Black said a man was knocking at our door then went to yours.'

Molly explained about Nathan and Jessica in a whisper as they trooped into the kitchen.

'What a lovely little girl! Lovely hair. Yours, is she?' said Bernie, addressing Doris.

'Chance would be a fine thing. Who'd have me? She's our old boss's daughter, isn't she, Moll?' said Doris in a bland voice.

'You used to work together?' said Bernie, looking surprised.

'Yeah! But no longer.' The last thing Molly wanted was Bernie knowing as much about her business as Jimmy and Cath. 'Doris, you could take her for a bit. I'll see you later.'

'There's no hurry,' said Doris cheerfully, glancing at Charlie. 'Gosh, that scouse smells good, wouldn't you say?'

'Great.'

'And who are you? Yer've got a smashing colour. Where d'yer go to find the sun?'

In no time at all the pair of them were chatting away about India, much to Molly's annoyance. She had no choice but to try and relax and be nice to Bernie, but her ears were straining for the sound of the knocker all the time.

Frank arrived next. 'You're late. They're already here,' she hissed. 'I'm going to have to stretch the dinner.'

'Can't help that.' He paused in the doorway at the sight of Jessica lying on the rug, asleep, clutching a rag doll. 'Is that kid still here? I thought you'd got—' He noticed Doris. 'Oh, you're here, too. Father not arrived then? I hope you haven't got her for the whole day, Moll.'

She ignored that remark, as she did her own guilt, and gently lifting her daughter, carried her upstairs. She placed her on their bed, kissing her before tiptoeing out.

As she dished up the meal, Frank said, 'I've signed up with the White Star Line, luv. I've got to report back at midnight tonight. Sorry, but that's the way it is.'

'We'd better not stay long then,' put in Charlie.

'Why?' asked Bernie.

He rolled his eyes and Frank grinned. 'There's no need to rush off yet, mate. You can eat your dinner first.'

As they ate the talk was of money and jobs. Charlie saw some difficulty, and so did Doris, in getting more work. 'The trouble is, I'm only small, see. At the moment I'm just helping me mam in the house,' she said.

'Then you'll make some man a good wife,' said Charlie. 'A woman's place is in the home. Isn't that right, Frank?'

'I've told Moll I don't want her going out working again. It's my job to look after her and the baby.'

'What baby?' said Bernie, dropping her fork.

'The one Moll's having.' Frank smiled at his wife across the table. 'It's going to be a boy, isn't it, luv?'

She nodded, wishing she could have kept that secret a bit longer. She bet Ma would know before she went to bed that night.

'Lucky you,' said Bernie enviously. 'I'm going to have to find a job. A nice shop job, I thought.'

She and Doris began to discuss what kind of shop and conversation became more general. Molly was silent, listening for that rat-a-tat-tat on the knocker which would announce the arrival of Nathan. But he still had not returned when the others left. Jessica woke up and the next person to arrive was Cath. 'Howdo?' she said cheerfully.

Molly eyed Frank, slumped in a chair by the fire, looking like a banger ready to explode. 'Let's postpone what you were going to say until tomorrow. He's sailing tonight,' she whispered to Cath.

'Not on your Nelly! With our Frank here you're bound to agree to what I say,' said Cath in a low voice. 'Who's the little girl? Pretty thing.'

The words were no sooner out of her mouth than the knocker went. 'I hope it's that kid's father,' growled Frank. 'It's like bloody Lime Street station in here with all the goings and comings. Isn't a man to get any peace in his own home?'

Molly rushed for the door, only for Frank to seize her by the shoulder and drag her back. 'Let me,' he muttered. 'If it's him, I want a word with him.'

'Oh, deary, deary me,' said Cath, raising her eyebrows. 'He's definitely in a happy mood. Who's he expecting?'

'None of your business,' said Molly hurriedly, seizing Jessica's hand and following in her husband's wake.

She was just in time to hear Frank say, 'Now listen, mate, don't be coming it here. I'm not having it.' His hands were balled into fists on his hips and he stood with legs braced like a bulldog ready to do battle.

'Sorry?' Nathan raised his eyebrows and shot a glance at Molly over Frank's shoulder. 'You're Frank, are you?'

'Dadda! Dadda!' Jessica freed her hand and sank to the floor. Seizing a handful of Frank's trouser leg, she pulled herself through his legs. He yelped, hitting out at her.

Nathan's eyes narrowed as he gathered her up in his arms. 'Don't you dare touch my daughter!' he said furiously. Jessica bent towards Frank and aimed a swipe at him.

'I didn't touch her!' he yelled, rubbing his leg. 'She bloody well pinched me and it hurt.'

'Watch your language, man,' said Nathan. 'There's a woman present.'

There was a deadly silence and Molly could almost see Frank's hackles rise. His muscular shoulders bunched and he said through clenched teeth, 'Don't you tell me what to do in my own house, Mr Collins. Just because you've got a bit of money, you think you own the whole of Liverpool.'

'No, I don't!' Nathan's face set in hard lines. 'You just back off. I'm not looking for a fight. I only came to pick my little girl up.'

'Well, you've got her now so you can go.'

'I'm going. I just want to thank Mrs Payne for taking care of her.'

Frank turned his head. 'D'you hear that, Moll? He's thanking you. But he should also pay you. You've put in a full day's work for that kid.'

'I'll pay her.'

'Let's see the colour of your money then?'

'I haven't got any spare cash with me but I'll see she gets it.' Nathan's tone was icy. 'Good night, Mr Payne. Good night, Molly.'

'How's your mother?' she called, relieved they hadn't come to blows.

'She's gone into a rest home in Formby,' said Nathan shortly. 'I've asked Doris to come back. Goodnight again.'

'Goodnight, Mr Collins. Bye-bye, Jessica.' She watched him walk away, her daughter's head resting on his shoulder, eyes staring unblinkingly at Molly as she waved one tiny hand.

Molly closed the door, relieved in a way that the day was over. As she turned she saw Cath standing in the kitchen doorway. 'So that's Mr Collins,' she said softly.

'And you can go, too,' said Frank, pushing past her into the kitchen. 'I don't know what you're doing here. I don't want you here.'

'Molly does,' said Cath. 'Don't you, Moll? She wants me to live with her. Be company while you're at sea.'

He looked at Molly, an almost comical expression of horror on his face. 'What's this? We can't have her staying here. She thinks she knows as much as I do. Too hardfaced for her own good.'

Cath grinned. 'Molly gets lonely when you're away. Isn't that true, Moll?'

'Yes,' she said woodenly. 'And Cath's willing to pay, Frank, and with the baby coming we need every penny we can get.'

'We're not that short. Anyway we mightn't stay here. I don't like that Doris and the rest of those McNallys here every minute of the day. I might just ask Ma to keep an eye open for a place by her for us.'

Cath looked alarmed. 'You must be mad,' she said rapidly. 'You'll never have a moment's rest, trying to keep the peace between her and Moll. They'll be forever at each other.' There was silence. 'But if you want to be a piggy in the middle, go ahead,' tossed in his sister. 'I don't care. I'm only thinking of Moll.'

There was another silence.

'We've no spare bed,' Frank said at last.

Cath winked at Molly. 'No need for you to worry about that, dear brother, I'll sort it out. And I'll keep me eye on Moll for you. She won't be losing this baby if I've anything to do with it.'

'OK,' he said roughly. 'But you can beat it for now.'

'Anything you say. Have a good trip – and I'll see you tomorrow, Moll.' Cath smiled and went out.

Molly stared after her, wondering just what her sister-in-law was up to. Was it true she only wanted to live here to be near Jimmy? Or was she a liar and her motives much deeper? Did Molly now have Ma's spy in her camp?

Chapter Nine

Cath arrived at seven o'clock the following evening accompanied by Jimmy pushing a handcart containing an old iron bedstead, a mattress and several mysterious-looking bundles. 'All my worldly goods,' Cath said, her expression mischievous.

Molly folded her arms across her bosom, heart beating fast, a mutinous expression upon her face. 'I don't want you here. You've destroyed my peace of mind.'

Cath promptly said, 'Come off it, Moll. You can't have any peace of mind. You're deceiving your husband with another man.' She lifted a bundle out of the cart.

'I am not!' Molly darted a look at two of her neighbours gossiping on the other side of the street. 'There is nothing, I repeat, nothing, going on between Mr Collins and me,' she whispered. 'And keep your voice down.'

Cath exchanged looks with Jimmy. 'D'you believe her?'

He looked pensive. 'I suppose I could have got it wrong. Still she's a shareholder in the factory and your brother doesn't know about that. And perhaps there was something going on between her and old Barnes instead. You know what they say about old men's darlings.'

Molly gasped and her arms dropped to her sides as she clenched her fists. 'How dare you? What kind of person do you think I am? I looked after Jessica, that's all, and he knew my mother. And if you really want to know the truth about me and Mr Collins – we came from the same village and went to the same school. *That's* why we're friendly.' They both stared at her and smiled. 'We believe you, Moll,' said Cath. 'Can we get past now and get this stuff inside?'

Molly glared at her, exasperated. 'You've got a nerve, you know that?' She moved a couple of inches to the side. 'Anyway, I haven't done anything to either of the back rooms. There's damp and neither of them have been painted for years *and* there's no oilcloth on the floors.'

'Thanks for letting us know,' said Cath sweetly, motioning Jimmy forward. He picked up two of the bundles and followed her inside. 'By the way,' she called over her shoulder, 'Ma knows about the baby so you can expect a visit. I didn't tell her, if you're wondering.'

Molly groaned, having a fair idea who had. That Bernie! She determined to be out the next few days.

Contrary to what she'd expected her sister-in-law seemed determined to be pleasant to her, handing over money for her board as soon as Jimmy left and adding that he knew where to get whitewash cheap and would do the walls of both rooms for her. 'And you don't have to thank me,' Cath said with a smile, settling herself in front of the fire with that evening's *Echo*.

'I don't intend to!' Molly took the kettle from the hob. 'I suppose you want a cup of tea?' she said tersely.

'Love one.'

'What did Ma say about your leaving?' Molly watched her, hoping to be able to read in her expression whether she was here on her mother's orders or not.

Cath lowered the newspaper. 'Tried to stop me but I'd had enough of her and our Josie. You've no idea how they carry on. Stop looking so worried, Moll. I'm sure we'll get on fine. I want to stay here so unless you go and do something completely shocking, I'll keep my mouth shut where our Frank and Ma's concerned about you know what.'

She could have screamed but was suddenly inclined to believe Cath. Molly didn't like the methods she'd used to get her feet under table, but she was here now and they were just going to have to make the best of it.

The next day, when Molly returned from the Free Library, her next-door neighbour told her she'd had a visitor. 'Scrawny little woman – said she was yer mother-in-law and that she hopes to find yer in next time.' I wish she'd said when, thought Molly, but decided Ma might have guessed she would try and avoid her if she'd given a date. As it was Molly didn't set eyes on her the rest of that week.

On Sunday Doris turned up in a horse-drawn cart. 'I've brought yer sewing machine, kid.'

Molly was pleased. 'I thought Nathan had forgotten about it.'

'Jimmy reminded him. And I've money for yer, too, for looking after Jessica.'

Molly's smile vanished. 'There was no need for him to do that.'

'There's a note with it.' Doris took an envelope from her pocket 'I did think of not giving it to yer. I don't want to be no go-between, you being a married woman.' Molly snatched the envelope from her and hurried into the house, slitting the envelope with one finger. A half crown fell out and she pocketed it before unfolding the sheet of paper.

> *Dear Moll,*
>
> *Having met Frank face to face, I can't say I like what I see. He's a handsome devil so I can understand why you were attracted to him, but you never said he was violent. I can only presume he's never hit you. But if he ever was to, you must leave him. What a mess this all is.*
>
> *I've managed to persuade Cook and Flo to come back as well as Doris, so things aren't too bad. The doctor reckons Mother's had some kind of brainstorm which led to a nervous collapse. Anyway it'll be some time before she's well again. I'm sending your sewing machine and have asked Mrs Arkwright about work. Jimmy will bring it.*
>
> *Yours, Nathan*

What did he mean, Frank violent? thought Molly. It must have been his aiming a swipe at Jessica that gave Nathan the wrong idea. He probably hadn't ever meant to hit her but would certainly explode if he saw this letter. Molly dropped it on the fire and watched it burn, supposing it proved Nathan still cared about her which was nice to know. Even though they must keep their distance.

The following morning Jimmy arrived bearing a large cardboard box. It contained cut out hangings and frontals in need of hemming and decorating. There were reels of different coloured cottons as well as embroidery silks and a roll of golden fringe. 'Four sets,' he said. 'Red, green, white and violet to cover the Church's year.'

She put aside her annoyance with him.

'You mean green for spring, etc? I've been going to church off and on for years but never thought about what the colours meant.'

He grinned. 'You've got a few things to learn then. Green's for the weeks following Pentecost and after Epiphany. White's Easter and Christmas. Red's Good Friday.'

'Violet?'

Jimmy's brow knitted then he clicked his fingers. 'Lent! Different colours for the different saints' days too. St James is red. I know that because I'm named after him.'

'It makes for a colourful church,' said Molly, washing her hands before fingering the material.

'I like a bit of colour meself.'

She nodded and said casually, 'How are things at the factory?'

'Not bad. We've had a visitor. Miss Charlotte Braithwaite no less. The boss took her round.'

Molly's hand paused on a length of purple cloth. 'What's she like?'

'Didn't have much to say to me. But the women seemed to think she was OK, asking about their work and telling them what was going on in the south where that Mrs Pankhurst and her daughter are creating trouble. She's one of those suffragettes, isn't she?' He shook his head uncomprehendingly. 'Wants to rule the roost – definitely anti men. It goes to show, doesn't it?'

'It doesn't go to show that's true of all women fighting for the vote and equal rights,' said Molly, eyes glinting. 'I agree with some of their aims and I'm not anti men. Although I reckon I'm as clever as half of them and quite capable of ruling my roost here.'

'That's heresy,' said Jimmy, hands on hips, shaking his head at her. 'You don't want to let your Frank hear you.'

Her eyes glinted. 'You shut up about my Frank and tell me when these are needed?'

'Next Friday. You'd better have them ready or there'll be hell to pay. Mrs Arkwright can be a real tartar.'

'They'll be ready.'

Molly set to work with enthusiasm. It was a real pleasure handling such lovely fabrics – and all for the glory of God. She enjoyed herself so much she gave no thought to Ma Payne, so that when the knock came she went to answer the door without thinking twice.

A familiar bony figure stood on the step in her long black coat, arms folded across her chest, handbag dangling from one wrist and coal scuttle hat pulled low over her brow. 'So I've caught yer in at last, girl. If I didn't know better I'd think yer've been trying to avoid me.'

'Looks like it, doesn't it?' said Molly, hating being disturbed.

Ma shook her head. 'Yer getting real hard-faced.'

'You mean because I'm sticking up for myself? Anyway I'm busy right now and who's to say I have to invite you in?'

Ma Payne's jaw dropped. 'But I've walked all this way.'

'More fool you.'

The older woman pursed her lips, cleared her throat and burst out, 'Now listen, girl, you're carrying my boy's babby and yer gonna need help when yer time comes.'

'Not from you I'm not! I've a proper midwife coming. One who's been recommended.'

'I'm glad to hear it,' Ma surprised Molly by saying. 'But yer'll still need help. And what's our Frank going to say about all this?'

'All what?'

'You chasing me out when I'm knackered.'

'I doubt he'd be surprised.' Molly made to close the door but Ma Payne wedged her foot in it.

'Where's yer Christian spirit? I'm an old woman and I'm weary after that walk.'

Molly sighed. 'Why don't you get your violin out?'

'I would if I thought it'd make a different.'

Molly couldn't help it, she smiled and gave in. 'One cup of tea and then off you go. I've work to do.'

'I wasn't thinking of pitching me tent.' Ma followed her in, looking about her. 'Haven't got much in the way of nick-nacks, have yer? Although that's a nice vase on the mantelpiece. I've got one like it that our Frank brought me. He's got nice taste has my lad.'

Molly lost patience with her. 'He's not *your* lad anymore! He's *my* husband!'

'OK! Keep yer hair on.' Ma sat down, pulling up her skirt and baring her knees to the heat of the fire. 'This is a lovely blaze. How can you afford to keep it going during the day? Our Cath's money, I suppose. How are yer both getting on?'

'Surely she's been to see you and given you a report?' said Molly, throwing a cloth over her work before her mother-in-law could make any comment about that. She also removed the pan simmering on the fire, replacing it with the kettle.

The older woman sniffed. 'Something smells good.'

'Bacon bones.'

'Yer don't want to be spoiling our Cath, yer know. She's an ungrateful faggot. Her leaving's had the neighbours jangling – they're saying things about me. I'm real annoyed with her. I had to tell lies, say our Frank had asked her to stay and look after yer.'

Was all this true and there was in fact no scheming going on between mother and daughter? It certainly sounded like it.

'Yer looking better than yer have done. When's the baby due? I reckon it must be May.'

'Then why ask?'

'Just want to make sure. Yer not very big.'

Molly stared at her. 'What are you suggesting?'

Ma had the grace to look uncomfortable. 'Boys are big,' she muttered.

'You weren't hinting at that. I'm small because I've been working blinkin' hard.'

'OK, OK! I believe yer.'

'So you should.'

Molly seemed to have taken the wind out of Ma's sails because she was quiet for a while. But not long enough. 'I've come to tell yer I went to that Burscough place. Not much there, is there? Not like Bootle.' She shivered. 'I hate the country. Anyhow, I couldn't find the poor wee mite's grave on me own, so I asked the vicar.'

'You what?' said Molly, having to sit down quickly because her knees went weak.

'I'd bought some flowers, hadn't I? I wasn't carrying them all the way home again,' Ma said pugnaciously.

'So what did he tell you?'

'Showed me the grave. Someone else had been putting flowers on it. He explained it was the woman who's buried there's brothers. And her husband occasionally goes, too.'

Of course! Nathan hadn't forgotten her as Molly wouldn't have forgotten Frank if he were really dead. Did Nathan ever see his brothers-in-law? For a moment Molly felt sick with worry, then realised that of course they couldn't have mentioned the sovereigns to him or he would have said something to her.

Ma was continuing, 'He told me all about how yer couldn't afford even a pauper's grave for little Mabel. I didn't like that, Moll. Yer should have got in touch. I didn't realise the poor mite actually lived for a few days. I thought she were a stillborn.'

'What difference does that make?' All this talk was making her remember the horror of it all.

'I want me grand-daughter to have her own place to rest,' said Ma, jutting out her chin. 'Besides she should be in the Catholic cemetery. So I went to see the parish priest, Father Eager.'

'You what!' Molly shot to her feet, eyes wide with dismay. 'What have you done? You haven't dug her up, have you?'

'Don't be daft, girl. They wouldn't let me without our Frank's permission.' Ma shook her head dolefully. 'Anyway, Father Eager's going to write to Frank and see what can be done.'

'You interfering old faggot!' cried Molly, trembling. 'How can you do this to me? Raking it all up, stirring up bad memories and while I'm carrying too? Isn't it bad enough that I bear the memory of my mam dying in childbirth?'

The little woman was defiant. 'I did what I thought was right.'

'You were interfering in something that's none of your business. She's mine and Frank's daughter, not yours.' Molly's voice broke and she pointed in the direction of the door. 'I want you out of this house.'

Ma did not move, sitting bolt upright clutching her large handbag to her bosom, two bright spots of colour in her cheeks. 'Well, I'm not going. You just calm down, girl. It's not good for the baby. And I want that cup of tea. I'm parched and me legs need a rest. I'll say no more about the other poor mite.'

'You've said enough.' Molly's voice shook.

'Well, as I said, I'll say no more.'

Frustrated, Molly looked at her with dislike. Without evicting the woman bodily she was not going to get her to move. What was she to do? What if Frank and his mother were to go there together and meet Em and talk to her, ask questions? Any suspicions Em might have had about the truth, she would feel morally obliged to divulge.

The kettle began to steam and Ma rose and made tea. She handed a cup to Molly who took it without speaking. Ma began to talk, chattering gaily on about how Bernie had found herself a job in a gown shop on Stanley Road and that everybody reckoned Charlie had a fancy woman because he was always disappearing without saying where he was going. Josie had another cleaning job but there wasn't a man prepared to take her on yet. Ma thought her own lumbago was getting worse.

At last she drained her cup and said she would be going. 'I'll be back, though,' she said, buttoning up her coat. 'Sorry if I upset yer.'

'I doubt it,' said Molly, shivering. 'And don't hurry back. In fact, I'd prefer it if you didn't come back. Ever.'

Ma sniffed. 'That's very nice, that is. But what I'd expect from yer, the mood yer in. This is our Frank's house and I'll not be banned from it.'

Molly saw her out. 'You stubborn, hateful woman,' she muttered, slamming the door behind her.

She was glad to pick up the red frontal she was embroidering with grapes and vine leaves, although she felt as if a cloud labelled 'doom' hung over her. She tried to vanquish it, think sensibly, but she couldn't. If Frank were to learn from Ma that the baby was buried in the grave of Mr Rich Man's wife, as he called Nathan, then he might well do as Ma asked. What if he confronted Nathan, and he got angry and flung back at Frank that he'd made love to Molly and the baby she was carrying could equally well be his?

For the next few days she worried herself sick, picking at her food and causing Cath to say, 'If you're not careful you'll starve that baby to death.'

With that Molly forced herself to eat and tried to put her anxieties to the back of her mind, but every time the postman was due she expected to see the priest's letter to Frank come through the letter box. She would burn it, she decided. The trouble with that, though, was that Ma was bound to ask him whether it had arrived or not.

A letter, though, was still conspicuous by its absence when Frank's ship docked and he breezed into the house. 'How's my best girl?' He put his arms round Molly, hugging her gently.

'Fine,' she said, wishing she could be overwhelmingly pleased to see him.

He scanned her face, frowning. 'You don't look fine.'

'I am. It's just that I get worried sometimes about the baby.'

'You're not to worry. This one'll be a bruiser. Are you eating properly? No strange fancies?' He smiled at her lovingly.

She forced herself to return the smile. 'Depends what you mean by fancies. I have yearnings for pickled beetroot. Do you want something to eat now? Was it a good trip?' She didn't like the fact that he was so solicitous of her. It made her want to burst into tears or blurt out the truth, and she must never do that. She wriggled out of his arms and went over to the fireplace.

'What's this?' said Frank.

Molly glanced over her shoulder and saw him pick up the lectern fall she was working on. She had already decided on the line she was going to take over her work. 'Oh, that. It's for the church,' she said casually. 'You didn't know I was a fine embroiderer, did you, luv?'

'No. But the machine... where did that come from?'

She decided this time she had to tell the truth. 'It's mine. I left it at Mr Collins's house in Blundellsands, though. I'd forgotten about it but Doris brought it here when Mr Collins sent me the money for looking after Jessica that day.'

'So he paid you? How much?'

Molly told him. 'I've put it away for the baby.'

Frank frowned. 'Put it in the poor box. I can provide for my own child.'

She was annoyed. 'Frank! You said I earned that money, I don't want to give it away.'

'You heard me, Moll.' His mouth set in a hard line. 'Do as you're told. And while we're at it – I don't mind you working for the church but if it's that that's making you look peaky all over again, then you can stop it.'

Stop the work she loved? She decided to give him something else to think about. 'I told you, I'm fine! Or I would be if Ma hadn't called and upset me.'

'Upset you?' He pulled off one boot. 'Tell me something new.'

'She wants to have the baby moved.'

'What baby?' He looked bewildered.

'Our baby, Frank. She wants to dig her up and transfer her coffin to the Catholic cemetery. I tell you, I haven't been able to sleep since she told me she was out at Burscough. The priest's going to write asking your permission but I don't want little Mabel disturbed, Frank.' Tears welled up in Molly's eyes and she flung herself into his arms.

'OK, luv, OK! Hush now.' He stroked her hair. 'Don't get yourself worked up.'

'I can't help it, Frank. She brought it all back to me. The pain and the loss and me alone without you…'

'OK, luv. I'll speak to her.'

'And you'll write to the priest? I can give you his name and address.'

He sighed. 'OK. I'll write to the priest. But you've got to try and understand Ma. She lost a few babies herself, you know.'

Molly did not want to know that. She did not want to think about Ma having suffered, needing sympathy and under-standing. But she was not going to tell him that and so made noises that could be taken for sympathy.

The two days they spent together were enjoyable and Cath kept out of the way. They went to see a show at the Rotunda and had a good laugh. Molly was able to forget her worries for a while. When he returned to sea she was in a much better frame of mind.

Mrs Arkwright was pleased with her work and sent her more. Molly placed the money she earned in a jam jar with the gold sovereigns, having prised up a floorboard in the corner of the empty bedroom. She found time to visit Doris in Blundell-sands and her heart swelled with pride as she played Patacake, patacake with her daughter, who was able to say more words now and was walking with confidence.

The weeks passed without sight nor sound of Ma, much to Molly's relief. Whatever Frank had said to her it must really have hit home. He docked next in time for the May Day celebrations and the pair of them went to town to see the annual horse parade, standing amongst the crowds watching the decorated floats and beribboned horses go. Then he returned to sea.

A week later the country was thrown into mourning when the King died from a pulmonary infection. 'The King is dead, long live the King', blazoned one newspaper. George V and his consort Mary now ruled Great Britain and its Empire.

The next day Molly went into labour.

She was alone in the house when her pains started because Cath was late arriving home. Feeling in need of another woman, Molly hurried over to Mrs McNally's house.

'Come in, luv. Started, has it?' she said sympathetically.

'I need someone to go for the midwife.'

'That's all right, luv. I'll send one of the kids out the street. Then I'll come back with yer to your place.'

A girl was soon despatched and Mrs McNally accompanied Molly home, describing her own second labour graphically.

An hour passed and there was no sign of the midwife. The girl reappeared, breathless. 'She's broke her leg! She can't come.'

'Why didn't she let me know?' said Molly, fear darting through her as she shifted her bulk uncomfortably.

'Now yer not to start worryin', girl. I'll pop out and get Gert. She does for some round here,' said Mrs McNally, patting her shoulder.

Molly had met Gert at the wash house. She was an untidy, skinny woman with a cigarette stuck permanently to her lower lip. Her breath smelled not only of cigarettes but rum due to her habit of constantly calling in at one of the numerous pubs in the area which opened at six in the morning and didn't close until midnight.

Molly moistened her lips which suddenly felt dry. 'No! I've heard jangling in the wash house about her.'

'Those tales are just to frighten yer, girl. Some women are like that,' said Mrs McNally soothingly.

'No,' repeated Molly stubbornly.

The older woman looked exasperated. 'Beggars can't be choosers, girl.' And with that she went out.

Molly knew the tales were probably exaggerated but she believed in the proverb 'No smoke without fire'. She walked up and down, wondering what to do, but it was enough coping with her contractions without finding another midwife at such short notice.

Mrs McNally reappeared, accompanied by Gert.

Molly looked at her and her heart sank. 'I've been told you've killed more mothers and babies than you've had hot dinners,' she said unsteadily. 'How do I know those tales aren't true?'

'Well, I haven't had that many hot dinners, queen.' Gert spoke out of the corner of her mouth, cigarette bobbing up and down in time with the words. 'You shouldn't be listening to gossip.'

A sharp laugh escaped Molly. 'I haven't got cloth ears and some people have loud voices!'

'Then yer don't want to believe everything yer hear.' Gert rolled up her sleeves. 'Yer looking bad and beggars can't be choosers.'

'I'm not begging!' Molly's eyes flashed with anger but the pain came again, causing her to groan. She picked up a cup and flung it at the woman.

Gert ducked and crossed herself before grabbing Molly's arm. 'Help me here, Eileen. She's getting hysterical.'

Molly wrenched her arm out the woman's grasp and leaned, panting, against the table. 'Don't you touch me!'

The door opened and to her relief Cath entered. To everyone's surprise she was followed by Ma. 'As if I didn't have enough on me plate,' whispered Molly.

Ma glanced at the two women then looked at her daughter-in-law. 'Having trouble, girl? You started?'

'Yes to both.' She was thinking that at least Ma wanted the baby born safely. 'And I don't want this woman here. I don't trust her.' Molly turned to Gert, saying almost triumphantly, 'This is my mother-in-law and you won't get anything past her. Make her wash her hands, Ma.'

'Don't you be worrying, girl. I'll see yer all right.'

Within seconds Molly was half-carried upstairs between Cath and her mother. She was helped on to the bed, undressed and told to rest. She tried to relax but could not for wondering what was going on between Gert and Ma. The door opened but it was only Cath. 'Where's Ma?' asked Molly.

'She's standing over that woman while she washes her hands like you asked. You OK?' Molly groaned as another contraction made itself felt, trying to curl herself up into a ball. Cath swallowed and looked nervous. 'Is it really bad, Moll?'

'Don't ask bloody stupid questions!'

'Sorry. But I don't know what to do.' There was a knock and Gert entered with Ma. 'Let's be having a look at yer,' said the former.

'Let me look at your hands?' Molly pushed herself up on her elbows.

'Come on, girl! I stood over her while she scrubbed them,' rasped Ma. 'Yer can trust me.'

Could she really? thought Molly wistfully, knowing the woman held no love for her. But she had no choice but to submit to the examination.

'Well?' she demanded. 'How far gone am I?'

'Yer've got some way to go yet, girl,' replied Gert, before dragging on Ma's sleeve and whispering in her ear. The two of them left the room.

Molly felt like screaming after them, 'Say what you've got to say in front of me.' But she felt certain she would be wasting her breath. She lost all track of time, existing in what felt like a circle of ever-increasing agony. She was aware of Cath by the bedside and reached out a hand to her. The girl took it and Molly gripped it tightly, unaware that she dug her fingernails in when the pain was really bad.

Cath disappeared for a while and Ma came and sat with her, mumbling over her rosary beads. Molly thought, I'm going to die! and was relieved when Cath reappeared and Ma left. The pain went on and on. Molly felt she was getting nowhere. She began to worry about the baby, gnawing on her lip so hard she could taste blood in her mouth.

The chirping of sparrows signalled the dawn and Cath whispered that she needed to go to the lavatory again. The two older women entered and Gert examined Molly once more, going outside with Ma Payne afterwards just as she had before. Something was wrong, Molly just knew it. As if in a dream she heard the familiar sounds of people going about their business in the street below but she was drifting on a sea of pain.

The door opened and Cath came back in. 'How are you feeling, Moll? Someone's come for Ma. Our Josie's gone and cut herself and is bleeding all over the place. Ma's going to have to go. And I should be leaving for work now.'

'I'm going to die,' whispered Molly.

'Don't think like that.' Cath's mouth trembled.

'Can't help it. It's taking too long and the pain's so bad.' She clutched at Cath's sleeve. 'You must do something for me. Ask Jimmy to tell Nathan – Mr Collins – the baby is—' Her words were cut off as she screamed, pain gnawing inside her like a rat.

Cath stared down at her in horror. Gert and Mrs McNally came hurrying in. Cath brushed past them and dashed downstairs and out of the house, running as fast as she could in the direction of Vauxhall Road. She had overheard her mother saying the baby was the wrong way round and that was why

Moll was having such a difficult time. She had lied to her about Josie. Ma had gone in search of a priest to baptise the baby in case it died. Poor, poor Moll! But Cath wasn't ready yet to give up on her. The two girls were getting on very well living together, better than either of them had imagined. Cath did not want to return to her mother's house.

Breath burning in her chest, she reached the candle factory. She ran through the door and banged on the counter. Jimmy's head poked through the hatch and he stared at her in surprise. 'What are you doing here, luv?'

She was so puffed she could hardly get the words out. 'Mr Collins! Molly's going to die if something isn't done.'

He came out from behind the partition and put an arm round her. 'Is it the baby?'

'Of course it's the bloody baby!' she cried. 'Those old women can't cope.' Her eyes filled with tears. 'Oh, Jimmy, she's in such pain. And she sent me to tell you to tell Mr Collins about the baby.' She pushed him. 'Go on! Tell him if he doesn't do something – get her a doctor or a better midwife – she'll die!'

Jimmy's mouth fell open. 'You mean there *is* something between him and her? That the baby...?'

'It must be that, mustn't it, if she's thinking of him and not our Frank at such a time? And there was us not really believing it.' She poked him in the stomach. 'Go on! He's got to help her.'

Without another word Jimmy went running up the corridor.

Chapter Ten

Molly was so exhausted she hardly had any fight left in her. She had tried pushing but, oh, it hurt so much! Then suddenly she was aware of a commotion in the street below and men's voices. Someone was hammering at the front door.

Gert and Mrs McNally gazed across the bed at each other and the latter got up and went downstairs, thinking it might be Ma with the priest. But no sooner was the door open than she was pushed aside. 'The mother?' said a man in a frock coat and striped trousers with the sharpest of creases. He was carrying a black medical bag.

'Upstairs,' said Mrs McNally, bewildered but thankful, wondering who had sent for him.

He hurried up the stairs, followed by a nurse and a younger man carrying some kind of large metal canister with gadgets attached. Nathan was just behind them. Mrs McNally stared in astonishment.

'She's still alive?' he said, looking pinched about the mouth.

She nodded, and he made to follow them up but she caught his sleeve. 'You'd better stay here, lad,' she said grimly. 'I don't know what she is to you, and I don't want to know, but you'll only be in the way up there. I'll make us a cup of tea.'

Upstairs the doctor was ordering Gert out of the way. He bent over Molly and examined her. 'It'll soon be over, my dear,' he said briskly. 'We're going to give you something to make things easier for you.' She thought he looked a strange kind of angel. A rubber mask was placed over her nose and mouth. It

168

smelled peculiar and for a brief moment Molly struggled against it. Then as the pain ebbed she went with it.

-

Molly emerged from what felt like a deep, dark well, aware of pain still though it wasn't anywhere near as bad as it had been. She forced her eyelids to open and saw Cath sitting next to the bed. 'My baby?' croaked Molly, throat as dry as the beach on a scorching day.

'It was a miracle,' Cath told her. 'He wasn't breathing when he came out but somehow *he* got him started. Or that's what Gert said.'

'He?'

'The doctor Mr Collins brought.'

Molly could scarcely believe it. 'How did he—?'

'I went for him, of course. I couldn't let you die. After the baby was born he sat here for ages with his head in his hands until you came round a bit. Then you drifted off again and Mr Collins left.'

'When was that?'

'This afternoon. You've been out of it for hours.'

Molly tried to remember what she had said to send Cath flying to Nathan for help and was frightened. 'Was Ma here?'

'Downstairs. She arrived with the priest and wanted the baby christened there and then. They nearly came to blows. Mr Collins wasn't having it and went on about you not being a Catholic. She demanded to know who he was and you'll never believe what he came up with.' Unexpectedly Cath smiled.

'What?' said Molly faintly.

'He said he was a vicar. She asked where his dog collar was and he said even vicars had holidays.' Molly stared at her and Cath giggled. 'He baptised the baby – and so did the priest.'

Molly thought, I must be dreaming, Cath's finding that funny. 'Why didn't you tell her the truth? Or are you going to hold this over my head to blackmail me into doing something else for you? Perhaps you want money this time?'

Cath went very still. Then she snapped, 'I find that insulting after I just saved your life. The baby was a breech. I don't know why I bothered! Frank's my brother, you know, even if he is a bossy sod and Ma thinks he's God's gift to mankind.'

'I'm sorry – I'm sorry!' Molly's face crumbled and she reached out one hand. 'But you're only here because you threatened me. What else am I to think?'

Cath gave a tight smile. 'Perhaps you're right to think I want something. I'll continue to keep my mouth shut about you and Mr Collins carrying on if you stay away from him from now on. Cross my heart and hope to die.'

Molly eased herself higher in the bed, wincing as she did so. 'I am not carrying on. It only happened once. Just before Frank came back from the dead. The baby could be Frank's or his.'

'Mr Collins obviously believes it's his,' said Cath, pulling a face.

'Obviously.' Molly snuggled down in the bed again and closed her eyes. 'You shouldn't have gone for him. You should have let me die.'

'The baby too?'

She sighed. 'No. But what if Ma goes on about him to Frank?'

'So what? You just say he was one of those exchange vicars from another part of the country. Although why I'm prepared to lie for the pair of you, I don't know.'

'Me neither. Perhaps it's something to do with Mr Collins being able to put Jimmy out of a job. They're not that easy to come by,' Molly was feeling extremely tired by now.

'You're more devious than me. I'll get the baby, shall I?' Cath's voice was gentle all of a sudden. 'For hours he's done nothing but sleep but he's awake now, fretting and sucking his fist.'

'Thanks.'

For several minutes after she left Molly lay, wishing she had been aware of Nathan here in the room. Would he be back? She pushed herself up, gritting her teeth and finding difficulty in moving her legs. She lifted the covers and peered underneath.

'They've tied your legs together,' explained Ma, standing in the doorway. 'Real fancy stitching you've got down there, according to Gert. You're to stay in bed and take things easy. Holy Mary, girl, yer still as white as a sheet! Lost a lot of blood according to Gert. You need to get some stout down yer.'

'Give me him here.' Molly held out her arms for her son.

With obvious reluctance Ma handed him over. 'I suppose our Cath's told you about his baptisms? I've never heard of such a thing in all my born days.'

'She didn't say what you'd named him,' murmured Molly, searching her son's face anxiously for similarities to Nathan. She stroked the corner of his Cupid's bow mouth and his lips puckered.

'George Francis,' said Ma.

'Nice.' Molly began to undo the buttons on her nightgown. She could not tell by looking at him who his father was. His hair was scanty and white blond. His eyes were dark but that didn't mean anything. His face was puffy so at the moment she could not say he was the handsomest of babies, but for all that her heart ached with love for him. He was her son and that was what counted at the moment.

She was aware of Ma, sitting on the bed gazing adoringly at George, and thought, If she can feel such love for this child, who am I to hold her faults against her? After all, I'm as much of a sinner as she is: a liar, a thief and an adulteress. God forgive me! As the baby began to suckle she tried to imagine Frank's face when he saw him.

–

'I knew you'd have a boy,' said her husband jubilantly, standing close to Molly, one hand caressing her shoulder as she cradled the baby. 'He's not a bad-looking little fella, is he?'

'He's a beautiful baby and he's baptised and everything,' said Ma proudly.

'So you were saying. Twice. That's crazy, but what's it matter? I must thank both of them.'

'Mine's gone back down south,' said Molly swiftly.

Ma dropped a soiled nappy in a bucket. 'D'yer want me to wash these for yer, Moll?'

She smiled. 'I think you've done enough. Your Josie'll be wondering where you are.'

'Ma's in her element.' Frank kissed the top of Molly's head. 'You don't know how it makes me feel, seeing the pair of you together. We're a proper little family now.'

'And little is how I want it to stay, Frank,' said Molly as his mother disappeared into the back kitchen.

'Here, Moll, let me hold him?' He held out his arms for George.

'Did you hear me, Frank?' Her voice trembled.

He rocked the baby gently. 'Look! His eyes have opened. He's staring straight at me.'

'Recognises his dad, that's why.'

'Dad! I'm a dad,' he crowed.

'Yes. And dads have responsibilities. I don't want any more children. Are you listening, Frank?'

'I'm listening but I'm not believing you. Women always say that after giving birth. I've heard other blokes talking about it. You'll love the kids, though, once you've got them.'

Fear made her persist, wanting this sorted out before another day passed. 'This has nothing to do with me not loving children. It's to do with me nearly dying.'

'So you had a hard time? I'm sorry about that, luv.'

'Sorry?' She almost choked on the word. 'Sorry? You don't know what it means. I'll say it slowly, Frank. I-nearly-died.

You-could-have-been-coming-home-to-my-funeral but for your Cath who fetched a doctor.'

He stared at her. 'How much did *that* cost?'

Molly almost burst into tears but instead decided to lose her temper. 'Is that all you care about – money? Your son and I could have been dead!'

'He cares but he doesn't believe you both nearly died.' Ma stood in the doorway of the back kitchen, sleeves rolled up, hands red with scrubbing, frowning at Frank. 'You listen to your wife, me lad. She's lost one baby and she nearly died having this one. Two babies in two years. How much suffering d'yer think a body can take? You just keep yerself to yerself for a while and give her time to get her strength back.'

He looked uncomfortable. 'When you say it like that, Ma, I get what you're saying. I'm sorry, Moll. We'll wait a bit.'

'Thanks. I'm glad you listen to your ma.' And she meant it too. There was a lot more she could have said but it could wait until another time. Frank's ship was on turn around and he would be back at sea tomorrow.

–

In the weeks that followed Molly found a certain contentment. The birth was behind her and Frank was keeping a rein on himself when he was home. She knew it was not easy for him but every time she thought about her confinement it was as if a dark cloud enclosed her, filling her with terror. She had not seen Nathan and tried not to think about him, but she could not help asking herself what had got into him that he should risk being in the house at such a time, never mind pretending to be a vicar? She could not help admiring such ingenuity.

She now felt fit enough to resume sewing and asked Jimmy to inform Mrs Arkwright. 'Are you sure?' he had the nerve to say to her.

'Mind your own business,' said Molly, tight-lipped. 'You just remember who's employing you.'

He said no more and next time she saw him he brought her a letter from Nathan, along with a plain oak cradle and more embroidery work.

She was delighted with the cradle, stroking the smooth wood with quivering fingers, imagining Nathan's hands touching the same places. But Frank would want to know where the cradle had come from. She needed to give some thought to her answer.

She opened Nathan's letter. It was short and to the point.

> Dear Molly,
>   Jimmy informs me you're looking a lot better now, otherwise I would, not allow Mrs Arkwright to send you work. The cradle is, of course, for George. How I wish I could see you, that things could be different and you were my wife.
>   Yours Nathan

'Yours, Nathan', she thought with a sigh, sinking into a chair. But of course he wasn't hers, and never would be in the present circumstances. She threw the letter on the fire, knowing she had to put him out of her mind.

Her days settled into a pattern as she healed and gained strength, her life revolving round her son and her work.

Frank came and went and seemed satisfied with Molly's explanation that her stepfather had sent the cradle for the baby. Her husband was patient and kind but as the months went by and she was still reluctant to allow him near her, she became aware of his mounting discontent. She began to have nightmares about being buried with an unnamed child – only they weren't dead! She would wake, retching, with the taste of soil in her mouth.

Molly's horror of childbirth grew so bad that she went so far as placing a pillow between Frank and herself when next he came home. He was furious, picking it up and swinging it at her. It caught her a glancing blow on the side of the head and she screamed, lost her balance and fell off the bed. The baby woke, crying. Frank told her to shut him up. Shaken, Molly picked up George and began to hush him.

Cath came dashing into the room. 'What's going on?' She glanced at Molly, seeing how distressed she was.

'None of your bloody business!' snarled Frank, shoving her out of the room and slamming the door on her. To Molly's surprise he dragged on his trousers. 'What are you getting dressed for?'

'I'm getting out of here. You want me to keep my distance so I will. That's what you want, isn't it? To be rid of me? It's not enough that I'm at sea more than I'm at home.' He looked at her as if he hated her and that shocked Molly. Until now she had taken his love for granted.

'You can't really believe that?'

'You're not bloody denying it, are you? I tell you, if you had another fella I'd throttle you.'

'You're crazy.' She didn't know how she kept her colour down and her voice steady. 'Talk sense, Frank. I'm scared silly of getting pregnant. Do you think I'd let anyone else touch me?'

He didn't answer but left the room, slamming the door. The baby started crying again. Molly soothed him and took him into bed with her, wondering when Frank would be back.

He did not return until morning. He did not say where he had been and she dared not ask. He looked dreadful and she felt sorry for him and filled with guilt, telling herself it was all her fault because of her cowardice.

'I'm off in a minute.' He glanced at her as he drained his teacup. 'When I dock next time, Moll, things had better be different or you'll regret it.'

The threat stifled her sympathy as well as scaring the life out of her. She went upstairs to see to the baby who was teething and when she came down again Frank had gone.

'I'm not going to ask what that was all about last night but can't you try and make him happy?' said Cath in a plaintive voice, resting her elbows on the table.

'I don't want another baby, that's what it's all about,' murmured Molly, rubbing her forehead where it ached.

'The next birth could be easier. I heard Ma say so. Surely this has more to do with your being in love with Mr Collins?'

'You're wrong!' Molly could not stop herself from blushing, though. 'You saw the way I was.'

'Of course I did.' Cath reached for her coat. 'But God help you, that's all I can say. A man must have his oats.'

'It's nice to know you care.' Molly's laughter was forlorn.

'I do, believe it or not,' said her sister-in-law fiercely. 'I love Jimmy and I know what it's like wanting someone but having to resist. But you must know you could twist our Frank round your little finger if you wanted to. Just try and work something out. I don't want to find your battered body at the bottom of the stairs.'

'You think that's likely?' Molly's tone was flippant despite the chill about her heart.

Cath forced a smile. 'No. But there must be a way of keeping him happy. Have a word with some of the women at the wash house.'

'They'd only tell me what I know already. Abstain on high days and very holy days and get him to be careful.'

'Try it then. Knowing what I know, I could make your life even more difficult than it is now.'

'And your saying that could get Jimmy the sack,' retorted Molly, hurt and dismayed, having come to believe she and Cath were becoming more like sisters these days, laughing at the same things and caring for each other. But maybe she was fooling herself, blood being demonstrably thicker than water. She watched a tight-lipped Cath reach for her coat and leave the room.

Molly picked up the poker and riddled the fire vigorously. She felt mean threatening Cath in such a way but it was only tit for tat. Still, she was going to have to think of a way of keeping Frank content or Cath might call her bluff.

The next time he docked Molly welcomed him with a kiss. 'Good trip?'

'Hmmm!' He pulled her against him. 'That was only a little kiss. Give me a proper one – and loosen up, Moll. You're too stiff.'

'Sorry, luv. It's my back. It's aching from carrying the baby around. I need a pram.'

'Well, buy one. Here.' He dug into his pocket and brought out a fistful of coins, stuffing them down her cleavage. Then he drew her back into his arms. 'I'm not an unreasonable man. There are ways and means of preventing you from getting in the family way again too soon.'

Surprised, she touched his cheek gently. 'You've been talking to your mates again,' she teased. 'You amaze me, Frank. What would the priest say?'

'I go to sea, don't I? He'll put it down to that if we don't have another kid for a couple of years. I'm not blind, Moll. I've seen women in Bootle dragged down, old before their time through having too many kids.'

She was touched and relieved. 'I'm glad to hear you talking like this, because I want something more for George. I want him to make his way in life and for that he needs to go to college. And children take a lot of money.'

'Hold on, Moll!' protested Frank. 'He's still only a tot and we don't want him looking down on us. Where is he, by the way?'

'Asleep upstairs.' She put her arms around her husband. 'Don't let's fight anymore. We must think of him. He's the most important thing in our lives.' She kissed her husband, twining her arms round his neck, fear making her determined to keep control of what went on between them. It wasn't easy but Frank went back to sea a happier man than when he'd docked. It was obvious to Cath whose manner towards Molly thawed overnight.

It was sometime since Molly had seen her daughter due to her decision to keep her distance from Nathan but Doris kept her informed of Jessica's well-being. But the day came when Molly could stay away no longer. She decided she must see her daughter for herself and took the train to Blundellsands.

She realised as soon as she saw Jessica that her daughter was well past the baby stage. Her hair had grown almost shoulder-length.

She was also capable of having a simple conversation and was able to show in no uncertain terms that she objected to George's presence. She pulled on his arms and blew in his face until Doris told her to stop. 'She's getting a real handful, doesn't like sharing the limelight,' she said apologetically.

'Does Mr Collins spoil her?'

'No, he's quite strict with her. Not that he has much time to spend in her company. He's always doing something. Never seems to be still for a moment.' Doris bounced George on her knee, smiling soppily at him and rubbing noses.

'You mean, to do with the business?' said Molly wistfully, knowing she would enjoy being more involved.

'Not just the factory. He works in the garden. I told him he should get himself another gardener since the last one died but he said he enjoys raking up the leaves and all that. He's planning on having a big bonfire when he's got a minute.' Doris shook her head dolefully. 'Have yer ever heard the like? I told him he was keeping someone out of a job.'

'It's a wonder you didn't suggest someone. One of your family or a friend, perhaps?'

Doris grinned. 'I did. And we'll see. Perhaps it's a daft idea of mine, but it's worth a try.' And she began to talk aboutelse.

For information about the factory Molly pumped Jimmy. It was he who informed her Mr Braithwaite was going downhill, weight just falling off him each time they saw him. The day came when he told her that Nathan's partner was dead. Molly wondered who would take charge of the Leeds factory now. Mr Braithwaite's daughter, perhaps?

She was to find out on her next visit to Blundellsands. The streets were shrouded in fog when Molly set out on a cold November's day. George was buttoned up inside her coat, so that only the tip of his nose was exposed. But by the time they arrived at their destination the sun had managed to break through the mist, casting trees and the last of the Michaelmas daisies and chrysanthemums in a golden glow. She was feeling more relaxed these days, less threatened. Even so she was not prepared when Nathan came into the kitchen. Molly's first instinct was to get up and flee. How could she stick to her decision if he was to get her alone and come closer?

Jessica danced over to him, mouth ringed with crumbs of gingerbread. 'Moll's here with her baby, Daddy. We don't like babies, do we?'

He swung her into the air, his eyes on Molly's face. 'How are you, Mrs Payne?'

'Fine, thank you.' Her voice sounded breathless. 'Yourself?' She realised she found him as attractive as ever.

'I'm well. But I'm afraid Mr Braithwaite died.'

'I know. Jimmy mentioned it.'

They could have been two business acquaintances, she thought.

He set Jessica down. 'I should have written to you. I intended to but things have been hectic.' He turned to Doris. 'I'm lighting the bonfire soon. Jessica can come and watch. Wrap her up, though. The wind's sharp.'

'Yes, Mr Collins.' Doris did not look at Molly as she took Jessica by the hand and left the kitchen.

'You're welcome to watch, too, Mrs Payne. If you don't think it's too cold for the baby?' he said politely. Before she could answer, he added, 'I know! Cook can look after him. It's nice and warm in here. We don't want him catching cold.'

Molly realised she wasn't getting the option of refusing. He was already lifting her outdoor clothes from the hook on the back of the door and helping her on with them.

They were both silent as they stepped outside, Molly aware of him staring at her. She rushed into speech. 'So poor Mr Braithwaite's dead?'

'I thought we'd agreed on that.' He seized her hand and ran with her along the side of the house until they were out of sight of any windows. Then, before she could protest, he drew her into his arms and kissed her with a thoroughness that took her breath away.

'What d'you think you're doing?' demanded Molly as soon as she was able to speak.

'I thought it was obvious. Reassuring myself that you're really OK.' He kissed her again and this time she had to bang on his chest to get him to stop. 'What's the matter now? There's nobody here to see us.'

'What's that to do with it?' she said weakly. 'I'm a married woman!'

'But your husband's not here.' He smiled lazily down into her eyes. 'And, as I said, there's no nosy neighbours to go telling him.'

'Nathan, we agreed to keep our distance.' Molly struggled to free herself. 'I'm very grateful – you saved my life and George's – but I have to go now.'

She pulled away from him but he yanked her back into his arms. 'Not yet. Let's talk business and then that conscience of yours will feel better.'

'I'll come to the factory. We'll talk there. It'll be safer. I must fetch the baby and go,' she gasped.

He shook his head slowly, grey eyes twinkling with amusement. 'And what'll Doris think then? And Cook and Flo? Only that I've done something to upset you.'

'Doris'll understand.'

His expression froze. 'You mean, she knows about us?'

180

'You haven't been exactly discreet. Besides—'

'No, I haven't, have I?' he said, grimacing. 'Her mother'll have told her about me turning up at your house. But I was terrified you'd die like Jess. That girlfriend of Jimmy's—'

'Cath, Frank's sister. She's told me I mustn't have anything to do with you. She was convinced we'd been carrying on. I've told her the truth and warned her you could sack Jimmy if she says anything. But if she were to find out we'd seen each other, she could call my bluff. So, I think I'll sell my shares and then we must never meet again.'

'You can't do that!' Nathan hugged her to him. 'I would sack Jimmy if she were to say anything.'

'No, I don't want that,' said Molly swiftly, resting a hand on his jumper. 'He's got no father. His mother needs his money.'

'All the more reason for the pair of them to see they can't threaten you. I need you in the company. Charlotte wants to be making decisions, having an equal say in how to run the business, and I'm not keen on the idea.'

'Why not? Just because she's a woman?'

'She has too much to say for herself – numbers Mrs Pankhurst and her daughters among her friends. She says she'll sell her shares elsewhere if I don't agree to do what she wants.'

'Let her then,' said Molly, deciding swiftly she didn't want Nathan and Charlotte having too much to do with each other.

His jaw set. 'I don't want strangers coming in. It wasn't the way my uncle and her father saw the business going.'

'So what are you going to do?' Molly said patiently.

His eyes softened. '*You* could try and persuade her that she owes a certain loyalty to her father's business, without necessarily wanting to run the place. Mr Hardcastle, our manager in Leeds, would do better without her constant interference.'

'Me! Why should she listen to me?' said Molly, feeling a thrill nevertheless at his wanting to involve her.

'You're a woman and a shareholder. Get her to realise she should be thinking of marriage, not being involved in running factories or this suffragette movement. Would you believe she's talking of sinking her money in the movement if I don't let her become a proper partner?'

Molly hesitated before saying reluctantly, 'Give her something to do then. After all, where would you be in the Embroidery and Garment room without a woman's knowhow?'

'Oh, Mrs Arkwright's different. She doesn't throw her weight around. And, by the way, I asked her about our mothers and the cousin.'

His change of subject surprised Molly, catching her unawares. She pulled away from him, the better to see his face. 'She knew the three of them?'

'Remember my telling you she worked in Colne with a cousin of Uncle William and my mother?'

'You think it's the same one your mother used to talk about?'

'Probably. His family were originally bargees but he wanted to earn more money so turned to weaving. The interesting thing is that his name was May.'

Molly felt a stir of excitement. 'Related to my father?'

'Possibly.'

'Did she mention my mother and yours having babies?'

He shook his head and smiled. 'She lost touch with the cousin after she married. It was after she was widowed and returned to the factory she discovered he'd died. So it seems it's possible we could be distant cousins.'

Molly's brow knitted. 'I wonder why your uncle never mentioned it?'

Nathan shrugged. 'We'll never know. A puzzle, isn't it?'

She nodded. They were silent a moment, then he said, 'Getting back to Charlotte, any suggestions?'

Molly considered. 'Perhaps she can start by doing a course in book-keeping then help you with the accounts?'

He looked amused. 'Oh, aye! I'll suggest it to her and see how she takes it. And now we've got that sorted out...' He pulled her back into his arms but Molly hastily pushed him away. 'Shhh! I'm sure I can hear Doris and Jessica.'

He froze. 'Damn! You're right. Let's head for the bonfire. At least we can appear to be behaving ourselves.'

They did just that so that when Doris and Jessica came round the corner of the house, Molly and Nathan were picking up twigs and throwing them on the pile of leaves and cuttings.

It was a beautiful bonfire and Molly enjoyed the glorious, crackling spectacle immensely, wishing that her life was always so exciting. She also found pleasure in watching her daughter's enraptured face.

All too soon the fire died down and Molly knew she must go.

'I'll be in touch,' said Nathan. 'There's bound to be a share-holders' meeting sooner or later to sort things out. You will come, Moll?'

'I shouldn't,' she said, fastening the baby into her coat. 'I can't imagine what Frank might do if he was to find out about us.'

'Take a chance,' urged, Nathan. 'After all, we're not going to be breaking any of the commandments. Do you think I'd put your life at risk? Or this fella's?' He stroked George's cheek.

Molly smiled, thinking that it might well be interesting being involved with decisionmaking at the factory. She threw caution to the winds. 'I'll be there,' she promised.

Chapter Eleven

It was Jimmy who told Molly there was a rumour going round the factory that Miss Braithwaite wanted the company to expand its church business by making chalices and the like. Apparently she had a friend who was a silversmith.

'And what does Mr Collins think of that?'

Jimmy took an envelope from an inside pocket and handed it to her. Molly shook her head at him in mock reproof for not giving it to her right away and left him and Cath to their own devices.

The letter was typewritten so she did not expect it to say anything personal but she was not disappointed by its contents.

> Dear Mrs Payne,
>   I am writing to inform you that there will be a meeting of the shareholders of Collins & Braithwaite on 9th January. It would be appreciated if you could be at the Angel Hotel, 22 Dale Street, for 12 o 'clock noon. Luncheon will be served before the meeting.

It was signed Yours sincerely, Nathan Collins and he had scribbled at the bottom: Put on your best bib and tucker.

The letter sounded rather officious but the last bit made her smile and she scribbled off a note saying she would be there and gave it to Jimmy. Best bib and tucker, she thought, instantly making the decision that she had to have something new to wear, however reluctant she might be to dig into the little nest egg she was building for George's future. For a moment she toyed with one of the sovereigns before dropping it back in the jar.

She bought a length of emerald green woollen serge to make a suit from a pattern of her own design. As she cut out the material she thought of Mr Barnes's generosity to her and of that time at Blundellsands when Nathan's mother had come and stood behind her while she sewed.

Not for the first time Molly thought about her conversation with Nathan on the day of the bonfire. At the time it had felt as if he was talking about two different people when he said they could be second or third cousins. It hadn't hit home. Perhaps because it wasn't so unusual in a country district where families seldom moved from their birthplace to marry close neighbours. But why had Mr Barnes and her mother kept quiet about that family tie? The only way of finding out, she supposed, was to ask Mrs Collins and Molly could not see herself doing that.

She dismissed the matter from her mind and carried on with her sewing, looking forward to the lunch at the Angel Hotel with a mixture of trepidation and excitement.

But Frank's ship docked on the morning of the 9th and he arrived at the house not in the best of moods. 'Do you realise how bloody hard I have to work for the pittance I get?' he said, handing over some housekeeping to her.

'I'm sure you work very hard, Frank,' said Molly, spirits sinking.

'*And* the lousy conditions some seamen have to work in?' He snapped his fingers in her face, almost catching her nose.

'I'm sure they're terrible. Frank, I've-'

'I tell you, trouble's brewing and we're going to have to tighten our belts. The Seamen's and Firemen's Union are demanding improved conditions from the shipowners, and if they don't meet our demands there'll be a strike.'

Her spirits plummeted even lower. That meant he would be home with no money coming in! 'Are you sure about this, Frank?'

'Of course I'm sure.' He scowled. 'The shipowners are lining their pockets while we men risk our lives day after day in cramped, filthy conditions. Yer've heard about swinging cats? Well, you couldn't even swing a mouse where me and me mate swing our hammocks.'

'OK, I hear you! But a strike, Frank? Is that wise?'

'We've got to do something. And I want you behind me – or right by my side.' He reached out for her, drawing her into his arms and nuzzling her ear. 'Let's go upstairs.'

'What? Right now?' Molly went rigid, experiencing a familiar fear. He was not going to be careful, the mood he was in. 'What about George? And I've shopping to do,' she stammered.

'He's OK in his pram and the shopping can wait.' He seized her hand, still smiling.

'Frank, no! Listen to me!' She dug in her heels; pulling against him. His smile vanished, and ignoring her plea he dragged her towards the stairs. Molly fought against him but he appeared oblivious to the blows she aimed at him, half-carrying her into their bedroom. His handsome face was set in rigid lines as he ordered her to undress. She shook her head, miserable with disappointment, unable to pull herself together, to think and behave sensibly.

'You want me to do it?' He took a step towards her and with trembling fingers Molly began to undo buttons, staring at him wide-eyed with terror.

Unexpectedly he sank on to the bed. 'Don't look at me like that, Moll.' His voice sounded raw. 'I remember the day when you'd come running into my arms as soon as we set eyes on each other. You couldn't get enough of me then.'

'I'm sorry. Really I am,' she whispered. 'But you frighten me when you get angry.'

'I love you! I don't want to hurt you. It's not me that's changed, it's you!' He looked so despondent and hurt that guilt almost suffocated her. She could not help but go over to him and put her arms round him, resting her chin on the top of his head. 'I don't know what the answer is, Frank. I'm real scared since the baby, you know that.'

'Don't be scared. I'll carry on being careful, honest. You've been OK so far, haven't you?' He put one arm around her waist and pressed his face against her breasts.

But for how much longer? she thought, stroking his hair, thinking of the green suit and Nathan expecting her. There was no chance of her making the shareholders' meeting now.

—

A month passed before Molly received another typewritten letter informing her this time that it had been decided that a small silversmith's workshop was to be installed in the Leeds factory. There was no handwritten footnote.

So Miss Braithwaite has got her way and Nathan is angry with me, she thought, throwing the letter on the fire. At least knowing that should make it easier for me to stick to my guns and stay faithful to Frank. She regretted having missed the opportunity to become more involved in the business but it was too late now. She had to put the factory and Nathan out of her mind.

When Frank returned from his next trip he was hardly in the house before he was out of it again. 'I've got a meeting, luv.' He kissed her on the mouth and held her against him for a moment before smoothing George's fair hair with an unsteady hand, telling him to be a good boy for his mother.

'Is it to do with the strike you mentioned last time?' asked Molly apprehensively.

'Yeah.' He went before she could ask anything else and she was filled with foreboding. All her savings would soon go if there was a strike.

Trouble came within weeks, much sooner than Molly had expected. In no time at all the shipowners were refusing to employ men belonging to the union. A strike began at

Southampton and swiftly spread to other ports throughout the country. She saw little of Frank because he was out at meetings all the time but to her relief after a few days the shipowners agreed to raise pay, recognise the union and permit delegates on board ships.

But the trouble was still not over. The seamen and firemen refused to return until the demands of other transport workers were met. There were riots in Manchester, Belfast and in Liverpool as the strikers were joined by a number of railway carters.

'Are you all daft?' demanded Molly, leaning on the table which was spread with a cold supper.

'I thought you'd understand, Moll,' said Frank, eyes alight. 'This is about us workers being brothers together. We can't allow the bosses to pay other men less than we get.'

'OK, OK!' she agreed with him but nevertheless worried about keeping a roof over their heads and food in their stomachs without having to resort to the money which she was determined to save for George's future.

On Merseyside railway workers stopped work and Lord Sheffield officially opened what was to become the city's most famous landmark, the Royal Liver Building. But there was little work at the docks because few ships were sailing or arriving. As for the construction of the new Gladstone Dock at Seaforth, that stopped altogether. Sugar and grain mills, tobacco warehouses and breweries, all closed.

Molly had thought Nathan might punish her for not turning up at the meeting by stopping her work but there was still some for her to do. Even so it was a struggle to make ends meet and she pawned several items of clothing and, reluctantly, one of the sovereigns. The latter she took to a pawnbroker's along Stanley Road, not wanting him asking questions as the local one in Athol Street might have done. Cath was laid off and Jimmy told both women that if the strikes didn't end soon then Collins & Braithwaite would be closing as well because supplies of timber and paraffin wax were dwindling fast.

At the beginning of August labourers and dockers in London came out on strike as a heatwave hit the country. People sweltered in temperatures as high as ninety degrees. In Liverpool dockers and railway workers withdrew their labour completely. As food began to rot in the holds of ships, police from other parts of the country were called upon to ease the situation. The policemen escorting supplies of food had missiles thrown at them.

Frank arrived home on the Friday to inform Molly that there was to be a demonstration in Lime Street. Tom Mann, chairman of the Liverpool Strike Committee, and Havelock Wilson, the founder of the National Union of Amalgamated Sailors and Firemen, were to speak from St George's Plateau.

Molly's mood had changed over the last few weeks and like a lot of women she felt angry that the railway bosses were refusing to sacrifice a little of their profits by giving in to the union's demands. If only they could spend a week or even a day experiencing the poverty-stricken lives of some of their employees' families it might stir their greedy souls, she thought.

So on a sunny and sultry Sunday morning she sat on the front step watching George chalking patterns on the pavement, waiting for her husband. 'Are yer ready, Moll?' Frank squeezed past her and stood in front of her, feet set a little apart, hands on hips.

She rose to her feet, shielding her eyes from the sun. 'Should I bring George? Or leave him with Doris's mother?'

Frank's brown eyes glowed. 'It's a great day for the working man, Moll! It'll be spoken of in years to come. He'll be able to say, *I was there!*'

She supposed he was right and felt a stir of excitement herself. They were living through history in the making. 'You'll have to carry him for a while then. His little legs won't be able to keep up.'

Frank hoisted George on to his shoulders and the boy clasped his hands over the man's eyes. Frank swayed about, holding his hands out in front of him. George chuckled and so did Molly, who was still looking for a likeness between her son and the two men. Frank grinned as he removed the boy's hands. 'It's going to be fun. There'll be banners waving and bands playing. One big family having a party.'

Molly had never seen so many people. Thousands and thousands crowded into Lime Street and on to St George's Plateau. They hung over the top decks of trolley buses parked in front of the North Western Hotel, where guests peered out of windows on to the scene below. Men and women had climbed on to the equestrian statues of Queen Victoria and Prince Albert and Frank helped Molly up on to the plinth of the Wellington Monument on Commutation Row at the London Road end of Lime Street.

He passed George up to her. 'You stay here, luv. I must find someone. I won't be long.' With those words he vanished into the crowd.

Molly gazed out over a restless sea of caps, straw boaters and bowler hats; the latter told her that there were others besides the working classes here, who perhaps saw it as a fight for justice. There were also barefoot street urchins, bent on picking a pocket or two. Some people were singing hymns, others bawdy songs. There was a feeling of expectancy in the air. She caught snatches of earnest conversation, jokes and laughter. Her own heart swelled with emotion as she held her son against her, looking out over that huge crowd.

But as time wore on and Frank still did not return Molly began to get worried. As the wait for the speakers continued, the atmosphere began to change. She had noticed odd groups of policemen around but did not expect things to turn ugly. As the minutes ticked by, however, the air became charged with tension and still there was no sign of Frank.

Several times Molly heard the sound of breaking glass but could not see where it was coming from. She knew something was going on near the railway station but again could not see exactly what. Then suddenly she noticed what looked like a whole battalion of policemen erupting from St George's Hall. As soon as they hit the crowd, which was jammed too tightly to get out the way fast enough, they began lashing out with their truncheons. Within minutes fights were breaking out all over the place. She clutched George to her, wondering what to do.

Like the wind whipping up a storm on the Mersey, the turmoil swept towards her. Some people made their escape along London Road, up Islington or down William Brown Street. Everywhere Molly looked there was pandemonium and a knot of panic formed in her stomach. She had to get George out of here but where was Frank? She could have hit her husband at that moment.

Then two policemen and a man stopped in front of the monument. The next moment the man climbed up beside her. He unfolded a sheet of paper and began to read out the Riot Act. He was hissed and booed for his pains.

As soon as he descended, Molly decided not to wait for Frank. But she had delayed too long. Soldiers appeared and the fighting grew fast and furious with mounted police charging the crowd close by. Then, unexpectedly, there seemed to be a lull in the tumult and a space opened up in front of her.

'Stay there, George, while I get down,' Molly ordered.

'Mam! Mam!' He held out his arms, stamping his feet impatiently.

Suddenly she was seized by the waist from behind and hit out furiously until a voice stopped her. She twisted and looked up into Nathan's face. 'What are *you* doing here? This isn't your fight.'

'Isn't it?' he shouted. 'I could go bust if we don't get supplies soon. What are you doing here on your own?'

'Frank went off somewhere. I have to get George away.'

Nathan turned to the boy and told him to jump.

George looked at his mother and she nodded. He threw himself at the man, who placed him on his shoulders, much in the manner that Frank had. Taking Molly's hand, Nathan began to force his way through the crowd.

It was hard because while some people were going their way, others were pushing from the opposite direction, wanting to see what was going on. At one point the crush was so bad Molly's hand was torn from Nathan's grasp. She panicked until she noticed George's head bobbing above the crowd. She elbowed her way towards him and managed to catch up with them both.

They forged on as if swimming against the tide until eventually they found themselves in a back alley off Christian Street not far from Scotland Road. 'There's going to be trouble on the streets for the next few hours,' warned Nathan. 'It's not over yet.'

'What went wrong?' cried Molly, breath coming in gasps. 'One minute everyone was so happy. The next it was chaos.'

'Too much anger and deprivation, too much waiting, and for some too much drink. And then there's the heat,' he said, beginning to jog with George clinging to his hair.

'What's the hurry?' gasped Molly. 'Frank's not going to get home before I do.'

'I want to board up the factory windows. There'll be bricks flying and I don't want the expense of having to replace glass.'

She stopped and stared at him. 'You're serious?'

'What d'you expect? Mob rules. There'll be more trouble before the day's out.'

She continued to, stare at him then took a deep breath. 'OK. I'll help you.'

Nathan raised his eyebrows, unsmiling. 'That's a surprise. After your not turning up at the meeting, I took it the factory wasn't important to you?'

'Frank arrived home that morning.'

'I see. Well, it's too late now.' He hurried on.

They came to the factory and she took George from Nathan, watching him unlock the door. They stepped inside and he locked it behind them. He strode along a corridor, vanishing inside one of the rooms to reappear a moment later with a crowbar, hammer and nails. He had taken off his collar and looked almost boyish. 'You're taking a risk, being here. I take it you know that?' he murmured.

'Frank doesn't know where I am. And who's going to tell him?'

'I meant, from me.' His eyes were steely. 'D'you know how maddening you are? I could strangle you sometimes.'

'If you're talking about the meeting again, I could hardly walk out on Frank.'

'You could have written and told me what happened.'

'What was the use? Anyway you wrote and I felt firmly put in my place.'

'I said nothing.'

'Exactly.' She was starting to get annoyed herself.

'Because I believed there was a legitimate reason for us to meet and was disappointed when you didn't come.'

Immediately her annoyance evaporated. 'I'm sorry, Nathan,' she said softly. 'But I am a married woman.'

'Don't keep reminding me,' he groaned. Molly sighed. 'Perhaps I shouldn't stay after all?'

He fiddled with the crowbar. 'It's up to you. But I need another pair of hands to pass things to me.'

She smiled. 'Does that mean you want me to stay?'

'Let's get on with it, shall we?'

Nathan led her out into the yard at the back of the building. In the distance Molly could hear shouting. 'They're coming closer,' she murmured uneasily.

He ran across the yard to where there were several wooden crates. 'Help me with these. Just keep a hold while I rip them apart.' He rolled up his shirt sleeves.

'You're not going to do it with your bare hands, are you?' she teased.

He grinned. 'Very funny. Just do as you're told.'

She did, finding pleasure in watching his rippling muscles as he tore the crates apart with the crowbar, afterwards piling up the planks of wood.

They went round to the front of the building where once more Molly had the task of holding things steady while this time he hammered the planks across the windows. As they worked she was aware of hurrying footsteps and could see groups of men on their way along Vauxhall Road. As they glanced her way she turned her back on them.

'It's time you went,' said Nathan, looking at her. 'I know there's only a chance in a thousand of Frank's spotting you with me but it could happen.'

She nodded. For a short moment their eyes met and his hand rested briefly on hers. Then she took her son's hand and walked away.

To her relief Molly arrived home to find the house empty. Putting a match to the fire, she watched the wood catch light before draining the lentils that were soaking, ready to make a cheap, nourishing pan of soup.

Cath and Jimmy came in a couple of hours later with news that mattresses had been set alight in Christian Street and that there were men on the roofs, ripping up slates and throwing them down on the police.

'Have there been any arrests?' asked Molly. 'Frank's still out.'

'The way our Frank's been lately, I wouldn't be surprised if he's in the thick of it,' said Cath, grimacing. 'When did you last see him?'

'Hours ago.' Molly frowned. 'Perhaps I should go and look for him?'

'It makes a change, you being worried about him.' Cath went over to the fireplace and lifted the lid from the pan simmering there. 'I'm starving. Is it OK for us to have some of this?'

'I could have done without that first remark,' said Molly tersely. 'Save some for Frank, and listen out for George in case he wakes.'

Molly stood on the corner of Athol Streep gazing along Scotland Road in the direction of town. Plenty of people were still making their way home but she could not see anyone who looked remotely like Frank. She asked several people whom she knew whether they had seen him but nobody had. They all spoke of men being injured in the clashes with police and soldiers, and of arrests being made. Concerned, she hurried home just in case somebody had popped in with news of her husband.

She met Jimmy coming in search of her. 'Some bloke's just called – Frank's been arrested. He's had a bang on the head and is in the cells under St George's Hall.'

Molly's fingers curled into her palms, nails digging into the skin. 'What did he do? Did the man say?'

'Rammed a Paddy-Kelly's helmet down over his ears.'

She relaxed a little. At least he hadn't used a bottle on the policeman or hit him with a slate. 'Did the man know when he'll be brought to court?'

'Didn't say, but they won't be going to the crown court. I'd stay away if I was you. There's bound to be trouble. You'll find out soon enough what's going to happen to him.'

Molly said impatiently, 'Don't be daft! He's my husband. I should be there.'

Jimmy stared at her and she glared back at him, daring him to mention Nathan and their supposed affair. Instead he said uncomfortably, 'He'll be out before you know it. It's only disturbing the peace.'

Assault more like, she thought.

Molly did not sleep well and was up early, thinking to buy a newspaper and see what it said about the riots. On the way she met Mrs McNally, who was obviously bursting with news.

'Have yer heard?'

'Heard what?'

'There was a pitched battle in Great Homer Street last night.'

Molly scowled. 'Blast! Why don't they know when to call a halt?'

'It wasn't to do with the demonstrations, girl. It was religion! One pint too many and yer know what some of them are like. Mention the Pope or King Billy and they're off. Anyway, the police and the soldiers were out again.'

Molly was fed up with it all. 'I'll have to go. Frank's been arrested and I need to find where the trial'll be held.'

'I can tell yer that, girl. I heard two Paddy-Kellys talking about it on Athol Street. It's at the new Juvenile Court in Dale Street this morning.'

Molly touched her arm in gratitude and hurried back to the house. She was just telling Cath what Mrs McNally had said when Ma turned up. Having heard about the disturbances, she had come to see if they were all right. When Molly told her Frank was in gaol she was blazing mad, waving her handbag and saying, 'Let's get down there now! I'm going to give them judges down the banks, arresting my son who's never so much as stolen a sweet! I brought him up respectable. What'll the neighbours say?'

'Probably think he's some kind of bloomin' hero,' said Cath, who last night had been almost as angry as her mother over her brother's arrest.

Ma darted a furious look at her. 'You watch yer tongue. He *is* a hero, but heroes get bleedin' martyred for the cause.' Her mouth quivered and she sniffed audibly. 'So if yer'll move yerself, Moll, we'll be on our way.'

'You'll look after George, Cath?' said Molly.

Ma put her arms round the boy, almost squeezing the life out of him. 'We'll take him with us. Might soften the judge's hard heart when he sees this little cherub.'

'Judges don't have hearts,' warned Cath.

Ma ignored her and carried a wriggling George outside.

But by the time they reached the Juvenile Court building it was all over. People were still milling around outside and the police were out in force but they were too late to see Frank. The two women managed to push their way through the crowd and speak to a clerk, who ran his finger down a list of names and told them Frank was to serve a month's hard labour in Walton Gaol.

'A month?' squealed Ma, and swung her handbag at him.

Molly grabbed it just in time. 'That's not going to do any good!' She turned back to the clerk. 'When can we see him?'

He looked at them over his wire-framed spectacles. 'In a few days, probably. Now, if you don't mind, I'm busy.'

'It's a bleedin' disgrace!' yelled the old woman.

'Shut up, Ma!' Molly dragged her away. 'You're not doing Frank any good.'

'I'd like to knock their blocks off,' she muttered, elbowing people out of her way. 'He was brought up respectable was my boy.'

Molly thought, If she says 'my boy' once more, I'll slay her! That boy is a man and should have thought twice about his wife and child.

'Poor little lad!' said Ma, squeezing George's hand. 'Thank the saints he doesn't know his poor father's a jailbird.'

Molly thought that probably when her son was old enough he wouldn't care about that. And perhaps she *was* being a bit hard on Frank. Perhaps he *was* a hero, fighting for better conditions for the working man. But right now she wished her husband had considered the consequences and not left her and George. But then, if he hadn't she wouldn't have met up with Nathan again and now be on better terms with him. In the meantime she wanted to get George home before more trouble broke out.

It was not long coming. Jimmy came hurrying into the house that evening with the news that a bread van had been looted and the rioters were at it again. 'There's fires burning all over the place and the Riot Act's been read. Blinkin' idiots! Wouldn't we all like some bread?'

'Too right,' said Cath, eyes bright. 'Perhaps we'd better go and snaffle some?'

'You've got no hope now,' said Molly, yawning. 'The police'll be out in force. I'm going to bed. I hardly slept a wink last night.'

But despite her weariness Molly still could not sleep. It was worry, worry, worry about whether the country was on the brink of civil war and how she was going to manage for money with Frank in prison. Eventually she dozed off, having decided she would pawn the last sovereign.

In the late afternoon of the following day a man came tearing down the street, yelling that the prisoners were being escorted along Vauxhall Road and the mob was going to try and rescue them. The next moment the houses virtually emptied as people rushed out into the street, Molly among them. She did not believe the prisoners would be rescued but she wanted to see Frank for herself, even if she was annoyed with him.

Hundreds of people were charging along, some armed with bottles and bricks and even the odd service rifle from the Boer War. It struck her suddenly that this could get really nasty. What the hell was she doing here? She couldn't be thinking straight. What about George, left behind with Cath? But it was too late to be having second thoughts now. She was caught up in the crowd and there was no escape.

Cavalry formed an outer guard for the roofless prison vans, inside which stood policemen and prisoners. Missiles aimed at soldiers and police went flying through the air. Soon rioters and soldiers were grappling with each other.

Molly kept her head down as much as she could, making her way along the pavement, pushing and shoving, dodging the odd missile that went astray. Then she heard a shot ring out and almost at her feet a man fell to the ground.

She stopped in her tracks, terrified, wishing herself out of it and back at the house. She stared at the soldier and his smoking gun. Then she was pushed aside.

Molly hurried on as she spotted Frank. His head was bandaged and his face pale. He looked very unlike himself. Her sympathy was roused, wondering how a man accustomed to the open seas was going to cope with imprisonment. She shouted his name and plunged into the melee around the van. A horse reared. A soldier cursed. She felt a blow on her shoulder which knocked her off balance. Struggling to her feet, she realised the prison van containing Frank had passed her by.

She looked after it. 'Frank!' she yelled. 'I'm behind you.' This time he must have heard her because he glanced over his shoulder. Then he was gone.

Someone took her arm and pulled her back. 'Are you bloody mad?'

She could scarcely believe her eyes. 'You again?'

'What the hell do you think you're doing?' Nathan's eyes were dark with fury. 'You could have been trampled by that horse.' Molly was trembling and in pain. 'Frank's in one of those prison vans.'

'So you came to see him?'

'He's going to prison. I am his wife!'

'I didn't think you cared that much.' There was a look on his face that brought her up short.

'Of course I care.' Molly's voice softened and she winced, putting a hand to her shoulder. 'He's injured. If I had a brother in that state, I'd be here.'

'He's hardly your brother!'

'I've just explained,' she said wearily. 'Surely you can understand? Aren't you still putting flowers on your wife's grave?' A bottle whizzed past her ear and Molly jumped.

'Let's get out of here,' muttered Nathan, pulling her up a side street.

Molly was starting to feel odd and her shoulder was throbbing. Her body sagged against his. 'I don't feel well,' she murmured.

'Neither do I. I thought you loved me?'

'What?' She looked at him, startled. 'Of course I love you. But I'm fond of Frank. How would it have been between us if you hadn't lost your wife?'

There was silence. Then he said, 'I met her eldest brother last time I was at the grave.'

Molly stiffened, feeling worse than ever. 'What did he have to say?'

'Talked of old times. It was Easter and we always had a big supper at the farm then. He sent Jessica a present afterwards. A gold sovereign.' Molly almost fainted. 'He mentioned some others and said he'd see to it she'd have enough to buy a diamond necklace for herself by the time she was twenty-one. He's a bit soft for a farmer is Arnold. How many of them think in terms of diamond necklaces instead of pig's swill or cow's milk? I put it with the others I found in a drawer in the nursery. That was careless of you, Moll. You should have told me about them being there.'

'I forgot about them altogether. Grief, I suppose. We both had other things on our minds and when I left it was in such a rush.' She hoped he would understand or at least pretend to.

'That's true.' He gazed down at her. 'You OK?'

'No. But I'll survive.' He must believe the coins in the drawer were all there'd been. She felt worse than ever now about the one she'd pawned.

'You were a fool to come here today but I envy Frank more than ever now.'

'You mustn't.' She stumbled, feeling dizzy with pain. Nathan put his arms around her and swung her off her feet.

'What are you doing? Someone might see us.' She gazed wildly about the street. Fortunately it was deserted.

'What the hell!'

She struggled but he gripped her tightly and carried on walking. Molly laughed weakly. 'You're crazy!'

'The whole town's gone mad.'

She gave up and relaxed in his arms but it was a relief when he set her down outside the pawnbroker's on the corner of Latimer Street. 'It was a daft thing to do, carrying me,' she said sternly.

'No dafter than you putting yourself in danger for a man who didn't think twice about deserting you and George on Sunday.' He brushed his lips against hers.

'I had a rescuer.' She caressed his cheek then turned and made for home.

Chapter Twelve

'That's a nasty bruise,' said Cath, dabbing witch hazel on the purplish swelling on Molly's shoulder. 'You surprised me, Moll. You're the blinkin' heroine of the hour, if you ask me. I never thought you'd put yourself in danger for our Frank.'

Neither had Molly but she wondered what Cath would have made of her meeting up with Nathan. It was the following morning and she could scarcely move her arm. If she'd had work she wouldn't have been able to do it. She gasped with pain as she flexed her fingers. 'Fool more like,' she murmured, but she felt more confident about herself somehow. 'I don't know what we're going to do for money. Mine's almost gone.'

'What about your shares?'

'Wrong time to sell.' Cath looked at her and she said, 'Don't say it. I haven't any intention of cheating on Frank. Anyway, we've got to carry on pulling together. Tommy Mann's threatening a general strike now.' She sighed. 'As if things weren't bad enough. The scavengers are out now. The streets are a mess.'

'Have you heard anything more about that man who was shot?'

'He wasn't the only one killed. Mrs McNally told me three are dead. One a young fella from Hopwood Street who was only putting shutters up to protect his property. He was hit by a stray bullet. He was getting married in a few weeks.' Molly went over to the window and stared out, tears in her eyes. For a moment neither of them spoke. Then she said, 'Where's George?'

'A couple of girls asked could they take him to Burroughs Gardens in the pram,' said Cath, adding, 'I suppose you could pawn that pram.'

'I could. Frank's not going to be pleased about it, though. Still, he's in prison so how's he to know?' And it meant she could hang on to the last sovereign.

'When are you going to visit our Frank?' Cath put the witch hazel into a cardboard box with a red cross on it.

'I'll decide when I see your mother. She's bound to call today.'

'There's no trams running.'

'Then we'll have to walk.'

—

'I never thought I'd live to see the day, girl, when I'd be visiting Walton prison,' said Ma, as they walked up Strand Road.

'Me neither. But there it is,' said Molly as they crossed the canal.

Soon they were hurrying through a maze of streets, discussing the situation in Liverpool. The threatened general strike had not materialised but there were warships in the Mersey and soldiers were guarding the power station which provided the hydraulics to open the dock gates. There had been looting before they took charge. Ships were arriving and departing but the dockers were still on strike. There again the soldiers had taken over.

The two women reached the footpath which ran through open fields to Hornby Road where the prison stood opposite the cemetery in the ancient parish of Walton. The streets were quiet today, the Corporation having enlisted five hundred special constables to ensure the peace. 'It fair breaks me heart to think of me boy shut up in such a place,' said Ma breathlessly as the gaol came into view.

Her boy again, thought Molly, but was able to sympathise with her mother-in-law somewhat today, imagining how she would feel if George were confined within its walls. Perhaps, too, she no longer felt such possessiveness towards Frank. She remembered reading that the grimy, red brick Victorian structure had been built around the same time as the potato famine. The sight of it was enough to chill her blood. She thought of the men who would never leave it again because they had an appointment with the hangman and shivered as they went through its gates.

But when she saw Frank she realised there was another kind of death to fear here. His eyes were lacklustre and in the short time since they had last seen him he had lost weight. 'Aren't they feeding you?' asked Molly, reaching out a hand towards him.

'I'm not hungry.' His voice was so low she scarcely caught the words.

'What did he say?' said Ma, cupping a hand over her ear.

'He's not hungry.'

The older woman's face worked as if it was about to crumple but she managed to say, 'You've got to make yerself eat, me lad! What kind of attitude is that to take?'

He shrugged, averting his eyes.

Molly started to feel annoyed with him. 'Your ma's right, Frank. You'll be out in less than a month and then everything'll be back to normal. You've got to stop feeling sorry for yourself and eat.'

'You mean, you'll still be there waiting for me?' This time he looked straight into her eyes.

The fury in his shocked her and caused her to stiffen. 'What's that supposed to mean?'

'One of me mates said he saw you with a bloke.' Frank's voice was sullen. 'What am I to think when you've been trying to keep me at a distance for I don't know how long?'

Molly glanced at his mother and said in a low voice, 'Well, it hasn't worked, has it? Anyway, I've spoken to lots of fellas over this past week. What day would this mate be talking about?

The day you left me stranded up the Wellington monument with George or the day they carted you off here and I got hit by one of the soldiers? I was glad of a Good Samaritan both times, Frank Payne. And why? Because you were too wrapped up in your cause to protect me. Perhaps you'd like to see my bruises?' She began to undo her blouse with her left hand. 'I've got a lovely one on my shoulder, shaped just like the map of Africa. It's a beautiful shade of yellow.'

'Stop that!' he hissed, shooting out his hand. 'I don't want my wife—'

'Then don't go accusing me of something that's not true,' Molly retorted.

There was silence and she could see he was having an inner struggle with himself. Eventually he mumbled, 'Sorry, Moll. I just feel mad when I think of you carrying on with that bargee.'

'Bargee?' She was flabbergasted and for a moment could not think who on earth he was talking about. Then, 'You don't mean Jack Fletcher?' she cried. 'He's old enough to be me dad, and besides I haven't seen him for ages. So stop being daft. Eat up your greens and come home ready to get back to work because we're going to be skint.'

Frank looked baffled. 'You really haven't seen him?'

'Of course I haven't. Anyway, I look upon him as an uncle.'

He appeared to pull himself together, easing back his shoulders and holding his head higher. 'Sorry, Moll. It's this place, it gets you down.'

She forced a smile. 'You just think of getting back to work.'

'I don't know if they'll take me,' he said gloomily, shoulders drooping again.

'Of course they will!' She knew she had to be positive. 'You're not a thief or a murderer. Now stop upsetting your mother.'

'Sorry, Ma.' He looked abashed.

She began to talk to him in a soothing voice.

Relieved, Molly sat back, letting the words wash over her, wondering who had mentioned Jack to him and why.

It was not until the two women had left the prison that Ma said, 'Was yer telling the truth back there, girl, about the bargee?'

'Of course I was telling the truth. D'you think I'd lie about it?' Molly hoisted herself up on to the top of the cemetery wall and sat there, holding her face to the sun. It was a warm day with a slight breeze and she felt much better now she was outside.

'Yer might.'

She opened her eyes and watched her mother-in-law take off her shoe to flick out a stone. 'I knew a lad once who got a nail through his shoe,' said Molly conversationally. 'He was dead within the week.' She stretched out her legs, gazing at the dust-covered tan boots, thinking how they had once belonged to Nathan's wife whose grave he still put flowers on. Her heart ached for him.

Ma gave her an exasperated look. 'What's any of that got to do with what I just asked yer, madam?'

'Nothing, I suppose. But I can tell you straight I haven't been carrying on with Jack Fletcher or any other bargee. And if you don't believe me, you can just lump it.'

'I didn't say I didn't believe yer,' said Ma placatingly. 'And I know yer did get hurt because our Cath told me about yer bruise. Said it was enormous.'

Molly smiled. 'That's OK then. Are you ready to go?' She lowered herself down from the top of the wall and dusted her skirts.

They began to walk towards the footpath. 'Why don't yer leave that house and come and live with me?' said Ma. 'We'll manage better altogether. I'll be able to look after George while you carry on with yer sewing. Our Cath can come back too. We'd all be better off.'

'I'll think about it,' said Molly diplomatically.

'Well, don't think about it too long,' grunted Ma. 'I've taken in a couple of lodgers and I'd have to give them notice to quit.'

Molly parted from her near the canal in Stanley Road, pausing on the bridge, glad to rest her weary feet. She glanced down at the water and remembered the morning she had escaped Ma's house. She thought of the real Jessica Collins buried in St John's graveyard and sadness swept over her. Poor little girl! But at least she lay with her mother and was in no danger of being moved since Frank had warned Ma not to interfere and written to the priest as well. Thank God he'd accepted what she'd said back at the prison. He'd given her such a fright at first. But where did he get the idea that she was seeing a bargee?

As if on cue a barge came gliding by. 'You couldn't give me a ride as far as Athol Street gasworks, could you?' called Molly, thinking it would save her feet.

'So long as thee's not in a hurry, lass,' said the boatman.

She glanced round to check Ma wasn't hiding nearby, spying on her, then made her way to the towpath. She accepted a helping hand aboard and settled herself in the stern, eyes on the boy leading the horse along the towpath, envious of what appeared at that moment to be a wonderfully tranquil life.

'I've seen thee with Jack Fletcher,' said the bargee abruptly.

'Not for a while,' said Molly hastily, but not surprised because he would know Jack and she vaguely remembered seeing him before. 'How is he?'

'Wife's just passed away.'

'Poor Uncle Jack.'

'I don't know if he sees it like that, lass,' rumbled the man, a smile creasing his tanned face. 'She was a bit of a tartar.' He paused, puffing on his pipe. 'He'll be getting another woman in her place. His youngest's getting married and living on the barge.'

Molly nodded. 'He's marrying Marie McNally who lives in our street.' Suddenly she remembered that she and Marie had hair almost the same colour and were of similar build and height. She would tell Frank that when she saw him again.

It wasn't too long before she was limping up Ascot Street. Mrs McNally was sitting on her front step with George perched on the lower one, watching a group of boys playing five stones. He jumped up when he saw his mother and held out his arms. Molly swung him into the air, wincing as she did so because of her shoulder. 'How's my beautiful boy? Have you been good?'

'Of course he's been good. He wouldn't dare be anything else with me,' said Mrs McNally with a chuckle. 'How did yer find yer man, girl?'

Molly sank on to the step beside her, glad that Mrs McNally had never said a word to her about Nathan's turning up on the day George was born. 'He's worrying about getting his job back… and Ma Payne wants me to go and live with her but I don't want to.'

'It never works, girl. Needs must sometimes but best on your own.'

'That's what I think. I just hope the strike finishes soon.'

'Me too. I'll be glad to have my man back on full time again.' Molly nodded.

'Our Doris was here.'

'How is she? It seems ages since I've seen her, with all that's been happening.'

'It's not that long, girl. But she had little Jessica with her. She's growing into a smasher. Behaved like a right little mother to George.'

Molly was surprised to hear it. Disappointed too. 'I'm sorry to have missed them.'

Mrs McNally seemed to hesitate before saying, 'Yer've only just missed them. They could still be at the factory. Yer'll have to take George with you, though, if you're going.' Molly was already getting to her feet.

She hurried down the street as fast as she could, giving George a piggyback. She was in luck. Doris was playing ball with Jessica in the forecourt where one of those noisy, foul-smelling horseless carriages was parked. Jessica caught sight of them and dropped the ball. She ran towards them just as Nathan came out of the factory, accompanied by a fashionably dressed young woman.

Molly put George down and caught hold of her daughter's hands as Nathan walked towards them. 'Molly, what are you doing here? Not that it's not nice to see you.'

'Mr Collins,' she said circumspectly, inclining her head, glad she had put on her Sunday best to visit Frank.

'So this is our other shareholder?' said his companion, gazing at Molly with a birdlike brightness in her eyes. 'It's about time we met.' She held out a hand. 'I'm Charlotte Braithwaite. How do you do?'

Molly had expected a Yorkshire accent but Miss Braithwaite spoke in well-modulated Standard English. They shook hands and Molly wished she could afford a hat as frivolous as the one Charlotte was wearing with its bird-of-paradise feathers and froth of veiling. 'It's nice to meet you. I've heard lots about you.'

'Not all good, I bet,' said Charlotte with a chuckle. 'Nat hates a woman who knows her mind.'

'That's not true. If her mind is running on the same lines as mine, that's fine.' He winked at Molly.

Charlotte's plump lips parted and her almond-shaped eyes widened. 'I saw that. I believe you and Nat are distantly related, Mrs Payne, and that's why Mr Barnes left you shares in the company?'

Startled, Molly glanced at Nathan but got no help there. She cleared her throat and decided to go along with what he'd said. 'Yes, we're second or third cousins.'

'You must join us for dinner so we can have a chat. That's all right, isn't it, Nat? I'm sure we can squeeze her into the motor.' Charlotte did not wait for his answer but loosened the veiling wrapped round the brim of her hat, and fastened it beneath her chin in readiness for the journey.

'Yes, do come, Molly,' he said with a gleam in his eyes.

She was not about to turn down the chance of a free dinner or the opportunity to spend time with him. Besides she was hoping to discover why he had lied about her being left the shares. 'I'll fetch George.'

'I'll get him.'

Before Molly could move Nathan swung her son up, whirling him round before placing him on his shoulders.

'I'm not pleased, Daddy,' said Jessica, running after them. 'I want you to lift *me* up there.'

'What's going on?' hissed Doris to Molly.

'What's it look like? I'm getting a free dinner.'

'Have yer forgotten yer've a husband?'

'No. Now shut up, I want to enjoy this. I've never been in a motor before.'

Doris's lips tightened but Molly turned her back on her. She desperately needed to forget her troubles for a while.

Charlotte slid behind the steering wheel and ordered Nathan to crank the engine. Jessica called to him, 'I'm going to have one of these one day, aren't I, Daddy?'

'Not if I have any say in it,' he said, handing George to Molly before inserting the cranking handle.

Doris closed her eyes, clutching at the seat with both hands as the motor shuddered into life. 'Give me me own two legs any day,' she muttered.

'It's progress, Doris.' Molly's face shone. Suddenly she felt alive and almost carefree. The last few weeks, no, the last couple of years, had been a terrible strain at times. Now for just a little while she was going to enjoy Nathan's company and her daughter's, as well as a meal cooked by a woman she rated as highly as Maggie Block on the gastronomic front. 'Drive on, Miss Braithwaite! Full speed ahead,' she called.

'You're a woman after my own heart,' shouted Charlotte, pulling down her goggles. 'Forward, Boadicea!' As Nathan climbed aboard the motor trundled forward.

–

'That was lovely,' said Molly, exhilarated despite her watering eyes and windburned face. She stepped down on to the driveway of Falconstone and turned to lift George down but Nathan was there before her.

'I'll take him,' he said, swinging the boy up into the air and holding him there a moment. George's arms and legs flailed in the air but he was laughing as he smiled down into the man's face. Nathan lowered him to the ground and called Doris over. 'Take George and Jessica to the nursery and give them tea.'

'Yes, Mr Collins,' she said woodenly.

'And tell Cook there'll be one extra for dinner.'

Doris went, muttering to herself as she seized the children's hands and led them round to the back of the house.

Molly was aware of her friend's disapproval but was determined to enjoy herself nevertheless.

'I'm glad you liked the trip,' said Charlotte, removing her goggles. 'I love speed.'

'That thing's a monster. Too powerful really for a woman.' Nathan inserted the key in the front door and stood to one side. 'After you two.'

'You really are maddening, Nat,' said Charlotte, easing off a glove. 'The automobile is the transport of the future and will be driven by women all over the country one day.'

'I'm sure you're right,' he said smoothly, 'as you are about so many things.'

'Now you're being sarcastic,' she sang, tapping him under the chin with her glove as she swept past him.

He ignored the remark. 'I'm sure you'd like to clean up, Molly? You've smuts on your face.' Before she realised what he was about he reached out and rubbed her nose. She pulled away, wondering what he thought he was doing with Charlotte there.

'Perhaps you'd like to borrow something to wear?' said the other woman.

'No, thank you,' said Molly with a smile. 'But I would like to wash.'

'Then I'd best take you up, seeing as Mrs Collins doesn't appear to have heard us come in.'

Molly whirled round and stared at Nathan. 'You didn't mention your mother was home?'

'She only arrived yesterday.'

'How is she?' Molly's newfound confidence was in danger of evaporating. Just the thought of that woman did something to her.

'I couldn't leave her there indefinitely, Molly,' he said gently.

That was no answer, she thought. 'Will she be joining us for supper?' Molly's voice shook in trepidation.

'Most probably. Don't worry about it. She's a lot better.' He left them then, taking the stairs two at a time.

'You know Mrs Collins, of course,' said Charlotte, as they followed him upstairs.

'Yes.'

'She's a most peculiar woman,' mused Charlotte. 'Comes out with the strangest remarks when you think she hasn't been listening. Was she like that when you last met her?'

'Yes.' Molly realised Charlotte must have no idea what her position had been in this house. Was that why Nathan had lied? Perhaps she should be grateful to him. After all, Charlotte would definitely have treated her differently if she'd known Molly was once a nursemaid.

'Still, she hasn't been well so we must excuse her. This is where we part. You'll find the bathroom at the very end of the landing.'

Molly limped to the bathroom, locking the door and resting her back against it, attempting to calm herself. Was Mrs Collins better, as Nathan seemed to believe, or was that wishful thinking on his part? What if she became violent again? What if she spoke of getting rid of Jessica and harped about her belonging to Molly? Would Nathan continue to pass her words off as madness? But she realised she would get no answers until she saw the woman for herself.

–

Molly sat at the oval mahogany dining table, her stomach rumbling with hunger. Mrs Collins was seated between Nathan and herself but so far his mother appeared not to have noticed her.

'Well, this is cosy,' said Charlotte who was wearing an Alice blue gown with a white broderie anglaise insert in the bodice and panels of the skirt. She looked pretty and was seated on Nathan's right.

No, you're quite wrong! thought Molly. For her the word 'cosy' conjured up a small room with the fire glowing red in the grate, children playing on a rug, and her with her boots off, toasting her toes with the man she loved beside her while rain beat against the window.

'It's at this time of day I most miss Papa,' said Charlotte with a sigh. 'Your father's dead too, I believe, Mrs Payne?'

'I never knew him,' said Molly, watching Flo ladle asparagus soup into her bowl. 'He died when I was only small, crushed between a barge and the lock wall on the Leeds–Liverpool canal.'

'How dreadful!'

'Dangerous places, canals,' said Mrs Collins, startling them both. She bent her head as she sucked up soup from her spoon. 'A body could easily go in. A foot in a coil of rope. Splash!'

Molly shivered. It was as if icy fingers were running up and down her back, like the keys on a piano.

'We're not near the canal so we don't have to worry about that, Mother,' said Nathan. 'You must stop living in the past.'

She made no sign of having heard him but continued noisily to drink her soup.

Roast chicken followed, accompanied by boiled potatoes, tiny new peas, carrots and turnips. Molly drowned her food in a pool of Cook's marvellous gravy, determined not to let Mrs Collins's presence spoil her meal.

Charlotte talked about the factory and her silversmith's venture. Nathan said little. He had opened a bottle of wine and filled their glasses. Molly took a sip of the amber liquid which glowed in the light of tapering candles in a silver candelabra set in the centre of the table. She chanced a look in his mother's direction and was met by an unblinking stare. Mrs Collins waved her fork in Molly's direction, dropping potato on the damask tablecloth, and said in a quavering voice, 'I've seen you before.'

'It's Molly May that was, Mother,' said Nathan.

'Ha, Mabel's daughter! I knew her father.'

'Tell me, Mrs Payne,' said Charlotte, smiling across at her, 'is your husband a man of education? Nathan tells me he's been involved in this most damaging strike, helping the working classes.'

Molly almost dropped her glass. She looked at Nathan. Was he inventing her a new background so she was more acceptable to Charlotte? Two could play at that game, she thought. 'Yes. He travels a lot and likes to read. Sir Arthur Conan Doyle is one of his favourite authors.'

'Sherlock Holmes?' Charlotte's eyes gleamed. 'I admire the plots. Although I'm certain a woman could do better.'

'If you mean women's minds are more devious, I'd agree,' said Nathan, downing half the wine in his glass and refilling it. 'Take Catherine Flanagan, for instance.'

'Who?' said Molly.

His gaze was fixed on her flushed face and she felt a fluttering in her stomach. 'Listen, Moll, and you'll find out,' he said softly. 'She wasn't going to let anyone get in the way of her making money. Even members of her own family.'

'Poison,' said Mrs Collins unexpectedly. 'Little girl.'

'That's right, Mother. My father told me the story. She was at the centre of a famous trial in Liverpool in the 1880s. She and her sister killed several people, including members of their own family. They'd insured them with several different insurance companies then afterwards collected the burial money.'

'Wasn't your father,' said Mrs Collins.

'Yes, it was. I remember exactly where he sat when he told me of it. He frightened the life out of me. I was only a kid then.'

'How did they poison people?' asked Charlotte, leaning towards him, face rapt.

'Soaked fly papers in water. Arsenic,' muttered Mrs Collins. 'Specks of it on the clothing. Have to wash them carefully.'

'Did they hang?' said Charlotte.

'Of course they did,' said Nathan, glancing at his mother. 'Someone got suspicious despite their moving to a different house before killing their last victim. The bodies were exhumed and as Mother said, they found arsenic. So should all poisoners perish,' he said with relish. 'Have you finished, Moll? I believe there's treacle pudding for afters. More wine?'

'So long as it's not poisoned.' She held out her glass.

He smiled. 'It's me that has the money so why should I poison you? But I've been thinking of helping you because of Frank's little trouble. I was wondering if you'd like Mrs Arkwright's job? Her sister's seriously ill and she has a young family. Mrs Arkwright feels it her duty to go and look after them.'

Molly flushed with pleasure. She did not know what to say. She would love the job. Sometimes she felt lonely working on her own. Her first instinct was to say yes, but commonsense soon came into play. What was he thinking of? What was she? How long did he think her husband was going to be in prison? 'I'd love it,' she said softly, 'but Frank's only going to be away a month.'

Nathan's face fell. 'Why don't you think about it? Stay the night here and sleep on it?'

'That's a good idea,' said Charlotte, nodding vigorously. 'Then we could take Mrs Payne into Liverpool first thing and she could speak to Mrs Arkwright before making up her mind. I'm all for us women being involved in business.'

Molly was tempted, she really was, but knew it just couldn't be. She couldn't expect Mrs McNally to look after George every day. 'I can't stay. My sister-in-law lodges with me and she'll worry if I don't go home.'

'Hell, Molly!' said Nathan, looking exasperated. 'She's not your keeper. Besides, how are you going to get back? There are no trains or trains. George can sleep in the nursery with Jessica.'

'No.' She panicked. God only knew what might happen between them if she stayed. She rose to her feet, pushing back her chair. 'Well, I'd best start now.'

'Let the girl go. She's no use to us,' mumbled Mrs Collins.

Molly glanced at her but saw nothing in her expression to worry her. 'They're the most sensible words you've spoken so far this evening, Mrs Collins,' she said in a low voice. 'Good night!' She moved towards the door.

Nathan stood up. 'Why don't you see if George is asleep? It'd be selfish to wake him. I'll come up with you.'

'Don't forget, we need to be out early tomorrow,' called Charlotte. 'There's a meeting of the Women's Social and Political Union in London which I mean to attend. It's a pity you can't come with me, Mrs Payne. I'm sure you'd find it interesting.'

'I'm sure I would,' Molly said without turning round. 'It really has been nice meeting you.' And she hurried into the hall.

Nathan was not far behind. Molly took one look at his face and fled upstairs.

'There's no need to run away from me,' he said, catching up with her at the top of the stairs. 'You couldn't have spelled it out more clearly that you don't want me fouling up your resolution to stand by Frank. But it won't do, Molly. George is too damn' much like me.'

She whirled round. 'He isn't!'

'I've a photograph to prove it in my room. Come and have a look?'

'No!'

'Why not? I'll keep my hands to myself, promise.'

'It's not that.'

'I don't believe you.'

'You can believe what you want.' She just wanted to get home. This whole day was proving traumatic.

He seized her arm. 'Well, you're damn' well going to look at it! I want a son and this photograph proves he's mine.' He seized her arm and hustled her along the landing.

'Even if it's true, why do you have to make things so difficult for me?' she said in a low voice.

'Don't you think this whole situation's difficult for me too?' He pushed open a bedroom door and pulled her inside, leading her across the room to a chest of drawers on which stood a framed photograph. 'This used to be my uncle's room, as you know, and this is me at three.'

She stared at the photograph and was immediately convinced. Yes, here was George's image almost. Nathan with fair hair, chubby-cheeked and glowering at the camera but with that way of holding his head to one side when he was angry.

'Don't you think he's got a look of Jessica too?'

Molly's heart turned over. She knew she couldn't admit to this. 'Who? You in this photograph?'

'George?'

'Oh, I thought you meant you here.' She laughed lightly. 'I could say yes but the shape of the chin's all wrong.'

'That's because he has your chin and your eyes, but for the rest I think he's growing to look like me here.' Nathan tapped the glass.

She could not admit it. What would he do if she did? What would Frank do? Oh, God! He might kill the pair of them. He'd assaulted that policeman and he'd tracked her down before when she went missing. She had to stop this right now, for all their sakes. And the best way was suddenly clear to her. 'If we're related then he will look like us both.'

Nathan's expression froze. 'I don't believe it! Why don't you want him to be my son? He could follow in my footsteps, take

217

over the factory after me. I could give you so much more than Frank.' He seized her by the arms. 'Stay here, both of you, not just for tonight but forever. Divorce Frank.'

'Divorce?' Molly was stunned.

'You can't love him,' said Nathan desperately. 'A man who's violent. He might beat George. It would be much better if my son was brought up with Jessica, half-brother and sister together. Eventually we could get married.'

It sounded wonderful. Molly was trembling inside, longing to do what he said, but it would create a terrible scandal. 'It would ruin you. Who's our main customer? The Church!'

She could see by his expression he had not thought of that. Then his face set and he squeezed her hand. 'I don't care. We'll move away. Find other customers.'

She was touched that he would be prepared to do that for her but couldn't let him. What had he said only months ago when Charlotte had threatened to sell her share in the business to strangers? He cared for that business. And what about Charlotte too? It could leave her in a mess. Theirs was a specialised business and would there be buyers interested in it, with the strike and the way everything was so unsettled? Molly put a hand to her head. And what about Jessica? Molly hadn't done what she had for Jessica to become the child of a poor man. She had to be strong.

'You can't do it. I won't let you.' She had to convince him that there was no future for. She took a deep breath to steady herself. 'I've made vows, Nathan, before God. I broke them once unintentionally, I mustn't do so again. Forget me and forget George. Besides, what kind of woman would people think me if I went off with a rich man while my husband was in gaol? It'd be a bit like the Bible where David wanted Bathsheba and got rid of her husband by sending him to the battle front.'

'If only I could!' Nathan's voice broke on a laugh.

They stared at one another and there was a long silence. Then he said in a bitter voice, 'You still love Frank.' Molly forced herself not to deny it. 'You've been stringing me along all this time.' Still she remained silent, lowering her eyes so she couldn't see the hurt and anger in his eyes. 'Go back to him. But he's not having George. I could keep him here right now and you couldn't prevent me. I will not have him catching some horrible disease in those miserable streets. I want him to have a good life.'

Molly's head shot up. 'So do I,' she said fiercely. 'But what do I tell Frank when he comes home? "Oh, your son's gone to live in Blundellsands? I thought it better for his health"?'

'You can tell Frank he's died.'

Her eyes widened in shock. 'You're mad!'

'Mad for my son like I was once mad for you, Molly. You think about it. I'd best join Charlotte. Come down when you've pulled yourself together.' He opened the door and slammed it after him.

Her legs felt like India rubber and she sank on to the bed. Never had she thought her own son would be the one to replace her daughter in Nathan's affections. But he was not going to have the boy. She slowly turned the handle of the door and listened to Nathan's receding footsteps. Then, when she knew he was downstairs, she tiptoed to the nursery. To her relief Doris was alone, sewing in front of the fire. 'So yer've come to show yer face, have yer?' she said grumpily.

Molly made no answer but went over to the cot and carefully lifted out her sleeping son. He murmured and his limbs twitched. She hushed him, suddenly furious with Nathan for frightening her into believing he could take George from her. 'I'm going out the back way. Will you lock the door behind me?'

'Fell out with him, have yer?'

'Ask no questions and I'll tell you no lies.'

'Suit yerself,' said Doris with a sniff.

'I'll tell you another time but not right now. Please, open the door for me?'

With ill grace, Doris did as she was asked. Once outside the house Molly realised it was going to take her hours to walk home with feet that were already sore. And what guarantee was there that when she arrived home Nathan wouldn't come chasing after her in Miss Braithwaite's motor? She must hide somewhere else until he calmed down. It was then she remembered Ma and the invitation to move in with her.

Chapter Thirteen

A weary Molly stumbled painfully up the step to Ma's house and hammered on the front door. She kept on hammering until a window opened overhead and Ma's voice shouted down, 'Who the hell is it?'

'It's me, Molly, with George. Open up and let us in.'

'Wharra yer doing here at this time of night?'

'I'm not telling the whole street. Let me in!' Despite her anguish Molly had desperately tried to think up a reason for arriving at such a time but her brain felt fuddled after the scene with Nathan and she could only hope inspiration would strike when she needed it.

The door opened and Ma stood there in a flannelette night-gown, her greying hair in plaits. 'What's happened?'

'Don't ask,' said Molly, wincing as she stepped over the threshold. 'My arms are breaking.'

Ma took George from her and went on ahead with him into the kitchen.

Molly fell on to the sofa. The pain in her shoulder was worse than ever and her feet throbbed rhythmically, almost in time with the agony in her shoulder.

'Here! Yer'll have to have him back while I light the mantle,' said Ma.

Molly cuddled her son, who seemed to be taking the night's adventure in his stride. He was awake and as she heard the faint hiss of the gas and the pop as it ignited she caught the gleam of his eyes. Poor little mite, she thought, he must be wondering what's going on.

'What is it? What are you doing here, girl?' said Ma, sitting opposite her. 'Looking for our Cath, were yer? Been and gone she has.'

'There was a man!' Molly was easily able to conjure up a sob.

'Hey, hey! We'll have no tears here.' Ma scowled at her. 'What have yer been up to while my lad's locked away?'

'I haven't been up to anything. Would I have George with me if I was up to something, like you say?' Molly's voice shook. 'Would I be coming to you?'

'Yeah, well,' said the old woman grudgingly. 'I can see yer upset.'

'Can I have a drink of water?'

Ma sniffed. 'You been drinking?'

'Communion wine.'

'Well, yer've got legs. Give me George here. Yer know where the tap is. I'm not going to be fetching and carrying for yer, girl.'

Molly handed her son over and hobbled towards the scullery. 'What's wrong with yer? Yer walking all funny. This man didn't get to yer, did he?'

Molly gulped down the water. 'No, thank God! But he frightened me so much I just grabbed George and ran,' she said, reentering the kitchen.

'Was this in the house?'

'No. On the lockfields by the canal. I've had to pawn the pram so I was taking a short cut. I was half-carrying, half-walking George when he came up to me and started talking.' She had no idea where this idea came from.

'Yer shouldn't be going down there. It's looking for trouble. Yer haven't been seeing that bargee, have yer?' Ma's tone was filled with suspicion.

Molly realised she'd talked herself into trouble and needed to think fast. 'God give me strength, Ma!' she said angrily. 'My feet are killing me and I come to you for help and all you do is accuse me of betraying Frank. Would I come to you if that were true? I can do without all these questions.'

'All right. Keep yer hair on,' she muttered. 'Have you any old sheeting? George needs changing and I'll have to bandage my feet.' Ma grunted. 'Yer nothin' but trouble. But I'll see what I can do.'

Molly removed her boots and then had to pull the feet of her stockings gently away from the skin where blood had caused the cotton to stick. Ma handed over some bits of rag, watching Molly as she bound the ruptured blisters.

'I thought yer'd come because you were seeing sense at last.'

'I had thought of staying.' Molly glanced across at her mother-in-law, who sat cuddling George.

'Yer'll have to sleep with our Josie then. Yer haven't give me notice, girl. I've still got me lodgers and I need their money.'

The last thing Molly wanted was to sleep with her sister-in-law.

Ma frowned down at her feet. 'They're a mess! You must have really got the wind up. Although I'm surprised you didn't scarper off to that Mrs McNally's.'

'I ran into church then decided not go home in case he was hanging around outside. I didn't want him knowing where I lived!' said Molly, lifting her head. 'So I headed for Stanley Road and just kept on walking.'

There was silence. Molly had a feeling Ma wasn't convinced.

'Have yer got any money?'

'How much d'you want?' parried Molly.

'I need yer keep. I'm not made of money.' Ma held out her hand, palm upwards. 'Yer've pawned the pram. Yer must have something.' There was a crafty expression on her face.

Molly hadn't expected this so soon. 'I've had to pay the rent and buy coal and food! I've nothing on me.'

'Well, that was stupid, coming here with nowt!'

'I am your son's wife and expected to be welcomed!' She tossed her hair back, eyes flashing. 'I can easily take George back home now I know Cath'll be there.'

'Hold on, hold on! Wasn't it my idea yer'd come to live here? I can wait. Yer can pawn that machine of yours to pay me.'

223

'I've a living to earn,' Molly said shortly, thinking of Mrs Arkwright and the job she had been offered. She could have wept for the future that might have been hers.

'Our Frank's not going to like yer working.'

'I don't like it that he's in gaol,' said Molly wearily, thinking the hour was too late for this kind of discussion. 'Why don't you go to bed and we'll talk in the morning? Me and George'll stay down here.'

Ma thrust out her chin. 'No, yer won't, girl. I'm not having you making the lodgers' eyes pop out when they comes down in the morning.'

Molly gave in, too exhausted to argue. It had been quite a day.

–

'What's *she* doing here?' demanded Josie, slumping in the chair opposite Molly and folding her arms across her high stomach.

Molly yawned, still tired, having spent an uncomfortable night in the double bed which the two sisters had once shared, with George sprawled asleep on top of her. Josie had spread her not inconsiderable bulk across most of the bed too so, although Molly had slept heavily for a few hours, she had woken early and in some discomfort.

'Did yer hear what I said?' said Josie when she received no answer.

'I explained to you when I accidentally woke you up,' said Molly.

'Don't remember. So why are yer here?'

'She's come to stay 'cos she's seen sense, so shurrup!' said Ma.

Josie fell silent, breathing noisily through her nose as she crunched into a slice of toast, eyes fixed on George. 'That babby doesn't look like our Frank.'

Molly felt the colour rise in her cheeks. 'Don't be daft! Of course he looks like him,' said Ma. 'It's just that he's only little and our Frank's a grown man. He's his own little self.' She beamed across at George. 'Aren't yer, boy? And him and his pa and us are gonna be one big happy family.'

'Our Frank's not going to be living here, too, is he?' There was dismay in Josie's voice.

'Of course he is!' Ma flicked her with the tea towel across the head. 'He's a good boy is our Frank.'

'He used to sit on me. I couldn't breathe.'

'That's because yer never shurrup. Another word and I'll give yer a good clout.' There was silence for which Molly was grateful. She wished she could go to sleep for a week. The quiet was short-lived. Josie was soon saying gleefully, 'Frank's in prison. He can't live here.'

'What did I say to yer, girl?' demanded Ma, clouting her across the head.

'Not on the head,' protested Molly, stirring herself to care. 'No wonder she's the way she is, poor thing.'

Josie began to blubber. Ma gave her another clout. 'Stop that noise.' She turned on Molly and said wrathfully, 'See what yer've done? Give her a bit of sympathy and she feels sorry for herself.'

'Nobody loves me,' moaned Josie, rocking to and fro.

'And nobody ever will if yer carry on making that racket.'

'You shouldn't hit her on the head,' Molly insisted, wiping George's face with a piece of rag.

'Keep yer nose out of it, girl. I know best how to handle me own daughter.' Her mother-in-law glowered at her.

'No wonder Cath left,' she murmured.

'Yer another one who can't shurrup!' yelled Ma across the table. 'Yer might as well sling yer hook then! I can't be doing with busybodies in me own house.'

Molly could scarcely believe her ears, thinking of the way Ma had interfered in so many people's lives. 'If anybody's a busybody, it's you.'

Josie gasped. 'The cheek of her, Ma! She should keep her nose to herself, shouldn't she?'

Molly laughed. 'I was sticking up for you, you soft thing.'

'Ma, she called me soft!' Josie clutched her mother's sleeve. 'Shall I hit her?'

'I heard her. And there's only one person allowed to do that and that's me. So get out!' ordered Ma, shooting out one skinny arm and digging Molly in the chest.

'I knew it wouldn't work,' she said, relieved.

'And I knew yer wouldn't last here long. D'yer think I believed all that rubbish yer spouted last night? Yer've been up to something. Got yerself a man.'

'You can believe what you like.' Molly stood up with George in her arms. 'See you again sometime. Thanks for the breakfast.' She got up and limped out of the house, thinking that in the light of day her fear of Nathan's taking George from her was nonsense.

Church bells were ringing as Molly passed the butcher's on the corner of Aintree Street. St Matthew's or St Anthony's must be having bell ringing practice, she thought. Either that or someone was getting married. It was a while since she'd been to church, having felt too much of a sinner. She wondered whether Cath would be in but it didn't really matter. The key was on the string behind the door and as soon as she was in she would put her feet up. Oh, blissful thought!

Molly was just removing her boots when Cath burst into the kitchen. 'So you've come home! I wasn't sure if you'd done a vanishing act like you did when you left Ma's that time.' She plonked herself on a chair and scowled at Molly. 'Where the hell have you been?'

'You didn't ask Mrs McNally?'

'Yeah, but she was cagey, just like you're being now. So where were you? Golly, why are your feet all bandaged?'

Molly gritted her teeth as she unwound the rags. 'Too much walking. I spent the night at Ma's. But she's hopping mad with me now because I've come home again. Her idea yesterday was that the pair of us should live with her.'

'I know, she's mentioned it. Barmy! But you weren't there when I called, so where were you?'

'At a friend's.'

Cath fixed her with a stare. 'I didn't know you had any women friends. And what about George? You didn't take him with you to see our Frank. You must have been chasing your tail going backwards and forwards. Why don't you try telling me the truth?'

Molly thought she might be needing Cath's help so said, 'OK, I went to Mr Collins's house in Blundellsands but I ran away. A little habit of mine. I did stay at Ma's. I'm not going to tell you what happened at Mr Collins's but we won't be seeing each other again. Although he just might turn up here asking for George. You mustn't let him in.'

Cath gave her a funny look. 'He's gone away. Didn't he tell you? Gone off to play soldiers, Jimmy said.'

Molly dropped the bandage. She had been frightened for nothing! She had forgotten it was that time of year. Why hadn't Nathan said? Had he forgotten in the heat of the moment? Or was it because he knew that by the time he returned from training camp Frank would be out of prison and it would be so much more difficult for her to do as he'd asked? He must have decided in an instant. Now he was gone, away for a month believing she had never loved him but still loved Frank. Molly put her head in her hands and wept.

'Come on, drink this up. It's not the end of the world.' Cath touched her shoulder and said with a trace of embarrassment, 'It might feel like it but people really don't die of broken hearts. So he doesn't love you anymore! Perhaps that's a good thing. You can get your marriage back together again when our Frank comes out.'

Molly pushed back her hair and wiped a hand over her wet face. What was the use of telling Cath she had it all wrong? Still, perhaps Nathan didn't love her anymore now. She sipped the scalding tea, wondering whether once the strike was over she would still get sewing work from the factory. Who was going to be in charge while he was away and Charlotte in London? She would ask Jimmy. In the meantime she needed to visit Frank before Ma got to him and told him her tale. Perhaps Cath was right and her heart wouldn't break? Her feet were another matter. She gazed down at them, knowing she would have to rest them for a few days at least.

Fortunately for Molly the trams were running within days as were the trains. The dockers went back but there was no work for Molly. When she asked Jimmy he told her Mrs Awkwright was staying on until they found someone else to take over her job but she'd said there wasn't enough work to be sent out. Molly wondered if that was true or whether Nathan had given orders to provide her with no more. Perhaps she was going to have to do what Ma had suggested and pawn her sewing machine.

In the meantime she awaited with trepidation her visit to Frank, having reached the conclusion that only the truth would serve her. Well, some of it.

Her husband looked more his old self, although he had lost some of his ruddy colour. 'Not long now, Frank,' she said brightly.

'No, thank God!' His fingers caressed hers. 'How've you been? How's Georgie?'

'Fine. Ma been in?' Molly was almost certain she hadn't because then his smile wouldn't have been so welcoming.

He shook his head. 'Told her I didn't want her coming here, getting upset. Have you seen her?'

'I stayed the night at hers the other week.' Molly took a deep breath. 'And I'm sorry, Frank, but I told her a whopper because I just didn't want her knowing all my business.'

He stared at her, frowning. 'Go on? What business is this?'

She lowered her voice to a whisper. 'I went to Mr Collins's house in Blundellsands. Now stay calm, Frank,' she said, as he half rose in his chair. 'I had George with me and I wasn't on my own. Miss Braithwaite, who owns half the business, was there and so was his mother.'

He sat down again, both of them aware that the warden had taken a step towards them. 'So?'

'Remember me telling you Mr Barnes, his uncle, left me some money? Well, that wasn't exactly the truth.' Molly fiddled with a button on her coat, wishing she didn't have to say the next bit. 'He left me shares in the company.'

A muscle at the side of Frank's jaw tightened and the expression in his eyes suddenly reminded her of Ma. 'You've kept that a secret all this time? It's not bloody well on, Moll! I'm starting to think I can't trust you.'

'I did it for George. I knew you'd want me to cash them and then they'd be gone. As it is, I have a regular amount of money coming in that I can depend on. Unless, of course, the company collapses, but that hasn't happened yet.'

'So you're telling me you've had money from these shares coming in and kept quiet about it?' His voice was dangerously low.

Colour flamed in her cheeks. 'I know what you must be thinking, Frank. But I'm glad I did it because I'd been saving the money for George's future and it's only that and my job that's kept us going for the last few months.'

'Your job?' He squeezed her fingers so hard she felt sure he was cutting off the blood supply.

'You're hurting me, Frank.' Molly squirmed in her seat.

'Too bloody right I'm hurting you,' he growled. 'What job's this? What did I say about you working?'

'It's the sewing I do for the church,' she gasped. 'I get paid for it. Collins and Braithwaite don't just make ecclesiastical candles. That's why I was at Mr Collins's house. He wanted to put me in charge of the Embroidery and Garment room at the factory. He thought it would help me out, with you in prison.'

'We don't need his money!'

'Yes, we do. Ouch! That hurts!' She glared at him and managed to pull her hand free. 'Your pride isn't going to keep the roof over our heads and put food on our table, Frank Payne.'

'You're determined to grind my self-respect into the ground, aren't you?' he snarled. 'Thanks a bloody lot!'

'You're wrong! Have some commonsense. D'you want me and George in the workhouse? And don't mention us going to Ma's again because it just wouldn't work. I've tried it, remember. In the meantime we've got to get by the best we can.'

'OK! You've had your say. Now I'll have mine. You're not going to work at *his* factory.'

'I turned the job down. Said you wouldn't allow it.'

For a long time Frank stared at her, a frustrated expression on his face. Then he said abruptly, 'The trouble with you is you've had too much of a free rein since we've been married. So I'm going to do what you asked me once: I'll give up the sea.'

Her heart sank. How was she going to cope having him home all the time? So far she had been lucky but she could easily get pregnant with him always around. There was no chance of him being careful then. 'What'll you do?' she whispered.

'Get a job in the wash house.' He hunched his shoulders. 'Georgie's growing, I should see more of him. Otherwise he won't know who his father is.'

Molly's heart missed a beat. She wondered what would happen if Nathan did turn up on her doorstep demanding to see *his* son. Perhaps she should just grab George as soon as she got home and make a run for it?

All the way there she was planning her escape. There was one gold sovereign left which she could pawn as well as her sewing machine. She would get the money and go...

Cath glanced over her shoulder as Molly entered the room. She was holding a sheet of newspaper in front of the grate, trying to draw in air from below to fan the slumbering embers into life. 'George isn't well,' she said.

Molly glanced at her son where he lay curled up on the sofa. His cheeks were flushed and his eyelids drooped. He was sucking his thumb. She placed a hand against his forehead and was shocked to feel how hot and dry it was. Fear cut through her like a hot wire. 'He's burning up!'

'He was like that when I picked him up from Mrs McNally's.' Cath folded the newspaper. 'That little girl was there too. The one Doris is nursemaid to. Pretty little thing. But then, we could all look good if we had money like that.'

'Was she mopey? Burning up like this?' Molly's imagination ran amok, Lord! What if she lost both her children?

'No. She was dancing round the kitchen, singing and making us laugh by pulling faces. She reminded me of someone but I couldn't think who...'

Frank, thought Molly, feeling another stab of fear. Then she told herself it was no use worrying about that, George was more important right now. 'I'm going to have to watch him. I'll keep him in bed with me tonight.'

Molly spent a restless night and in the morning her son was still feverish and burning hot. Sweat out a fever, she thought, but it seemed crazy, piling clothes on to the bed and making him hotter still. She decided to act on her instincts and sponged him down with cold water, continuing to do so most of the day. The two nights that followed he was so fretful and hot she could not rest. But on the fourth day when morning came she noticed immediately that his face was covered in spots. She struggled into a sitting position and lifted his nightgown. More spots. He opened his eyes and smiled sleepily up at her. She returned his smile and felt his forehead. It was still hot but also slightly damp.

Molly scrambled out of bed. 'You stay there, sweetheart. I'm going to fetch Mrs McNally. She'll know what's wrong with you.' It could be measles or perhaps scarlet fever. She didn't have the experience to tell.

'Yeah. It's measles all right,' said the older woman as soon as she set eyes on George. 'Yer'll need to keep him in with the curtains closed. It can affect the eyes.'

So there could be no running away just yet, thought Molly with a sinking heart. Fortunately Cath was back at work so they had some money coming in. As well as that the neighbours, sympathetic to her plight and thinking well of Frank, gave her little gifts of tea, sugar, milk and potatoes, while Mrs McNally brought in the odd bowl of soup or a couple of bacon ribs.

Molly was grateful even though she did not feel like eating. George's throat was terribly red and sore which resulted in a hacking cough. She pawned her last sovereign and called in the doctor. He prescribed a cough linctus and told her to give the boy plenty of drinks.

Mrs McNally dropped by the same day to say Doris had been on a flying visit. 'Little Jessica seems to be sickening for something. So I told her about George.'

Poor child, thought Molly, hoping she wasn't suffering as much as her brother. 'Is Mr Collins still away? And how's Mrs Collins?'

'Oh, he'll be back any day now. As for the old woman, Doris says she's fine if a bit confused. I was to tell yer as well that Charlie's working there now.'

'Charlie! You mean Charlie McGuire?' Molly's eyes widened in amazement. 'How's that come about?'

Mrs McNally grinned. 'Our Doris has been trying to get him a job there for ages but it was only the morning Mr Collins went away he said Charlie could come. That maybe it would be a good thing to have a handyman around the place. He does a bit of everything, does Charlie. Marvellous when yer think he's only got one hand. Nice bloke.'

Molly wondered if wedding bells were in the air but kept quiet. A couple of days later Ma turned up. It seemed she had heard about George and was prepared to forget their differences. Unfortunately half an hour later Molly had another unexpected visitor. 'Uncle Jack!' she said in amazement on opening the door.

The bargee's weatherbeaten face creased into a smile. 'I heard through our Rob that thy little lad had the measles so I brought him a slate and chalks to keep him happy while he's stuck in.'

'That's kind of you,' said Molly, hesitating only a moment before inviting him in.

As soon as he entered the kitchen it was obvious Ma's suspicions were aroused. Jack's attire proclaimed the bargee. She cleared her throat noisily. 'Who's this then?'

Molly realised there was nothing for it but to make the introductions. 'Uncle Jack, this is my mother-in-law, Mrs Payne. Ma, this is Jack Fletcher. He was a friend of my parents.'

'Yerra bargee?' said Ma.

'Aye, I am that, missus.'

'Seen plenty of yous lot out Bootle where I live.'

'Happen the canal goes through there,' he said with a smile, sitting alongside George and handing him the slate.

As she poured him a cup of tea Molly felt certain Ma was putting two and two together and coming to the wrong conclusion. Why had she been so stupid as to mention the lockfields and a man that evening? Perhaps it had been the wine that had caused her to say such things?

'Mamma, duck!' said George.

'He's quick, lass,' said Jack.

'That's a new word for him. You've been good for him.'

He grinned. 'I don't know about that.' The man drained his cup. 'I'd like to stay, lass, but I'll have to be going. Have a schedule to keep to.'

Molly saw him out.

'Don't say it, Ma,' she warned as she went back inside.

The old woman sniffed, getting to her feet. 'Don't yer worry, girl. I'm saving all what I've got to say until my boy comes home.'

'I thought you might.' Molly tossed back her hair and folded her arms. 'Well, there's nothing in Uncle Jack's being here, so put that in your pipe and smoke it!'

'I will, girl, don't you worry. And I'll see meself out.'

'No. *I'll* see you out. I want to make sure you've gone!'

Affronted, Ma marched out of the house.

After that all the fight went out of Molly and she collapsed on the sofa. Trouble, that's what she faced when Frank came home. Trouble with a capital T. Should she scarper? Where could she go? The money from the sovereign was gone. Perhaps it was time to face up to life as it really was? She had flung at Nathan the fact that she had made vows before God. Perhaps it was time she seriously set about honouring those vows? Many of the neighbours considered Frank some kind of hero. He deserved a hero's welcome. If nothing else it might get her off the hook.

–

It was with this thought in mind that Molly flung herself into Frank's arms as soon as she set eyes on him. 'I'm so glad you're home, luv. I've done your favourite dinner: spare ribs, fried potatoes and cabbage.' She gave him a dazzling smile.

He held her at arm's length, his jaw set. 'I must go to prison more often. Only, would I be getting this kind of welcome if you didn't have a guilty conscience over a certain bargee?'

Molly's smile faded. 'You went to Ma's before coming here?'

'It was on my way and I wanted her to know I was OK. I also wanted to know what it was you said to her.'

Molly turned away from him and went over to the fire. 'She told me she didn't believe me.'

'She believes you're a liar. And that you were down at the lockfields seeing that bargee!' His expression was suddenly thunderous. 'So what have you got to say for yourself, girl?'

Molly realised there was no point in getting angry. It would only ignite further fury in him. 'Only what I've said before. Uncle Jack's like a father to me.' Her voice was low.

'So you keep saying. Perhaps it's a father you're really looking for? Because your own pa died when you were only a little girl.'

Words suddenly rang in her head. A *body could so easily go in. Afoot in a coil of rope. Splash!* She shook her head to rid herself of the picture the words created. She cleared her throat and concentrated on Frank. 'That's not true. Of course I wish my father had lived, but I'm not looking for a father. You can believe what you want but it's not true.'

'I don't know what to believe.' Frank's head drooped and he sounded hopeless all of a sudden.

'Well, try believing something that makes sense. Do you think I'd go risking getting with child by another man when I'm scared out of my wits of such a thing?' She took a step towards him. 'Believe me, Frank.' She placed a hand on his shoulder.

'I want to believe you.'

Again she put her arms round him. 'Believe me.'

He reached up and pulled her down on his knee and kissed her. Then, without a word, he lifted her up and carried her upstairs. She could only say weakly, 'What about George? A couple of girls have taken him to the park. They might come back.'

'Then they'll knock and one of us'll have to answer it.'

Molly said no more. She had put clean sheets on their bed in preparation and the smell of the wash house was on them. In a way it was like so many other times when he'd arrived home from sea but never had she felt she must prove to him that he was the only one in the world for her. It wasn't true but her life wasn't going to be worth living unless he believed it. She remembered the act she'd had to put on when the real Jessica had died and summoned up all her resources to convince him she really cared for him.

Later, as she watched him devour his food, Frank smiled across the table at her. 'Another baby, Moll. That's what you're missing.' She was silent, fingers tightening on her fork. Her son's illness had gone some way to convincing her that another baby mightn't be such a bad thing. If she had lost George her arms would have felt empty indeed. Still she was scared. 'George needs a brother or sister,' continued Frank. 'And I'll be around to help you now. I won't let you die, Moll.'

She half-smiled, thinking, He believes he's God now. 'What about getting a job?'

'My old priest came to visit me in prison and I told him what I planned. He brought me paper and envelopes and the like and saw that my letters got into the right hands.' She was impressed by his determination. 'So which wash house are you going to?'

'Burrough's Gardens.'

Molly stared at him. 'But that's local!'

'That's what I want. I'll be able to come home in the middle of the day and see you and George.' His eyes glinted at her. 'Be a proper father to him, and husband to you.'

She said lightly, 'If I thought, Frank, you were only doing this to keep an eye on me, I'd be really cross.'

'Molly, sweetheart!' He reached out across the table to her. 'I want to be with you. What's wrong with that? You should be pleased to have me around more. It's what you've always said you wanted.'

She did not believe him. He didn't trust her and for that she only had herself to blame.

Shortly afterwards he left the house. She expected him back in an hour or two but he was still out when the girls brought George home and Mrs McNally dropped by.

'I've been up at the wash house. Your Frank's there. All the women are making a fuss of him, saying he's a hero for going to prison. He's lapping it up. Singing along with the Mary Ellens, putting on the Irish as if he was one of them. "I'll Take You Home Again, Kathleen" and all that. It's a real turn up for the book, isn't it, him getting a job there? Yer have to be pleased, girl?'

'I do, don't I?' She smiled, thinking if she had to force a smile anymore that day her face would crack.

Frank swaggered home four hours later with a grin almost as big as a banana on his face. 'And where've you been?' Molly said quietly, placing his supper plate on the table.

'Started work right away. Doesn't that make you happy, Moll? Money coming in at last.'

'Deliriously.'

'Then where's your smile?' he teased, prodding her gently on the back of the hand with his fork.

She snatched her hand away just as Cath walked through the door.

His sister stopped abruptly on seeing Frank. 'So you're home?'

'And got a job.'

'Already?' She looked relieved. 'When d'you sail?'

'Tell her, Moll. Tell her that her big brother is going to be around from now on so there'll be no messing about with that Jimmy in this house.' Cath's face fell and without a word she turned and left. 'Perhaps she'll get Jimmy to marry her now. Or go back to Ma's,' said Frank.

But Cath did neither and Molly was relieved she was staying, not wanting to be alone with Frank in the evenings.

In the days that followed she was on pins. Jimmy had told her that Nathan had returned from training camp so she half-expected him to turn up on her doorstep. His knowing Frank was home just might drive him to do something crazy, such as demanding his son and flinging her misdemeanour in Frank's face. But weeks passed and there was still no sign of him.

Then one murky October Sunday Cath arrived home from an outing with Jimmy.

'Have you heard?' she said.

'Heard what? You and Jimmy tying the knot?'

Cath said with a smile, 'I'm working on it. I thought you might have seen Doris. I only said hello. It's Jimmy who told me the news but she'll probably know more. Maybe she'll drop in?'

'What are you talking about?' Molly untied her apron.

Cath glanced around. 'Our Frank out?'

'He's taken George down to the Pierhead to see the ships so you can say what you want.'

Cath's expression sobered. 'There's a rumour going round the factory that Mr Collins and Miss Braithwaite are getting married.'

Molly sat down abruptly, her apron falling to the floor. For a moment she was devoid of speech before managing to catch her breath. 'It's only a rumour then?'

Cath nodded and said uncomfortably, 'But perhaps it's just as well he marries someone else, Moll? It'll help you to put all you felt for him out of your heart.'

Molly stared at her then laughed. 'You've no idea! I'll go and see Doris.' She almost ran out of the house and over to Mrs McNally's.

Doris opened the front door and immediately the light in her eyes dimmed. 'Yer'd best come in. I thought it wouldn't take long before yer heard.'

'It's true then?' said Molly, a tremor in her voice.

'Yeah. I don't think it's a love match, though,' she said hastily. 'It's for expediency. Or that's the word Charlie used.'

'And what's that supposed to mean?' Doris screwed up her face. 'I think it means useful. Her being a suffragette, she doesn't like men that much, does she? Come and have a cup of tea and I'll tell yer all about it.' She linked her arm through Molly's and dragged her into the kitchen.

'She's told yer then about her and Charlie?' said Mrs McNally, sitting with her other daughters, skirts turned up, warming her legs in front of the fire. 'I don't know where the money's coming from for the do.'

'You and Charlie!' Molly turned to her friend. 'You two are getting married as well?'

She nodded, facing her mother. 'And, Ma, I've told you not to worry. Me and Charlie'll see to it all. He's got a bit of money put by. We don't want too much of a fuss – him with only one hand and me with me bow legs. It'd be like a freak show.'

Molly was feeling terrible but she squeezed Doris's hand. 'I think it's lovely! Best news I've heard for a long time. When's it to be?'

'Spring, of course.'

'And Mr Collins's wedding?'

Doris's expression changed and she said with dismay, 'I thought you said you knew? They're already married, luv. By special licence yesterday.'

Molly's heart seemed to turn to stone. Her whole body felt numb. It was all over then. Nathan didn't love her and would not be claiming George. With Charlotte he could have another son. And where that would leave Jessica she didn't want to think about.

Chapter Fourteen

Molly sat at her sewing machine, hands motionless on the white crêpe-de-chine chosen by Doris for her wedding dress. She imagined her daughter, who was celebrating her birthday today, one day walking down the aisle wearing something much more extravagant. Hopefully she would be marrying someone who could keep her in style.

'You'll never get that finished, sitting there like that,' chided Frank.

Molly jumped and her hand moved the wheel. 'Is there something you want?'

'I'm taking George to Ma's. Yer not much company at the moment and I don't want him playing up at the McNallys' all the time with their grandkids.'

'He doesn't!' Molly was annoyed, feeling Frank had cast aspersions on her mothering skills. She knew he wanted her pregnant, guessed that he saw her failure to conceive as a black mark against his manhood, which was stupid when due to the miners' strike and the shortage of coal the wash house was closed. The last thing they needed at the moment was another mouth to feed.

'I'll be bringing him in for bed soon,' Molly murmured.

'Why? It's Saturday night. The streets are alive. He'll enjoy the outing. It'll be a real treat. You'd enjoy it too,' he said gruffly. 'Why don't you come, Moll?'

'I can't – I've got to get this done. The wedding's only a week away.' Her voice softened. 'But thanks for the thought.'

'OK. Please yourself,' he muttered. 'See you later.'

'Don't keep George out too late!'

There was no answer and she heard the front door slam.

Molly eased her back before settling down to machining again but could not recapture her dream. Instead she thought of Jessica of whom she had seen little since Nathan's marriage. According to Doris, Charlotte Collins had kept on her father's house in Leeds and she and Nathan apparently went to and fro between the two houses, taking Jessica with them. At the moment they were staying in Blundellsands.

Molly finished her machining and settled down in front of the fire with the gown on her knee and a card of lace in her hand to trim the mandarin collar and the sleeves. Charlotte was still not pregnant either and Molly speculated about how Nathan must feel about that, him wanting a son. She wondered about her own ability to conceive, deciding that maybe George's passage into the world had damaged her. If she couldn't get pregnant that meant an end to her anxieties about childbirth and sex.

She began to set neat stitches, looking forward to the wedding and wishing she could afford a new hat. She planned on wearing the green suit she'd made for the lunch at the Angel, and had made herself a peach-coloured blouse with a crossover bodice from a remnant bought in the market. She was not charging Doris for making her gown. It would be her wedding gift.

–

To Molly's relief the board outside the newsagent's announced an end to the miners' strike the following day. There was also news of the White Star liner *Titanic*. That evening Cath drew Frank's notice to an article about the liner in the *Echo*. With coal now available to stoke *Titanic*'s boilers, the White Star line was taking on crew at hiring halls in the main ports of the British Isles. 'What d'you think, brother? What wouldn't you give to serve on such a ship?'

'You wanting to get rid of me?' Frank took the newspaper from her.

The two women watched his handsome face as he read the article. 'You must miss the sea?' said Molly.

'It'd be bloody strange if I didn't. It was my life for years.' There was suddenly an air of excitement about him as he threw down the newspaper and made for the door. 'I'm going out.'

The two women exchanged glances. 'D'you think he'll sign up?' said Cath.

Molly shrugged, wishing he would, knowing the three of them would be happier if he went back to sea.

Frank made no mention of the *Titanic* when he returned and it sailed from Southampton without him on board. He was grumpy for days so Molly presumed he had tried to sign on but had been rejected. Poor Frank, she thought. It was a shame.

He would be working on the day of the wedding now, so could not attend the ceremony, but Ma was to be there as a friend of the bridegroom's family. Naturally Bernie would also attend as sister of the bridegroom. Ma bought George a sailor suit in anticipation of the event and for his birthday in May.

Full of a pleasurable anticipation, knowing she looked her best, Molly entered the church holding George by the hand. She was brought up short on seeing the back of Nathan's head. Her heart began to thud. Doris had made no mention of his being here. Molly sat down in the nearest pew, hoisting her son on to her knee. She lowered her head as if in prayer but her eyes were fixed on Nathan, and on Jessica sitting beside him. She looked for Charlotte but could not see her.

The service passed in a blur with Molly inwardly rehearsing the polite words she would say if she and Nathan happened to bump into each other. But when he came and stood alongside her as she kept an eye on George, who was playing with other children while the wedding photographs were being taken, the polite sentences died on her lips.

'You look lovely,' he said, as if the words were torn from him.

He had surprised her. 'You-you don't look so bad yourself. Wh-Where's your wife?' Molly hated herself for stammering. It was something she had not done for a long time.

'In London.' He smiled. 'Where's your husband? I believe he's finished with the sea.'

'Yes. He's working at the moment. That – that's why he's not here.'

'You must be pleased you've got him home all the time?'

Was he being serious? She could have told him the truth then. Instead she kept silent. Hadn't she lied enough to the two men in her life?

'Perhaps you're not?' murmured Nathan. Still she was silent. 'I'll take it that you're not then. D'you know how long it is since I've seen you, Molly?'

She nodded, wondering why he didn't appear to hate her. She kept her eyes fixed on the children, knowing she might betray how she felt if she looked at him. Jessica had joined them now in playing tig. Molly thought it was her daughter who was the lovely one in a primrose eyelet-embroidered frock and yellow ribbons in her hair.

'Seven months, three weeks and four days,' said Nathan.

At that Molly stared at him and then wished she hadn't because he was looking at her in a way that made her feel breathless. 'I thought you'd want to forget me,' she said in a low voice.

'I tried and I couldn't. Even if Mother didn't ramble on so about your mother and father and his brother.'

'His brother?' She hadn't known her father had a brother.

'Yes,' said Nathan softly. 'He's the cousin Mrs Arkwright knew, the one who died of stomach trouble. I got the impression from her ramblings that she felt a lot for him. We could have been first cousins, Moll.' He paused. 'Why did you run away the way you did?'

She gazed down at the toes of the tan boots, heeled and soled twice now, thinking that didn't answer the question why Mrs

Collins had hated her mother. And what about the baby she had mentioned being taken from her? 'You threatened to keep George. I couldn't bear to lose him. Just like I didn't want you to lose the factory. I knew it meant a lot to you.'

'Is that why you said all those things? Because you didn't want me giving up the factory?'

'You might have lived to regret it.'

'You meant more to me, Moll. You both still do,' he said, glancing at George. 'But I suppose you did the right thing. I love the business. I'm sorry I got steamed up and frightened you.'

She smiled, her heart seeming to swell with love for him. 'You should have told me you were going away the next day. I wouldn't have been so frightened.'

He took her hand and squeezed it gently. 'It won't happen again.'

They were both silent, gazing at each other. Molly felt a fluttering in her stomach and slowly withdrew her hand. She cleared her throat. 'Jessica's growing into a proper little girl now.'

'Lottie's very fond of her. She takes her places, keeps her away from Mother.'

Jealousy stabbed Molly to the heart. 'Does Jessica like her?'

'I'm sure she does. Which is all to the good, don't you think? Lottie's a match for Mother anyday. She knows what she did to Jess so watches out for any sign of trouble on that front. That was one of the reasons I married her. The other—'

'I can guess the other,' Molly said swiftly.

There was silence.

'How's Frank with George?'

She wished he hadn't asked. 'Like any father with a son.'

'Damn him!' said Nathan savagely. 'But he can't give him money, can he? I could help you there.'

'No, you mustn't,' said Molly hastily. 'If Frank were to find out he'd get all suspicious again. As it is he'll be at the party this evening. Are you going to be there?' She wished he would be, thinking how lovely it would be to dance the night away.

'No.' Nathan grimaced. 'Best I'm not, don't you think? Jessica wanted to see the wedding because Doris and Cook have been going on about it. I've business to attend to and I'd best be on my way. I'm glad I've seen you again, Moll.'

She nodded, tightness in her throat. There were suddenly tears in her eyes. 'Don't look like that,' he said quietly. 'You make me want to—'

'Go! Just go!' She fluttered a hand in his direction.

He hesitated, then turned and walked away. She watched him swooping on Jessica and despite her yells of protest carrying her out of the church yard.

'So who's he?'

Molly spun round to find Bernie McGuire standing behind her. Her heart sank. Somehow she managed to pull herself together. 'You don't know your brother's boss?' she said in a mocking voice.

Bernie's eyes widened. 'So that's him? You two seemed friendly.'

'I used to work for him.' Molly moved away, only to collide with Ma.

'Did I recognise that bloke or not?' demanded her mother-in-law. 'Wasn't he the vicar who baptised our George along with the priest?'

'Molly's just said he's our Charlie's boss,' put in Bernie, almost eagerly.

I should have lied, thought Molly. I can see Ma's brain ticking over. 'Likenesses are strange, aren't they?' she said. 'We're all supposed to have a double somewhere.'

'Yer don't say?' said Ma, eyes as cold as those of a dead fish on a slab. She put an arm through Bernie's and drew her away.

Molly's expression was grim as she collected George. She had little hope of Ma and Bernie keeping their mouths shut, but there was nothing she could do about it right now.

'So how did the wedding go?' asked Frank. 'A couple of oddities they are, if you ask me.'

'The bride looked radiant,' said Molly, irritated by his comment. 'Even your mother looked halfway to decent in a navy dress and a straw hat with an artificial rose. I think her eyesight's going, though. She kept mistaking the guests for other people.'

'Bernie's not still wearing black, is she?' said Cath, elbows on the table as she ate a jam butty.

'She was wearing one of those new hobble skirts with buttons unfastened to the calf,' said Molly. 'Less dangerous than the first ones that came out but much more daring.'

'Perhaps she's already got a new man in her life?' Cath turned to her brother. 'What d'you say, Frank? You must hear things when you go to Ma's.'

'You don't think I listen to women's gossip, do you?'

'Of course you do,' said Cath, winking at Molly. 'So tell us the latest?'

'Why don't you ask her yourself?' he said abruptly, getting to his feet. 'I'm going to have a shave.'

'Ah! The party!' said Cath with glee, pushing back her chair. 'I'd best get ready, too. You'll be going down the pub with all the men first, I suppose, Frank?'

'That's right. I'll see you two later.'

It was much later and the party had spilt out on to the street where a piano was brought round on a handcart from the home of one of Doris's relations. A tall, sharp-nosed woman was thumping its keys for all she was worth and people with drinks in their hands were singing along in various pitches. Molly saw Frank in the thick of it leading a chorus of 'There I Was, Waiting at the Church'. It wasn't long before he was having a word with the pianist and had launched into a solo rendition of 'The Soldiers of the Queen'.

'Our Frank's in his element, isn't he?' drawled Cath, raising her eyebrows.

Molly agreed, swaying in time to the music with George in her arms. 'That's what he was doing when I first set eyes on him. I thought he was wonderful.' She was just praying he would not take anything Ma said tonight seriously.

'Then you got to know him,' said Cath, squeezing her shoulder. 'Here's Jimmy. We're going to dance as soon as our Frank shuts up.' She moved off.

With a wide-awake George struggling to get down, Molly wandered around, greeting people and exchanging news. The gathering got louder and louder and from somewhere a fiddler and a youth playing a penny whistle appeared. People danced some more, and when they paused for breath Frank got up on a step and launched into another song. Molly wondered how much he'd had to drink but it wasn't often he indulged. She overheard more than one woman saying he sang luv'ly.

There was a tap on her shoulder and she turned to see Jack Fletcher. 'Hiya! I never thought to see you here,' said Molly, smiling.

He pushed his cap to the back of his head. 'I thought I'd just look in. Doris's mam said to, seeing as how our Rob was here.' He tickled George in the ribs and the boy giggled. 'How's my wee lad coming on?'

'He can draw a duck that's recognisable, thanks to you, as well as a boat.'

The man chuckled and dug into his trouser pocket, bringing out a ha'penny. 'Here, lad, buy theeself some sweeties.'

'That's kind of you, Jack,' she said softly. 'But then, you're a kind person.' The words were hardly out of her mouth before Frank loomed up out of the crowd.

'What are you doing, making up to my wife?' He swayed in front of them.

Oh, no! thought Molly. 'We're only talking, Frank,' she said quietly.

'Only talking? You think I believe that?' There was an ugly expression in his eyes. 'This is the man you say is like an uncle

247

to yer? Well, I don't believe that. Like I don't believe Mr Collins is a vicar as well as a factory owner. What was he doing in my bloody house when George was being born? You tell me that, girl?' He grabbed a handful of Molly's blouse, forcing her against him and almost hitting George in the eye with his elbow.

'Stop it, Frank!' she gasped, placing a protective hand over her son's face.

'Let her go!' said Jack, seizing Frank's arm. 'Are thee crazy, man? I'm old enough to be her father.'

Frank released Molly and, turning, crashed a fist into Jack's face, sending him flying. Almost immediately Rob appeared. 'Who the hell do thee think thee's hittin'?' he demanded.

Frank shot out his fist again and caught him on the nose. Blood spurted from his nostrils but the younger man barely paused to wipe it away with the back of his hand before launching himself at Frank. With her heart hammering fit to burst, Molly bent to help Jack to his feet. Already a circle was forming and people were taking sides. A man was offering odds and soon money was changing hands.

'What's going on?' demanded Ma, accompanied by Josie.

'As if you didn't know!' said Molly in an angry voice. 'Why couldn't you keep your mouth shut?'

Ma bristled. 'Don't you be blaming me, girl, for yer own sinning. Who's this young fella my Frank's fighting? Have yer been carrying on with someone else now?'

'No, she hasn't! That's my son,' said Jack, touching the side of his jaw gingerly.

'And he's *my* husband,' said Doris's sister Marie, bobbing up next to Molly. She was rolling up her sleeves and there was the light of battle in her eyes.

'Is she goin' for our Frank, Ma?' said Josie, jutting out her bottom lip. 'I'm not having that.' She brought up a plump arm and caught Marie a clout across the face with the back of her hand.

There was a concerted gasp from those close by. The next minute there was a free-for-all. Molly was caught in the crush,

George squashed against her breast. He struggled to lift his head, gasping for breath. She was reminded of that time in Lime Street and, panicking, dug an elbow into one of the pugilists and pushed and shoved her way through in an attempt to escape the crowd. In the distance she heard a warning shout and blasts from police whistles. It was enough to cause the party to break up and scatter.

She ran for home with George in her arms and managed to open the front door, giving it a backward kick to close it before hurrying through into the kitchen. Sitting her son on the table, she saw friction burns on his cheek and his lip was bleeding. 'Mad, mad, mad!' she cried. 'I could kill him!' She ran into the back kitchen for water and a cloth.

She was cleaning George's face and whispering soothing words to him when Jimmy and Cath entered the room.

'Holy Mary!' said Cath, her eyes shining with excitement. 'But it's crazy out there.'

'You don't need to tell me,' said Molly, still furiously angry with Frank, Ma and Bernie.

'They're fighting the Paddy-Kellys now,' said Jimmy, grinning. 'There're going to be a few sore heads in the morning.'

'There'll be some spending the night in the bridewell,' said Cath. 'I wonder what started it? Religion, I bet.'

'Your Frank started it,' raged Molly. 'Just because Jack Fletcher spoke to me. And don't look at me like that, the pair of you! I haven't done anything.' She stood up with George in her arms. 'I'm taking him to bed now. If Frank comes in I don't want to speak to him. He can sleep in a chair.'

'I'm not telling him that,' said Cath, rolling her eyes. 'He'll probably land me one and tell me to get out.'

The door knocker went and Molly hurried towards the stairs, calling over her shoulder. 'I'm not answering that.'

But it was Charlie. Hearing his voice, Molly retraced her steps. 'Frank's been arrested,' he gasped. 'So've Rob and his dad and a couple of dozen others.'

'Where's Ma and Josie?' asked Cath, exchanged a swift glance with Molly.

A grin lit Charlie's face. 'Josie was carted off, swearing like a trooper. Your ma was running alongside, aiming blows at the three scuffers trying to hold on to her. I'll be off now. It is me wedding night after all.'

'I am sorry, Charlie,' said Molly stiffly. 'It's ruined your party.'

'Naw! it livened it up. Reminded me of me early days in India. Tarrah! I'll let meself out.'

'I suppose I'd best go and see if Ma's OK,' said Cath reluctantly.

Molly hoped they'd put her mother-in-law in prison too. The troublemaker! She went upstairs with George, glad that tomorrow Frank would have a monstrous hangover. It served him right. At least her reckoning with him was postponed. But what was she going to do when it did come? How could she explain Nathan's presence in the house the day George was born? Say that he was her cousin? He'd think it strange about her father having a brother she'd never even heard about? Was it in fact wise to hang around and wait for Frank tomorrow? She thought of Jack Fletcher, hit in the face on her behalf and clapped up in gaol. Just for speaking to her. She would have to wait and see how he was, at least.

She put George into his cot and stood there, holding his hand and singing *Rock-a-bye-baby* until his eyes closed. There were tear-stains on his face and she felt moisture in her own eyes. She wiped it away, thinking of Nathan. As she smoothed back George's tangle of golden brown hair and said a prayer, she felt weighed down with worry all over again. Yet knowing that Nathan still cared for her helped a little bit. Even so there could be nothing between them. He had a wife, and besides it was too risky with Frank knowing what he did now.

She went downstairs and sat gazing into the empty fireplace, waiting for Cath to return. An hour passed and still she waited. Eventually she decided Cath wasn't coming so she went to bed.

She slept late and when she woke it was to the sound of church bells. She found George still sleeping so hurried into Cath's room but her bed had not been slept in. Molly went to the dairy for milk then woke George.

It was noon and still Frank had not arrived home, so leaving George with her next-door neighbour, Molly walked to the bridewell in Athol Street to enquire after her husband and the Fletchers.

'The bargees have been let out with a caution,' said the policeman, leaning across the counter towards her. 'But your husband's been transferred to the cells at St George's Hall. He'll be appearing in court Monday morning.' His voice was stern. 'He put a good man in hospital with serious stomach injuries.'

'One of yours, you mean?' Molly was dismayed, feeling herself to be partially to blame.

'Yeah, that's right. And seeing he's already got a black mark against him, he could be doing some time.'

It was a shock. Molly felt as if the room was spinning round and clung to the counter. 'You OK, luv? You got kids? Anything we can do to help you and them?' It was from this bridewell that help in the form of clothing and food was given to the poverty-stricken children of the area.

'Only the one.' Everything steadied around her. 'If you could let me know what time and which court, I'd appreciate it?'

'Not sure, luv. But there isn't anything you can do for him so why don't you go home and I'll let you know what happens? Give us your address.'

'It doesn't matter,' she said, managing a faint smile. 'I'll find out for myself.' She thanked him and left the bridewell.

When Cath turned up later in the day she was looking very determined. 'I'm in the doghouse,' she said, 'and it's all *your* fault.'

'Ma found out it was you who went for Mr Collins the day George was born?' guessed Molly.

'She had words with Mrs McNally at the wedding break-fast and it all came out.' Cath frowned. 'Why didn't you tell

251

me there was more to it than your talking to Mr Fletcher last night?'

'I was too angry. Anyway, did she tell you why she didn't tell Frank as soon as he arrived at the party?'

'No. Perhaps she was delaying because she didn't want to hurt him. I think it was Bernie who pushed her into it.'

'That's what I thought too.' Molly tapped one foot on the oilcloth. 'So where did you stay last night? You do know Frank's got to go to court?'

'At Jimmy's mother's. And, yes.' Cath hesitated. 'Will you be letting Mr Collins know what's happened?'

Molly looked at her calmly. 'Why should you think that? *He's* a married man now. What kind of woman d'you think I am? When are you going to accept that, except for that one time, I've never slept with him?'

'OK! I'm sorry,' said Cath, flushing. 'It's just that—'

'Just that nothing! And you can tell Jimmy I don't want what's happened to Frank getting back to Mr Collins. If he asks after me, tell him I've moved away.'

'What!'

'You heard me.'

Cath looked puzzled. 'So you don't love him?'

'That's none of your business.'

'Where are you moving to?'

'I'm not sure yet.'

'Right.' Cath twisted her fingers together. 'If you're moving, me and Jimmy would like this house. We're fed up of waiting to afford a do so we decided last night to have a simple wedding and look for somewhere to live.'

Molly felt some of the strain ease, especially at the back of her neck. 'That's fine by me. Although I might not go just yet. I've made no definite plans.'

'It doesn't matter. I'm sure we can rub along together.'

'Right. You two can have the double bed in the main bedroom and I'll take yours.'

'You mean it? Your bed!' said Cath, incredulously. 'What'll our Frank say?'

Molly smiled wryly. 'I doubt he'll say anything to me. I won't be hanging around waiting for him to smash me in the face.'

She stood up. 'You hungry? I'll do us something to eat then let's try and forget things for a few hours.'

–

The following morning Molly caught a tram to Lime Street and managed to slip into the back of the courtroom at St George's Hall. She was just in time to hear sentence being passed on Frank. He was to go to prison for three years' hard labour for grievously harming a police officer.

Three years! Three whole years! Relief, guilt, regret, sorrow… Molly experienced all those emotions. She felt she should have been on trial along with Frank in a way. He'd been wrong to jump to conclusions and hurt Jack Fletcher and that policeman, but her behaviour in deceiving him had driven him to it. What should she do now? He surely needed support and he was her husband. She stared down at him as he was being escorted out of the court. At that moment he caught sight of her. The coldness and anger in his expression chilled her to the marrow.

The news of Frank's sentence did not even make the Stop Press of the Liverpool *Echo*. Its pages were full of the unthinkable. A few hours after Molly and Cath had discussed their plans the great liner *Titanic* sank after hitting an iceberg. All those working in the engine room lost their lives.

Life's strange, thought Molly, as tears rolled down her cheeks, grieving for the newly dead and bereaved. If Frank had never gone to prison in the first place he might have been on that liner. Instead he was alive and she was still married to him. God only knew what he might do to her when he came out. She was just going to have to make sure he couldn't find her.

Chapter Fifteen

'What are you doing?' demanded Cath.

'What's it look like I'm doing?' Molly folded the blouse and placed it on the pile of clothing to be knotted in a sheet.

'I thought you'd stay a bit longer. At least until me and Jimmy get married.'

'Sorry.' Molly lifted the bundle and made for the door.

Cath followed, clattering down the stairs behind her. 'But why so soon?'

Molly placed the bundle next to another one of bedding in the kitchen. 'I go into a shop and the conversation stops straightaway so I know they're talking about me. I've caught snatches of the gossip on the street. "It's always the quiet ones,"' she mimicked one of her neighbours to perfection. '"And he's such a luv'ly man. It's all her fault, the little tart!"'

'I know,' said Cath unhappily. 'Jimmy says it's going round the factory too.'

Molly was horrified. 'How? Surely he didn't…?'

'No, of course not! It's more than his life's worth. I'd clock him one. I reckon it's Doris's dad who knows about Mr Collins playing at vicars now. The way things are going it won't be long before Mrs Collins gets to hear about it. Although they're both in Leeds at the moment. Jimmy's telling people there's nothing in it but they'd rather believe there is. You know what they're like.'

Oh, Lord! thought Molly despairingly, hoping it wouldn't get back to their customers as well.

'So where are you going?' said Cath. Molly glanced at the clock.

'Back where I came from. Jack Fletcher's picking me up because I want to take my sewing machine – and the single mattress, if you don't mind. I don't want anything Frank paid for.'

Cath sighed. 'Talk about history repeating itself. Jack's coming here is going to give them something more to jangle about, too. Don't forget his name's been bandied around as well.'

'He says he doesn't care. That he's flattered.' Molly smiled for the first time in days.

'Where'll you stay?'

'With Rob and Marie. Uncle Jack sleeps on the boat more often than not. Marie said she'll look after George while I find a job.'

'And I'm going to miss you,' said Cath forlornly.

'I'm going to miss you, too. Despite our not starting off on the right foot.'

For a moment they stared at each other and then they hugged. 'If things don't work out, you can always come back,' said Cath in a muffled voice against Molly's shoulder. 'You can bet they'll be tearing someone else's reputation to shreds by next week.'

Jack and Rob arrived ten minutes later. Molly was aware of the neighbours watching and muttering amongst themselves as the two men carried out her possessions. Jack shouted, 'Hasn't thee anything better to do?'

A couple sniffed and went indoors.

Jack, Molly and George were just about to turn the corner into Latimer Street when Mrs McNally came tearing after them. 'Why didn't yer come and say tarrah?' she panted. 'Here, take this.' She handed Molly a newspaper-wrapped parcel. 'They'll do for yer teas.' Molly was suddenly near to tears and she hugged her. 'There now, girl, we all make mistakes,' said

Mrs McNally roughly, patting her back. 'You just take care of yourself and little George. And don't forget, my door's always open to yer whatever my fella might say.' She waved until they were out of sight.

Rob had hung a swing from a pair of hooks embedded above the cabin doorway and George pattered over to it. He was soon swinging back and forth, singing away like a chirpy little sparrow.

At least he seems unaware of the big changes in our lives, thought Molly thankfully. She gave the swing a push every now and then as warehouses gave way to housing. They came to Bootle and she thought of Frank incarcerated in prison and tried not to feel guilty, telling herself that perhaps she was taking too much of the blame on her own shoulders.

Housing gave way to fields and the air was sweet except when they passed the Litherland tannery where a barge was tied up unloading animal hides. 'Pooh!' said George, pulling a face.

Jack called her down into the cabin to have a bite to eat and a cuppa. She slid past George and gazed about her with pleasure. The interior contained a range for cooking and heating, a cupboard with a folding table and long seats at the sides. At the forward end, hidden by crochet-work curtains, she knew there was a folding crossbed. There were ample cupboards and lockers. No space was wasted and it was all decorated with paintwork and graining. She thought Nathan would be interested in that. She liked the lace plates and shining brasswork best.

'How snug you are here, Uncle Jack. I envy you,' said Molly, accepting a doorstepsized bacon butty from him.

'Well, thee's always welcome to come for a ride with me anytime. Thee knows that, lass.' His expression made her feel slightly uncomfortable and she was glad when Rob called down for someone to bring him a cuppa and a butty at the wheel.

The house where Marie and Rob lived backed on to the canal. The tiny bedroom Molly was to share with George overlooked a garden where potatoes, onions, cabbages and carrots had already been planted. They would sleep on the floor on the single mattress. For now her sewing machine was of no use to her. Molly needed to earn money some other way before she could think of finding customers and sewing from home. Hadn't she tried that before when last she was here? Her heart ached as she remembered those days when she had her daughter with her and saw Nathan most days.

She found herself a job repairing grain sacks, Ainscough's flour mill being conveniently situated next to the canal a few minutes' walk away, which meant she could see George at lunch time. The mill was lit by electricity, powered by a gas engine. She thought of Nathan and his plan one day to produce electrical fittings for churches and wondered if it would ever get off the ground. She could only hope the scandal she was running away from would not ruin his business.

A couple of the older women she worked with remembered her mother. 'Married one of the May twins. Now they were a match all right.'

'My father was a twin?' Molly was astounded, wondering why nobody had ever mentioned that to her.

'Aye, that's right.' The woman smiled. 'Mabel went out with one, Hetty Barnes with t'other. She would have married Tom if he hadn't died young. Followed him all the way to Colne she did to get a job near him. Broke her heart it did when he died. She went a bit queer afterwards and her family brought her home. Threw her cap then at your ma's fella and then there was an almighty row. It caused quite a stir at the time because there was gossip going round, but old Collins married her so she was OK.'

So that was why her mother and Mrs Collins had fallen out, thought Molly. But what about the baby Nathan's mother'd talked about? Why had marrying old Collins meant she was OK? Could she have been pregnant? Whose baby was it if she was? For a moment Molly went hot and cold, wondering if she and Nathan shared the same father. Then she remembered Mrs Collins rambling on about them taking her baby away from her. So perhaps she had been pregnant but her husband had got rid of the baby? If that was so Nathan was truly Mr Collins's son. Molly felt weak with relief. It explained a lot and she found herself feeling unexpectedly sorry for Nathan's mother.

Molly relaxed and carried on with her work. It was easy, too easy, but the sacking rough so that sometimes it split the skin down the sides of her fingernails. She did not complain but rubbed lard into her hands when she hurried home to see her son. He cried after her for the first few days and that upset her but Marie was like her mother in that she stood no nonsense and soon he settled down and made friends with the other children in the street.

Molly's days fell into a routine that was undemanding if tedious. On Sundays she took George to church, determined to try and get herself back on to the straight and narrow. There she met Em. Molly had forgotten that she went to St John's.

'So you're back?' she said, catching up with Molly in the churchyard. 'It's nice to see you, lass. How are you doing?'

'OK.' Molly flashed her a smile, glad that Em did not hold their last disagreement against her. Yet still she worried that the older woman might have guessed she'd swopped the babies so wanted to be on her way. But Em was not going to let her slip away so quickly.

'What a lovely little boy. Yours, is he? You remarried?'

'Yes... no!' Molly was flustered. 'My husband was found and came back. He's back at sea now. You'll have to excuse me, Em, I've got to go.' She hurried away.

Molly did not return to church for a few weeks but eventually felt a need to be there in the old familiar setting, to sing hymns and find comfort and challenges in the words of the liturgy as she sought forgiveness and peace with God. But she always sat in a back pew so she could get out quickly and avoid Em. As for George, he started in the tots class at Sunday School.

She was kept informed about what was happening to Cath and the McNallys as Marie went at least once a week to visit her mother. From one such trip to Liverpool she returned with the news that Cath and Jimmy were at last getting married and Molly was invited. Also that Mr Collins had called at the house several times.

Molly's heart missed a beat. She longed to see Nathan but knew she could not chance going to the wedding in case he attended in the hope of seeing her. So she told Marie to say thank you and give them her best wishes. She would have sent a gift if there had been money to spare but that was something in very short supply. Her son was sprouting up and after giving Marie their keep there was little over. As it was she had to pawn the green suit she'd made for the lunch she'd never attended in order to buy him a pair of shoes.

One day there was to be a Fletcher gathering at one of Jack's sons' homes. Molly was invited but as it was the day of the Sunday School outing to Southport and she had to have George at the meeting place round about the same time she excused herself. After seeing him off, she decided to pick some flowers and visit Nanna's grave.

It was peaceful as she walked along the path with only the sounds of birdsong and the breeze swaying the branches of trees. She placed the wild flowers on the grave then stood a moment, remembering, before making her way to that other grave where the real Jessica was buried. It came as something of a shock to find Nathan there and immediately her heart beat accelerated.

Even though the turf softened her footsteps he must have heard her because he turned and smiled, not looking the least bit surprised to see her. 'Hello, Moll. Why did you run away again? I told you if you ever needed help you were to come to me.'

'You were in Leeds.' Her voice shook. 'Besides it was impossible. You must know what people were saying about us?'

'I'm sorry you were put through all that. I should have ignored you at the wedding but I couldn't. I was too damn' glad to see you.'

She understood. Hadn't she felt the same? 'How did you know I was here? Or is it purely coincidence and you're visiting your first wife's grave?'

His eyes gleamed and he dug his hands into his pockets. 'A bit of bribery. I couldn't get anything out of that sister-in-law of yours but now she and Jimmy are having a baby and have moved into his mother's street, I decided to see what I could get out of him by offering him a better position with a rise in wages.'

She could not help smiling. 'You're devious! Everything all right at the factory then?'

'If you mean, have things blown over, yes.' He rested one hand on top of his wife's gravestone. 'Although I had a sticky interview with a couple of clergymen. But I repented of my sins and seeing as how I appeared to be living amiably with my wife and hadn't run off with you, I've been forgiven.'

'So you and Charlotte are getting—' She did not finish the sentence, aware that they were being watched. It was Em visiting one of the other graves and fright churned Molly's stomach. 'I-I'll have to go,' she stammered and began to make her way to the gate.

Immediately Nathan followed her and suddenly Em was there as well. 'Moll! Mr Collins, how nice to see you. Is all well with you and the little girl? We heard you'd married again?'

'Everything's fine, thanks,' he said politely.

Molly could see he had no idea who Em was and wanted to tug on his sleeve and get him away quickly before she said something that would remind him of those sad days.

'Any children?' said Em.

He glanced at Molly. 'A son,' he said.

She wished one of the graves would open up and swallow her. How could he be so bold! If Em had known he was married, she must be getting her information from somewhere! Perhaps she'd find out that Nathan had no children with his wife. She might put two and two together now she'd seen them in each other's company and then the Lord only knew she might feel it her Christian duty to denounce Molly to the church. 'I'll have to go,' she muttered, and hurried through the gateway.

Nathan caught up with her and took hold of her arm. 'What's frightened you, Molly?'

She looked back and saw there was no sign of Em now. Was the woman a witch to vanish just like that? She had given Molly a terrible fright. Perhaps she was being irrational? Why should Em bother checking up on them at all? Her life had nothing to do with theirs. Even so the sight of the woman made Molly nervous every time she saw her.

'Answer me, Moll!' demanded Nathan. 'What is it about that woman? I thought I recognised her and she obviously knows us.'

Molly nearly died of fright. 'Nathan, I'm making a new life for myself here and I don't want to have to leave. Please go away.' She looked up at him, a pleading expression on her pale face.

His mouth softened. 'Why should you have to leave? Not that it can be much of a life for you here.' He looked her up and down. 'Those clothes and clogs... Let me give you some money, Moll?'

'I don't want your money,' she said agitatedly. 'And the clogs are the ones *you* gave me.'

'And you've kept them all this time?' He smiled and touched her cheek with the back of his hand.

His caress sent a shiver through her. 'Don't,' she whispered. 'You shouldn't have come. I was beginning to settle down.'

'Hell, Moll!' he said huskily. 'We've seen each other once in twelve months. Haven't you missed me? There isn't a night goes by when I don't think about you.'

'Of course I've missed you.' Her voice shook. 'But there's nothing I can do. There's your wife to think about now.' She carried on walking in the direction of the canal.

'We're not living amicably. Our marriage is a sham.'

Molly whirled round to face him. 'She knows about us?'

'It's nothing to do with that. It wasn't so bad at the beginning. Lottie was interested in me and Jessica then. She saw us as a challenge. She liked the house and taking an interest in the factory. But now she's fed up with Mother and gets bored easily when she's home too much.'

'Where is she now?'

'London again. I see little of her.' They had reached the Packet House Hotel and Nathan began to make his way down the steps to the towpath despite its starting to rain.

'Can't you make her stay at home?'

He raised his eyebrows. 'It's obvious you don't know Lottie. Besides it's more restful when she's not around. She works Mother up into rages.'

Molly was alarmed and forgot her newfound sympathy towards his mother. 'She doesn't take it out on Jessica, does she?'

'No!' He gazed at her in concern. 'I know you're fond of her but don't worry. Jessica would tell me if there was anything wrong. She's a chatty little thing. Always singing and dancing. She's having proper lessons now.' He touched her cheek again. 'You've gone pale. What did I say?'

She forgot Frank and even his daughter. Nathan's physical presence was suddenly overpowering, reminding her of how he'd made love to her once and how happy her life had been then. She trembled as he stroked her neck with a gentle hand. 'Accept help from me, Moll. If not for yourself then for George. To think I brought you to this! If I hadn't gone along to the house the day he was born, none of it would have happened.'

'No! It's my fault.'

'How's it your fault?'

She was silent, tempted to tell him the whole truth and get it off her conscience but fear of his being shocked by her deceitfulness stopped her from speaking. Suddenly she realised they were getting very wet and that they were only a few feet from Jack's barge. There would be no one aboard now. She dived on to the boat and went through into the cabin. There she sat on one of the side seats with a locker beneath which served as an extra bed. Nathan followed. The interior was warm. Probably Jack had used the range that morning to cook his breakfast. The smell of fried bacon and eggs still hung in the air. 'I've always loved these boats,' said Nathan, sitting next to her.

The breath was suddenly tight in Molly's lungs as he reached out and took hold of her chin, turning her face so that she had to look at him. 'Stop being frightened, Moll. The last thing I want to do is hurt you.' Slowly, almost hesitantly, he brought her face up to his and covered her mouth gently with his own. She felt a fluttering like a moth's wings inside her.

His lips, cold and damp from the rain, pressed a little harder. When she still did not push him away, he very firmly kissed her again, forcing her head back until it rested against the cushions. His hands caressed the column of her neck, parting to wander slowly over each of her shoulders, then her breasts and stomach. She had the strangest feeling that she was floating. It was almost as if her mind had left her body and yet she was experiencing every sensation.

The sound of feet on the deck took them both by surprise. Surely it couldn't be Jack back already? They stared at each other and stood up at the same time. She hurried out of the cabin followed by Nathan and came face to face with Jack.

Molly blushed and would have gone past him if Nathan had not caught her hand andher back. 'Mr Fletcher, Molly was showing me your boat. It's really neat inside.'

'What are thee doing here, lad?' said Jack, scowling. 'Where's thy sense? Hasn't thee caused her enough trouble?'

The muscles in Nathan's face tightened. 'I don't see how that's any of your business. But if you must know why I'm here,

263

Molly's due some dividends from her shares in the company and I wanted to check that I had her address right.'

'I–I'd almost forgotten about my dividends until he came,' she said. 'The money'll buy me a new pair of shoes.'

Nathan smiled and from an inside pocket extracted an envelope. He held it out to her. 'Enjoy spending it, Moll. I'll see you again.' He raised his hat and bade them both a good day before going on his way, whistling.

Molly had an absurd desire to giggle and was smiling as she turned to Jack. 'I hope you don't mind my showing him the boat?'

'Thee's a fool, Moll, if thee takes up with him again,' Jack growled.

Her smile faded. She had no wish to hurt Jack by telling him to mind his own business. She was fond of him but could not let him rule her life. Then he surprised her by seizing hold of her and pulling her into his arms. 'Marry me, Moll? Let me take care of thee and little George. He needs a father.' She struggled. 'Uncle Jack, let me go! Are you mad? I'm already married.'

It was obvious by the expression on his face that for a moment he had forgotten but he recovered quickly. 'Then thee shouldn't be messing about with *him*,' he muttered, releasing her.

'I'm not messing about.' Molly smoothed the sleeve of her frock.

'Then what were you doing in the cabin?'

'Nothing of which I'm ashamed,' she said, annoyed at being questioned.

'You love him?'

She did not answer but jumped off the boat on to the towpath and walked away. Jack had spoiled what had been lovely between her and Nathan and she was hurt and angry.

As she lay sleepless on the mattress beside George that night she knew she would have to leave Burscough. It was pointless staying anyway now Nathan had traced her. Besides, she was scared stiff of Em's mentioning any suspicions she might have about Jessica's not being his daughter. She herself might be utterly wrong in thinking Em suspected something but she could not risk it. What if Nathan rejected Jessica because she was Frank's daughter? The thought horrified her.

Then there was Jack's behaviour. She felt embarrassed every time she thought of what he'd said and done. But at least he'd made her face up to the truth that she and Nathan probably would have committed adultery if he hadn't turned up. Her whole body ached for Nathan but she would return to Liverpool. The news he'd given her of Cath and Jimmy had made that decision easier. She wouldn't have to face her old neighbours and would write Nathan a very circumspect letter, thanking him for her dividends, which were generous, and telling him that their case was hopeless and they might as well call it a day.

–

Cath was delighted to see Molly and George. 'I've really missed you and I've had so many people asking about you, all concerned.'

'You mean, I've still got some friends?' she said wryly.

'Maggie Block for one. She's after giving you some work. Wants a frock made. Apparently she remembers what a good job you made of Doris's wedding dress.'

Molly's spirits lifted a little. She wanted work and this was a start. If she made a good job of the dress Maggie might allow her to place an advertisement in her window. There were surely plenty of people in the area who wouldn't have heard the gossip about her? And even if they had, they'd probably have forgotten her name by now. She went to see Maggie that evening, determined to have a go at building up a business this time.

It was fortunate Molly had her dividend money because customers didn't immediately come knocking at the door in droves. Only gradually, by word of mouth and advertising in shop windows, did her business grow. It was a struggle. As much of a struggle as trying to forget Nathan, but she persisted.

She was just thinking she had succeeded when he turned up on the doorstep, rain dripping from the brim of his hat and with a parcel under his arm. Molly gazed at him through the window, uncertain what to do. He was definitely a sight for sore eyes but what was he doing here and could she cope with all the emotional turmoil of resuming their relationship?

He banged on the knocker a third time then suddenly noticed her face at the window and shouted, 'Let me in, Moll! It's wet out here.'

'I'm thinking about it,' she called.

'Don't think too long or I might go away.'

She went and opened the door, keeping him waiting on the step a moment longer. 'You're doing it again, you know. Turning up just as I'm managing to get by without you,' she said crossly.

'I've brought you work. Now let me in or I'll change my mind.'

Molly held the door wide and he stepped over the threshold. She closed the door behind him and immediately knew she had made a wrong move if she was to keep him at a distance. In the confined space of the lobby their bodies touched and the smell of him, mingled with the scent of his sandalwood soap and wet wool, was almost too much. She moved away quickly as a small voice piped up, 'Mam, who's that man?' Molly hesitated before saying, 'He's brought some work for me so run along in.'

'What's he got in that box?'

'I told you, work. Now in!' She ushered George into the kitchen.

Nathan followed. 'Next time I come, I promise I'll bring you a present, son.'

'Don't you go making him promises you won't be able to keep,' warned Molly, trying to ignore the treacherous warmth about her heart.

'I saw your advertisement in Maggie Block's window. How are you doing-?'

'I'm glad of this work to be honest,' she said, placing the box on the table next to her sewing machine and hoping that Cath would not return from the shops just yet.

He rested one elbow on the mantelshelf and glanced around. 'This is cosy. Nice fire. I could get you your own place like this.' There was a glint in his eyes the like of which she had seen before and she knew he had not accepted that it was over between them.

'No, thanks. I'm trying to stick to the straight and narrow. Stop making it difficult for me.'

Nathan frowned. 'It's difficult for me, too.'

They were both silent and Molly wanted him to go even as she wished he could stay.

He sighed. 'Does that have to mean we don't see each other at all?'

'Yes!' she said emphatically. 'It wouldn't be sensible to see each other.'

'How about just now and then?' he persisted. 'Say once a month, just so you could keep me informed about George's welfare.'

She was silent, not sure what to say to that, but thought he deserved some reward for bringing her work. Besides it would give her something to look forward to and bring colour to her life. She threw caution to the wind. 'When and where? It would have to be away from here.'

He smiled. 'The Pierhead, a week on Sunday?'

Molly thought, we sound like a courting couple making a date, and said swiftly, 'I'll have to bring George. Cath and Jimmy need Sundays to themselves.'

'OK.'

'Now you'll have to go,' she said, pushing him out before Cath arrived on the scene.

They went to New Brighton and had lunch on the Ham and Egg Parade. Nathan bought George a toy boat and both of them enjoyed his delight. She daydreamed about Nathan, living for the next time she saw him. Their destination was Sefton Park where George sailed his boat on the lake. Their meetings were bittersweet. It was like being married but without the necessary togetherness. They visited Liverpool Zoo and Nathan said, 'Jessica would have loved this. I did think of bringing her.'

Warning bells rang in Molly's head. 'She might mention us to Lottie or your mother,' she said uneasily.

'Doesn't George ever mention me?'

'So far I've managed to steer him clear.' Cath asked no questions which meant Molly told her no lies. Nor did her sister-in-law enquire where she had suddenly got work from.

'Where next then? Is there any chance of an extra meeting – one in the evening? Just the two of us?'

Molly met his eyes and said weakly, 'No. We said we'd be sensible.'

'Dinner, Moll. Or the theatre. That's all,' he said persuasively.

It sounded so innocent. 'Slip a note in when you send me work.'

Nathan's note arrived the day Cath was safely delivered of a daughter. Both parents were euphoric while George was grumpy and sought solace in Molly's bed every night. She found having him there a comfort but would have preferred his father. She envied Jimmy's and Cath's happiness but at least the note was some consolation. There was a variety show on at the Empire that Nathan thought she would enjoy. Molly decided it was just up her street and made herself a new frock. They went to the early performance and afterwards to the Angel for dinner.

'I missed out last time,' said Molly, sitting back after spooning up her last mouthful of chocolate mousse. 'That was lovely.' Her eyes shone with pleasure.

Nathan took her hand, stroking the back of it with his thumb. 'I'd like us to see more of each other. I'd like to make up to you for so many things you've missed out on.'

'And how do we do that?' she said, caught offguard.

'Come and work for me at the house?'

She stared at him, speechless.

His eyes twinkled. 'I say work because I know you've got your pride.'

'Lottie?' she managed to get out.

'She's away more than she's home. You can look after Jess. Be a companion to Mother.'

He must be joking! she thought, fear welling up.

'We'd see each other every day, Moll,' Nathan said urgently. 'We're second cousins. You could be there as part of the family. Weren't we happy when you lived at the house before?'

'Yes, but—'

'It's better than meeting once or twice a month.'

'Yes, but—'

He frowned. 'You don't want to do it?'

'I can't.' She got to her feet hastily and said unhappily, 'I knew we couldn't go on the way we were.'

'Of course we couldn't. But I thought with Doris having a baby it was the perfect excuse for you to come back and look after Jess.'

'What! Doris and Charlie?' She stared at him. 'I never thought they'd manage it.'

'She's kept it a secret for a while, apparently. Moll, sit down,' he urged. 'Getting back to us – you're still fond of Jessica, and George would be company for her.'

A dream come true, thought Molly. But he was being ridiculous. Lottie must have heard the rumours and even in a marriage such as theirs she wasn't going to be that tolerant. But that wasn't the worst of it, of course. What if, as soon as his mother saw Molly, she went on about that likeness between Jessica and her again? Sometimes Molly thought her fear of Nathan's finding out the truth went beyond the realms of reason but she could not help it. She would rather stop seeing him than risk things going wrong for her daughter.

'No!' she said harshly. 'It was a lovely dinner and I really enjoyed the theatre, but no, no, no! Lottie would think I was there so we could carry on, and we probably would. We have to stop, Nathan.'

'Dammit, Moll! Why do you always have to be thinking of other people?' he said, exasperated.

'I'm not! I'm thinking of myself. My reputation matters to me.'

'OK. You've made your point.' His voice was as harsh as hers. 'Then nothing changes?'

'Yes.' She tilted her chin. 'We stop seeing each other alto-gether. It's the only thing that makes sense.' And on those words she walked out.

Chapter Sixteen

Doris's baby was due towards the end of July and Molly found that of more concern to her than the assassination of an Austrian Archduke in a small Balkan state. She had not seen anything of Nathan recently and although she missed him, kept telling herself she had done the right thing.

The baby, a boy, was delivered safely. Charlie was as proud as Punch when he came to tell them. 'Mr Collins gave Doris a whole guinea for the baby before he went off to training camp in Wales. And he's given us an extra room on the top floor.'

Molly's heart missed a beat. She had almost forgotten about his being in the Reserves. 'When did he go?'

'Just this morning. It'll do him good. The missus came home last week and she's always at the old woman. If it weren't for Miss Jessica, his life wouldn't be worth living.' Charlie glanced at Molly and said gruffly, 'Our Bernie's been visiting Frank by the way. I've told her it's wrong but she can't see it.'

Molly wasn't a bit surprised. In a year's time Frank would be out of prison and there and then she decided to see if she could ask for a legal separation. The life she'd shared with him seemed to have been led by a different person and since Bernie had obviously taken him up it was doubtful Frank would want to live with Molly again.

She decided to visit Doris and the baby as soon as she had a moment. With Nathan away there would be no chance of bumping into him and she could see how Jessica was getting on for herself. But there was a wedding dress and four bridesmaids dresses to be made first.

It was August Bank Holiday before Molly had the chance to go to Blundellsands. Cath and Jimmy were taking the ferry to New Brighton and she could not help noticing they were snappy with each other. 'What's wrong with you two?' she asked as she brushed her hair before going out.

Cath burst out, 'He says he's going to enlist if there's a war. Have you ever heard anything so stupid?'

Molly stared at her in amazement. 'Why on earth should there be a war? Who are we going to fight?'

Cath raised her eyes ceilingwards and said, exasperated, 'You've been at that bloody sewing machine too long!'

'Cath!' protested Jimmy. 'It's not nice for a woman to swear.'

She ignored him. 'Or are you blind, deaf, and dumb, Moll? It's been in all the newspapers. Germany's invaded Belgium and we have a pact which was drawn up blinking years ago to defend them. The Government's sitting in Parliament today trying to decide what to do.'

'Well, we're not at war yet,' said Jimmy hastily. 'So let's go and enjoy ourselves. See you later, Moll.'

War! Could there really be a war? Suddenly it was a matter of urgency that she see Nathan. A month had passed so surely he would be home now? All the reasons why she shouldn't see him were no longer important at the thought that he might go off to war.

She dragged a struggling George away from the pavement where he was playing with a friend. 'Wanna play!' he wailed.

'We're going on the train. You'll enjoy that.'

His cries stopped and she hurried him to Sandhills station.

There was a lovely breeze cooling their faces as they walked up Blundellsands Road in the direction of the sea. Swinging on her hand, George smiled up at Molly, sniffing the air. 'We're going to the sands. I can smell the sea.'

'We've got to visit Uncle Nathan first. And maybe we'll see your Auntie Doris and her baby,' said Molly, her chest tight with apprehension.

He wrinkled his nose. 'I don't like babies! But I won't hurt it because I want to play on the sands.' He squeezed her hand and brushed his lips against it.

My little love, she thought, comforted.

There was no answer at the front door so Molly went round the back and found Doris with the baby sitting in the garden. Charlie was stretched out in a deck chair, reading a newspaper.

'What's this? Not working?' said Molly, forcing a smile.

'While the cat's away.' Doris got up and came towards her. 'Mr Collins had to rush off to Yorkshire as soon as he was home. Something to do with business. They've all gone with him.'

Molly felt sick with disappointment. Right now decisions were being made in Parliament that might mean Nathan's going off to fight the Hun. That couldn't happen, surely? On such a beautiful day the prospect of men killing each other seemed utterly impossible.

Chapter Seventeen

Molly glanced over her shoulder as Cath entered the kitchen, carrying her daughter Lucy and waving a newspaper in her free hand. 'It's war,' she said grimly. 'And Kitchener's asking for volunteers.'

'No!' said Molly, dismayed.

'He's only asking for single men between the age of nineteen and thirty at the moment, although Jimmy's in the street now talking about doing his bit. There's dozens like him can't wait to go.'

Molly thought, Nathan will be amongst the first being in the Reserves, and felt sick.

'I don't know what I'm worrying about,' muttered Cath, putting down her daughter. 'The French and our regular army'll probably see them off before any of the new recruits are even trained.'

'You're right.' Molly felt relieved. They probably wouldn't call on the Reserves straightaway either.

Cath sat at the table. 'Stupid to worry when there's probably no need. But we might as well make the most of this breakfast. Food prices are going up. Sugar'll be double the price tomorrow. George, give your Uncle Jimmy a shout. Tell him his breakfast's ready.'

Jimmy's eyes were ablaze with excitement when he entered the room. He sat at the table, humming 'We're Soldiers of the King'.

Molly and Cath exchanged glances and raised their eyebrows but kept their mouths shut. The next day he came home at lunch time with the news that Mr Collins had received a letter from the War Office telling him to report for active service.

'You saw him?' said Molly, rising from her seat.

'No. Mrs Collins came in to tell us. He had to go immediately, the lucky dog!'

Cath made an exasperated noise and told her husband to shut up and talk of something else.

'No,' said Molly, putting a hand on his arm. 'Tell me – where did he have to report?'

He shrugged. 'I don't know. She didn't say and I didn't think of asking. Does it matter? You can't go chasing after him, Moll.'

'As if she would!' said Cath indignantly. 'She might have been meeting him on the sly a while ago but she wouldn't chase after him.'

'How did you know?' asked Molly.

'I'm not daft. You'd come back looking different. Not exactly starry-eyed, but I knew.' Cath glanced at Jimmy. 'So shut up, you, about war.'

Molly walked out of the room, wishing she could have Nathan safely with her right now. She was going to have to keep in closer touch with Doris to find out how he was getting on. It was unlikely he would write to Molly herself after the way she had walked out on him.

A recruiting centre was set up in the Old Haymarket and most evenings in the *Echo* there was an advertisement stating *Your King and Country need YOU*. Despite Kitchener's stating the war could be a long one, young men from Liverpool's shipping and business offices rushed to volunteer. Lord Derby called them the Pals. A month later an advertisement appeared in the *Echo*, saying married men and widowers with children could now volunteer. Jimmy was one of the first and was soon off to Lord Derby's green acres at Knowsley Hall where, dressed in civvies and shouldering a broomstick, he began his basic training.

Lucky Frank, he was out of it, thought Molly, as reports of the war filled newspapers daily and she worried herself sick about Nathan. One minute victories were being claimed. The next there were heavy losses and the need for more men was being announced. Molly collared Doris the next time she visited her mother, asking after Nathan and how Jessica was in his absence.

'He's written to her. He's just outside Hull now at a training camp. He tells her mainly about the presents the townspeople have given them: fruit, chocolate, cigarettes, books and magazines.' Doris ticked them off on her fingers. 'Not bad being a Tommy, is it? He's a lance corporal now, yer know? They want him to stay over here and train the men. It's unfair,' she said indignantly. 'Charlie went and volunteered but they wouldn't have him because of his hand. He's real upset.'

Molly agreed it was unfair but like most women prayed the war would be over by Christmas.

It wasn't. And by then she knew Nathan had decided to have a go at the Boche. He sailed to Le Havre in November and made it sound very jolly to Jessica, writing about sipping *vin blanc* and practising his French.

'I don't suppose it's all fun, though,' said Doris seriously. 'He mentions the cold and I read in the *Echo* about some of them soldiers having frostbite in the trenches. I've taught Jessica to knit and turn a heel and she's busy making him some socks.'

Molly was proud of her daughter and wondered at Nathan for risking his life when he had her to think about but she supposed it was what he had been trained for and now he wanted to put it into practice.

She was curious to know how they were managing at the factory but Jimmy was no longer around for her to ask. Cath and his mother were busily knitting for him and trying to keep their fears at bay. Already the *Echo* was displaying photographs and names of Merseysiders killed on active service.

It was towards the end of January 1915 that Molly discovered that Nathan was in Boulogne where he was having treatment for trench foot. The news came via Doris through her sister. Rob

Fletcher had joined the navy at the outbreak of war and was serving on a troop carrier. Apparently he'd asked Nathan about the fighting and he'd made jokes about Fritz and whizzbangs and sausages. She guessed, though, that it was no joke at the front.

Molly was busy during the weeks to come. Miss Lightfoot, who was now in charge of the Garment and Embroidery room, turned up at the house, asking could Molly do some more work for them? She was pleased about that as it had petered out after she'd stopped seeing Nathan.

In March news came that Jimmy had been killed in action. 'That's it then, isn't it?' said a white-faced, pregnant Cath, crushing the telegram and flinging it on the fire. 'He's gone. He did his bit all right, didn't he?'

'Oh, Cath, I'm so sorry,' said Molly, putting her arms round her, thinking this kind of news was the last she needed.

'Not as sorry as I am or his mam will be.' Tears thickened Cath's voice as she struggled to control herself.

'You cry,' whispered Molly, her own mouth trembling. 'It'll be better for you.' Cath sobbed on her shoulder and tears ran down Molly's own cheeks as she imagined how she would feel if Nathan were killed.

After that sad news Cath was out of the house more often than she was in it, spending time with Jimmy's mother, the pair of them comforting each other.

Miss Lightfoot called again, although more often than not a messenger brought work to Molly. They talked and when the other woman realised Molly was a shareholder in the business, she said, 'You should be having more of a say in things. There's talk of changes coming.'

'What kind of changes?' It was well over a year since Molly had received a report or any dividends from Mr Taylor.

'To do with the war. We're getting work from the factory in Leeds. That's why you're so busy. There's talk of them using their building for the war effort.'

'In what way?'

'We haven't been told. Maybe you should ask Mrs Collins?'

'Do you see much of her?'

'More than we used to.'

Molly was thinking of acting on what she'd said when Doris called. She told Molly that Nathan had been gassed and shipped home to a hospital in Birmingham. As well as that Frank was out of gaol and had now moved in with his mother. 'And yer know why that is, don't yer?' she said grimly.

'To be near Bernie, I imagine,' said Molly, who was more concerned about Nathan.

'Perhaps you should prepare yourself for a visit from your husband?' said a concerned Doris.

Molly thanked her for the thought, and after she'd left decided not to wait for him to call but to take the fight into his corner by asking for a legal separation.

The next day she took a tram to Bootle. Ma opened the door just wide enough to poke her head out and glare at Molly. 'Took yer time coming, didn't yer? Well, yer too late. He's gone.'

'Gone where? To live with Bernie?'

'To sea, of course,' she snapped. 'His country needs him. And Frank's never been a boy to shirk his duty.'

Astonished, Molly turned on her heel and walked away.

It was a few days later that a German submarine sunk the passenger liner *Lusitania* and it occurred to Molly that Frank could have been killed. The whole of Liverpool was thrown into mourning and many women in her neighbourhood lost husbands or sons. People went on the rampage smashing and raiding the premises of German owned butchers, and music shops despite their proprietors having lived in the area for years. It appeared that the despised enemy, whom the press consistently mocked and belittled, were far more powerful and daring than most of them had believed. There was not going to be any quick solution to end the war as the Government had initially promised, and there were definitely more changes afoot on the home front.

Miss Lightfoot called again, informing Molly that this week's work was to be her last. There was talk of the factory being closed down. Molly thought how Nathan had worked to make it prosper and came to a decision. Two days later with her finished work in hand, she put on her Sunday best and walked to the factory. She was fortunate enough to arrive just as Lottie was stepping down from her motor.

'Mrs Collins!' called Molly. 'May I have a word?'

A frown creased the other woman's smooth white brow as she stared at Molly. 'I feel I should know you, but—'

'Molly Payne. It's a few years since we met. I'm Nathan's second cousin and a shareholder in the company.'

Charlotte's expression altered. 'I thought you'd gone off somewhere? There were rumours.'

Molly felt embarrassed but wasn't about to back down. 'Well, you shouldn't believe everything you hear. I've heard you're planning on closing down this factory?'

Charlotte looked startled. 'Who told you that?'

'Does it matter? I want to know why. Whether it's something to do with the war effort?'

'Ah!' Charlotte smiled. 'I suppose you're thinking about your dividends? Well, I can tell you that things are looking up.' She clapped her hands and rubbed them together.

Molly smiled. 'I'm glad to hear it. But I still want to know what your plans are?'

Charlotte hesitated. 'Perhaps you should come inside and I'll ask Miss Jones to bring us some tea.'

Molly followed her to the office which had once been Nathan's and memories came flooding back. She longed to see him. After sending the secretary to make them tea, Charlotte waved Molly to a chair and sat down behind Nathan's desk.

'How many uniforms do you think an army needs, Mrs Payne?'

'Thousands, I should imagine.'

Charlotte smiled happily. 'Thousands and thousands! We've turning our whole factory in Leeds over to making them. We need more machines there and I just won't have the time to be travelling backwards and forwards.'

'I see. Does Mr Collins know?'

Charlotte's eyes slid away from Molly's and there was a pause before she said with a smile, 'Of course. He realises that with him gone and most of the men, we won't have the manpower to keep this factory going.'

'You said manpower? It's women who work in the Garment and Embroidery room.'

There was a pause. 'I know that but with more men leaving soon—'

'How do you know they'll be leaving?'

'The call for more volunteers will soon be going out. Lord Curzon has said we're no where near the end of this war. Sacrifices are going to have to be made. The Church will have to wait for its cassocks and albs and candles.'

'He said that?'

'No, no. You *are* funny!' Charlotte laughed. 'Our French allies are covering themselves in glory, trying to hold back the Hun. They're losing thousands of men. We have to get more involved. So there's going to be a need for more uniforms, more guns and more shells. We're fighting evil, Mrs Payne, and with God's help our wonderful, brave men will defeat the enemy!'

Molly was completely taken aback. 'I thought you were a suffragette, only interested in votes for women and their cause?'

'I am. And this is the way to do it.' Her eyes shining, Charlotte leaned across the desk towards Molly. 'Mrs Pankhurst says we must get behind our men. Show them where their duty to their country lies. As I said, as more of them march off to war, women are going to have to fill their posts. We'll show them we're equal to the task and just as good as they are!'

'I see. And does Mr Collins know how you feel?'

Before Charlotte could answer there was a knock on the door and she called, 'Enter!' Miss Jones came in with the tea tray and Charlotte sent her out again.

Molly took a biscuit and nibbled on it before saying, 'Mr Collins, how is he? I heard he was gassed and in hospital in Birmingham.'

Charlotte fixed her with a stare. 'Where do you get your information from?'

Molly smiled. 'I have my spies.'

'Well, they haven't kept you up to date. He's now down in Eastbourne convalescing at Summerdown Camp.' Charlotte sighed. 'He wants me to take Jess there as soon as the school holidays start. It's a bore, really.'

'Perhaps I could take her for you?' said Molly, surprising not only herself.

'You?'

'I'm very fond of Jessica. I've known her since she was born.'

Lottie blinked rapidly. 'I don't know if I was ever told that. Or maybe I was. I've forgotten. What happened to your husband? Wasn't he one of the heroes of the riots a few years back?'

'He's at sea now. Like you, I'm having to make my own decisions. I have my own clothing business.' That was true in a way, although it sounded grander than it actually was. 'I've been working flat out and could do with a holiday in the South.'

Charlotte held her gaze a little longer before smiling. 'Yes, I suppose you could take her, seeing as she knows you.'

'I'll need some money. I've had no dividends for the last year. And I'd like that money, please.'

'Of course! It'll be a relief not to have to worry about my stepdaughter. What with Nat's mother to keep my eye on as well as a business to run, I don't know whether I'm coming or going. Nat's sent me the names of some hotels in Eastbourne. I'll book you and Jess into one.'

'And my son as well, if you would,' said Molly, getting to her feet. 'I'll come and see you again as soon as school's finished.'

She did not know how she got out of that office without throwing her arms in the air and dancing. She was going to spend time in Jessica's company, and hopefully sort out a few things with Nathan as well.

When she told Cath, her sister-in-law smiled. 'I don't blame you for going to see him. Make the most of it. Who knows if you'll ever see him again?'

'It's not like that,' protested Molly, reddening. 'It's purely business. I don't trust that woman. She's got the bit between her teeth and wants to run the Leeds factory flat out and sod Liverpool. I didn't believe her when she said Nathan knew what was going on.'

'Would she have agreed you could go down there if that was true? She must realise you'll tell him.'

'Why? In her eyes I'm not going down on business, I'm looking after Jessica.'

'When in fact you're going to tell Mr Collins?'

'Of course,' said Molly with a smile.

But when Molly next saw Charlotte she had changed her mind. 'I've decided I should see Nat after all. I mean, he's suffered for his country,' she said with a sigh. 'I should be a good wife to him.'

'Then you won't want me,' said Molly, the sunshine going out of her day.

'Oh, you must come too!' Charlotte's bright blue eyes widened. 'I'd appreciate your company. It'll be easier for me driving if you're there to make Jessica behave — and I can tell you all about the Movement.' Molly was surprised but did not argue. Better to be going than to be left behind.

–

Summerdown Camp was about a mile outside the town of East-bourne, nestling at the foot of Beachy Head. It was surrounded by a wire fence but inside the army huts were set among gardens bright with flowers. Charlotte parked the motor outside the gates and they were directed to the hut which Nathan shared with several other men.

They found him sitting outside in the sun, reading a newspaper. He was clad in blue trousers, white shirt and red tie, the same as most of the men were wearing. The legs were turned up at the bottoms as the trousers were much too long for him. Molly felt very peculiar as she paused to watch him, allowing Charlotte to go ahead with Jessica. The girl broke into a run, shouting, 'Daddy, Daddy!'

Nathan's head turned and he rose to his feet, catching Jessica to him as she reached him. He hugged her tightly, kissing her hair. There was an expression on his face that caused a lump to rise in Molly's throat.

'You look a fright, darling,' said Charlotte. 'Isn't there a tailor in this town?'

He made no answer, eyes going past her to where Molly and George waited. 'Perhaps you'd like to fix them for me, Moll?' he said with a glimmer of a smile. 'You're the seamstress.'

'I'm on holiday.' She smiled, relieved he was not going to hold that last farewell against her. She held out her hand.

Nathan clasped it firmly. Molly realised he was trembling. 'How are you? You look—' She searched for words as her eyes scanned his face.

'A wreck?' he supplied with a rueful grin.

'You said it.' She managed to infuse amusement into her voice. 'But you're alive and that's the main thing.'

A shadow crossed his face but all he said was, 'How about a cup of tea?'

'We thought we'd take you out,' said Charlotte, eyes going from his face to Molly's. 'I've the motor outside. That's if you don't mind being seen in town like that? Although I did think to bring you a change of clothes – just in case you only had your uniform. And I've brought you some money as requested.'

'If you'd seen me covered in mud a few months ago you wouldn't have recognised me,' he said lightly. 'In comparison today I'm fragrant and look devilishly smart in this gear. I'll just get the jacket to go with the trousers. Come in and see our Home Sweet Home.'

The four of them trooped after him into the hut, Jessica clinging to his arm; George pressing close to Molly's skirts as he glanced around. The beds were neatly made, the asbestos walls bright with hand-painted pictures displayed above the bed heads.

'Pussy cat,' said George, pressing his finger against the head of a tiger.

'It's a tiger, silly,' said Jessica in superior tones. 'And it could eat you up in one bite!' She snapped her teeth at him.

He snapped back.

'Oh, do behave, you two,' said Charlotte irritably.

'Who's the artist?' asked Molly, looking at the other pictures with a marvelling eye.

'We all do our bit,' said Nathan, shrugging himself into a blue jacket. 'Shall we go?'

Charlotte took them back to their hotel where they had tea in a dining room overlooking the sea. There were plenty of people strolling along the Grand Parade taking the air and Molly would have found it relaxing if Nathan had not been sitting a foot away from her. As it was she was having difficulty keeping her eyes and hands off him. She sensed a great change in him and it made her feel divorced from reality. The discreet chink of china cups, the tiny fancy cakes on stands, the murmur of subdued conversation, the chandeliers and the southern voices, were all a far cry from home.

After tea he suggested they take the children crabbing on the rocks below the promenade. 'Then you'd best carry on wearing that awful suit,' said Charlotte. 'Unless you want me to get one of the maids here to make it more presentable while you're out?'

'You're not coming?' he said.

'Darling! Crabbing is hardly my style.' She smiled sweetly at him. 'But you enjoy yourself. I'll have a snooze. I'm tired after driving all the way here, despite the stopover.'

'You're a Trojan,' he said, brushing her cheek with his lips.

He and Molly were silent as they made their way to the beach. They stopped on the way and he bought buckets and spades, handing them to the children. George's face lit up. 'Thanks!' For a moment he hesitated, as if remembering something. Then he dashed down to the beach with Jessica.

The two adults followed at a more sedate pace. It was several minutes before Nathan broke the silence. 'What's going on? How is it you're here with Lottie? I was never so surprised in my life as when she told me you were coming.'

'I had to see you. I've been worried sick about you. That time I walked out on you—'

'Forget it. You're here now, that's all that matters. But you didn't say any of that to Lottie, I take it?' There was that old glint in his eyes.

'No. I just offered to look after Jess. Did you know she's planning on closing the Liverpool factory?'

'Yes. Mr Taylor wrote to me.'

Molly was dumbfounded. She had thought Charlotte would have played her cards closer to her chest. Or maybe Nathan had spies in the company? 'And you're in favour of it?'

'At the moment I don't really care. You wanted to know how I am.' His eyes clouded. 'I'm one of the lucky ones. We thought we heard the order to retire and scarpered when we saw this yellow-green cloud coming towards us from the German lines. It was...' His voice trailed away and Molly saw beads of sweat break out on his face.

She slipped her hand into his and squeezed it gently, realising that the war was the only thing that had been on his mind for months. 'Wicked and cruel, that's the Hun! They're devils who have to be stopped.'

Nathan looked down at her and she waited for him to agree with her but instead a shout of laughter burst from him and, keeping hold of her hand, he ran with her to the beach where the children were already digging in the sand.

Perhaps his mind's going? thought Molly. But he seemed perfectly normal as he talked to the children about the sands at Blackpool. She felt tender, almost maternal towards him as she sat, hugging her knees, gazing at the three of them. She felt happy. Here were the most important people in her life.

Molly wanted her time in the South to be carefree but at the back of her mind there were always her feelings for Nathan and a determination to broach the matter of the factory closing again. It was getting time alone with him that was the trouble. Charlotte took them out most days in the motor to nearby Pevensey or Hastings, never seeming to want Nathan to herself. It was as he had said, their marriage was a sham.

In the evenings they had dinner and drinks and made conversation with other people at the hotel. There were plenty of wounded soldiers there who seldom spoke about the front, only talking of their off duty experiences in French villages or towns.

The day before they were due to return to Liverpool Jessica and George were asked to join a party of other children. Molly thought that she should offer to let Charlotte spend the last day with Nathan on her own. But, holding a hand to her forehead, she drooped against her pillows in bed and whispered, 'I've got this terrible headache. D'you think you could see Nat and tell him I can't come today? But I'll definitely bring Jess to say goodbye in the morning before we go.'

'Of course,' said Molly, relieved.

Immediately she went and asked reception if she could have a picnic for two. Then she put on the cream blouse and green skirt she had made for the Whit holiday that year and hurried over to the camp.

Nathan saw her coming and came to meet her. 'What's up?'

'The children have gone to a party and Lottie has a terrible headache. I've brought us a picnic. I thought you might know somewhere we could go. If that's what you'd like to do?' she added, feeling shy all of a sudden.

'Right!' he said, eyes bright. 'I'll get my jacket.'

He reached for her hand as they struck off from the rear of the camp and Molly did not pull away. Neither of them spoke as they climbed to the top of Beachy Head. Once there they sat together in the long grass. 'The factory in Liverpool,' she began.

'You want me to keep it open?'

'Yes.'

'Then I will. You'll have to work out how it's to be done.' He drew her to him and kissed her.

Only for a moment did Molly consider the moral aspect of what they were doing. Then she thought of how she loved him and how she would feel if he was killed before they had known their happiness again.

Nathan eased her down on the ground, unfastening her blouse. She drew his head on to her breast, remembering his face as he'd talked about the cloud of gas at the front. She determined to help him forget such horrors. There was no discussion about how far they should go.

Afterwards they sat, having their picnic, looking out over the Channel to France. They talked about the children. She told him about Bernie and Frank and her thoughts on getting a separation.

'A divorce, Moll?' said Nathan. 'Nothing's going to be the same after the war. If I survive I'm going to ask Lottie for one too.' He gathered her into his arms once more.

'Listen, I'll write to my solicitor and ask him to make over a quarter of my shares to George immediately.'

'But, Nathan—'

'Shush! You'll be his trustee and have the right to vote on his behalf. And I'm leaving another quarter to you in the event of my death.'

She couldn't believe it. What would Mr Taylor think about Nathan's changing his will? What would Lottie think? But probably she wasn't going to get to know. It seemed impossible that Nathan would die. 'Don't talk about dying! I can't bear it.' She put her hand over his mouth.

He kissed her fingers. 'I have to. In a way I hate it that the Leeds factory will make money from this lousy war but you keep the Liverpool one open. Even if it's only making candles and selling incense burners.'

Molly nodded. 'Will you tell Lottie what you've decided about Liverpool?'

He threw back his head and laughed. 'And have her make your life a misery all the way home! No. She'll find out soon enough from Taylor.'

After that they were silent for a while, avoiding any other mention of the future, watching small airships patrolling the Channel on the look-out for German U-boats. Molly wondered if they would ever see each other again.

Chapter Eighteen

Molly found it a wrench saying goodbye to Jessica but her daughter asked if George could come and play at her house.

Lottie was in full agreement. 'Come Saturday week and we can talk.'

Molly wondered whether she would be as cordial when she received the letter from Mr Taylor about the Liverpool factory. She went into town to see him and at the same time visited the Parisian Photo Company, as Nathan had asked for a picture of George and herself. She sent it off on the day of their visit to Blundellsands.

Lottie appeared to be in a good mood. Apparently there was a sale of silk on at Lewis's and she had been shopping. 'I had a lovely time. I'll show you what I bought later. But first we must talk business.' She waved Molly to a chair. 'I've had a meeting with Nat's solicitor and he wants you more involved in the business. Says it will help me out as well as you. He's made over some shares to George as well. I never realised he was Nathan's godson?'

'Oh, yes,' said Molly, crossing her fingers and thinking, So *that's* how he explained away his actions.

Lottie sighed. 'Mr Taylor has his spies apparently and Nat says I'm to keep the Liverpool factory going. What are your opinions on that?'

Relieved she seemed so amenable, Molly said, 'I think we could find different work for the women on the sewing machines and I don't mean uniforms. I hate saying this but black's going to be the dominant colour for a lot of women this season.' She cleared her throat. 'Did you know there've been over forty-two thousand casualties in the Dardanelles alone? I know many of them are from the colonies but even so a lot of our men were killed. And if our business were to grow, it would give some war widows a means of support, too.'

Lottie smiled. 'You're right. There's a market there and someone's got to fill it.'

'Perhaps we should be thinking of taking on more women in the candlemaking room, too, while we still have some men to train them? Although that'll depend on how much paraffin wax we're able to lay our hands on with the German U-boats so busy. There could be a shortage – and the same with timber, silver and cotton.'

'I never realised that.' Lottie put her chin in her hand. 'Clever you.'

Molly flushed. 'Not really. I didn't even think about it until we got back and I heard another ship had been sunk.'

'I'm pretty certain we have materials stockpiled. We'll just have to hope we don't run out before the end of the war.' She stood up and smiled. 'And now that's sorted out, come and see what I bought in the sales.'

They went upstairs and on the way met a much older Mrs Collins. She appeared to have shrunk, lost teeth and looked generally feeble, only mumbling indistinctly as they passed. Molly was relieved she did not appear to recognise the visitor.

They entered Lottie's bedroom where lengths of striped oriental satin in green and heliotrope were draped over a chaise-longue. Lottie picked up a length of material and held it against herself. 'What do you think? Could you make something up for me?'

'Easy,' said Molly, thinking it was one way to make up for having committed adultery with her husband.

When she returned home it was to find the house full of women: Jimmy's mother, Mrs McNally – and, heavens, Ma Payne with Lucy on her knee! Instantly she realised what must have happened as Jimmy's mother smiled through her tears. 'It's a boy. Dead quick, she was. And she's calling him after his dad.'

Molly took the stairs two at a time and found Cath resting against the pillows, her son cradled in her arms. 'Hiya! You've missed all the excitement.' She gazed lovingly down at her child. 'What d'you think? Just like his dad?'

Molly's eyes filled with tears and she could not speak as she sat on the bed and touched the baby's soft cheek. At last she managed to find her voice. 'I see Ma's downstairs?'

'Yes, I thought I should make things up in case anything went wrong. She's quiet for her, though. I expected her to rave at me for sticking by you but she hasn't and neither has she mentioned our Frank. I haven't asked but maybe something's happened to him.'

'She'd have told you. It's probably his carrying on with Bernie. She's realising he's not the altar boy she's always thought. Although I'll probably get the blame for that too,' said Molly cheerfully. 'Want a cup of tea?'

'So where've yer bin?' said Ma Payne belligerently after the other women left. 'I thought yer'd be looking after me daughter?'

'We look after each other.' Molly sat down, George resting against her knee, staring at Ma.

She stuck out her tongue at him and he smiled. The old woman sighed. 'He's growing up and our Frank doesn't know him. Not that he isn't more like yous than my boy.' It was as if she'd forgotten the possibility of Nathan's being George's father. 'How's Frank? Does he write?'

Ma grunted and pushed herself out of the chair. 'As if you cared! I'd best be going. Our Josie'll be wondering where I am.'

'Shall we be seeing you again?'

'Yeah, well, yer just might. Can't let Jimmy's ma be taking that new grandson of mine over.'

Within weeks the call for skilled men to work in munitions went out. People were going to have to work harder, the news-papers said. A new law was brought in cutting drinking hours on Merseyside. Molly smiled to herself as she unpacked rolls of black bombazine. There were plenty in Liverpool who weren't going to be pleased about that!

Lord Derby, director of recruiting, began a new drive for men to replace those who had fallen at the front. At the same time there were articles in the *Sunday Herald* about THE WAR AND THE SOUL. The Church preached about Christ's sacrificial death on the cross in his fight against the Devil, but the last thing Molly wanted was Nathan making the ultimate sacrifice.

He returned home for six days' draft leave, looking healthy and fit. Molly met him at the factory but with Lottie there could do no more than ask how he was and where he was heading.

'Gallipoli. I've no wish to return to Flanders,' he said, smiling faintly. 'No rain and mud there. It'll be nice and warm.'

She was silent, remembering that the 1st Lancashires had suffered heavily there in the early months of the year.

They showed him round the factory and he seemed satisfied with what they were doing. There were plenty of orders for mourning clothes coming in and they were keeping up the candle production.

That evening Nathan came to call on Molly. Cath made herself scarce, taking the children with her. Molly smiled at him and took both his hands in hers, placing them round her waist. 'Thoughtful, isn't she? I don't know what she thinks we're going to get up to.'

'I'm sure she knows.' He crushed her against him and kissed her hard before lifting her off her feet and carrying her upstairs.

Molly felt a stirring in the pit of her stomach as he put her down. That old attraction that had drawn them together in the beginning was still very strong. They kissed almost as if they wanted to devour each other. He nibbled right down her arm to her fingertips. It tickled and made her laugh. 'That's what I like to hear,' he murmured, 'you laughing.'

'Haven't had much to laugh at for a long time.'

'No. I'll have to make it up to you one day.' He undressed her with impatient fingers before carrying her over to the bed.

She watched him strip, the evening light playing over his supple body, hardened with training for battle. There was no thought in her mind of anything but pleasing him. When he lay beside her she turned, fitting the contours of her body against his in an act of remembrance. They touched each other all over as if to make sure nothing had changed since last they were together. Then he rolled her over on to her back and their lovemaking was frenzied.

Afterwards they lay quietly holding hands. 'I wish I didn't feel so guilty about Lottie,' murmured Molly. 'We're friends now. Did she ask where you were going?'

'No. She wasn't interested. So stop worrying and just think of us.'

She was to see him twice more before he left and their parting was awful.

–

By the end of November women tram conductors had made an appearance on Merseyside and Molly and Lottie had taken on more female workers. Christmas came and Molly was ready for a couple of days off. The Rotunda theatre had been closed for a while but it promised to be open on Boxing Day, showing *Cinderella*.

'That's just what we need,' she said to George.

'Us too,' said Cath. 'I'll get Ma and Jimmy's mam to meet us there.'

But even at the pantomime they couldn't forget the war. Ma told Molly that Frank's ship had been torpedoed but he was safe. 'They've given him another ship. One of them troop carriers. I don't think he's too happy about that. Prime targets they are.' Molly agreed but thought wryly that Frank seemed to have more lives than the proverbial cat.

She received a letter from Nathan, in which he sounded almost happy, writing about children diving for money in their birthday suits. She thought of George who swam in the canal in next to nothing. Nathan had seen dolphins in the Aegean and wrote about Aussies with plenty of money to spend and of the gambling that went on into the wee small hours. *I tell you, Moll, we could have made a fortune supplying them with candles.*

In spring she received another letter saying he was heading north for more *vin blanc.* Her spirits drooped. That could only mean Flanders. But she pulled back her shoulders and told herself she must not think the worse. Instead she thought of the war ending and his getting a divorce and one day marrying her. She must ask Ma for the name of Frank's ship and write to him soon. Surely he would want to marry Bernie?

-

In August Frank turned up at the factory, taking Molly utterly unawares. She did not know what to expect and found herself gripping her fountain pen like a dagger as she stared across the desk at him. He was still as handsome as ever but he looked older, new lines of strain about his mouth and eyes.

'Ma told me you were working here. I thought we needed to talk.' He swayed as if he had been drinking.

'Why don't you sit down before you fall down?'

He did not answer and there was an expression in his eyes that vanquished her fear. Getting up, she pushed him into a chair at the other side of the desk, realising as she bent over him that it was rum he'd been imbibing. 'What's up? War getting to you?' He did not answer. 'You wouldn't be the only one, Frank. There are many others finding it all too much.'

He dropped his head in his hands and his shoulders shook. She fought against feeling pity for him but after a moment placed a hand on his shoulder. 'It'll be all right, Frank. You'll cope.'

He shook his head. 'You've no idea, have you, Moll? Ma didn't tell you,' he said brokenly.

'Tell me what?'

'Bernie's dead. Died having my child.'

Molly was truly shocked. 'Oh, my God,' she whispered. 'Poor Bernie.'

'A boy.' His hands dangled at his sides. 'Her ma's looking after it. She won't let me see him, though. Won't even look me in the face.' His eyes were bloodshot and damp. 'The worst thing about it, Moll, is that I never loved her. I only went with her because I was so bloody furious with you.'

That annoyed her. 'So you're blaming me?'

'Bloody hell, yeah! If you hadn't carried on with snotty-nosed Mr Collins, I'd have kept meself to meself.'

Her eyes flashed. 'I didn't carry on with him as you put it while I was with you, Frank. It was just the once, when you were supposed to be dead. I was too scared to tell you about it. I thought you'd beat me. Kill me even.'

'You should have waited longer. I loved you.'

'I was in love with you once but it's over now.'

He glanced about him and muttered, 'You only love him because he's got all this. But if you're thinking you can shack up with him once this war's over, you can forget it. You're still married to me.'

'Don't threaten me, Frank.' Her eyes flashed. 'I'm not scared of you anymore. I can get a divorce on the grounds of your adultery. Now go! I don't want to see you here again.'

He dragged himself out of the chair and for a moment she thought he would go for her and stepped back, brandishing the fountain pen. But he stumbled towards the door.

She hurried after him and closed it, resting her back against it. Something inside her wanted to cry even though she was angry with him. He looked so terrible and she did feel to blame. But there was no going back. She would write to Nathan and tell him of Frank's visit and that it looked like her divorce could turn out to be nasty.

Not long afterwards Molly received a postcard postmarked Birmingham saying that Sergeant Nathan Collins had been wounded and was being transported to Manchester. It was signed by a clergyman. It did not say where the hospital was and she worried about how to find him but the following morning she received a brief letter from Nathan himself saying he was at Lower Broughton School. She arranged for Miss Lightfoot to take over and took a train to Manchester, worrying herself silly in case Nathan might have lost a leg or worse.

She found him with all his limbs intact, although one leg was in a cast and heavily bandaged.

'Hello, luv.' She bent and kissed him but his lips were cold and unresponsive and Molly's heart sank. What could be wrong?

'I'm glad you've come.' His voice sounded odd.

'A whole string of horses wouldn't have kept me away.' She covered the hand that lay on the coverlet with her own.

He gazed down at their hands before lifting his head and the pain in his eyes frightened her. 'What's wrong? Your leg? You're not going to lose it, are you?' Her voice rose.

'No. Although it'll put me out of the war. A sniper's bullet's shattered the thigh bone. Reach into that drawer. There's an envelope there. Take it out and open it.' His voice was colourless and somehow that scared her even more. She wished he would tell her what was wrong.

Two photographs fell out of the envelope. The one of herself and George, and another of Jessica. 'Photographs,' she murmured.

'Aye. I didn't see the likeness straightaway.' His voice was like ice. 'The photo of Jessica's new. I thought how alike the three of you were but I still didn't twig.' Molly felt as if she'd turned to stone. She'd never thought her worst nightmare would come true in such a mundane way. 'I showed them to one of the blokes on the way here. He thought you were my wife and Jessica our daughter. Then I looked at her photo closely and realised there was nothing of me or my first wife in her. What have you to say to that, Moll?'

She could not look at him as she searched for the right words. There weren't any. She could only whisper, 'You must have guessed why I did it?'

'No! You're not getting out of it like that!' he yelled. Several heads turned. 'You tell me why you swopped my daughter for your own?'

She looked at him then, trembling, holding her hands against her chest where she was hurting inside. 'I was scared! I had nothing! I thought I'd end up in prison – be accused of killing your daughter because she died in my care.' Her mouth quivered. 'She-she just didn't want to live. I tried so hard.' Tears started in her eyes as she remembered. Heads were turning and people were whispering.

'You should have told me!' said Nathan through clenched teeth.

'How? Wh-When your uncle acc-accepted and loved her an-and you were growing to love her too? I thought y-you could give her so much more than I could.'

'Thought how much *you* could get out of us as well!' His eyes were dark with fury and hatred.

'No!' She stumbled to her feet and rested her hands on the back of the chair. 'If you r-remember I'd already left b-before your uncle died b-because Frank came back.'

'Aye, and you left Jess for him! A fine mother you are!' She winced and jerked back her head as if he had slapped her. 'And you weren't even honest with him. Or were you? Perhaps the pair of you thought this up together to get your hands on my factory!' Her eyes widened in horror.

'How c-could you th-think like that? I've had nothing to do with Frank for years!'

'Liar! Have you forgotten you wrote and told me he'd been to the factory?'

She laughed hysterically. 'Would I have told you that if I had something to hide?'

'I don't know. I don't know you anymore.' He slumped against the pillows.

'You could take my word for it!' she whispered.

'How can I take your word for anything when you've been deceiving me for years?'

'I was scared you'd stop loving me.'

'You trust where you love. Perhaps I've deceived myself and you never loved me at all? You were only after what I could give you all the time.'

That was ridiculously unfair! The pain of it was suddenly too much for Molly and now she was angry. 'Maybe you're right. Your war's over. You can look after your own bloody factory from now on!' She left him, blinking back the scalding tears as a nurse hurried past her towards Nathan.

Chapter Nineteen

Molly was still trembling as she sat on the train. She had started to believe that things could work out for them. A divorce wouldn't be easy and would take years but it was something to get through like an illness. She had dreamed of herself and Nathan living with the children under one roof. How dare he insinuate she was a lousy mother! She'd show him! Tomorrow she would go to Leeds and bring her daughter home.

Her anger got her safely back to Liverpool without breaking down. She wanted to smash things, to rant and rave, to weep. But what good would that do? She had to face up to the truth. She had disowned her daughter and deceived Nathan.

What was she to do? How could she make matters right? It couldn't be in Jessica's best interests to take her away. How would she feel? But perhaps Nathan would disown her and Molly would have no option but to take her back. She tried to imagine her daughter's feelings when Nathan told her he wasn't her daddy. Molly went hot and cold, picturing her disbelief and bewilderment, her sense of loss. Surely it was too much for a child to cope with? And if Nathan could not accept her explanation, how could Jessica? Would she think Molly didn't want her and was only thinking of herself?

And what about George? Perhaps Nathan would come and take him? Maybe she should leave Liverpool and this time go where he'd never find them.

Molly sighed heavily. No. She must not do anything in haste. It was acting in haste that had got her into this mess. She must leave it to Nathan to make the first move. The same with the business. Despite what she had said to him, she could not leave things at the factory to fall apart. She cared too much. She must give him time to sort things out. But she would write to Lottie in Leeds, requesting that she ask Nathan to find someone else to take over the Liverpool end of the business.

Work was to be Molly's solace during the painful days that followed. Although she wondered each morning whether this would be her last in the factory there was no word from Nathan, Lottie or Mr Taylor. What was happening? Had Nathan told Jessica the truth? What should she do? Try and see him again? No. Molly could not bear the thought of his looking at her with such loathing and pain in his eyes. What about the shares he had given to George? Should she send them back? No! she thought stubbornly. He was Nathan's son. The income from them she would save for his future. He must not suffer for her mistakes.

Weeks of worry and uncertainty passed before Molly received a letter from Mr Taylor, saying that his client would appreciate it if she closed the factory down. Now the end had come she was stunned and without a second thought left the building and made her way to the solicitor's office in North John Street. The cleaner was just leaving and Mr Taylor about to seat himself behind his desk when Molly stormed into his office and threw the letter on his desk. 'I consider that ungrateful and rude,' she panted.

'Mrs Payne, really! What *is* the matter?'

'If you don't know then I don't know who should. I've worked my guts out, keeping that place going.' Molly sat down abruptly. There was a silence in which tears rolled down her cheeks.

A large, white handkerchief appeared within her line of vision. Without looking up she took it and wiped her damp face and blew her nose. 'I'll launder it and bring it,' she said in a muffled voice.

'There's no hurry. I assure you my client does not intend any ingratitude or rudeness. You wrote saying you did not wish to continue to run the factory and as Mr Collins will not be coming back to Liverpool just yet, he thought it best to do what you suggested. The powers that be consider that once he is fully recovered he will be able to drill and train the new volunteers for the front. At the moment he is convalescing in Yorkshire with his wife and daughter.'

Molly's head slowly lifted. Nathan must have been unable to face Jessica with the truth. Perhaps he still loved her daughter? Oh, she hoped so! 'Could you write and ask if he really wants the factory closed down? It's doing well, as you know. I'll stay on if it's his wish.' She stood up and held out her hand. 'Thank you for giving me your time, Mr Taylor.'

He smiled gravely as he shook it. 'It is my pleasure, Mrs Payne.'

Molly went out into the sunshine, heart-sore but feeling much more able to cope. Nathan had not rejected her daughter in the eyes of the world and for this she was grateful. It was obvious there was not going to be a divorce for the moment. But what about when this terrible war was over? What then? Would time alter things? Could Nathan ever forgive her? As she passed black-clad women in Dale Street, Molly thought, I'm sick of black. If Nathan agreed to keep the factory open and in her charge she would make a change. Most women wouldn't stay in mourning indefinitely and subdued colours would be the way ahead: greys, mauves and blues, in plain and simple styles.

Within days she received a letter from Lottie saying she could keep the factory going.

Molly wondered what was going on in Nathan's head. She still loved and missed him and found it hard to accept that she had lost him. But he must have calmed down and forgiven her enough to allow her to continue working. For that she was grateful. Now she had to live her life without him.

Molly had given Frank little thought during the last few months so that it came as something of a shock when Ma called to tell her that the troop carrier he had been serving on had been torpedoed and he was reported missing. Molly could only think that the news had come too late for her to feel anything but numb disbelief. Within days, though, she had another visitor with news of Frank. Jack Fletcher.

'Long time no see,' Molly said drily, having long forgiven him.

His weather-beaten face turned the colour of beetroot. 'I'm sorry, lass. I behaved like an old fool that time and I've been too embarrassed to visit thee since.'

'So what are you doing here now?'

'I thought I'd best let thee know that Frank's been picked up, along with our Rob.'

She couldn't believe it! 'That figures,' she said finally. 'He has nine lives, Frank has. But I didn't realise they were on the same ship?'

'Aye, lass. Worked in the stoke hole together. If they hadn't been off shift at the time and on deck they wouldn't have survived. Strange when thee thinks how they wanted to bash each other's head in at Doris's wedding. Jealousy's an evil thing.' Jack had the grace to blush as he realised what he'd said and left swiftly.

Ma called in on Molly and Cath some weeks later to say Frank was home. 'He's only a shadow of himself and is behaving all queer. I don't know what I'm going to do with him,' she complained. 'He had a bad bang on the head, yer know.'

'Our marriage is dead, Ma,' said Molly firmly. 'I don't know what you think I can do about him.'

She grumbled on about a wife's duty but Molly ignored her. It was not to be the last of Ma's visits, however. Every time she came it was to complain about Frank. It seemed he was incapable of holding a job down. 'He gets me down, moping about. He's all nervy. I can't be doing with it. I've Josie to look after as well as the lodgers, and I've had to get meself a cleaning job. It's going to kill me! Couldn't yer take him back? You're his wife. It's yer duty.'

Molly did not want Frank back but when he turned up on her doorstep one evening, looking like the dregs of mankind, she realised that perhaps she owed him something. He was after all the father of the daughter she had given away to another man. 'You can stay but I'm not sleeping with you,' she told him firmly.

'I couldn't do anything if you did,' mumbled Frank 'Nothing seems to be working properly. Not me head, nothing.'

Molly bought another single bed and Frank slept in George's room. He was no trouble but she could never forget he was in the house. He was constantly muttering to himself but did not actually cause her any extra work. He looked after himself, even cooking and taking the washing to the wash house, mumbling about the cockroaches he'd had to crunch through in the boiler room when he'd worked there. He would make her a cup of tea when she came in but they never had any conversation beyond hello, thank you or goodnight. Molly found this unnerving at times but couldn't help pitying him, remembering the man he once was.

Cath decided to move out. 'I can't cope with his mutterings and that vague expression he wears. For all we know he might turn violent again. Jimmy's mam's said several times it would be more convenient if I lived with her.'

Molly still had not heard anything from Nathan and as it looked as if the war could be coming to an end, she got in touch with Mr Taylor.

'Ah! I'm glad you phoned me, Mrs Payne. I was going to write to you. Mrs Collins will be paying you a visit next Thursday week before she goes on holiday.'

'What about Mr Collins?' said Molly, deeply disappointed.

'He's having some kind of operation on his leg. In a few weeks' time he'll be in touch.'

Immediately Molly began to worry about Nathan, wondering what kind of operation this was. She hoped he wouldn't lose his leg. But Lottie would know what was happening. Molly could ask her when she arrived next week.

She could not help smiling when Lottie drove up to the factory on a motor bike with sidecar attached, wearing goggles, a long leather coat and the kind of helmet airmen wore. 'You can't say that's one of the latest fashions,' Molly told her, hiding her amusement.

'Sensible, though. And I've become immensely sensible,' said Lottie, shaking out her hair.

Molly smiled. 'Is it sensible to ride such a thing? And those clothes… not very feminine.'

'Who cares? Haven't we proved we're equal to men? Anyway,' Lottie strode into the factory alongside Molly, taking her leather gauntlets off on the way, 'everything OK here?'

'Fine. How's Nathan? And Jessica?'

'Blundellsands, seeing Grandma. Then we're going up to the Lakes.' She sat down in front of the desk. 'How's your husband? Have you heard from him?'

Molly glanced at her secretary and sent her out for tea and biscuits. 'Yes, I've got him back living with me. His mother didn't want him. Frank's in a bit of mess. Nerves shot to pieces. Torpedoed twice.' She paused. 'How is Nathan, really? You haven't talked about the operation.'

'Oh, he's fine. Back home,' said Lottie carelessly. 'All the staff are fussing over him. He's got to rest his leg.'

'Poor Nathan.'

'Nonsense! He's enjoying himself. You know how men love being mothered.'

She left an hour later.

Molly had barely been in the building five minutes the next day when she was called to the telephone. 'It's Mr Collins,' whispered Miss Jones. 'He sounds terribly upset.'

Molly's heart missed a beat as she lifted the mouthpiece. 'Nathan?' she said tentatively.

'Molly, something terrible's happened. Lottie's crashed that damned machine of hers. She's dead and Jessica's unconscious in hospital. I thought you might want to go and be with her.'

304

Molly's knees buckled and she had to sit down. 'She's not going to die?' Her mouth felt as dry as a husk.

He did not answer, saying only, 'I'm sorry to break it to you like this but there was no other way. I'm hoping to get there myself but I'll have to find someone to drive me.'

'Where is she?' croaked Molly.

'Kendal. You should be able to get a train.'

'How did it happen?' She wanted to keep him talking just a little longer, gaining strength from the sound of his voice.

'Apparently there was a thunderstorm. The police said there'd been a lot of rain in the area round Shapfell. Lottie lost control avoiding a motor lorry. I'll have to go now. I want to get there as quickly as I can.' The line went dead.

'What is it, Mrs Payne? Shall I get you a cup of tea?' offered Miss Jones.

'Yes… no.' Molly stood up, one hand to her head. 'I'm going to have to take a couple of days off. I must see Miss Lightfoot, she'll have to take over.'

'But what's happened? Who's hurt?'

Molly stared at her. She wasn't seeing her secretary's face, only her daughter's. 'Mrs Collins has been killed,' she said, and hurried out.

Frank was not in the house so she packed a few things and left a note for George, eight now and mature for his years, before catching a tram to Exchange station. As she sat on the train she was aware of how scared she was of what she might find at the end of her journey. At the same time she was comforted by the thought of Nathan's getting in touch with her.

When she reached the hospital the Sister refused to let her on to the ward. 'Only family,' she decreed.

For a moment Molly considered telling her truth, that Jessica was her daughter, but Nathan arrived just at that moment. She gazed at him hungrily. Pain was etched into the lines of his face and, like Frank, he looked older than his years.

He brushed the nurse aside, took hold of Molly's arm and limped into the ward with her. She could hardly believe it was his hand on her arm. 'I've forgotten my stick,' he said gruffly, as if reading her mind.

The nurse hurried after them. 'Go away, woman!' roared Nathan. 'Isn't it enough that my wife has been killed? Mrs Payne has known my daughter since she was born. Now out of the way.'

'Mr Collins,' she chided. 'I just wanted to tell you that your daughter's regained consciousness and which bed she's in.'

He stared at her then smiled. 'I apologise. I was very rude.'

She blushed and went on ahead of them, stopping at a bed right at the end of the ward. 'Here she is.' The nurse smoothed the folded down sheet. 'Don't get her too excited.' She hurried off with a whisper of starched linen.

Jessica's eyes opened and she gazed up at them. 'Hello, Daddy. Mrs Payne, what are you doing here?'

Nathan sat on the chair at her bedside, his bad leg straight out in front of him, and in a gentle voice told her what had happened. Jessica burst into tears and Nathan put his arm round her as the girl buried her head against his chest.

Suddenly Molly could not bear it. Nathan did love Jessica and the girl loved him. They belonged together. She felt like an outsider. She left them alone, feeling an aching sensation inside her, and thinking what a fool she had been to forfeit her rightful place at Jessica's bedside. She went to the station but the train wasn't due for a couple of hours so she wandered aimlessly about the town, thinking of what she had lost.

Nathan found her standing on a bridge overlooking the River Kent. He was angry at first and she didn't blame him. 'Why didn't you stay? What the hell do you think I sent for you for? It hasn't done my leg a bit of good, chasing round trying to find you.'

'I'm sorry. But I felt I had no right to be there,' said Molly firmly.

'In God's name, I gave you the right when I rang you up and asked you to come,' yelled Nathan. 'I know I accused you of all sorts of things that time in the hospital but it came as a hell of shock and I was hurt. And look at me when I'm damn well shouting at you!'

Molly lifted her head and smiled faintly. 'I don't blame you for what you said. I deserved it. You're far more her father than I am her mother. You were right when you said I was a lousy parent.'

He lifted one hand and let it drop. 'Did I really say that?' His tone was milder.

'Not in so many words but that's what you meant and I agree with you.'

He said, exasperated, 'Stop sounding so bloody virtuous! We've got to talk but let's go down to the bank where I can sit.' He took her arm as he had earlier and leaned on it. 'I hated you for not trusting me with the truth but I think I understand now why you did it. But on top of that you got me to love another man's child. And bloody Frank's at that!'

'I never did it to gain anything for myself You have to believe that,' she said intensely.

'Of course I believe it. I haven't forgotten the times you wouldn't accept money from me.'

They were silent a moment.

Then Molly said with a sigh, 'I wanted the rearing of my own child. Instead, I've let other people be more of an influence in her life. I wanted her to have the kind of future money could bring. I wanted her to have you for a father, too. I love you both, Nathan. Giving her up was a real sacrifice.'

He nodded. 'How's George?'

Molly's face lit up. 'He keeps me going when I feel down.'

They had come to the seat and both sat down, gazing at the fast-flowing river.

Nathan broke the silence. 'So where do we go from here now Lottie's dead? She told me what you said about Frank. How the hell could you take him back?'

'I've asked myself that a thousand times. But perhaps if you saw him you might understand. Ma can't cope with him. Cath

307

has enough on her plate. There's no one else but me. We don't share a bedroom or anything like that but he needs someone to look after him.' She remembered the look she occasionally caught in Frank's eyes. 'He's a lost soul,' she whispered. 'A lost soul,' she repeated desperately. 'And I feel partly to blame for that. I've messed his life up as well as yours and mine.' She jumped to her feet, feeling terrible about what she was going to do. 'Forgive me, Nathan, but I must go. I'm sure Jessica's going to be all right now.'

'You're going?' He looked at her in disbelief.

She hesitated. 'I remember you telling me once that you took on Miss Lightfoot because she had a crippled mother. She hadn't the experience for the job but she needed the extra money it brought. Well, Frank's a mental cripple and he needs me. I love you, believe me, but you have Jessica to love you as well. Frank has no one.' She turned away.

'Moll! Don't go, please!'

His plea almost broke her but she kept on going, knowing she might never be happy again.

Chapter Twenty

It was on the train going home that she decided she would have to leave the factory. She had made a fair amount of money and so she decided to find a shop with a work room on Scotland Road and buy a few secondhand sewing machines on which to continue to make women's clothes; nothing too fancy or expensive. The kind of dresses, skirts and blouses for which there was a ready market. Perhaps eventually she might be able to afford a shop selling high-class fashions in Bold Street.

So she did just that, asking Mr Taylor to inform Nathan of her decision. She felt certain it would be easier for them both this way. In the days that followed, every time she set eyes on Frank she felt angry with him because she wanted Nathan. She still half expected to hear from him. Perhaps he would write to her angrily. Demand she give up George. But the only communication she received was through his solicitor, and that was about the business. Perhaps he had not believed her when she'd said she loved him?

Molly was grateful for one thing at least: that George and the man he regarded as his father kept each other company when she was busy. More often than not he and Frank could be found at a place the locals called Sebastapol where games of pitch and toss went on, or near the canal watching the barges being loaded. Sometimes Frank would join the boys swimming in the 'scaldies' at the back of Tate's sugar refinery, the water warmed by a factory outlet. She thought how different her son's life would have been if Frank had not survived when his ship was torpedoed. Then hated herself for almost wishing her husband dead.

One day Molly was surprised to see Jack Fletcher enter the house together with Frank and George at the end of a long day. 'What are you doing here? What's Frank done?' she said, immediately fearful.

Jack smiled. 'Hasn't done anything, lass. He wants to come on the barge with us.'

'You're joking?'

He shook his head. 'I don't think it's such a bad idea. Mrs McNally tells me thee'll be worrying about him once the lad's back at school. Young as he is, she tells me George keeps his eye on Frank but he's strong enough to help me load and unload. So what does thee think, Moll? I thought this was one way I could make things up to thee for that time. Will I take him off thee hands?'

'Oh, Uncle Jack! I could kiss you,' she said, and did. He blushed but she knew he would not take it seriously as he might have done once.

The next time Molly saw Mrs McNally, she thanked her. 'You don't know what a difference it's made. The worry was always there at the back of my mind. Frank's even sleeping on the boat now so I have no cares about him at all.'

'I'm glad to help yer, girl.'

'How's Doris?'

'She's getting on OK. Still looking after the old lady. Sees Mr Collins sometimes, but he doesn't look happy, she says.'

Molly felt a familiar ache at that but she had made her bed and had to lie on it.

–

As she cut through a swathe of white satin for a first communion dress Molly thought of Nathan, longing for the feel of his arms about her. Ever since Mrs McNally's mention of him she had felt restless. When she was home in the evenings she was unbearably lonely. George was often down by the canal talking to the bargees. Occasionally at weekends he would hitch a ride with Jack and Frank and be away all night.

Sometimes she would walk along the towpath in the early morning before going into the shop. At such times she would see her husband. The hard physical work of shifting coal had improved Frank's physique and hours in the open air had brought back the colour to his cheeks but his mental capacity was still limited.

There was a knock at the door and Molly went to answer it.

Mrs McNally stood there, obviously bursting to tell her something. 'I doubt yer've heard,' she said, 'Mrs Collins died and is getting buried beside her husband in that place up Lancashire. Our Doris said I was to tell yer.'

Dead? The old woman's dead at last! Molly thought frantically. Will Nathan sell the house and the factory? Cut all ties with Liverpool, live in Leeds and never come back? She had to see him. Even if it was just one last time. She would attend the funeral. After all, if his mother had never mixed up the babies in the first place she would not have loved and lost Nathan, and neither would she have George.

Having made up her mind, Molly decided to give herself a whole new look. She had her hair cut shorter and for a change bought, instead of made, herself a shorter length frock and matching coat in grey trimmed with fur. She had sworn never to wear black again.

On the morning of the funeral she inspected her face in the mirror and thought she looked washed out so applied the new cosmetics she had bought. Then she faced George. 'How do I look?'

'Not like you,' he said frankly, porridge spoon halfway to his mouth. 'More like one of those film stars you see at the cinema.'

'Thanks, son.' She smiled, ruffling his hair. 'You get on straight to school after you've finished breakfast.'

'Yes, Mam. Where are you going?'

'A funeral. Jessica's grandmother. Do you remember her?'

He looked thoughtful. 'Yee-es. She lives in that big house by the sands. Uncle Nathan's her dad. Why is it we don't see them anymore?'

'People drift apart. Live different lives,' Molly said lightly, pulling on her gloves.

'I think it's Dad. When he wasn't around we saw them.'

Her cheeks burned. 'That was because I used to work for Mr Collins. Anyway, I'll have to go now.'

George shrugged on his jacket. 'Mam, it's Friday. Let me come with you. I'd like to see them.'

She hesitated, thinking Nathan would probably like to see him too. 'You've got school.'

'You could give me a note on Monday, saying I was sick.'

'That's dishonest.'

'Just this once,' he pleaded.

She thought how nice it would be to have his company. 'OK! But you'll have to hurry.'

They were out of the house in minutes and made their way down to the canal. 'Hello, you two!' Molly called to the men.

'Good, thee's early and looking lovely as ever,' said Jack, smiling. 'We hardly recognised her, did we, Frank?'

'No. Who is she?' he said, chuckling.

'Thee wife, dafty!' Jack shook his head at Molly. 'Don't take any notice of him. He's in one of his queer moods today, finding everything funny.'

She pecked her husband's cheek, pitying him.

'Gerroff!' he said, scrubbing his face with his knuckles and hunching his shoulder. 'Ma won't like it.'

'You see little enough of her these days,' she said, accepting a cushion from Jack and making herself comfortable on the wooden seat. 'You'll just have to put up with me. I am your wife, more's the pity.'

He chortled. 'Got no wife. Live on the boat with Jack. No wife.'

She gave up and contented herself with watching the bank slide by, imagining the moment she saw Nathan.

Memory after memory trickled into Molly's consciousness as they approached St John's church. Why torture herself? There wasn't a thing changed since last she had met him. Suddenly she was nervous, thinking he might be angry to see her there after the way she'd left him in Kendal. She might have turned back if George had not been with her.

Then she caught sight of Nathan climbing out of a motor and was glad she'd come. He was as lean as ever, still drawing on that restless energy with which she had once been so familiar.

'That's him, isn't it? That's Uncle Nathan?' said George.

The man's head turned. 'Molly?' From the expression on his face he did not quite believe the evidence of his own eyes.

'Yes. It's me,' she said ungrammatically. 'I hope you don't mind us coming?'

'Of course not.' He walked slowly towards them, leaving those in the motor to get out without his help. 'How are you?' His eyes strayed to George and stayed there for several moments.

A voice called, 'Daddy!'

He glanced over his shoulder and then faced Molly again. 'Now's not the time to talk. I've got to bury my mother. You'll follow us in?'

'Yes. I suppose I should have worn black after all. I'm going to stick out like a sore thumb.' Her gaze fixed on the girl dressed in the black woollen suit with a large floppy black tammy set on top of her long brown hair.

'That's Jessica,' whispered George, as they followed him in. 'I remember she used to boss me about.'

Molly sat in a pew where she had a clear view of the back of Nathan's head. She gazed at his neatly cut hair. Despite its shortness it curled in the nape of his neck. As if in a trance she saw herself twisting those curls round her little finger and felt his head nestling in the palm of her hand. His lips were on hers and she was back in the nursery where they had made love on that golden August day the year Jessica was born. In a way it seemed a long time ago and yet in another no time at all.

The congregation stood for a hymn and she rose, catching sight of her wedding ring as she opened the hymn book. The organ launched into 'Crimond' and she was thinking of Frank now and the grief and pain their relationship had brought them. But without their marriage there would have been no Jessica. Oh, what was she going to do? What was she to say to Nathan? She just did not know. Agitated, she knew it was going to be terribly painful, speaking to him again. Nothing had changed. She was still married.

She decided not to wait for the coffin and chief mourners to leave first at the end of the service but pulled on George's arm while the last hymn was being sung, whispering for him to come.

'Why?' he mouthed.

'Just come.'

'What's up?' he asked as soon as they were outside the church.

'I don't want to talk about it,' said Molly, a tremor in her voice. 'Let's go and see if Jack and Frank are still at the bridge.'

'But aren't we going to talk to Uncle Nathan and Jessica?' He sounded disappointed.

She made no reply. George scowled. She tried to ignore him and carried on walking. They had almost reached the Packet House Hotel when she spotted Jack and Frank sitting in a patch of sunshine, supping a pint apiece.

'Thee's back quick,' said Jack.

'It's that woman again.' Frank's thick eyebrows twitched as he stared at Molly over the rim of his tankard.

'It's thee wife, dafty,' said Jack in long-suffering tones, getting to his feet.

'I didn't see any point in staying once the service was over,' said a breathless Molly. 'Mr Collins will have his guests to see to.'

Jack wiped the bench with a red handkerchief. 'Here, lass, sith thee down.'

Gratefully, Molly sank onto the bench. 'I'm feeling a bit shaky. I wouldn't mind a sherry, Uncle Jack?' She unfastened her handbag.

Jack disappeared inside the pub and Frank, glancing at Molly, hurried after him. There was silence except for a thrush singing its heart out in a nearby sycamore and the faint quacking of ducks from the canal below. George wandered down to the canal bank. Molly was suddenly in no rush to move. She closed her eyes, tired, having had little sleep last night, working herself upcome to the funeral and see Nathan.

Someone shook her shoulder. 'I was nearly asleep then, Jack,' she murmured.

'It's not Jack.'

Her eyes flew open as she recognised the voice. 'How did you know I was here?' she whispered.

'I didn't. Although I did wonder where you'd run off to,' said Nathan, a bitter note in his voice. 'We're having the funeral feast here. You and bloody Jack Fletcher! I should have guessed.'

Molly was about to deny there was anything between them when Jack came out of the inn with Frank. They both stopped, staring at Nathan. She wondered if Frank recognised him, but then, didn't he have enough trouble recognising her as his wife?

'Mr Collins, you know Mr Fletcher and my husband,' Molly murmured.

'Very funny, Moll,' said Nathan, glaring at the two men.

Frank dropped his head on one side. 'People I dunno in the pub. Don't like them. Boat. I'm going back to the boat.' He ambled away in the direction of the steps.

'I'd best go after him,' said Jack, handing Molly her glass before hurrying in his wake.

Molly made to follow but Nathan seized her hand and drew her inside the pub. 'Think what you're doing! People are staring! Haven't we caused enough scandal?' she said.

'Never mind that! I see what you mean about Frank — but Jack Fletcher? Tell me the truth?'

'It's not what you think. He takes care of Frank for me. They live on the boat.'

The anger died in his face. 'Where's George? I could help you with him.'

She stiffened. 'I don't need your money. I'm building up a nice little business of my own.' She had been a fool to come. It would be so much more difficult carrying on now she had seen him again.

'I could still help you.'

'I don't want your money, Nathan. The dividends are enough. Please let me go?'

He relaxed his grip but still kept hold of her hand. 'Divorce Frank! Marry me?' he urged. 'You've got grounds.'

'I'd have to have him committed and he's happy with Jack.' She sighed. 'So that's how my life is but at least I've got George to compensate me and you've got Jessica.' She glanced around. 'Where's she?'

As if in answer to her question Doris appeared in the doorway. 'Mr Collins, come quickly! Miss Jessica's fallen in the water. She ran away from me when she saw George and's been messing about on the edge of the canal. He's gone in after her!'

Molly wrenched her hand out of Nathan's and pushed past Doris. Once outside she raced for the bridge, pausing for a second there. The breath caught in her throat as she saw her son and her daughter thrashing about in the water and she was filled with fear. Then she saw a man swimming towards them.

'You go down ahead,' yelled Nathan, who'd followed her. 'Damn this leg!'

She fled down the steps and tore along the towpath. Suddenly she realised the man in the water was Frank. He was swimming on his back, with Jessica clutched to him, heading for the bank. George was swimming alongside them.

Molly sank to her knees on the grass and took her daughter from her husband. The girl sobbed uncontrollably. Molly hugged her to her breast. 'There now, sweetheart, you're safe! Mammy'll take care of you.' She rocked her back and forth.

'Mam?' gasped George, dragging himself onto the bank. Water streamed from his clothes and his face was pinched with shock.

She stared at him, wondering if he'd heard what she'd said.

At that moment Nathan reached them. 'Is she all right?' he panted, face tight with pain.

Molly could not have spoken to save her life as Jessica lifted a tear-stained face and held out her arms to him.

Nathan took her and shook her. 'Never bloody play the fool near water again!' he yelled, before crushing her to him.

Molly stumbled to her feet and drew George into her arms. 'Well done, son,' she whispered, pressing her lips against his wet hair. 'You were very brave.'

'Where's Frank going?' gasped Doris as she reached them.

Molly had forgotten Frank for a moment but now she looked for him. He was swimming across the canal towards Jack's boat – straight in the path of a flyer heading their way.

'What's he doing?' said George. 'Can't he see that flyer?'

'He-He saved my life.' Jessica shivered in Nathan's arms. 'Who is he?'

Molly released George. For a while she had looked upon her husband almost as an extra child. She must warn him. But something was blocking up her throat. She began to move but her legs felt peculiar. It was as if she was running through treacle.

Jack was suddenly there on the deck of his boat. 'What's going on?'

Molly found her voice. 'Frank, look out!' she screamed.

The boat caught her husband such a blow on the head that the sound vibrated across the water. He went under. The other bargee suddenly seemed to realise something was wrong. Jack shouted to him. He was looking over the side of his barge. Frank's arm surfaced for a moment then vanished. Jack dived overboard and so did the other bargee.

Molly could not take her gaze off them. Nathan, Doris and the children crowded round her. She was dimly aware of onlookers shouting from the bridge. When the two bargees eventually found Frank's body she knew without doubt that her husband's luck had finally run out.

Jack came over to them, a weary, sad expression on his face. 'He's gone, Moll. He ended up a poor bloody eejit but he made me laugh sometimes and I got used to having him around. I'll see his body gets taken home.'

'He was a hero, Mam,' said George, face strained, bottom lip quivering. 'Jess was struggling that much she was dragging me under.'

'It was all my fault,' said the girl, tears filling her eyes. 'I was singing and dancing on the edge, daring George to copy me.'

'You deserve a good spanking, young lady,' said Nathan severely, his arm still round her. 'As for Mr Payne, he deserved a medal.' He turned to Doris. 'Take the children up to the hotel. See they get hot drinks. Borrow blankets. I'll see they're returned.'

Molly stared at him, glad he was making the decisions. She was starting to feel very odd. Her brain was buzzing with questions. Why had Frank done it? What had gone on in his poor, mixed-up head when he saw George struggling with Jessica in the water? She could understand his saving her son but he'd actually saved Jessica. Was it possible he could have seen something of herself in the girl? Or was it his old self, dancing and singing, he had thought of when Jessica messed about on the water's edge? He must have been on the deck of Jack's barge, watching them, to have dived in so quickly. Her vision blurred as tears filled her eyes. She remembered Frank as she had first seen him. She had mourned once for that Frank, now she would mourn for the Frank who'd saved her daughter's life.

'You OK, Moll?'

She looked up at Nathan and nodded, wiping her eyes. 'It's been a bit of a day,' she said shakily. 'I want to go home. Could you take me, please?'

'Whatever you say.' He sounded weary as he put his arm around her. They leaned against each other as they walked towards the bridge. 'Why do you think Frank did it, Moll? He couldn't have recognised her, known she was his daughter, could he?'

'How could he?' Yet still she wondered, although she told herself it couldn't be.

'Dancing and singings acting the fool. She doesn't get that from me,' said Nathan.

They were silent a moment, Molly deciding that he like she was probably thinking they would be reminded of Frank every time Jessica indulged in a song or a dance for a long time. 'She's still more your daughter than his,' Molly murmured. 'You've had the rearing of her.'

'You've said that before.'

'And I'll go on saying it,' she replied robustly.

He smiled faintly and they were silent for the rest of the way.

–

It was not until the motor drew up outside her house after dropping off Jessica and Doris that Nathan said, 'I was thinking of starting up something different here at the factory in Liverpool.'

'Oh?' said Molly, who was still feeling a bit odd despite forcing down several sandwiches and a couple of schooners of cream sherry.

'Electrical fittings. Remember?'

Of course she remembered. 'We both thought it a good idea at the time.'

'I still think it's a good idea,' said George, who was sitting in the back seat wrapped in a blanket. 'Perhaps when I'm bigger and leave school, Uncle Nathan, you can give me a job?'

Nathan smiled at him. 'I don't see why not. Now get indoors and into some clothes.'

'Yes, sir!' The boy jumped out and hurried over the step, the edge of the blanket trailing on the ground after him.

Molly watched him open the door with the key on the string, aware that Nathan was gazing after him too. Is he thinking, This is the child that's really mine? she wondered.

'The children,' he murmured.

'Yes?' She stared at him.

'I wish we could tell them the truth but how do we explain you're Jess's mam and I'm George's father?' He frowned, one lock of brown hair dangling over his forehead.

'I don't know,' said Molly, kissing him and suddenly having a flashback to the moment on the bank when she had dragged Jessica out of the water. 'We know the truth, surely that's all that matters? We'll just have to be the best parents we can be to both of them.'

He nodded and they kissed again.

Perhaps from this day on Jessica will always be another man's child to him despite what I said earlier, thought Molly. She could almost feel the changeover being made. George his son, Jessica her daughter. Although perhaps it wasn't going to be as simple as that?

'If I come to see you in a couple of days, Moll, you won't turn me away, will you?' he said in a slightly mocking voice.

'No, I won't turn you away,' she said with a faint smile.

'Perhaps you might even say yes if I ask you to marry me?'

'Perhaps,' she teased, touching his cheek.

Nathan caught her hand and kissed her fingers. 'See you soon.'

She stepped down from the motor and waved until he was out of sight, telling herself that George and Jessica probably couldn't have distinguished between Molly and Mammy in the heat of the moment on the canal bank. Their secret was safe. She sauntered indoors, dreaming of the future when she and Nathan, Jessica and George, were living under the same roof, a normal, happy family.

Acknowledgements

For help with my research I would like to thank – my son Iain, my cousin Patsy Marshall, her friends and staff at Burscough Library, Don Hyman of Crosby Writers Club and his ninety-year-old father-in-law Charlie Williams, and last but not least, Hayes & Finch Ltd who've been supplying my church with candles for years!